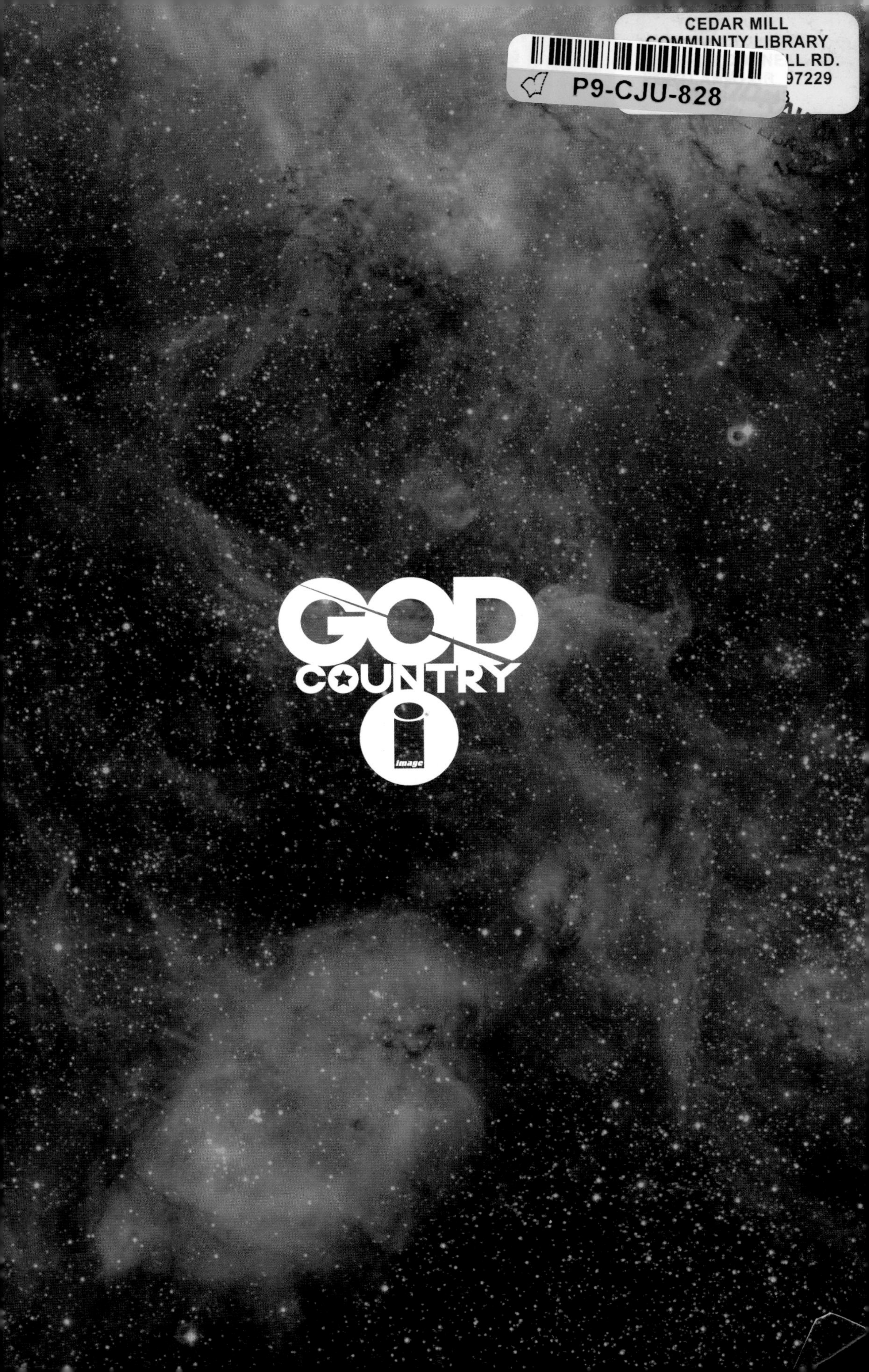
GOD
COUNTRY
image

DONNY CATES
WORDS

GEOFF SHAW
ART

JASON WORDIE
COLOR

JOHN J. HILL
LETTERS & DESIGN

GERARDO ZAFFINO
SERIES VARIANT COVERS

GD COUNTRY

IMAGE COMICS, INC.

Robert Kirkman - Chief Operating Officer · Erik Larsen - Chief Financial Officer · Todd McFarlane - President · Marc Silvestri - Chief Executive Officer · Jim Valentino - Vice-President
Eric Stephenson - Publisher · Corey Murphy - Director of Sales · Jeff Boison - Director of Publishing Planning & Book Trade Sales · Chris Ross - Director of Digital Sales
Jeff Stang - Director of Specialty Sales · Kat Salazar - Director of PR & Marketing · Tricia Ramos - Traffic Manager · Sue Korpela - Accounts Manager · Drew Gill - Art Director
Brett Warnock - Production Manager · Leigh Thomas - Print Manager · Branwyn Bigglestone - Controller · Briah Skelly - Publicist · Aly Hoffman - Events & Conventions Coordinator
Sasha Head - Sales & Marketing Production Designer · David Brothers - Branding Manager · Melissa Gifford - Content Manager · Drew Fitzgerald - Publicity Assistant · Vincent Kukua - Production Artist
Erika Schnatz - Production Artist · Ryan Brewer - Production Artist · Shanna Matuszak - Production Artist · Carey Hall - Production Artist · Esther Kim - Direct Market Sales Representative
Emilio Bautista - Digital Sales Representative · Leanna Caunter - Accounting Assistant · Chloe Ramos-Peterson - Library Market Sales Representative · Marla Eizik - Administrative Assistant

IMAGECOMICS.COM

GOD COUNTRY. First printing. August 2017. Published by Image Comics, Inc. Office of publication: 2701 NW Vaughn St., Suite 780, Portland, OR 97210. Copyright © 2017 Donny Cates and Geoff
Shaw. All rights reserved. Contains material originally published in single magazine form as GOD COUNTRY #1-6. GOD COUNTRY™ (including all prominent characters featured herein), its logo and all
character likenesses are trademarks of Donny Cates and Geoff Shaw, unless otherwise noted. Image Comics® and its logos are registered trademarks and copyrights of Image Comics, Inc. All rights reserved.
No part of this publication may be reproduced or transmitted, in any form or by any means (except for short excerpts for review purposes) without the express written permission of Image Comics, Inc. All
names, characters, events and locales in this publication are entirely fictional. Any resemblance to actual persons (living or dead), events or places, without satiric intent, is coincidental. Printed in the USA.
For information regarding the CPSIA on this printed material call: 203-595-3636 and provide reference #RICH –735731. For international rights inquiries, contact: foreignlicensing@imagecomics.com.
ISBN: 978-1-5343-0234-1. ISBN Fried Pie Exclusive: 978-1-5343-0445-1. ISBN Newbury Exclusive: 978-1-5343-0449-9. ISBN DCBS: 978-1-5343-0450-5. ISBN Jesse James/Hypno Comics/A Comics Shop
Exclusive: 978-1-5343-0451-2. ISBN Acme Comics Exclusive: 978-1-5343-0452-9. ISBN Scalefish Comics Exclusive: 978-1-5343-0453-6. ISBN Forbidden Planet /Big Bang Exclusive: 978-1-5343-0460-4.
ISBN Convention Hardcover Exclusive: 978-1-5343-0448-2.

SPECIAL THANKS: **SCOTT ALLIE**

FOR DAD

★

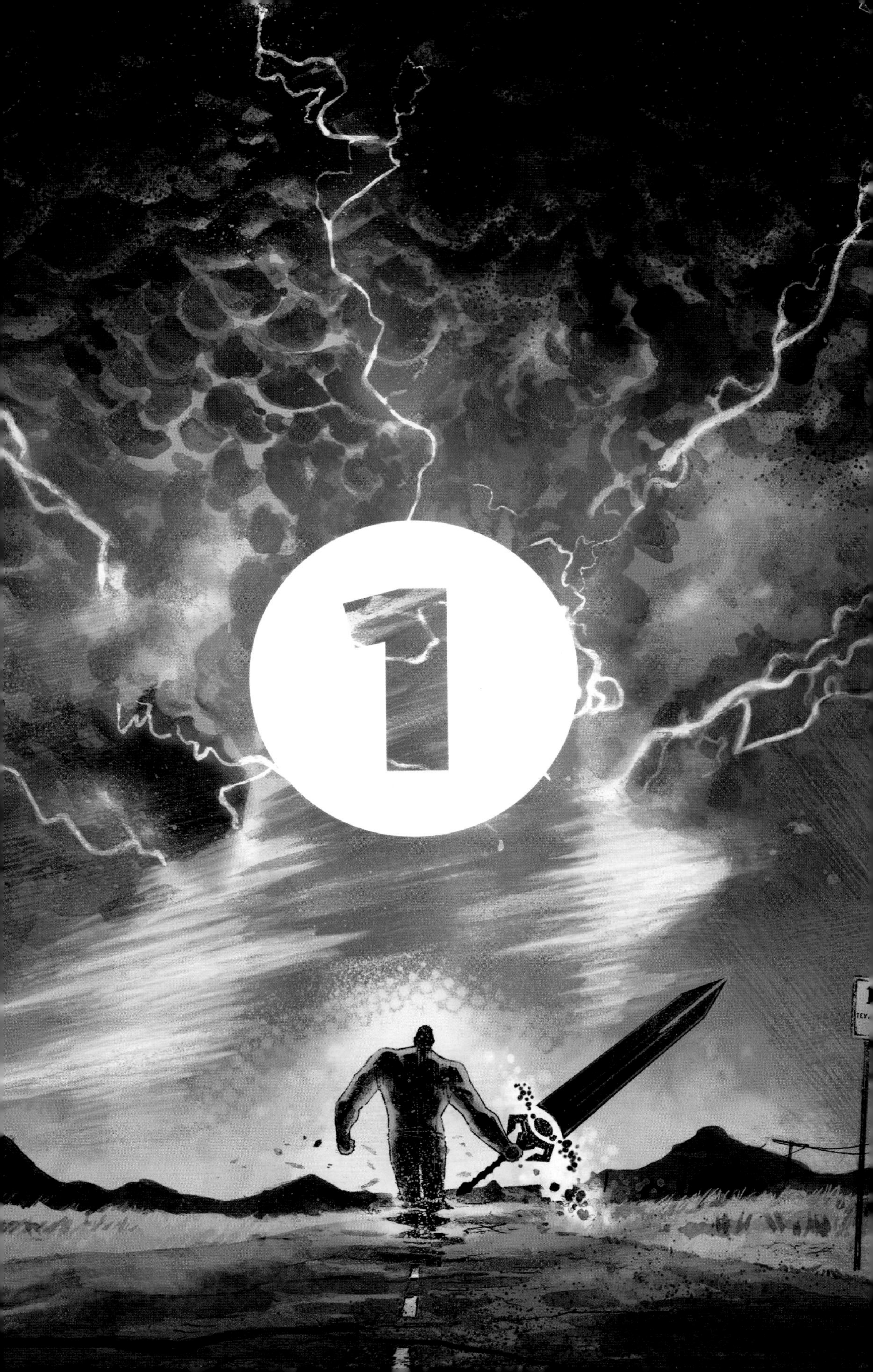
1

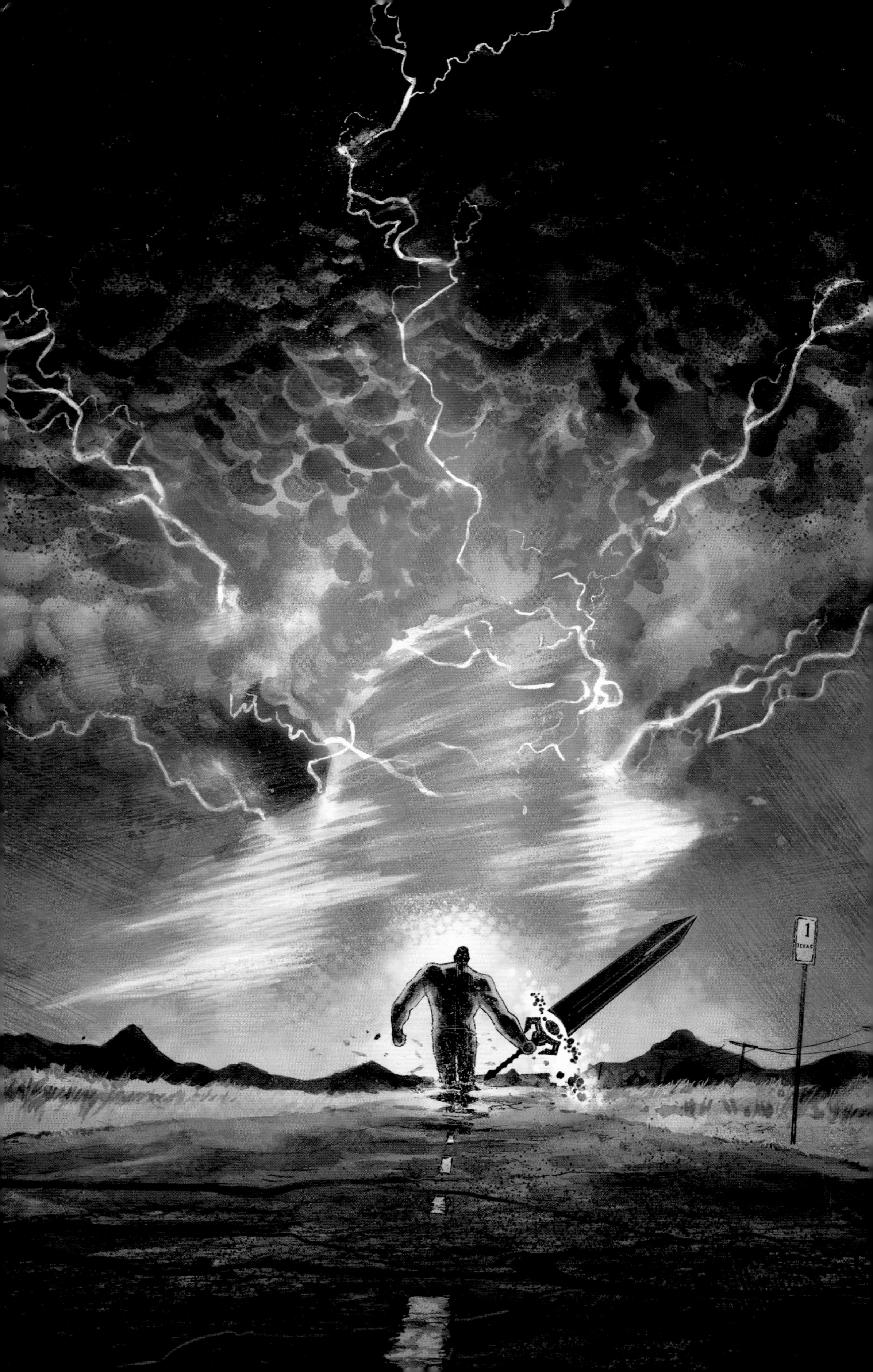
1
TEXAS

"The wrath of God lies sleeping. It was hid a million years before men were and only men have the power to wake it. Hell ain't half full. Hear me. Ye carry war of a madman's making onto a foreign land. Ye'll wake more than the dogs."

Cormac McCarthy
Blood Meridian: Or the Evening Redness in the West

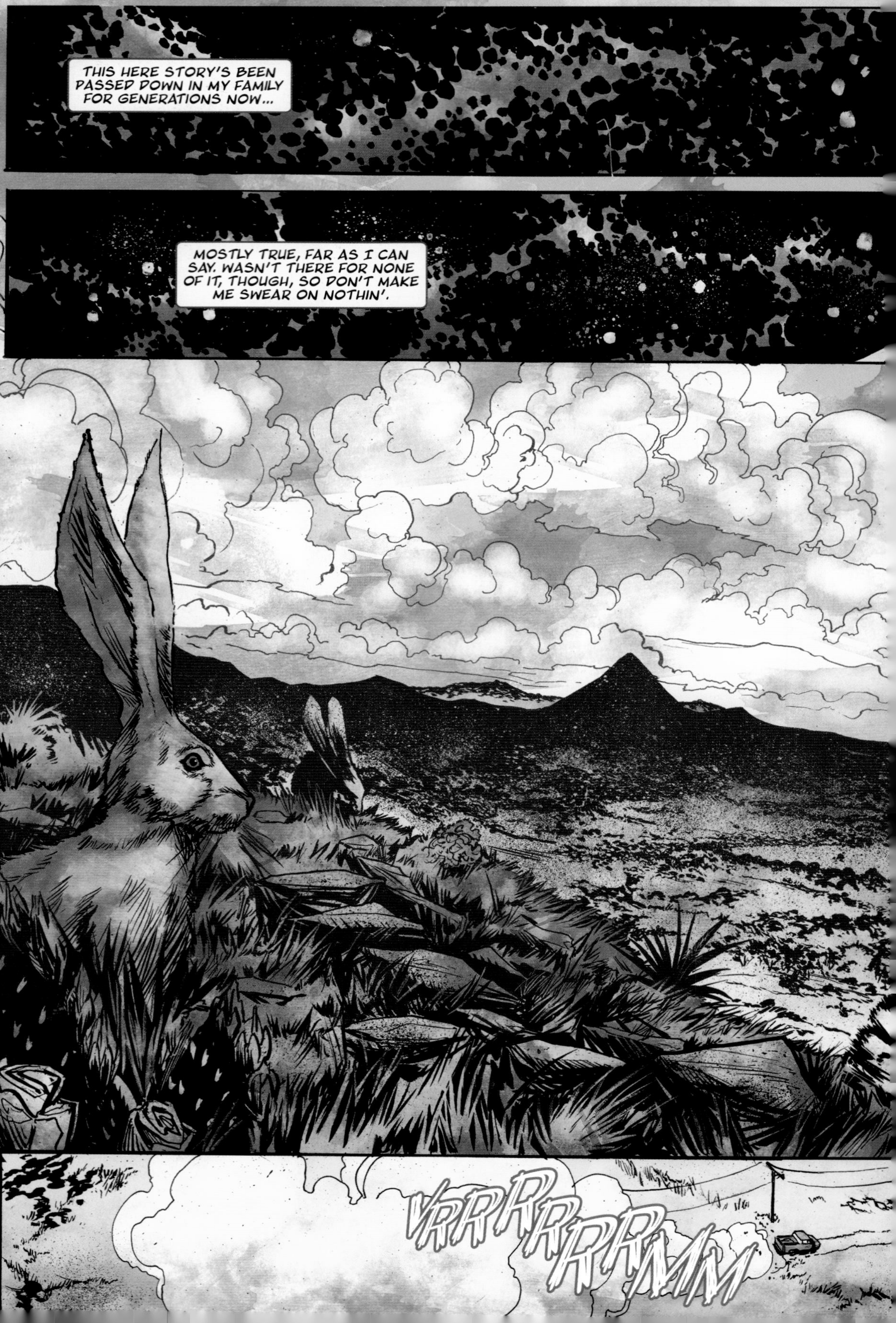
THIS HERE STORY'S BEEN PASSED DOWN IN MY FAMILY FOR GENERATIONS NOW...
MOSTLY TRUE, FAR AS I CAN SAY. WASN'T THERE FOR NONE OF IT, THOUGH, SO DON'T MAKE ME SWEAR ON NOTHIN'.
VRRRRRRRMM

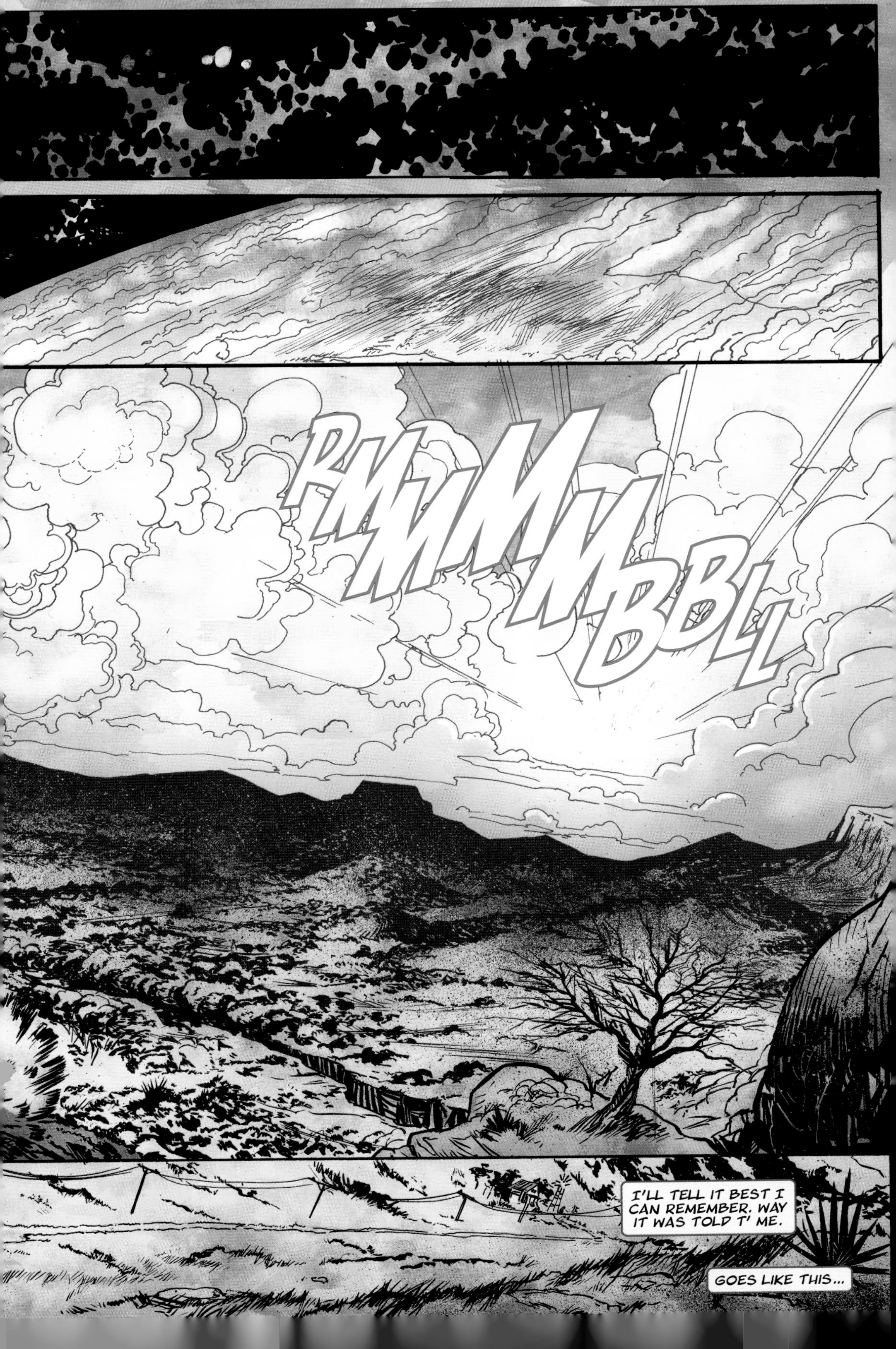
RMMMMMBBLL
I'LL TELL IT BEST I CAN REMEMBER. WAY IT WAS TOLD T' ME.
GOES LIKE THIS...

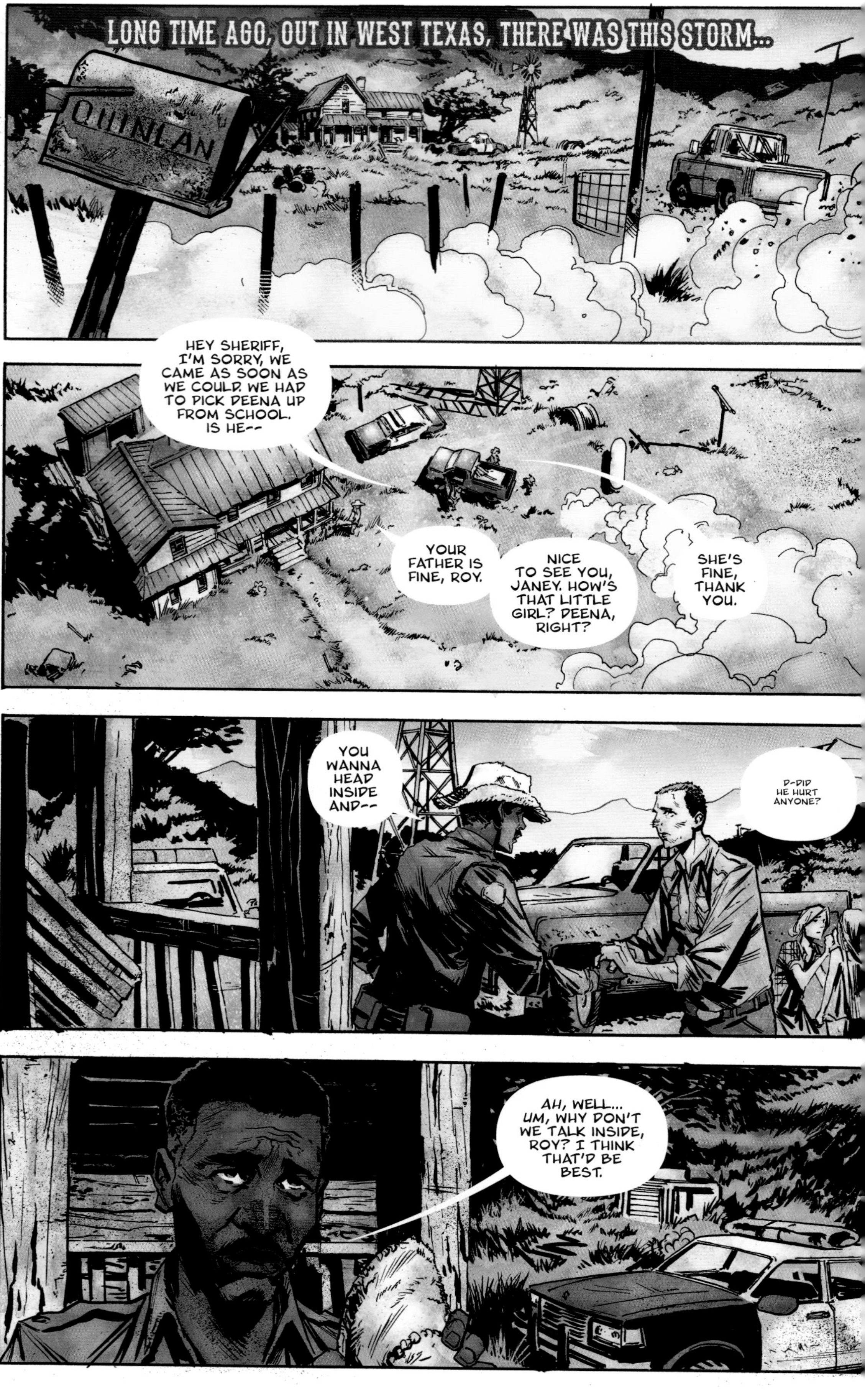
LONG TIME AGO, OUT IN WEST TEXAS, THERE WAS THIS STORM...
QUINLAN
HEY SHERIFF, I'M SORRY, WE CAME AS SOON AS WE COULD. WE HAD TO PICK DEENA UP FROM SCHOOL. IS HE--
YOUR FATHER IS FINE, ROY.
NICE TO SEE YOU, JANEY. HOW'S THAT LITTLE GIRL? DEENA, RIGHT?
SHE'S FINE, THANK YOU.
YOU WANNA HEAD INSIDE AND--
D-DID HE HURT ANYONE?
AH, WELL... UM, WHY DON'T WE TALK INSIDE, ROY? I THINK THAT'D BE BEST.

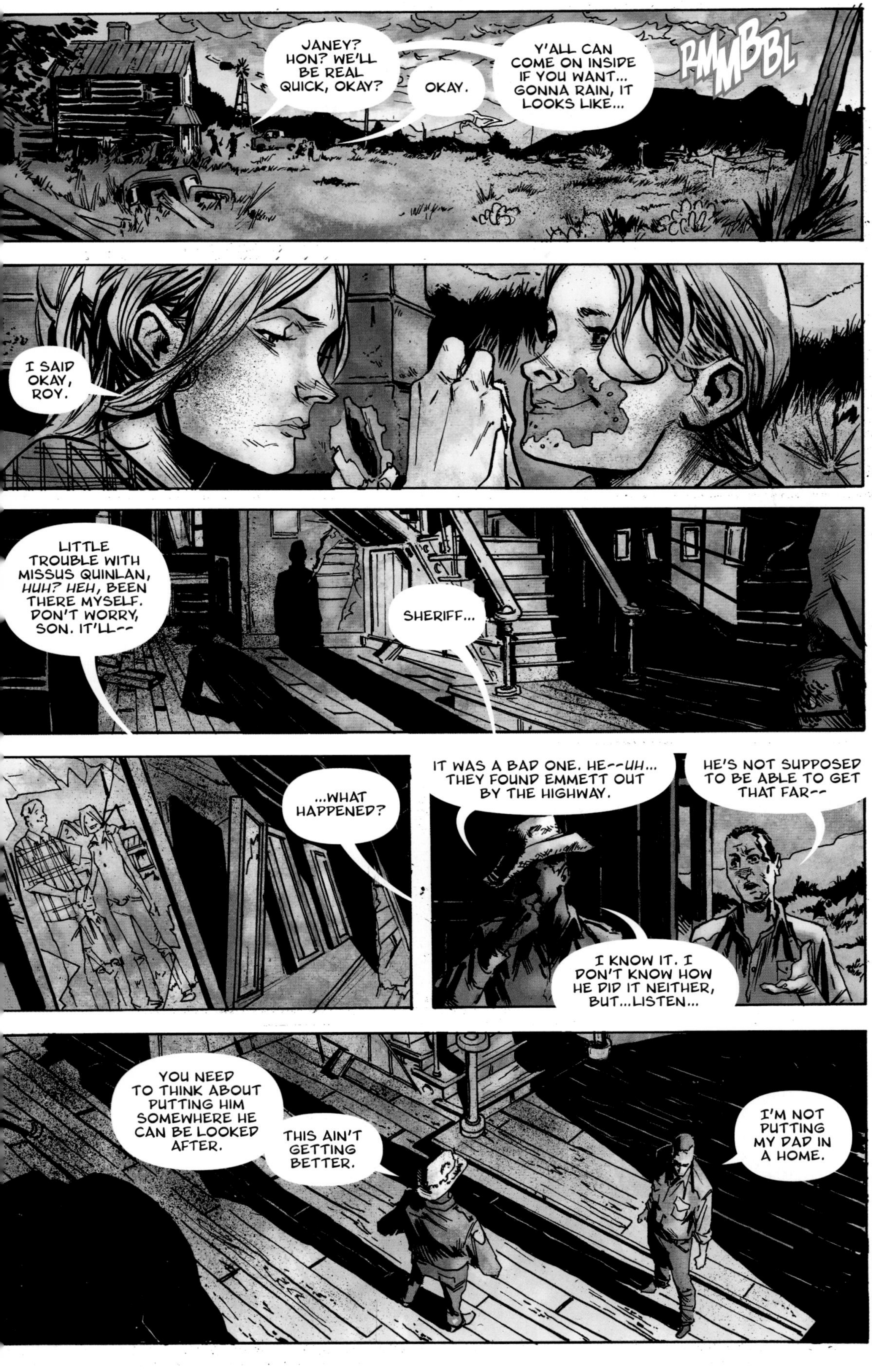
JANEY? HON? WE'LL BE REAL QUICK, OKAY?
OKAY.
Y'ALL CAN COME ON INSIDE IF YOU WANT... GONNA RAIN, IT LOOKS LIKE...
RMMBBL
I SAID OKAY, ROY.
LITTLE TROUBLE WITH MISSUS QUINLAN, HUH? HEH, BEEN THERE MYSELF. DON'T WORRY, SON. IT'LL--
SHERIFF...
...WHAT HAPPENED?
IT WAS A BAD ONE. HE--UH... THEY FOUND EMMETT OUT BY THE HIGHWAY.
HE'S NOT SUPPOSED TO BE ABLE TO GET THAT FAR--
I KNOW IT. I DON'T KNOW HOW HE DID IT NEITHER, BUT...LISTEN...
YOU NEED TO THINK ABOUT PUTTING HIM SOMEWHERE HE CAN BE LOOKED AFTER.
THIS AIN'T GETTING BETTER.
I'M NOT PUTTING MY DAD IN A HOME.

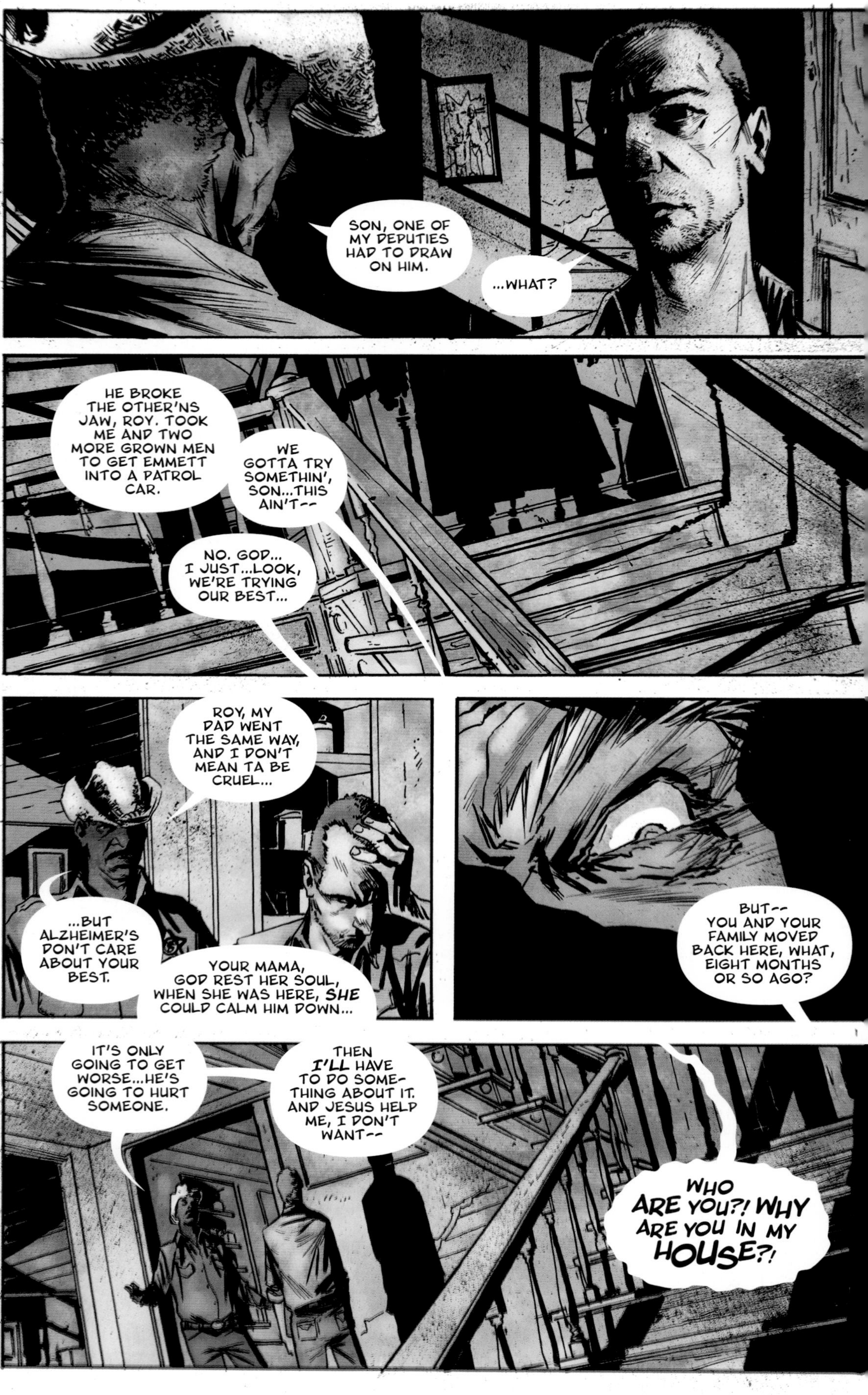
SON, ONE OF MY DEPUTIES HAD TO DRAW ON HIM.
...WHAT?
HE BROKE THE OTHER'NS JAW, ROY. TOOK ME AND TWO MORE GROWN MEN TO GET EMMETT INTO A PATROL CAR.
WE GOTTA TRY SOMETHIN', SON...THIS AIN'T--
NO. GOD... I JUST...LOOK, WE'RE TRYING OUR BEST...
ROY, MY DAD WENT THE SAME WAY, AND I DON'T MEAN TA BE CRUEL...
...BUT ALZHEIMER'S DON'T CARE ABOUT YOUR BEST.
YOUR MAMA, GOD REST HER SOUL, WHEN SHE WAS HERE, SHE COULD CALM HIM DOWN...
BUT-- YOU AND YOUR FAMILY MOVED BACK HERE, WHAT, EIGHT MONTHS OR SO AGO?
IT'S ONLY GOING TO GET WORSE...HE'S GOING TO HURT SOMEONE.
THEN I'LL HAVE TO DO SOME-THING ABOUT IT. AND JESUS HELP ME, I DON'T WANT--
WHO ARE YOU?! WHY ARE YOU IN MY HOUSE?!

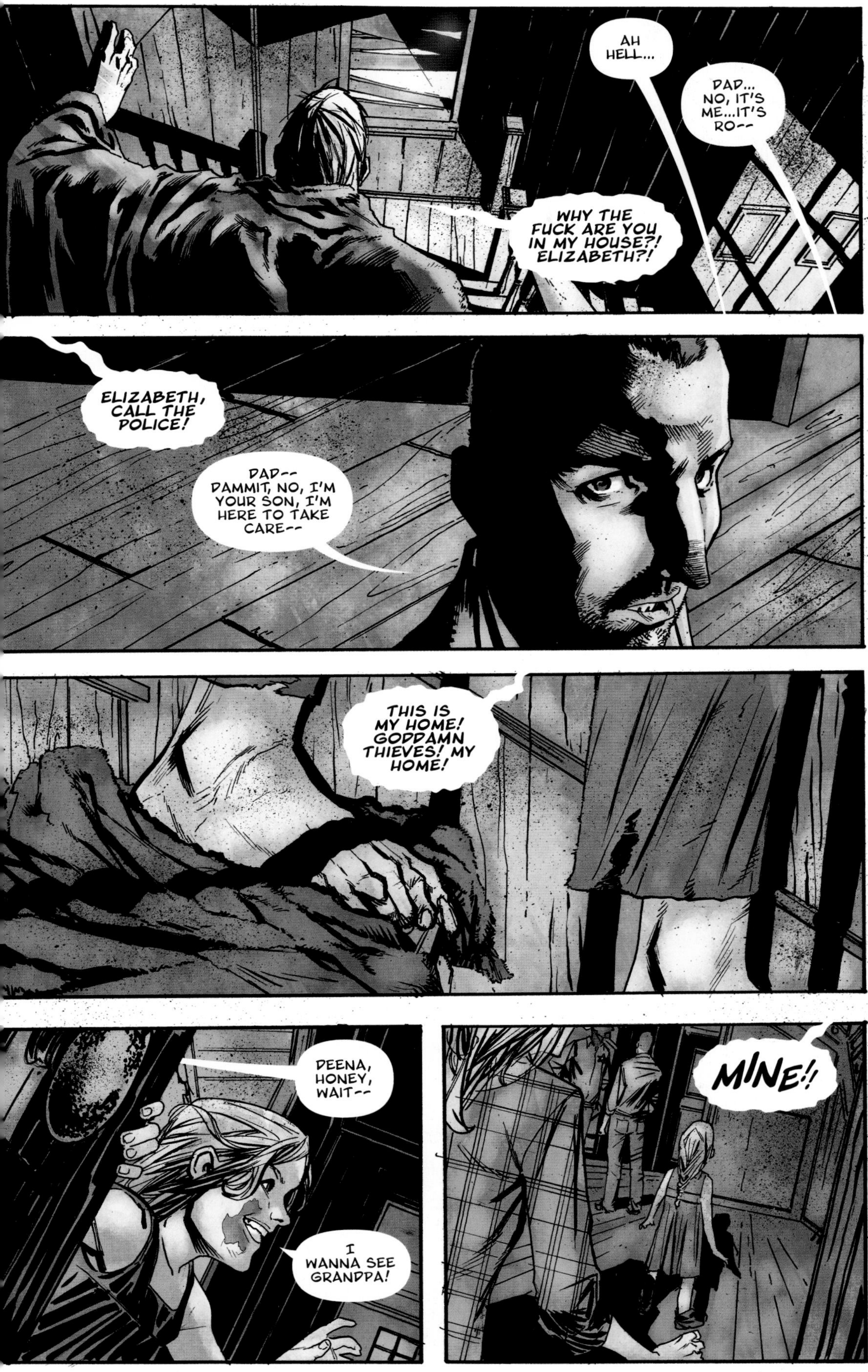
AH HELL...
DAD... NO, IT'S ME...IT'S RO--
WHY THE FUCK ARE YOU IN MY HOUSE?! ELIZABETH?!
ELIZABETH, CALL THE POLICE!
DAD-- DAMMIT, NO, I'M YOUR SON, I'M HERE TO TAKE CARE--
THIS IS MY HOME! GODDAMN THIEVES! MY HOME!
DEENA, HONEY, WAIT--
I WANNA SEE GRANDPA!
MINE!!

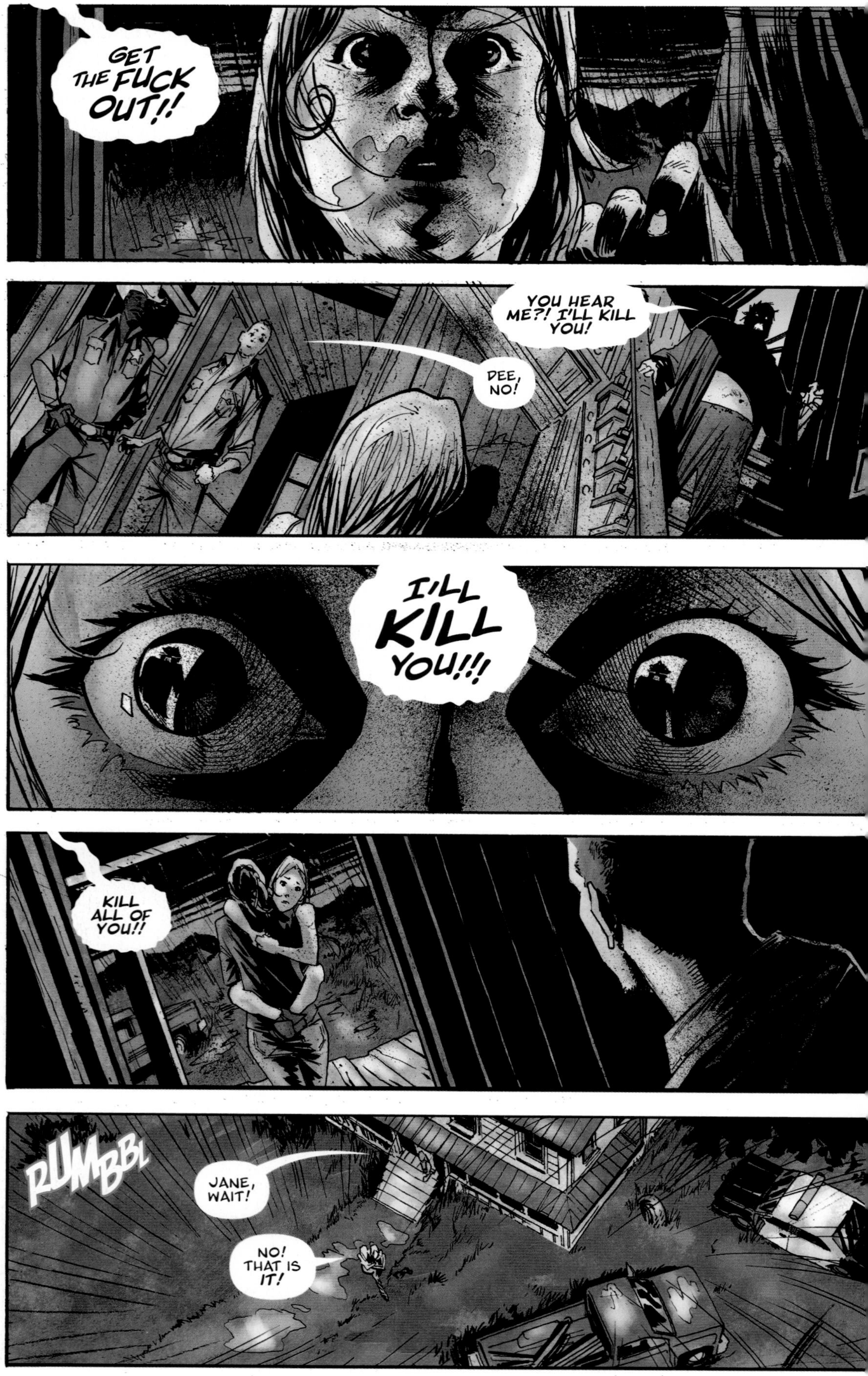
GET THE FUCK OUT!!
YOU HEAR ME?! I'LL KILL YOU!
DEE, NO!
I'LL KILL YOU!!!
KILL ALL OF YOU!!
RUMBBL
JANE, WAIT!
NO! THAT IS IT!

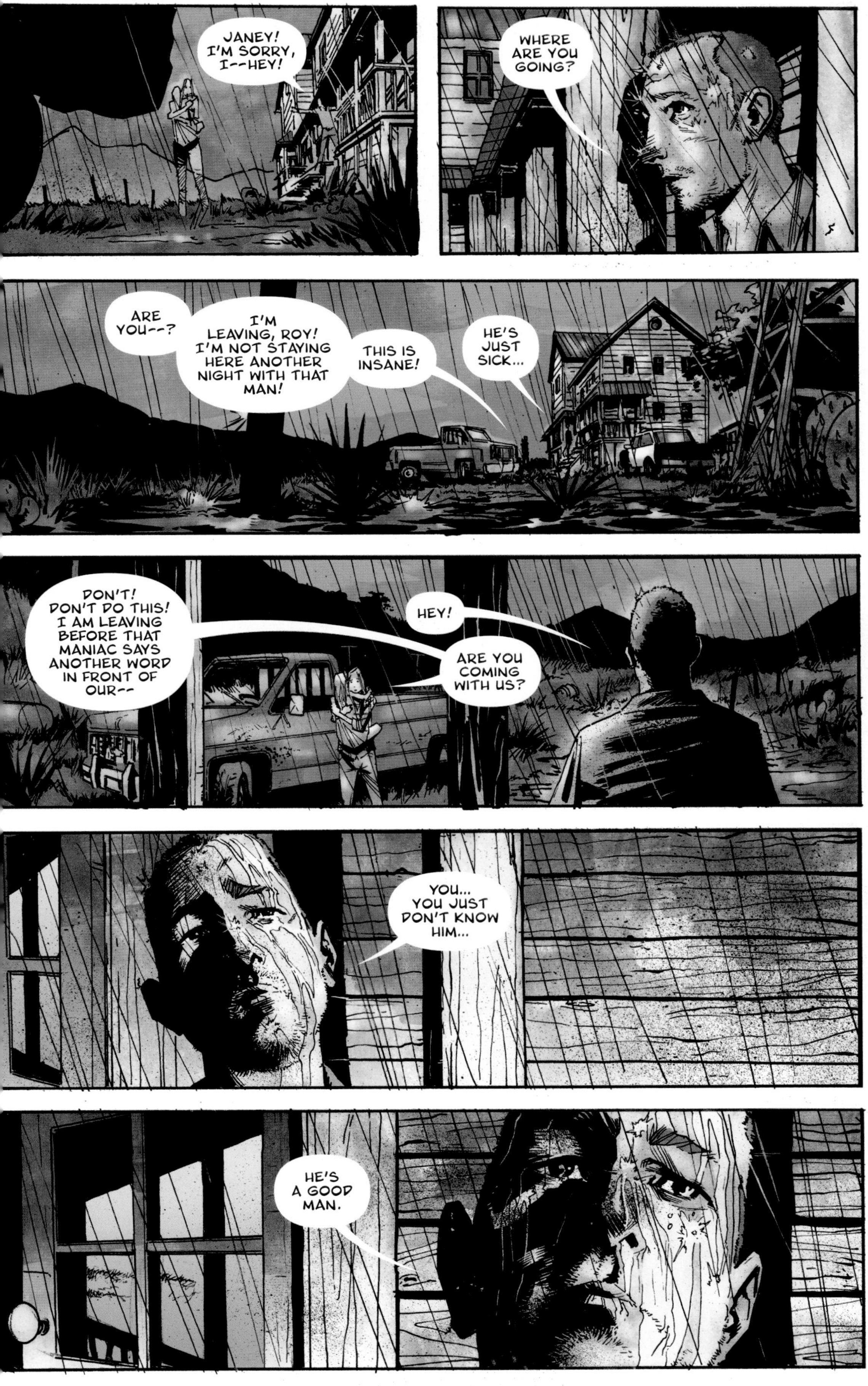
JANEY! I'M SORRY, I--HEY!
WHERE ARE YOU GOING?
ARE YOU--?
I'M LEAVING, ROY! I'M NOT STAYING HERE ANOTHER NIGHT WITH THAT MAN!
THIS IS INSANE!
HE'S JUST SICK...
DON'T! DON'T DO THIS! I AM LEAVING BEFORE THAT MANIAC SAYS ANOTHER WORD IN FRONT OF OUR--
HEY!
ARE YOU COMING WITH US?
YOU... YOU JUST DON'T KNOW HIM...
HE'S A GOOD MAN.

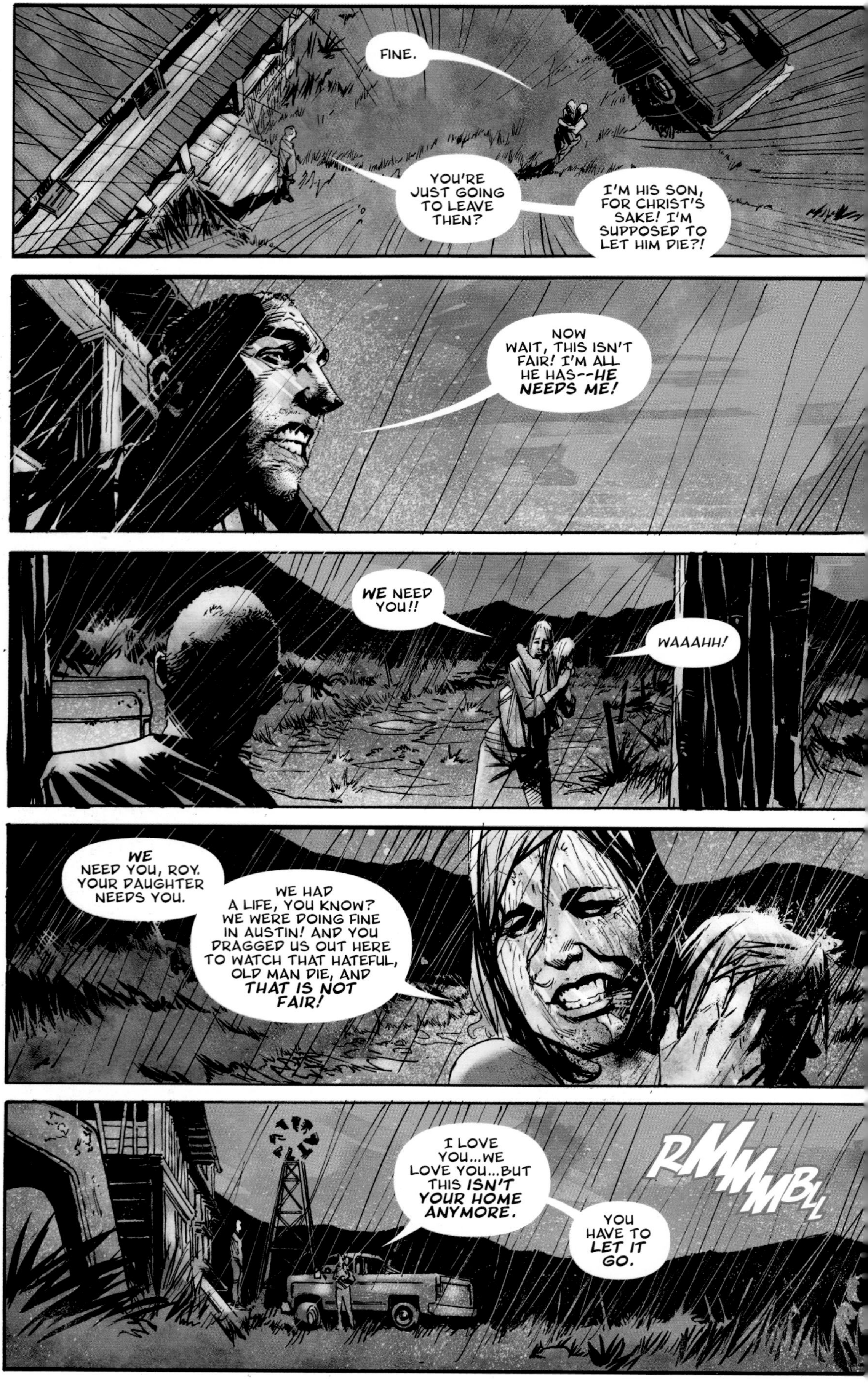
FINE.
YOU'RE JUST GOING TO LEAVE THEN?
I'M HIS SON, FOR CHRIST'S SAKE! I'M SUPPOSED TO LET HIM DIE?!
NOW WAIT, THIS ISN'T FAIR! I'M ALL HE HAS--HE NEEDS ME!
WE NEED YOU!!
WAAAHH!
WE NEED YOU, ROY. YOUR DAUGHTER NEEDS YOU.
WE HAD A LIFE, YOU KNOW? WE WERE DOING FINE IN AUSTIN! AND YOU DRAGGED US OUT HERE TO WATCH THAT HATEFUL, OLD MAN DIE, AND THAT IS NOT FAIR!
I LOVE YOU...WE LOVE YOU...BUT THIS ISN'T YOUR HOME ANYMORE.
YOU HAVE TO LET IT GO.
RMMMBLL

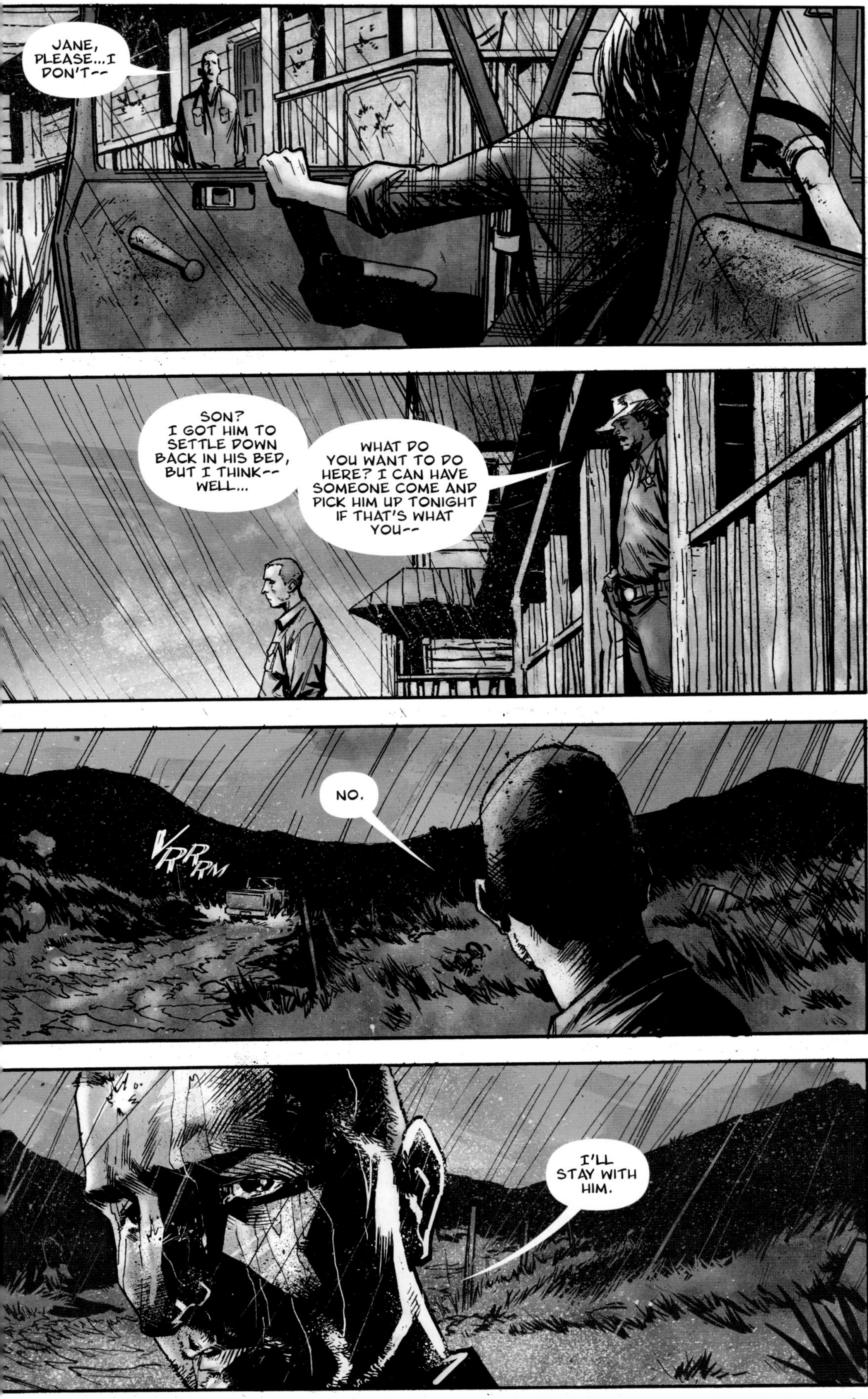
JANE, PLEASE...I DON'T--
SON? I GOT HIM TO SETTLE DOWN BACK IN HIS BED, BUT I THINK-- WELL...
WHAT DO YOU WANT TO DO HERE? I CAN HAVE SOMEONE COME AND PICK HIM UP TONIGHT IF THAT'S WHAT YOU--
VRRRM
NO.
I'LL STAY WITH HIM.

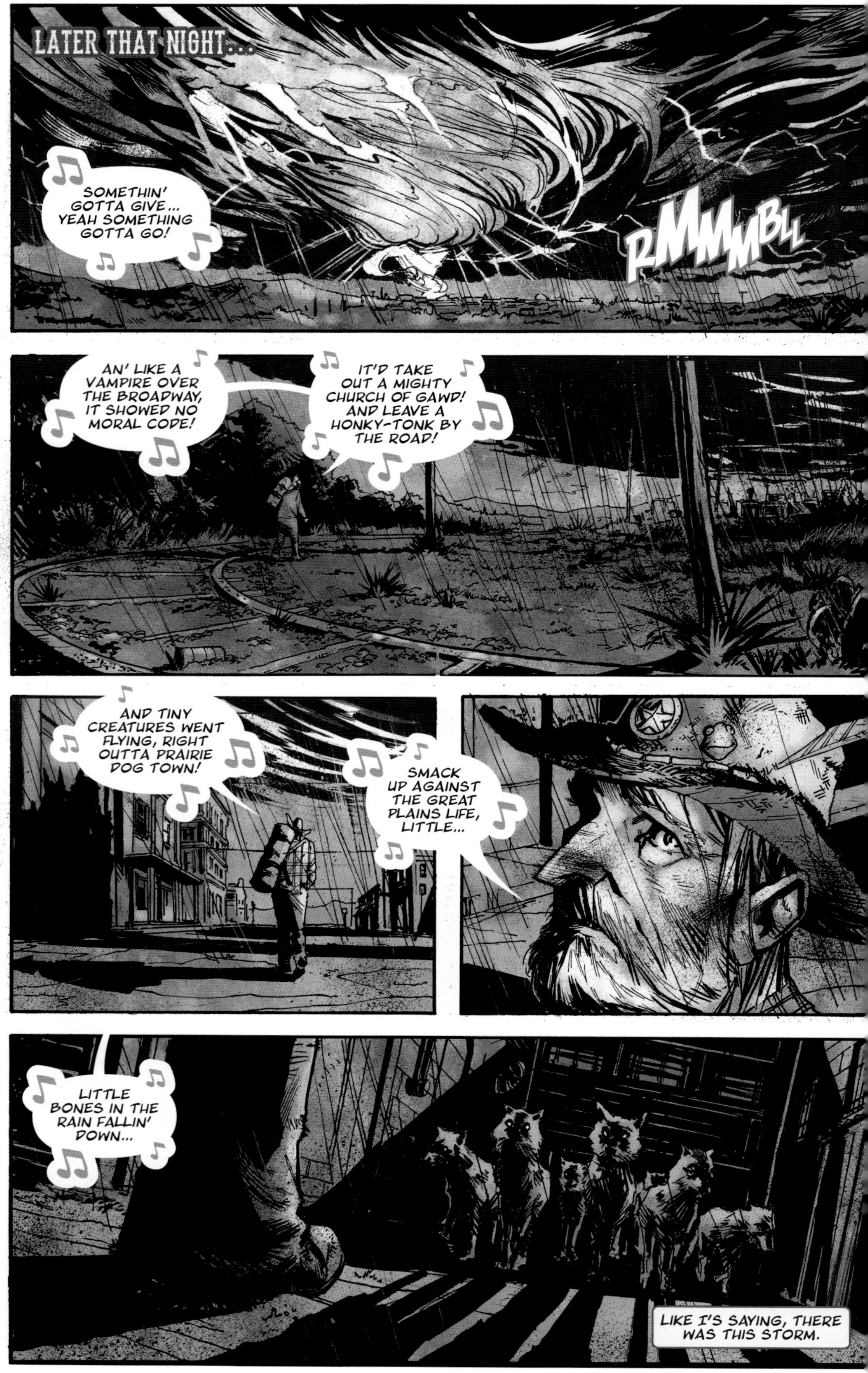
LATER THAT NIGHT...
SOMETHIN' GOTTA GIVE... YEAH SOMETHING GOTTA GO!
RMMMBLL
AN' LIKE A VAMPIRE OVER THE BROADWAY, IT SHOWED NO MORAL CODE!
IT'D TAKE OUT A MIGHTY CHURCH OF GAWD! AND LEAVE A HONKY-TONK BY THE ROAD!
AND TINY CREATURES WENT FLYING, RIGHT OUTTA PRAIRIE DOG TOWN!
SMACK UP AGAINST THE GREAT PLAINS LIFE, LITTLE...
LITTLE BONES IN THE RAIN FALLIN' DOWN...
LIKE I'S SAYING, THERE WAS THIS STORM.

WASN'T LIKE NONE THAT COME BEFORE IT...OR ANY THAT EVER CAME AFTER.

N-NO!

COME OUTTA NOWHERE. AND IT BROUGHT SOMETHING ALONG WITH IT.

HEH HEH...HOW DO YA LIKE 'AT?

THE TORNADO SIRENS RANG TOO LATE TO HELP ANYONE, BUT RANG THEY DID.

RRRRRBBBLLL

THA HELL ARE Y'ALL RUNNING AWAY...

SCREAMIN' AND ROARIN' THROUGH THE THUNDER AND RAIN...

G-GOOD LORD...

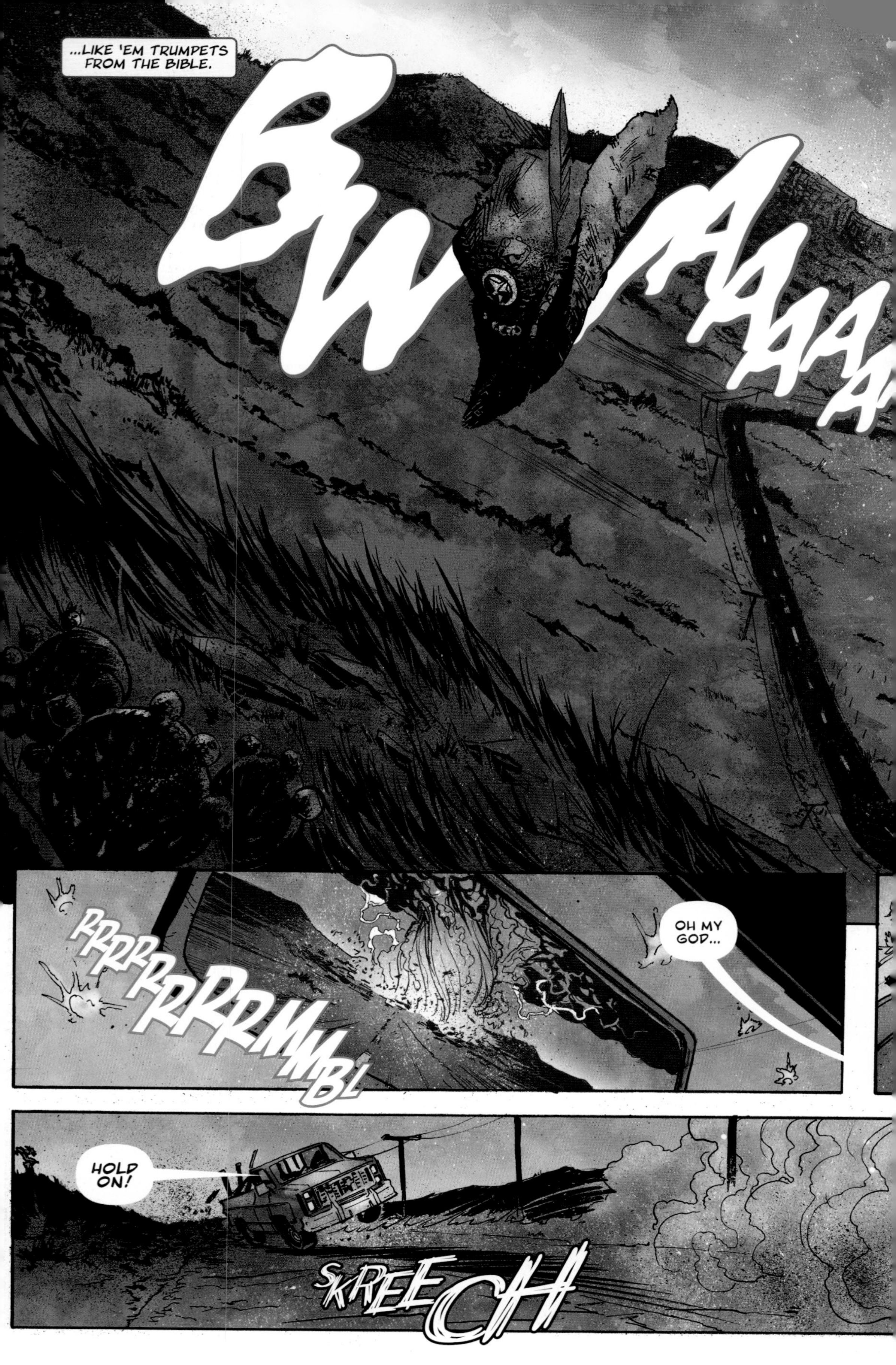
...LIKE 'EM TRUMPETS FROM THE BIBLE.
BWAAAAAA
RRRRRRRRRMMMBL
OH MY GOD...
HOLD ON!
SKREEECH

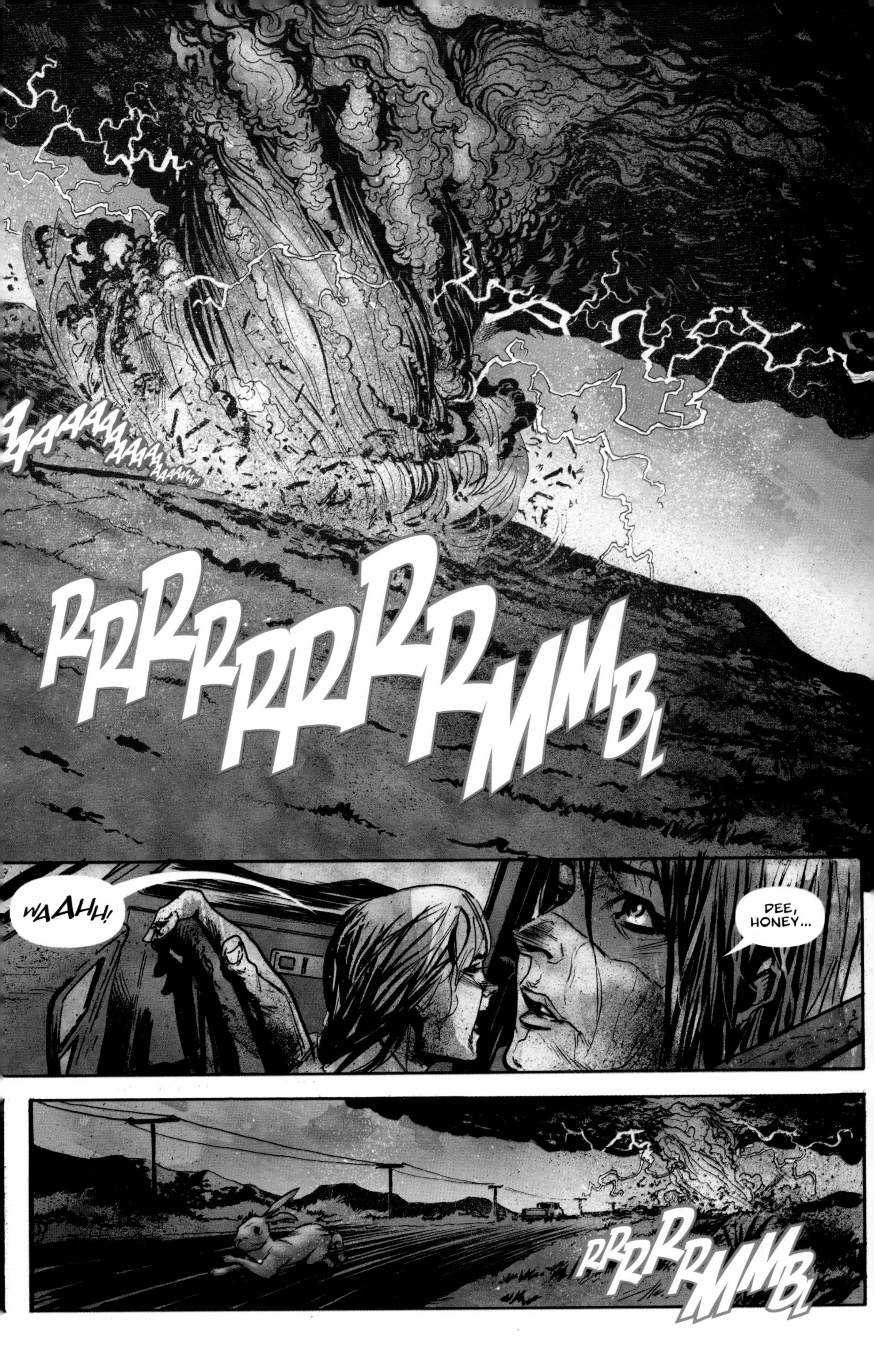
AAAAAAAAAAAAAAAAAHH!
RRRRRRRRRMMBL
WAAHH!
DEE, HONEY...
RRRRRMMBL

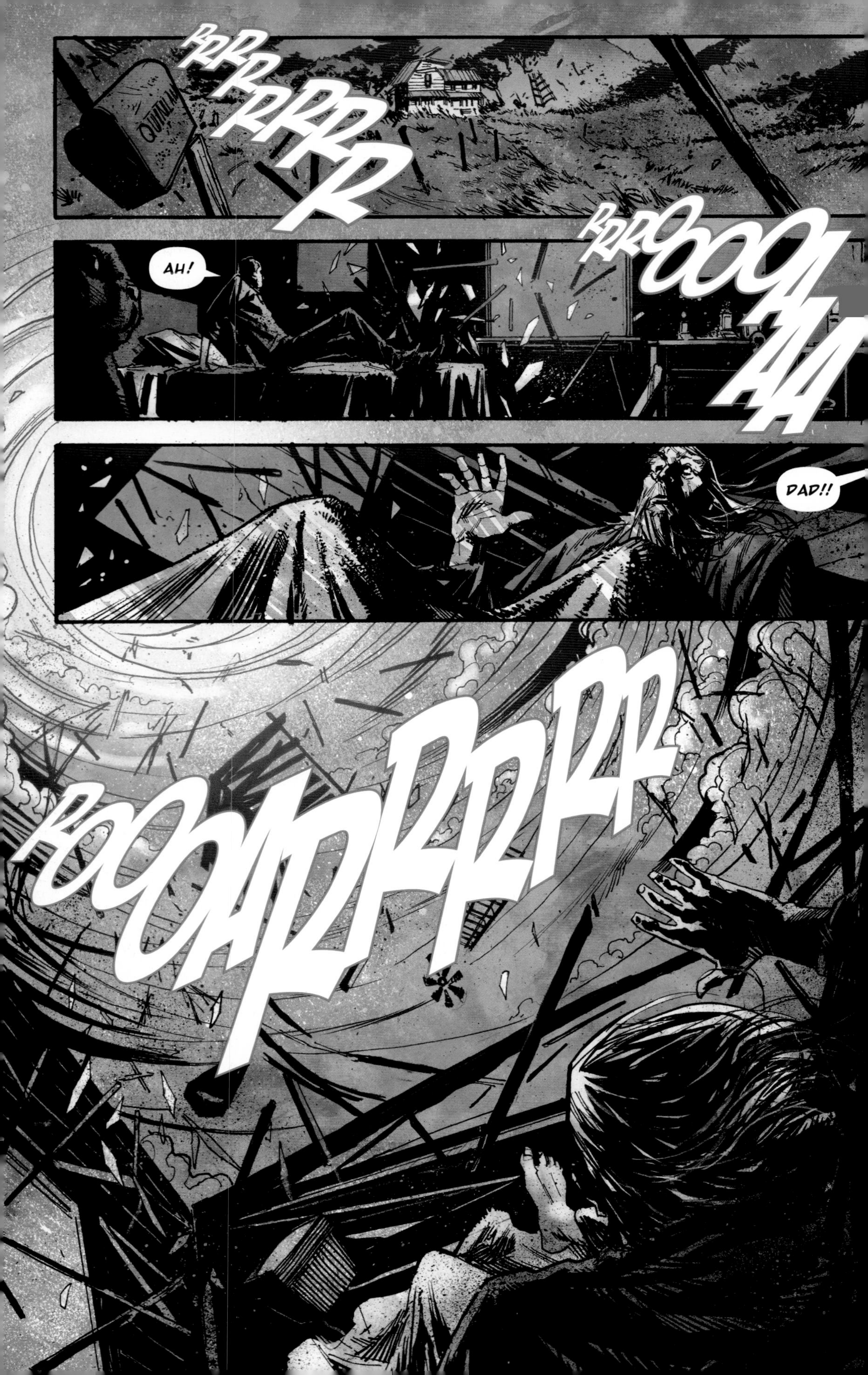
RRRRRRRR
QUINLAN
AH!
RRROOOGAAA
DAD!!
ROOAARRRRR

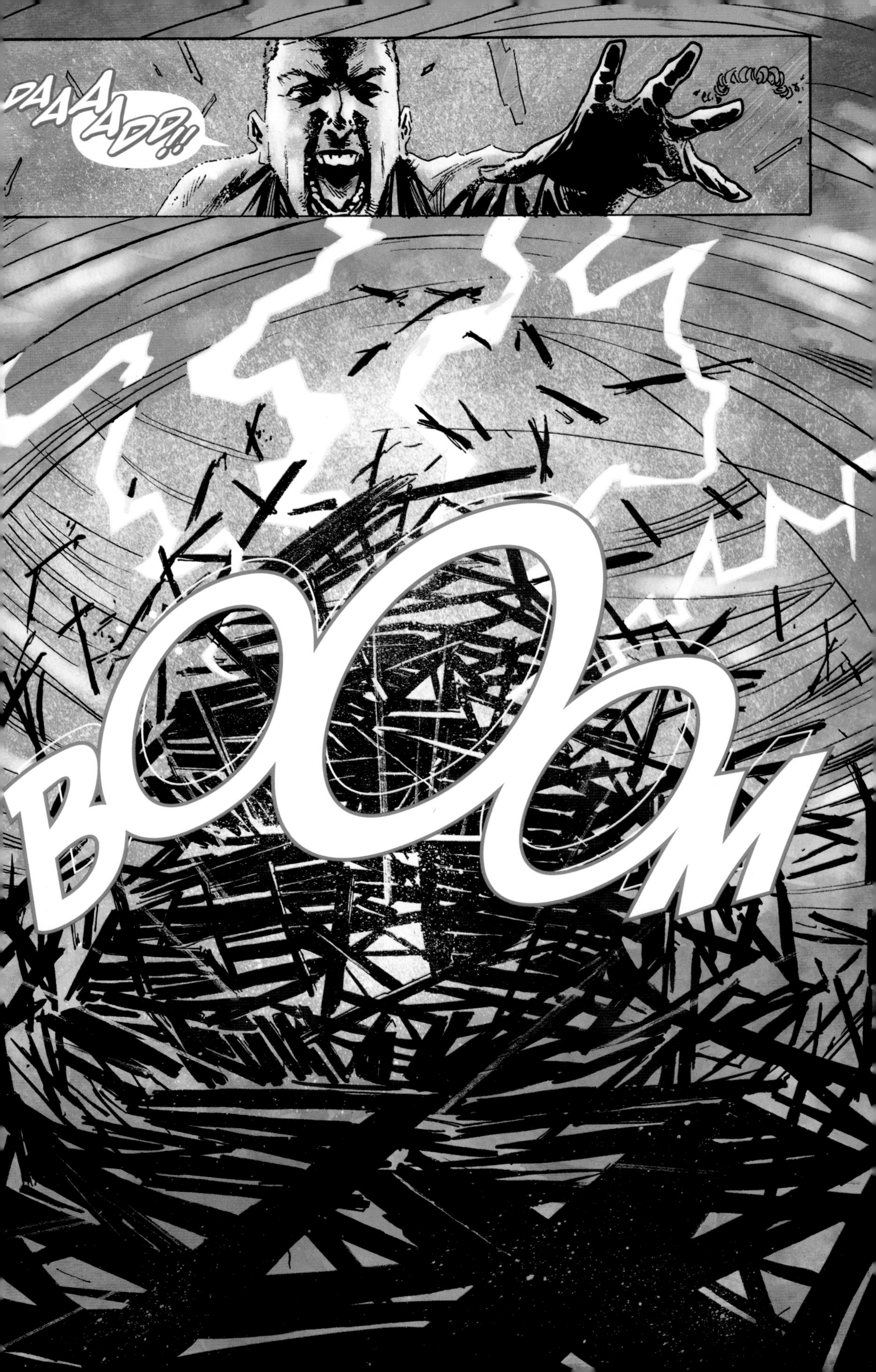
DAAAAADD!!
BOOOOM

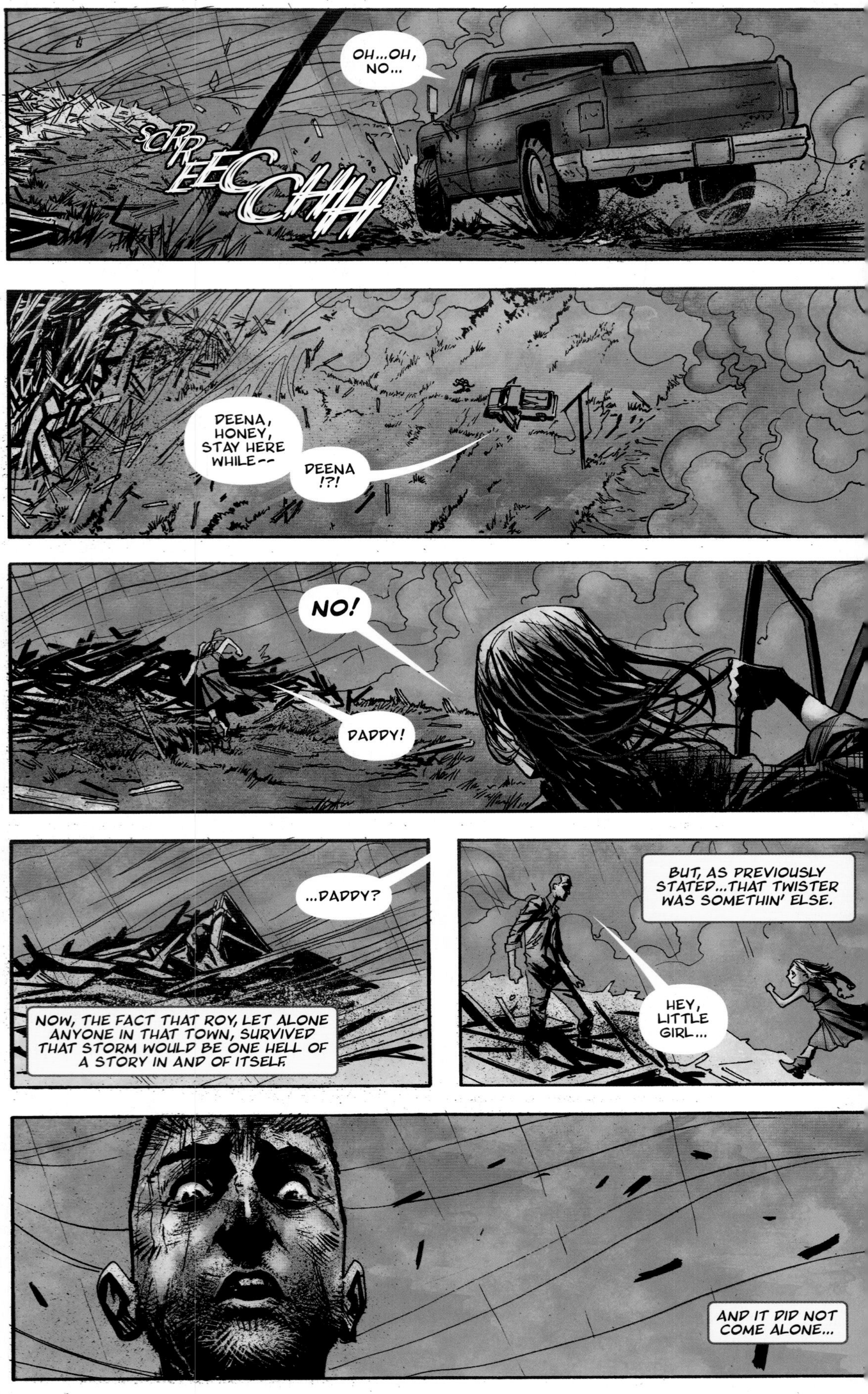
OH...OH, NO...
SCRREECCHHH
DEENA, HONEY, STAY HERE WHILE--
DEENA !?!
NO!
DADDY!
...DADDY?
NOW, THE FACT THAT ROY, LET ALONE ANYONE IN THAT TOWN, SURVIVED THAT STORM WOULD BE ONE HELL OF A STORY IN AND OF ITSELF.
BUT, AS PREVIOUSLY STATED...THAT TWISTER WAS SOMETHIN' ELSE.
HEY, LITTLE GIRL...
AND IT DID NOT COME ALONE...

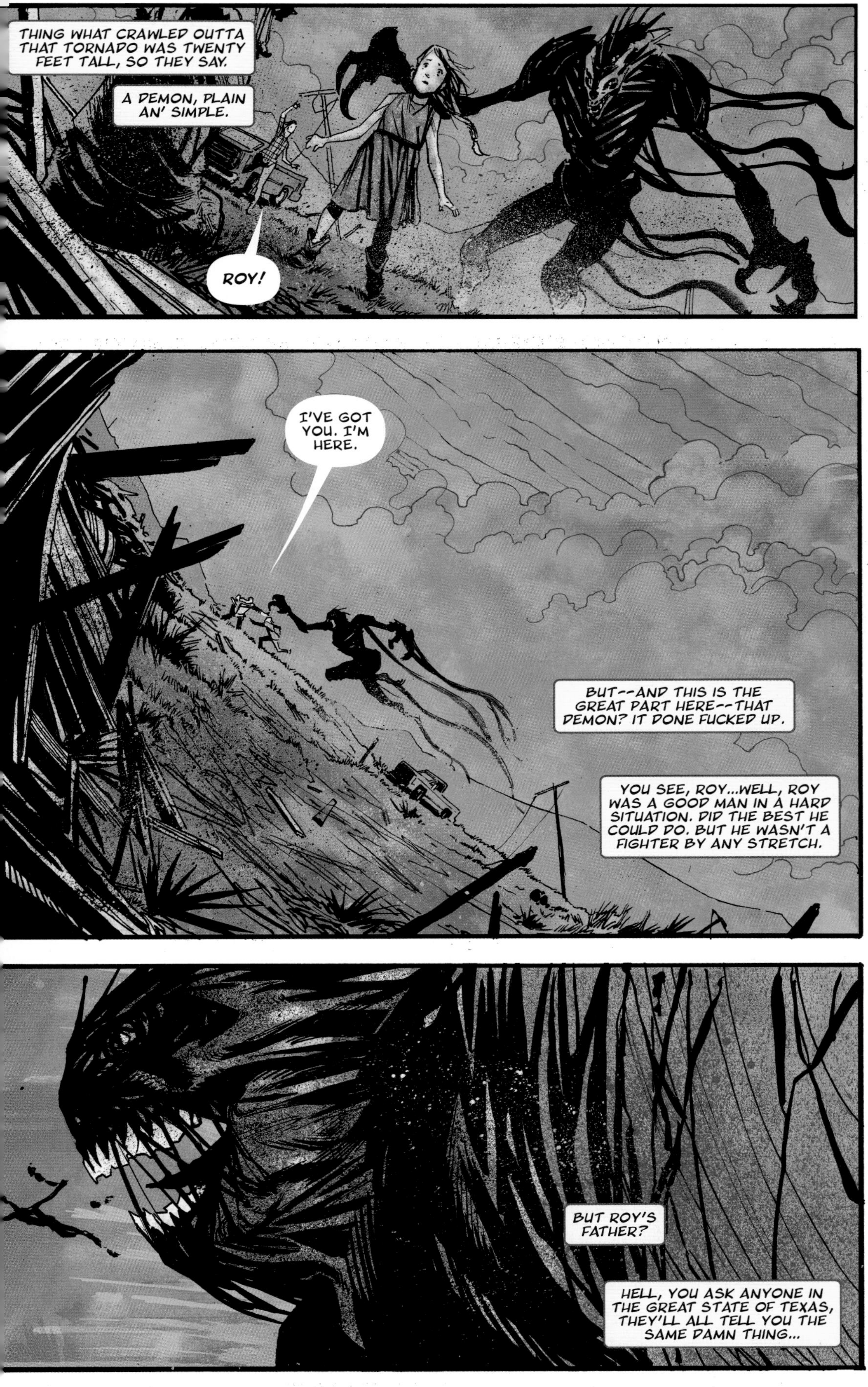
THING WHAT CRAWLED OUTTA THAT TORNADO WAS TWENTY FEET TALL, SO THEY SAY.
A DEMON, PLAIN AN' SIMPLE.
ROY!
I'VE GOT YOU. I'M HERE.
BUT--AND THIS IS THE GREAT PART HERE--THAT DEMON? IT DONE FUCKED UP.
YOU SEE, ROY...WELL, ROY WAS A GOOD MAN IN A HARD SITUATION. DID THE BEST HE COULD DO. BUT HE WASN'T A FIGHTER BY ANY STRETCH.
BUT ROY'S FATHER?
HELL, YOU ASK ANYONE IN THE GREAT STATE OF TEXAS, THEY'LL ALL TELL YOU THE SAME DAMN THING...

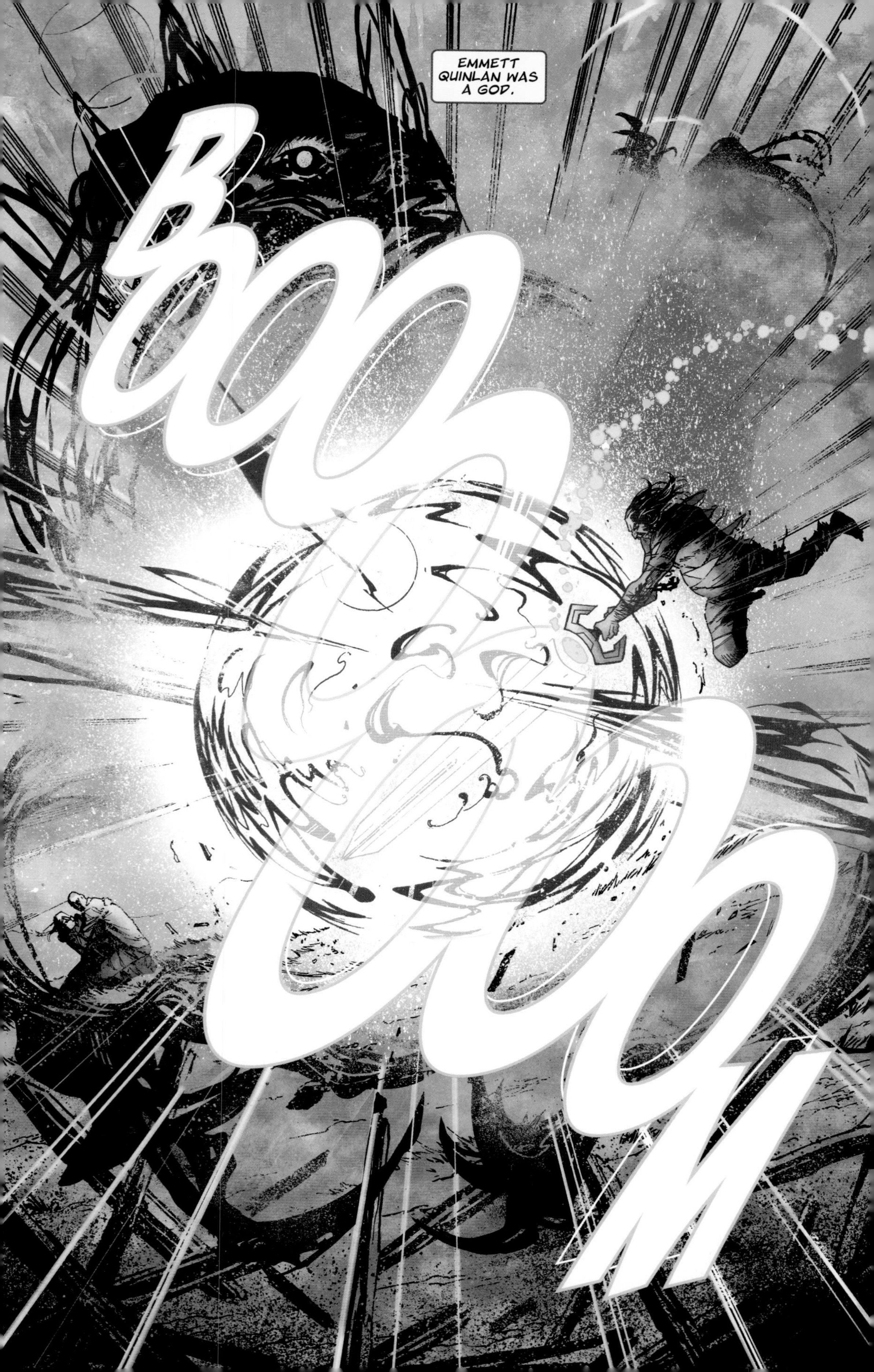
EMMETT QUINLAN WAS A GOD.
BOOOOOM

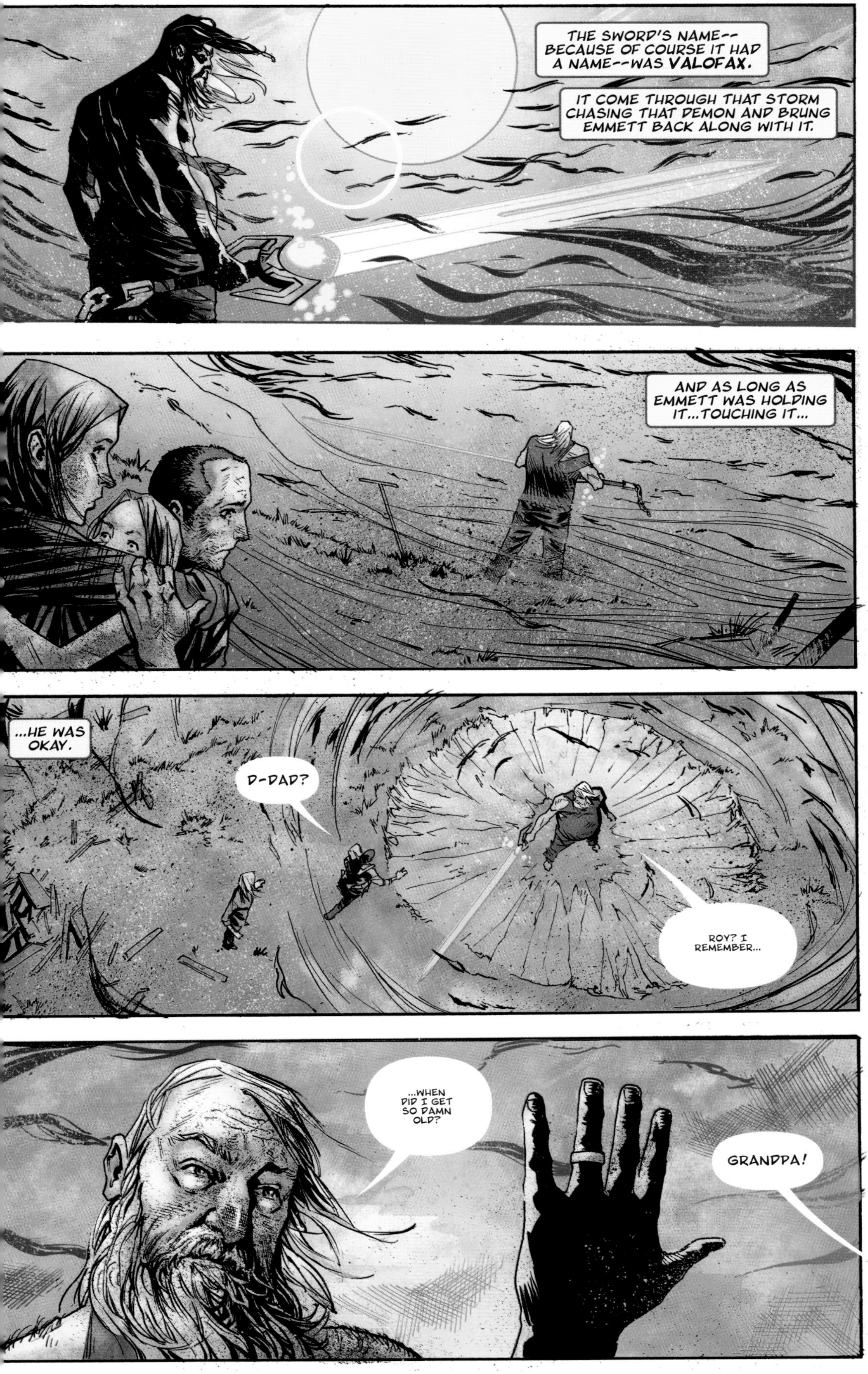
THE SWORD'S NAME--BECAUSE OF COURSE IT HAD A NAME--WAS VALOFAX.
IT COME THROUGH THAT STORM CHASING THAT DEMON AND BRUNG EMMETT BACK ALONG WITH IT.
AND AS LONG AS EMMETT WAS HOLDING IT...TOUCHING IT...
...HE WAS OKAY.
D-DAD?
ROY? I REMEMBER...
...WHEN DID I GET SO DAMN OLD?
GRANDPA!

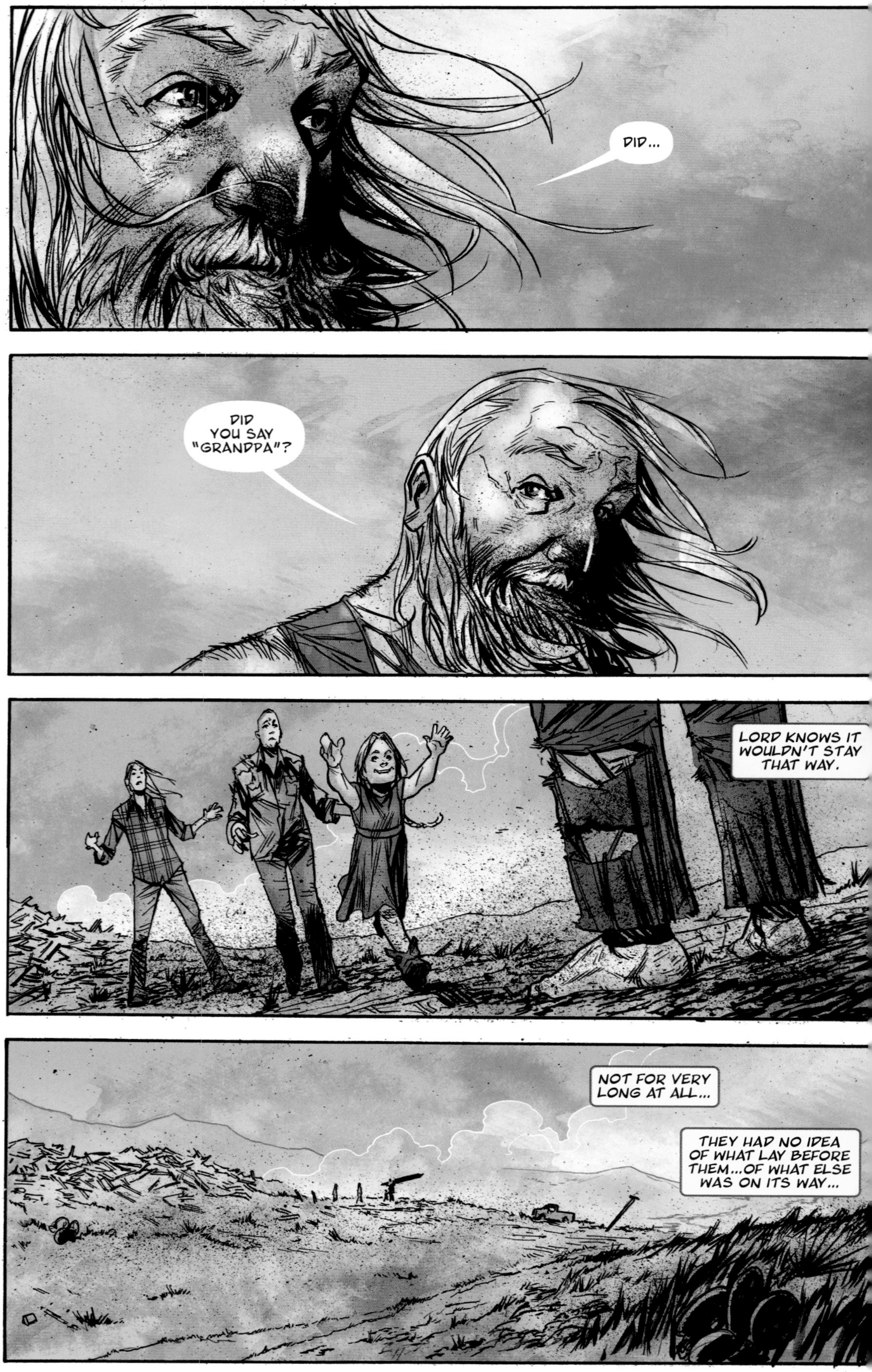
DID...
DID YOU SAY "GRANDPA"?
LORD KNOWS IT WOULDN'T STAY THAT WAY.
NOT FOR VERY LONG AT ALL...
THEY HAD NO IDEA OF WHAT LAY BEFORE THEM...OF WHAT ELSE WAS ON ITS WAY...

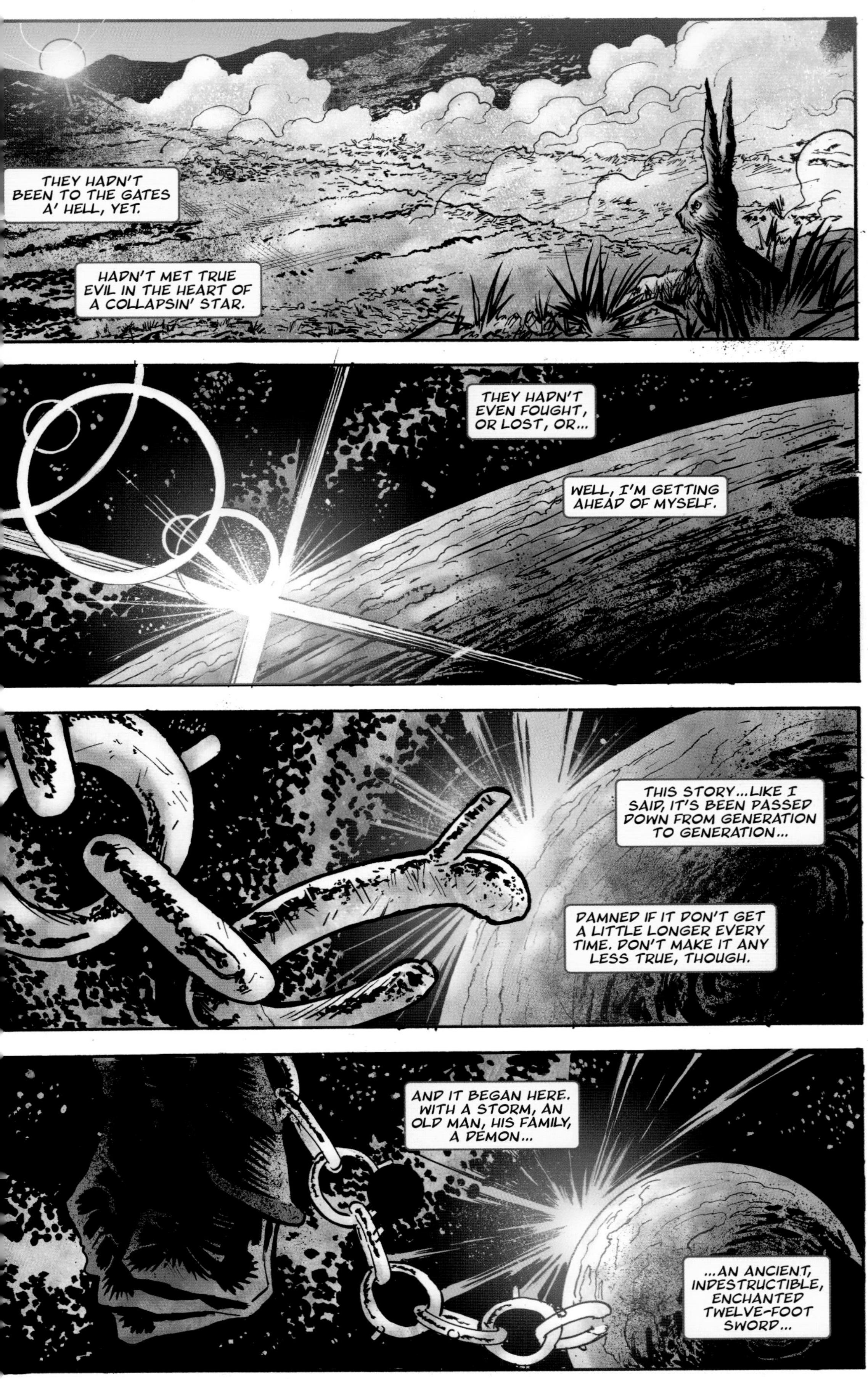
THEY HADN'T BEEN TO THE GATES A' HELL, YET.
HADN'T MET TRUE EVIL IN THE HEART OF A COLLAPSIN' STAR.
THEY HADN'T EVEN FOUGHT, OR LOST, OR...
WELL, I'M GETTING AHEAD OF MYSELF.
THIS STORY...LIKE I SAID, IT'S BEEN PASSED DOWN FROM GENERATION TO GENERATION...
DAMNED IF IT DON'T GET A LITTLE LONGER EVERY TIME. DON'T MAKE IT ANY LESS TRUE, THOUGH.
AND IT BEGAN HERE. WITH A STORM, AN OLD MAN, HIS FAMILY, A DEMON...
...AN ANCIENT, INDESTRUCTIBLE, ENCHANTED TWELVE-FOOT SWORD...

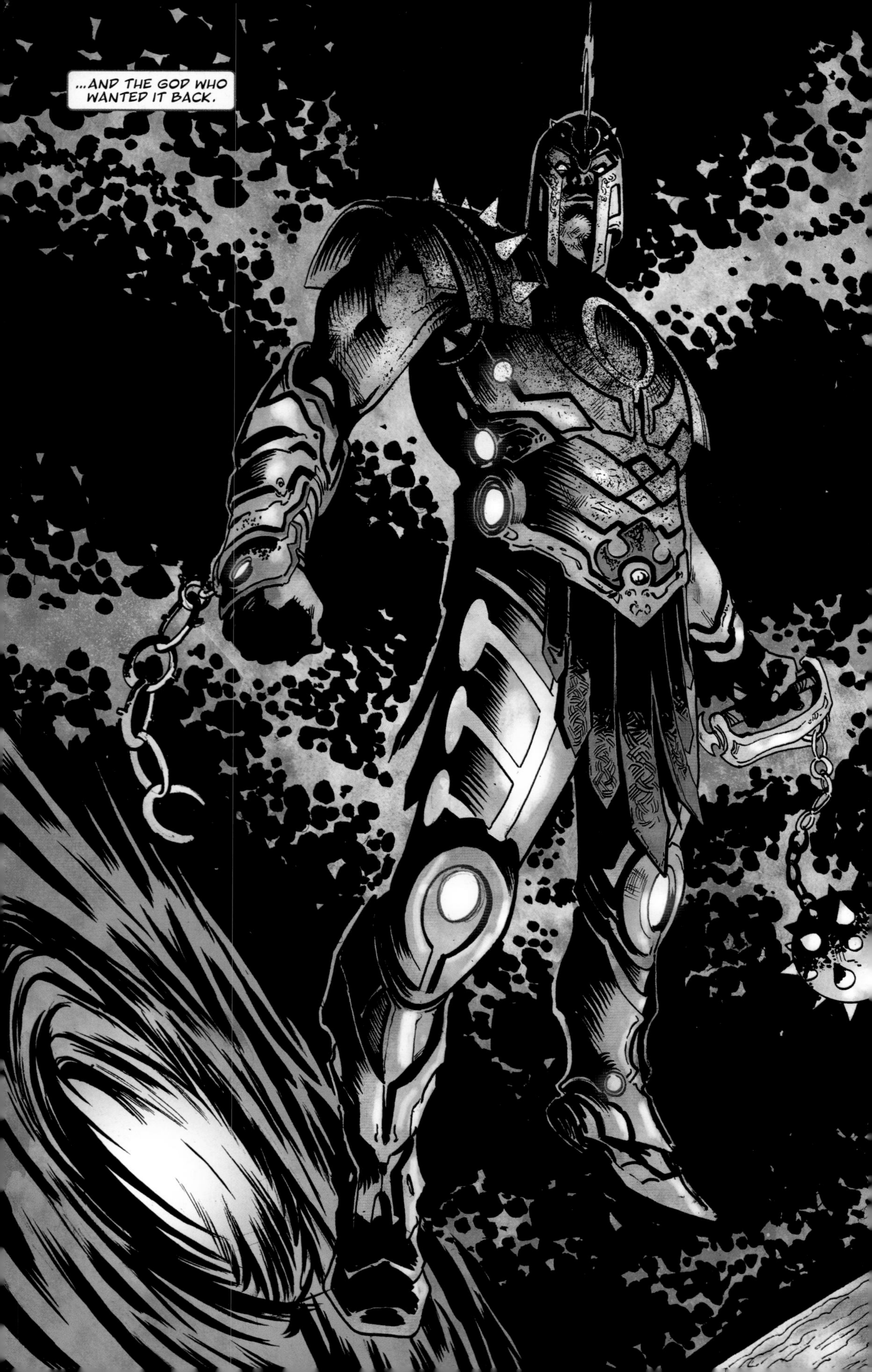
...AND THE GOD WHO WANTED IT BACK.

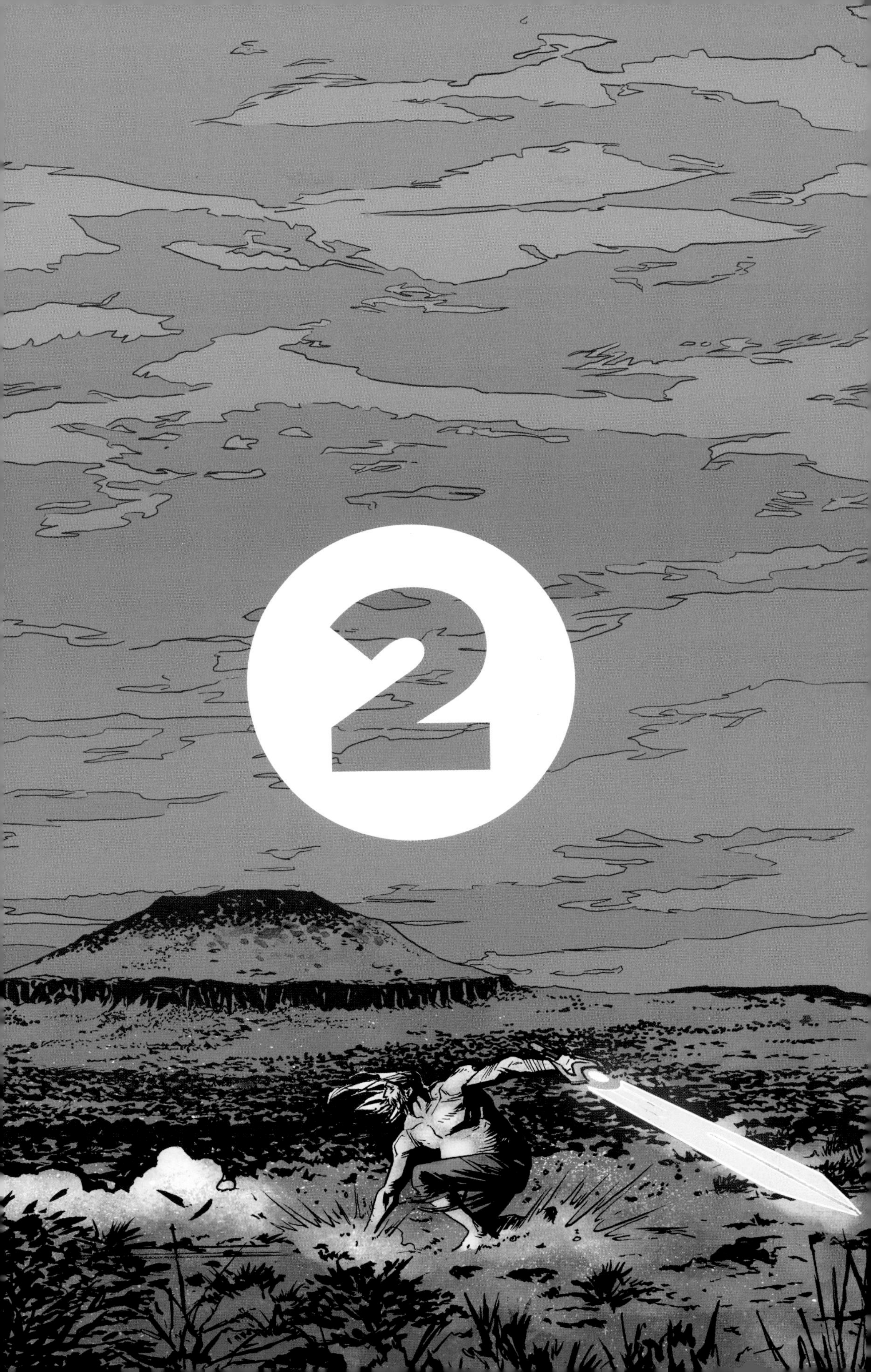
2

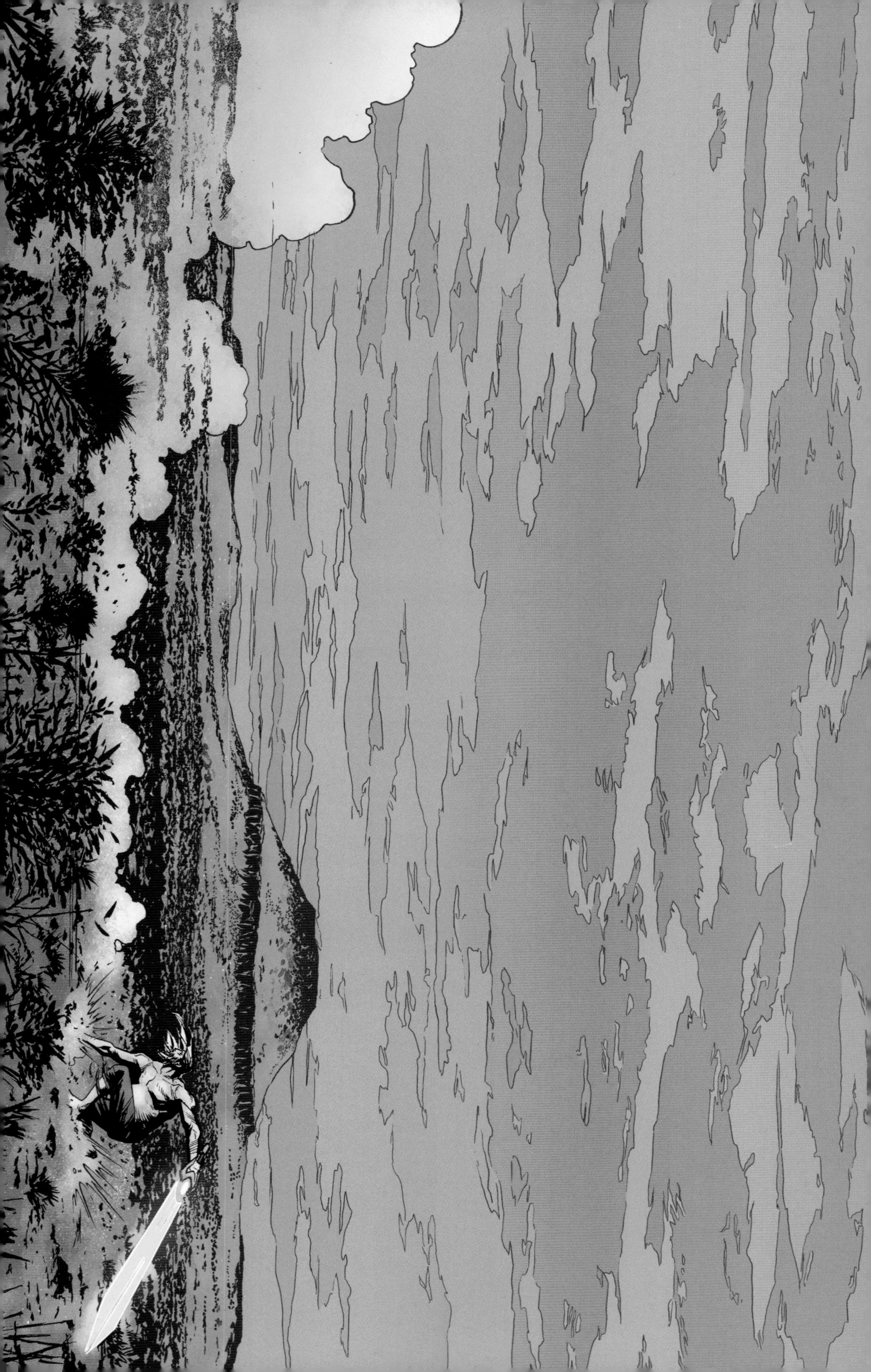

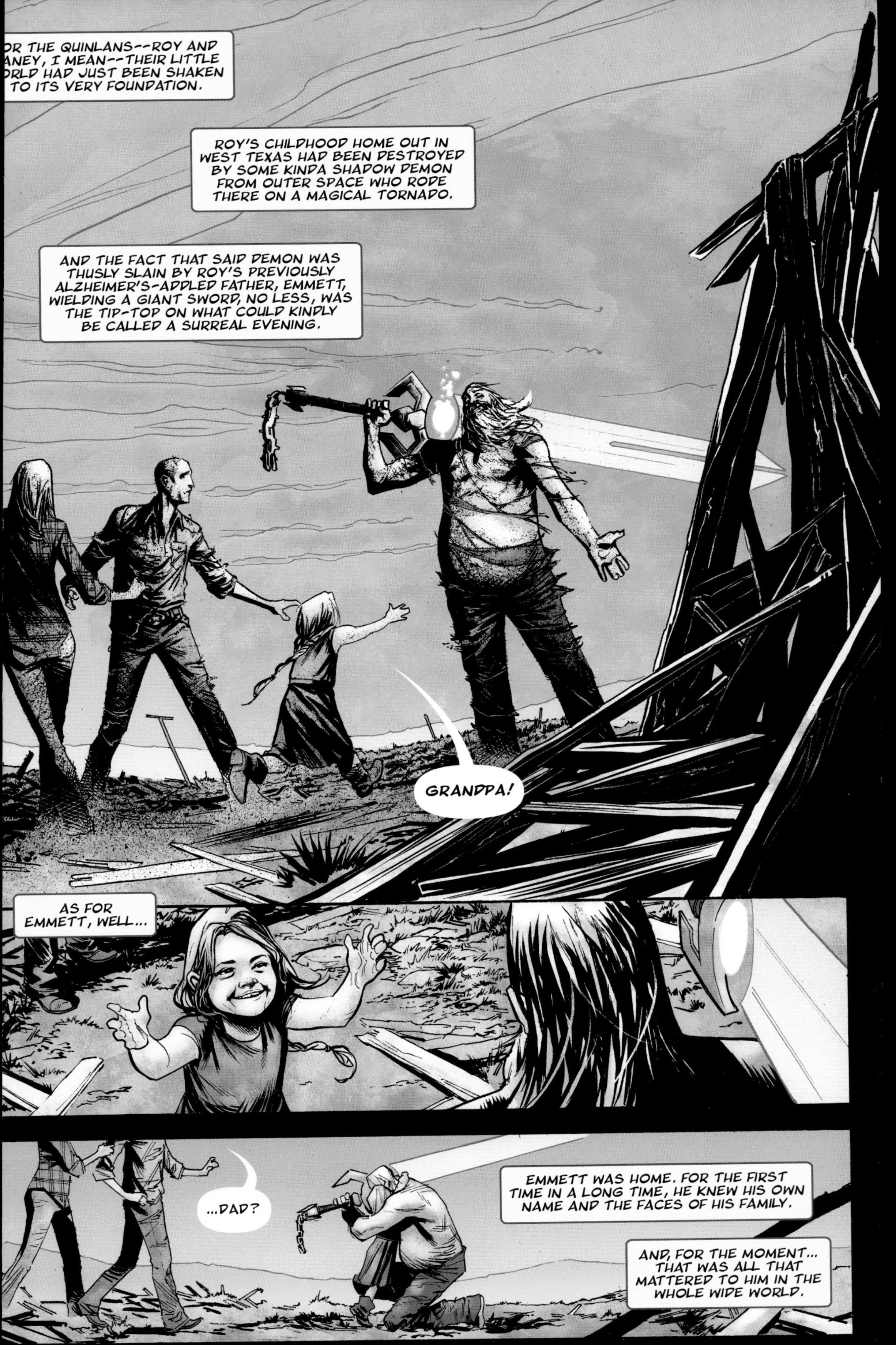
OR THE QUINLANS--ROY AND
ANEY, I MEAN--THEIR LITTLE
ORLD HAD JUST BEEN SHAKEN
TO ITS VERY FOUNDATION.
ROY'S CHILDHOOD HOME OUT IN WEST TEXAS HAD BEEN DESTROYED BY SOME KINDA SHADOW DEMON FROM OUTER SPACE WHO RODE THERE ON A MAGICAL TORNADO.
AND THE FACT THAT SAID DEMON WAS THUSLY SLAIN BY ROY'S PREVIOUSLY ALZHEIMER'S-ADDLED FATHER, EMMETT, WIELDING A GIANT SWORD, NO LESS, WAS THE TIP-TOP ON WHAT COULD KINDLY BE CALLED A SURREAL EVENING.
GRANDPA!
AS FOR EMMETT, WELL...
...DAD?
EMMETT WAS HOME. FOR THE FIRST TIME IN A LONG TIME, HE KNEW HIS OWN NAME AND THE FACES OF HIS FAMILY.
AND, FOR THE MOMENT... THAT WAS ALL THAT MATTERED TO HIM IN THE WHOLE WIDE WORLD.

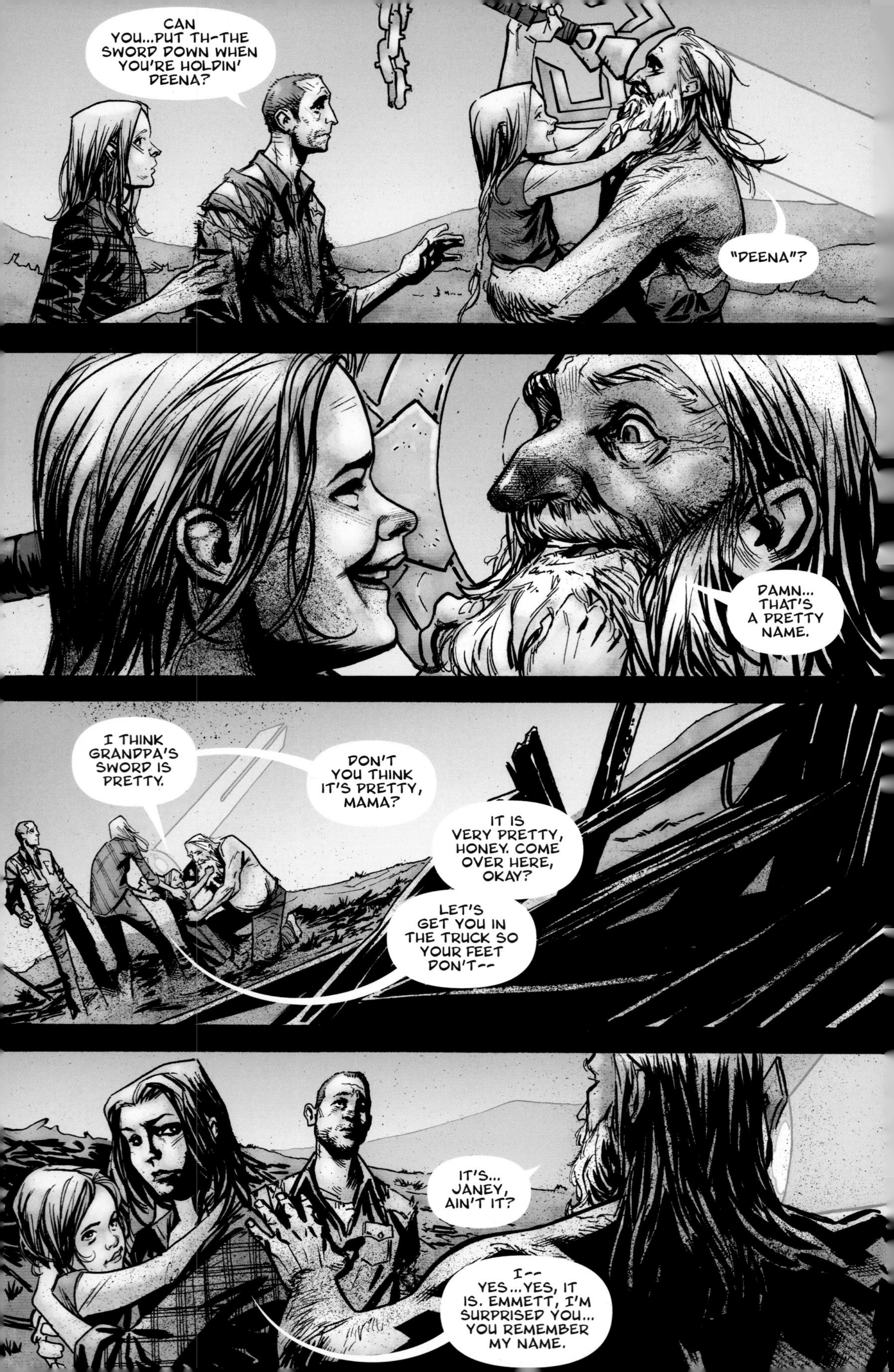
CAN YOU...PUT TH-THE SWORD DOWN WHEN YOU'RE HOLDIN' DEENA?
"DEENA"?
DAMN... THAT'S A PRETTY NAME.
I THINK GRANDPA'S SWORD IS PRETTY.
DON'T YOU THINK IT'S PRETTY, MAMA?
IT IS VERY PRETTY, HONEY. COME OVER HERE, OKAY?
LET'S GET YOU IN THE TRUCK SO YOUR FEET DON'T--
IT'S... JANEY, AIN'T IT?
I-- YES...YES, IT IS. EMMETT, I'M SURPRISED YOU... YOU REMEMBER MY NAME.

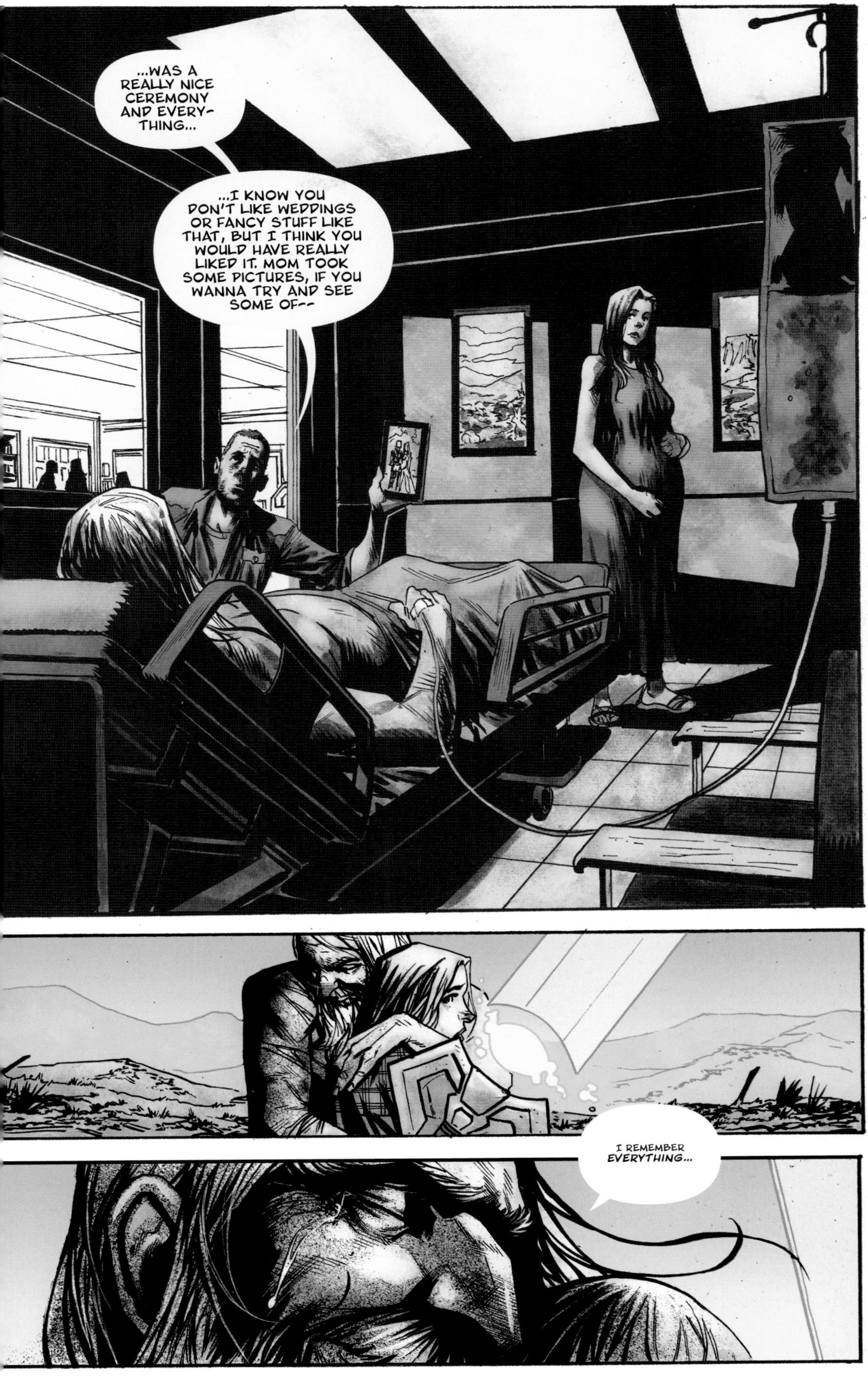
...WAS A REALLY NICE CEREMONY AND EVERY-THING...
...I KNOW YOU DON'T LIKE WEDDINGS OR FANCY STUFF LIKE THAT, BUT I THINK YOU WOULD HAVE REALLY LIKED IT. MOM TOOK SOME PICTURES, IF YOU WANNA TRY AND SEE SOME OF--
I REMEMBER EVERYTHING...

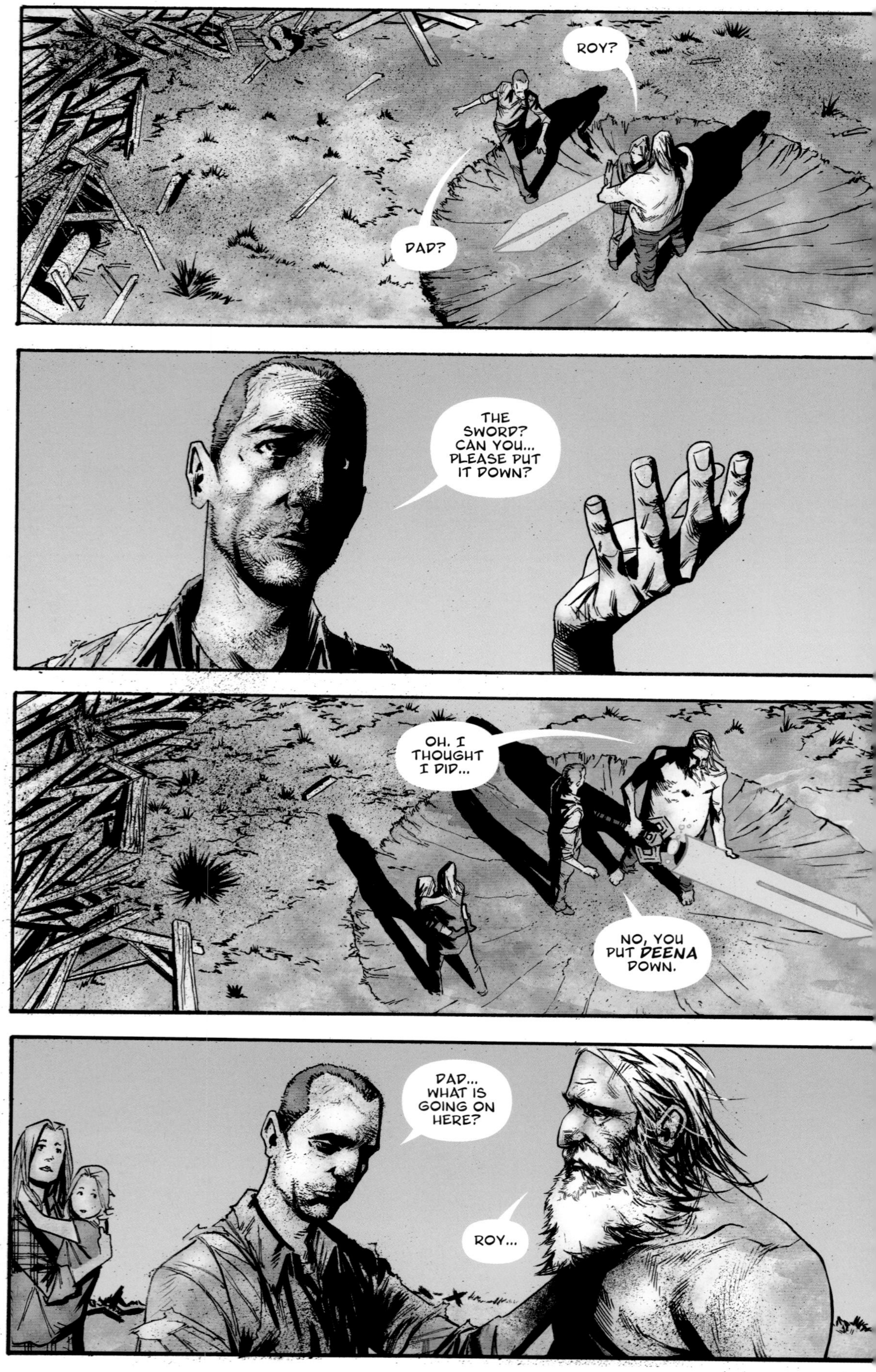
ROY?
DAD?
THE SWORD? CAN YOU... PLEASE PUT IT DOWN?
OH. I THOUGHT I DID...
NO, YOU PUT **DEENA** DOWN.
DAD... WHAT IS GOING ON HERE?
ROY...

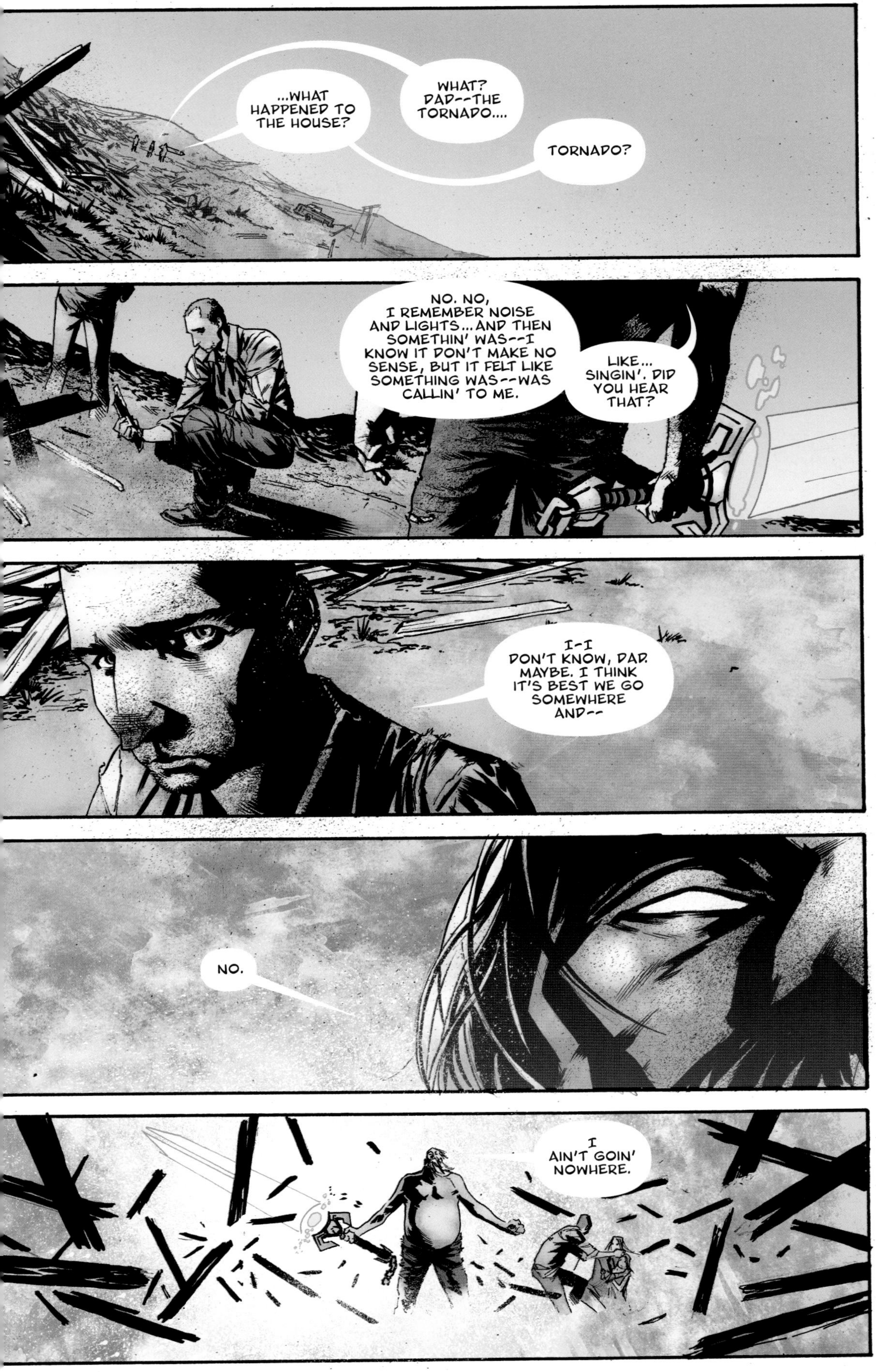
...WHAT HAPPENED TO THE HOUSE?
WHAT? DAD--THE TORNADO....
TORNADO?
NO. NO, I REMEMBER NOISE AND LIGHTS... AND THEN SOMETHIN' WAS--I KNOW IT DON'T MAKE NO SENSE, BUT IT FELT LIKE SOMETHING WAS--WAS CALLIN' TO ME.
LIKE... SINGIN'. DID YOU HEAR THAT?
I-I DON'T KNOW, DAD. MAYBE. I THINK IT'S BEST WE GO SOMEWHERE AND--
NO.
I AIN'T GOIN' NOWHERE.

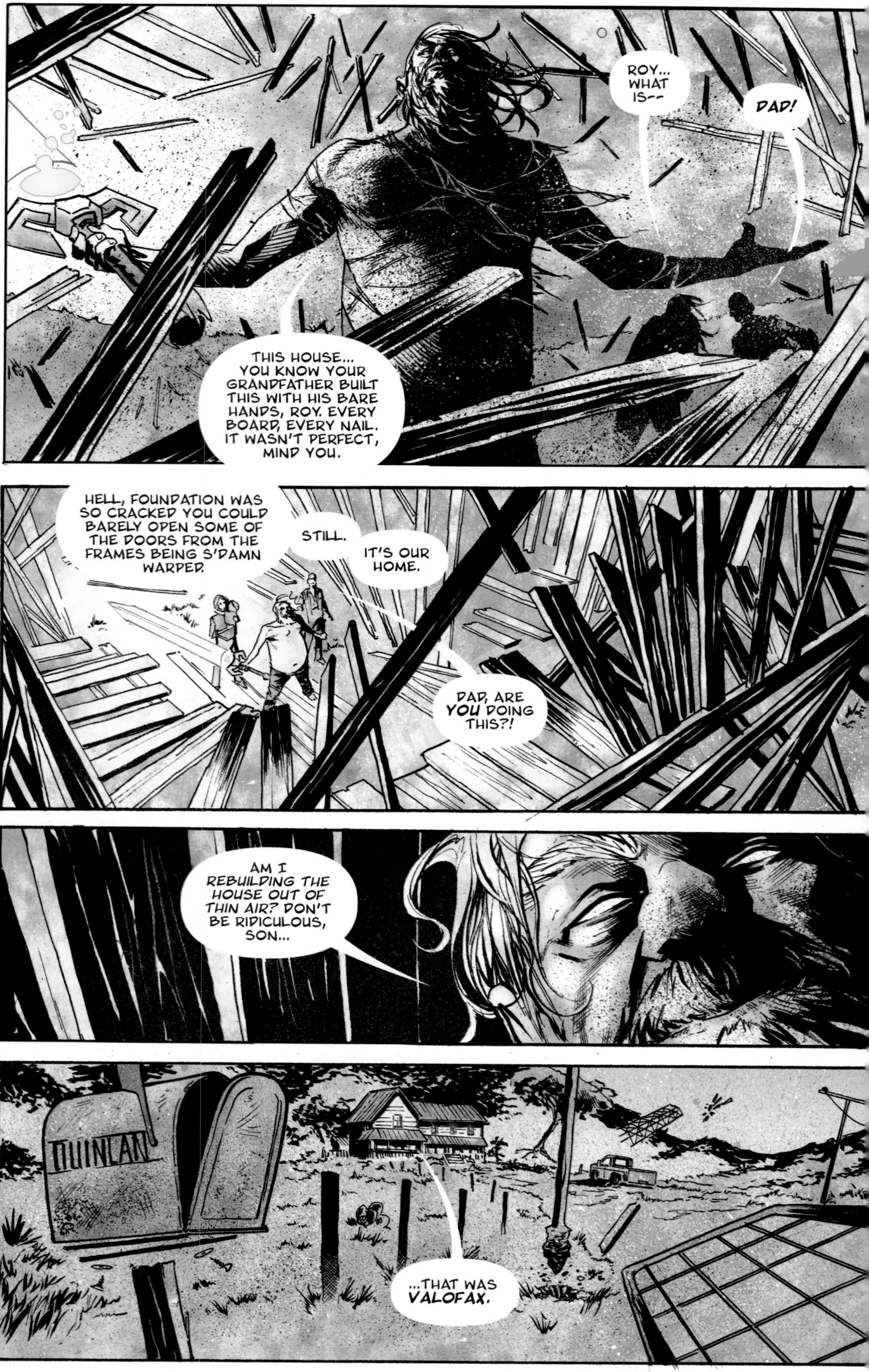

ROY... WHAT IS--
DAD!
THIS HOUSE... YOU KNOW YOUR GRANDFATHER BUILT THIS WITH HIS BARE HANDS, ROY. EVERY BOARD, EVERY NAIL. IT WASN'T PERFECT, MIND YOU.
HELL, FOUNDATION WAS SO CRACKED YOU COULD BARELY OPEN SOME OF THE DOORS FROM THE FRAMES BEING S'DAMN WARPED.
STILL.
IT'S OUR HOME.
DAD, ARE YOU DOING THIS?!
AM I REBUILDING THE HOUSE OUT OF THIN AIR? DON'T BE RIDICULOUS, SON...
QUINLAN
...THAT WAS VALOFAX.

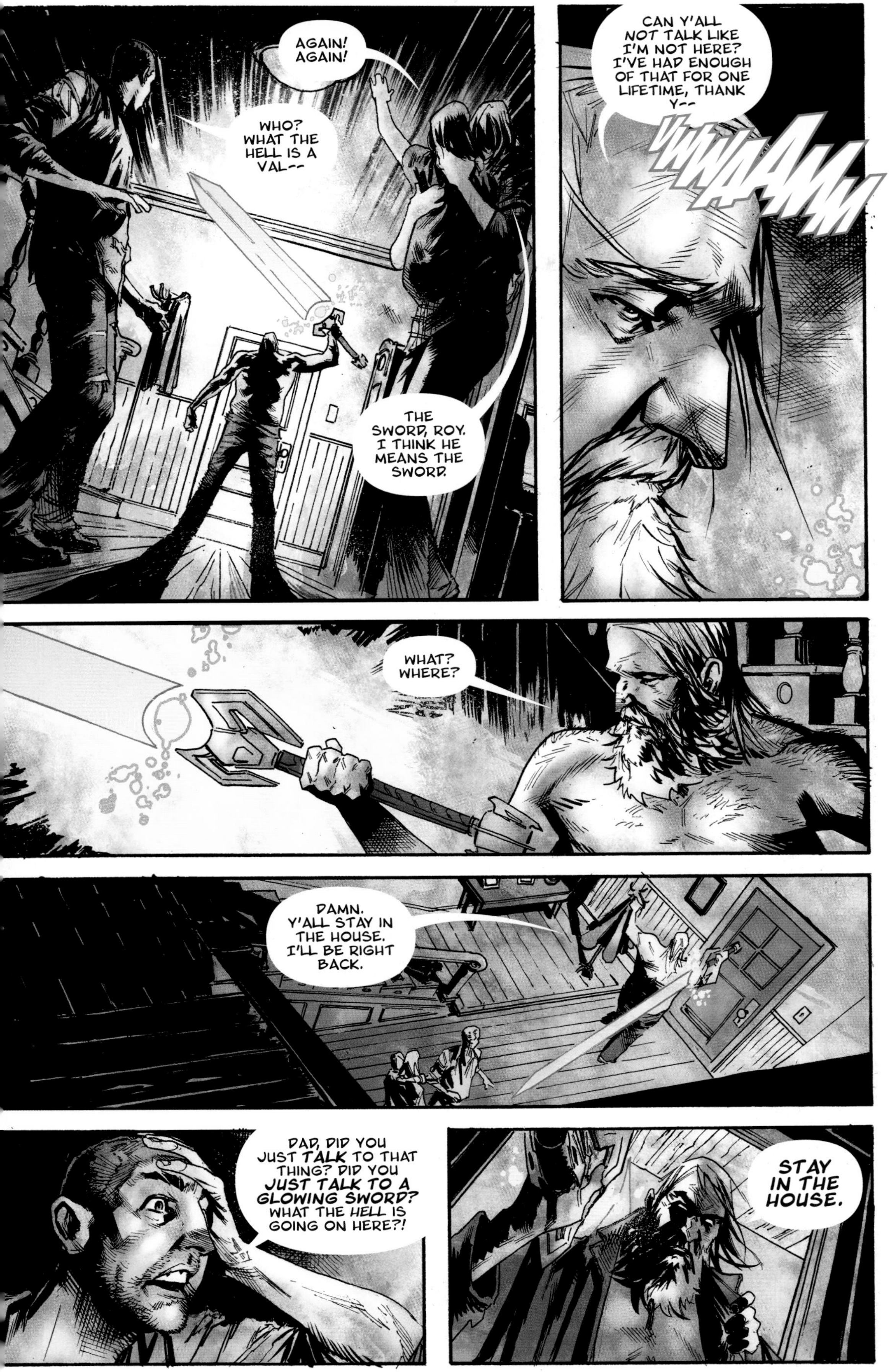
AGAIN! AGAIN!
WHO? WHAT THE HELL IS A VAL--
THE SWORD, ROY. I THINK HE MEANS THE SWORD.
CAN Y'ALL NOT TALK LIKE I'M NOT HERE? I'VE HAD ENOUGH OF THAT FOR ONE LIFETIME, THANK Y--
VWAAAMM
WHAT? WHERE?
DAMN. Y'ALL STAY IN THE HOUSE. I'LL BE RIGHT BACK.
DAD, DID YOU JUST TALK TO THAT THING? DID YOU JUST TALK TO A GLOWING SWORD? WHAT THE HELL IS GOING ON HERE?!
STAY IN THE HOUSE.

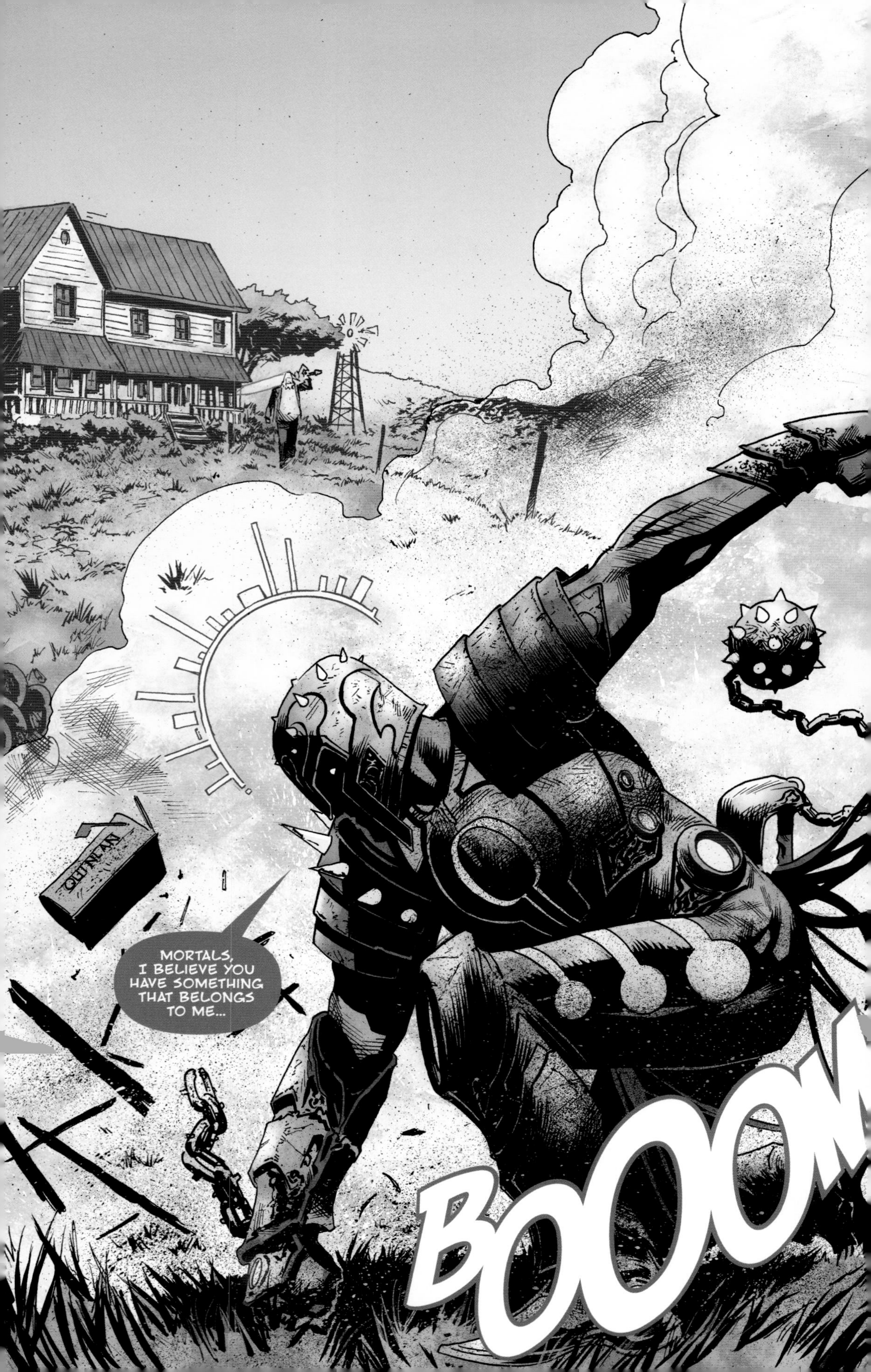
MORTALS, I BELIEVE YOU HAVE SOMETHING THAT BELONGS TO ME...
BOOOM

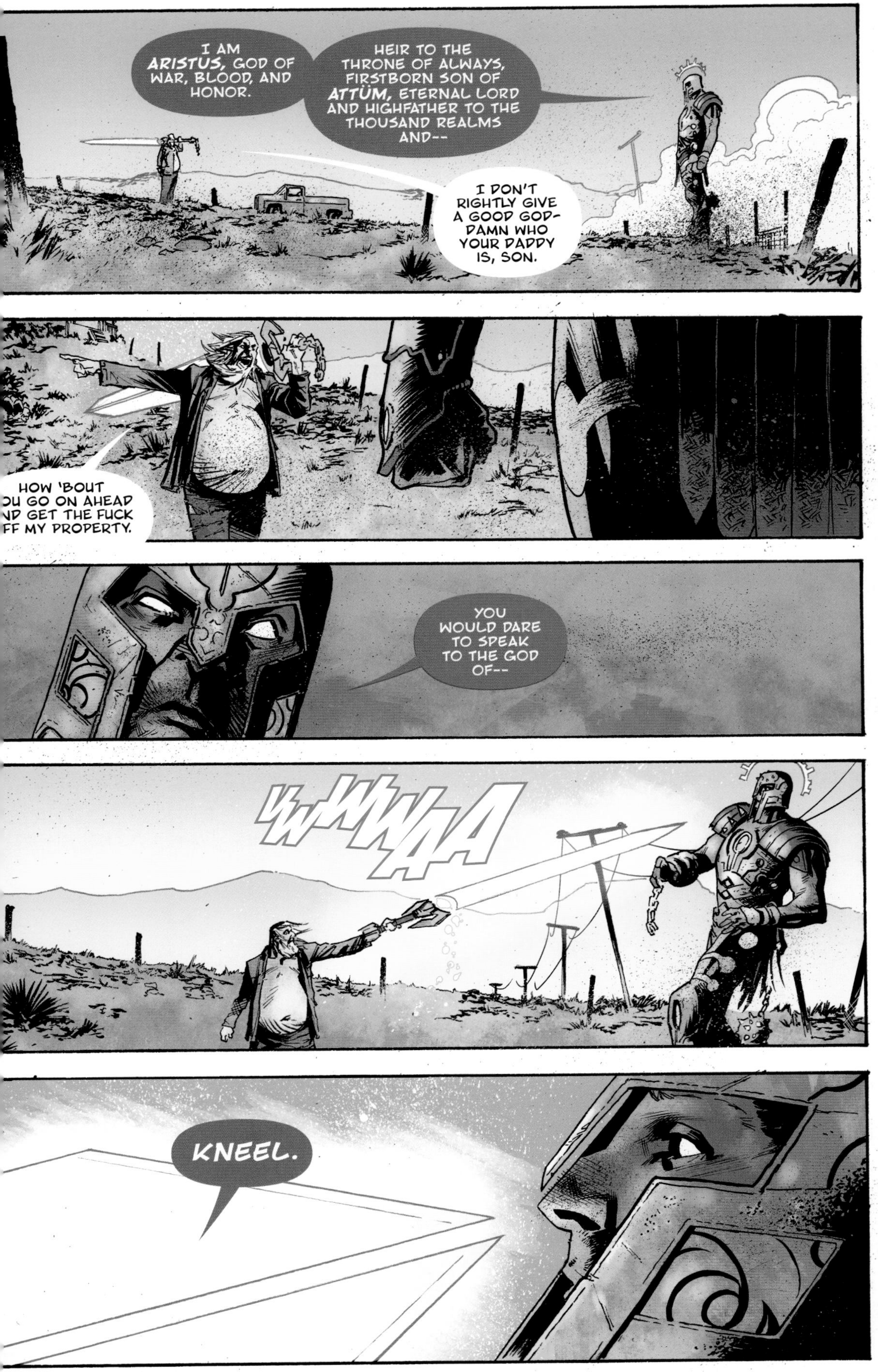

I AM ARISTUS, GOD OF WAR, BLOOD, AND HONOR.
HEIR TO THE THRONE OF ALWAYS, FIRSTBORN SON OF ATTÜM, ETERNAL LORD AND HIGHFATHER TO THE THOUSAND REALMS AND--
I DON'T RIGHTLY GIVE A GOOD GOD-DAMN WHO YOUR DADDY IS, SON.
HOW 'BOUT OU GO ON AHEAD ND GET THE FUCK FF MY PROPERTY.
YOU WOULD DARE TO SPEAK TO THE GOD OF--
WWWWAA
KNEEL.

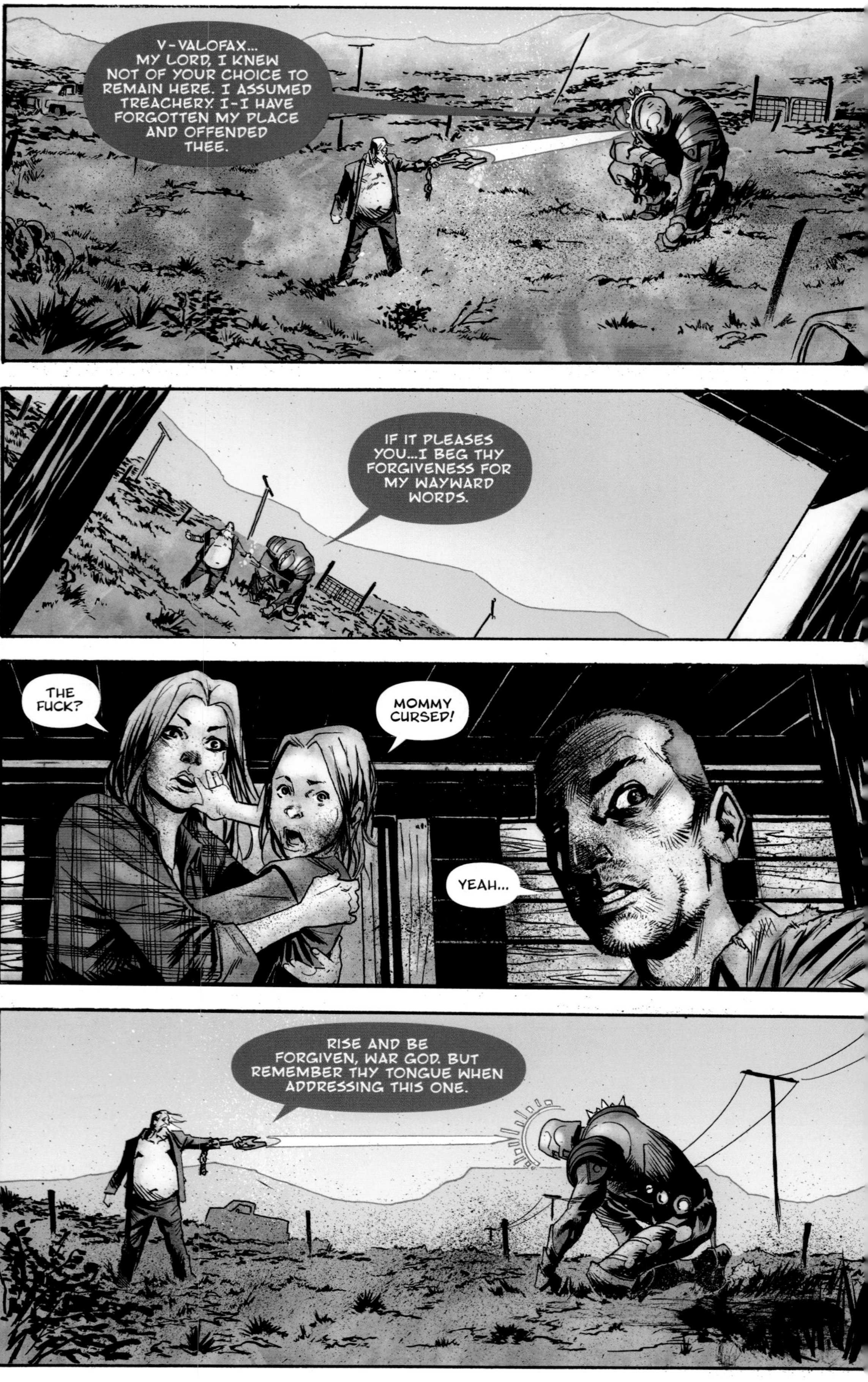
V-VALOFAX... MY LORD, I KNEW NOT OF YOUR CHOICE TO REMAIN HERE. I ASSUMED TREACHERY. I-I HAVE FORGOTTEN MY PLACE AND OFFENDED THEE.
IF IT PLEASES YOU...I BEG THY FORGIVENESS FOR MY WAYWARD WORDS.
THE FUCK?
MOMMY CURSED!
YEAH...
RISE AND BE FORGIVEN, WAR GOD. BUT REMEMBER THY TONGUE WHEN ADDRESSING THIS ONE.

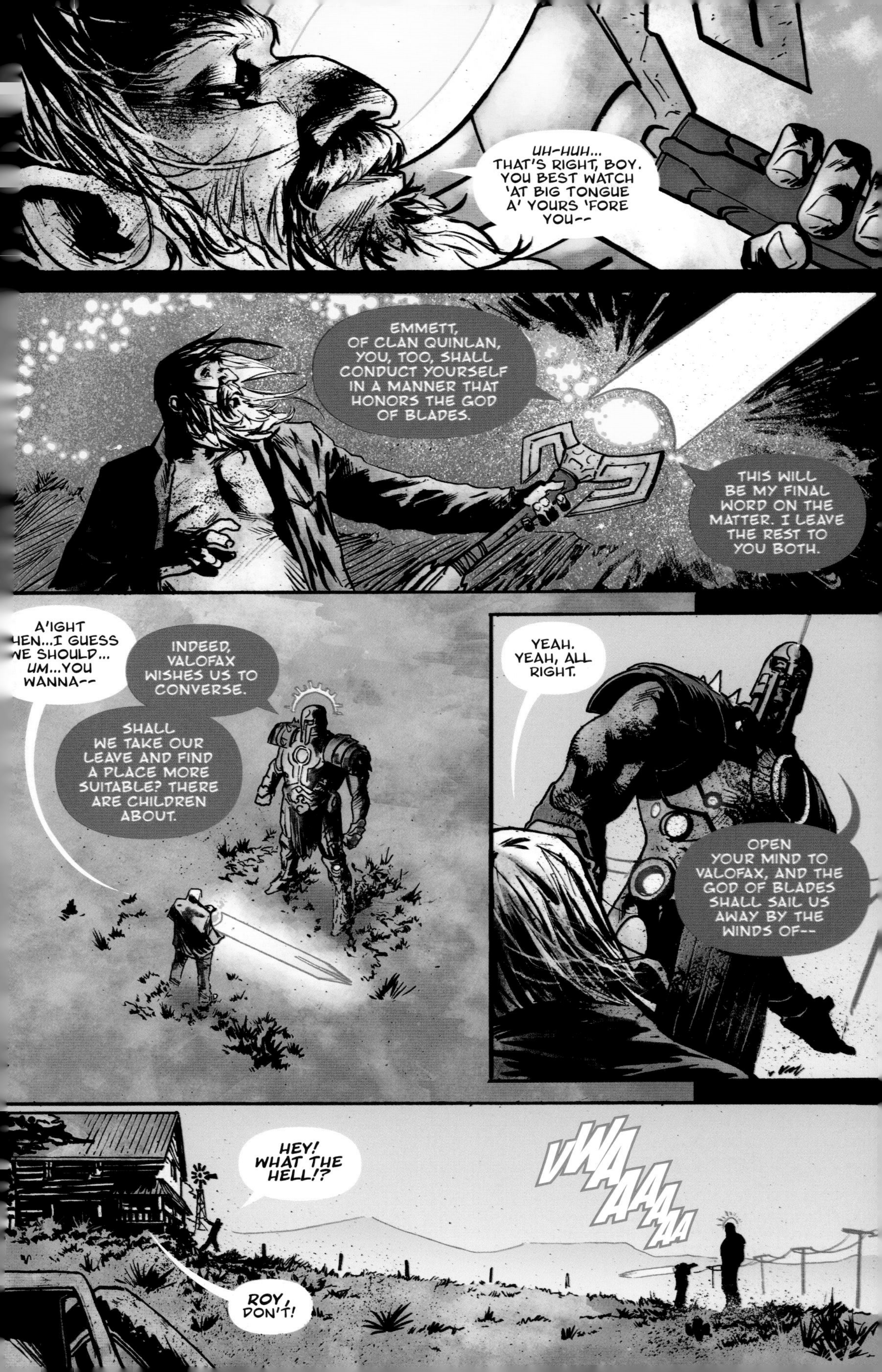
UH-HUH... THAT'S RIGHT, BOY. YOU BEST WATCH 'AT BIG TONGUE A' YOURS 'FORE YOU--
EMMETT, OF CLAN QUINLAN, YOU, TOO, SHALL CONDUCT YOURSELF IN A MANNER THAT HONORS THE GOD OF BLADES.
THIS WILL BE MY FINAL WORD ON THE MATTER. I LEAVE THE REST TO YOU BOTH.
A'IGHT HEN...I GUESS WE SHOULD... UM...YOU WANNA--
INDEED, VALOFAX WISHES US TO CONVERSE.
SHALL WE TAKE OUR LEAVE AND FIND A PLACE MORE SUITABLE? THERE ARE CHILDREN ABOUT.
YEAH. YEAH, ALL RIGHT.
OPEN YOUR MIND TO VALOFAX, AND THE GOD OF BLADES SHALL SAIL US AWAY BY THE WINDS OF--
HEY! WHAT THE HELL!?
VWAAAAAAA
ROY, DON'T!

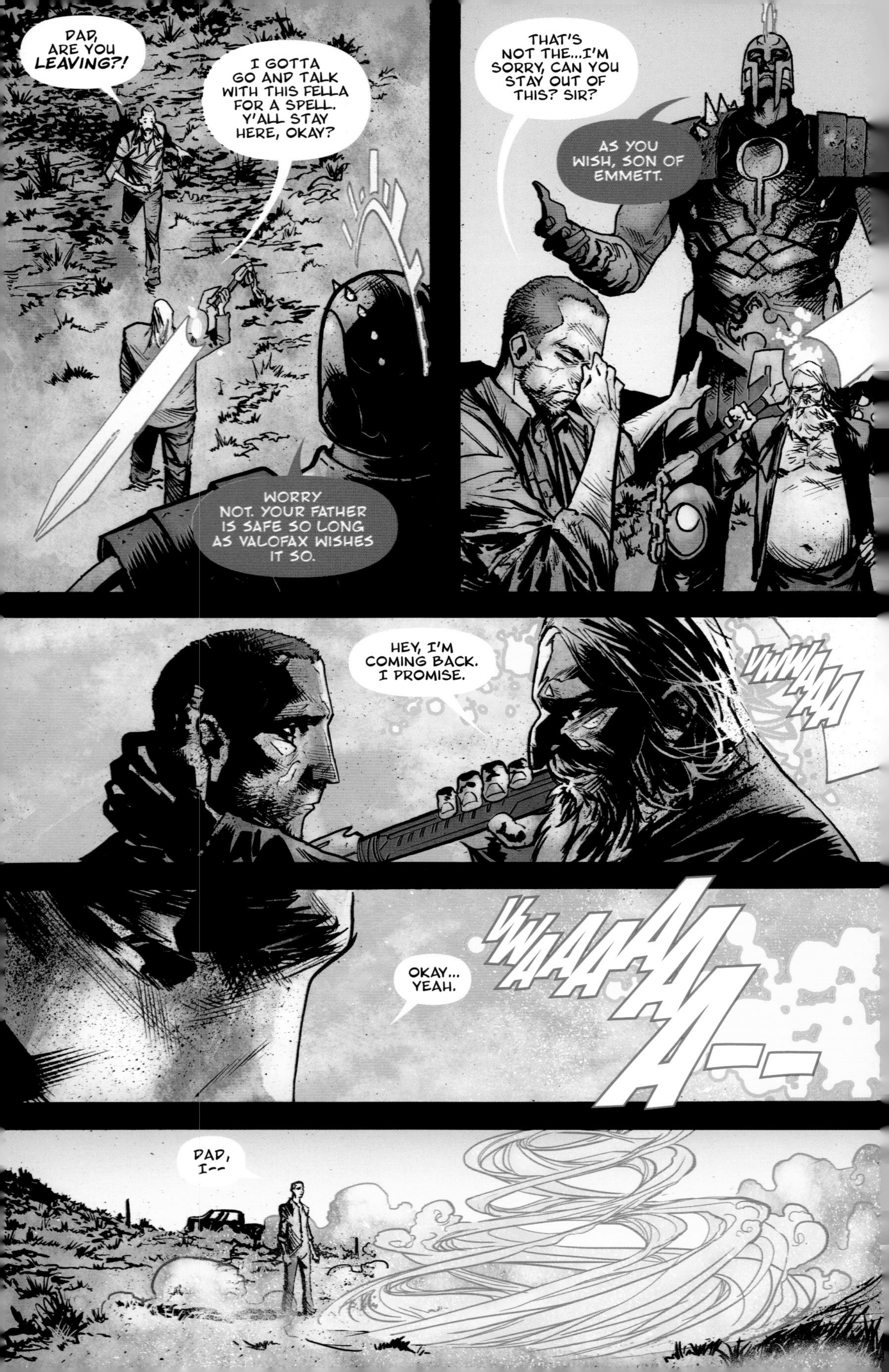
DAD, ARE YOU LEAVING?!
I GOTTA GO AND TALK WITH THIS FELLA FOR A SPELL. Y'ALL STAY HERE, OKAY?
WORRY NOT. YOUR FATHER IS SAFE SO LONG AS VALOFAX WISHES IT SO.
THAT'S NOT THE...I'M SORRY, CAN YOU STAY OUT OF THIS? SIR?
AS YOU WISH, SON OF EMMETT.
HEY, I'M COMING BACK. I PROMISE.
VWWAAA
OKAY... YEAH.
VWAAAAAAAA--
DAD, I--

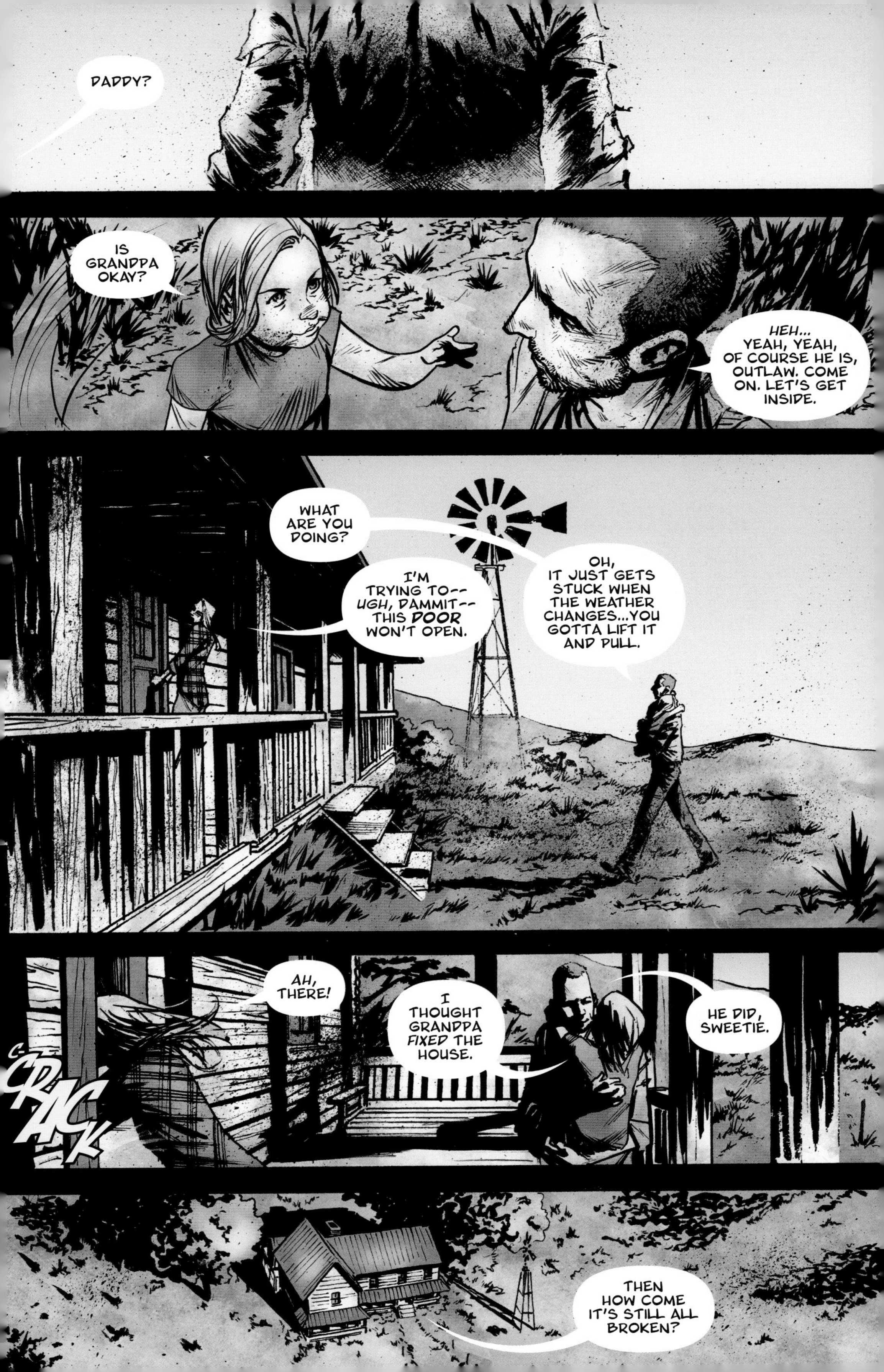
DADDY?
IS GRANDPA OKAY?
HEH... YEAH, YEAH, OF COURSE HE IS, OUTLAW. COME ON. LET'S GET INSIDE.
WHAT ARE YOU DOING?
I'M TRYING TO-- UGH, DAMMIT-- THIS DOOR WON'T OPEN.
OH, IT JUST GETS STUCK WHEN THE WEATHER CHANGES...YOU GOTTA LIFT IT AND PULL.
C-CRACK
AH, THERE!
I THOUGHT GRANDPA FIXED THE HOUSE.
HE DID, SWEETIE.
THEN HOW COME IT'S STILL ALL BROKEN?

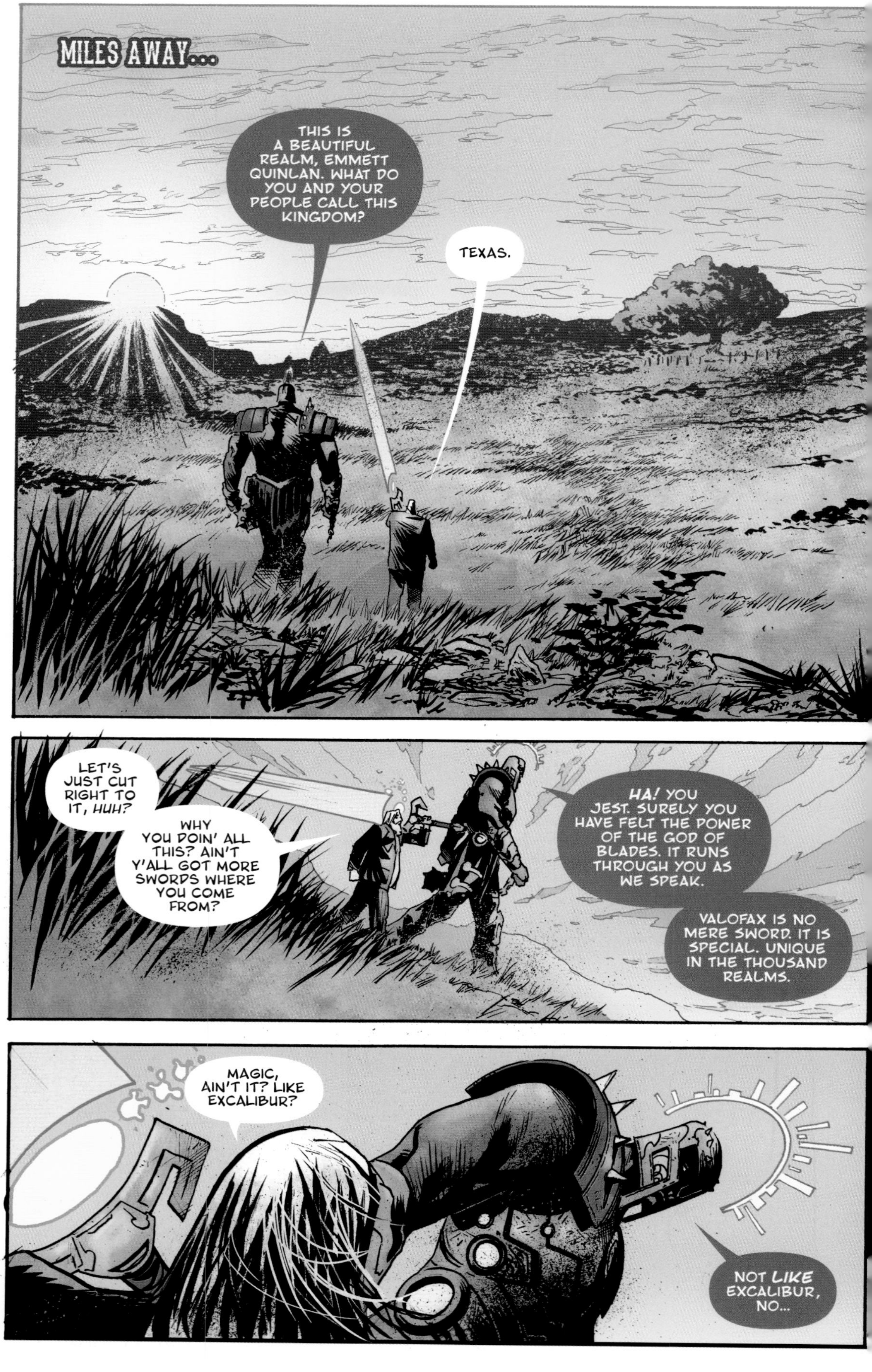
MILES AWAY...
THIS IS A BEAUTIFUL REALM, EMMETT QUINLAN. WHAT DO YOU AND YOUR PEOPLE CALL THIS KINGDOM?
TEXAS.
LET'S JUST CUT RIGHT TO IT, HUH?
WHY YOU DOIN' ALL THIS? AIN'T Y'ALL GOT MORE SWORDS WHERE YOU COME FROM?
HA! YOU JEST. SURELY YOU HAVE FELT THE POWER OF THE GOD OF BLADES. IT RUNS THROUGH YOU AS WE SPEAK.
VALOFAX IS NO MERE SWORD. IT IS SPECIAL. UNIQUE IN THE THOUSAND REALMS.
MAGIC, AIN'T IT? LIKE EXCALIBUR?
NOT LIKE EXCALIBUR, NO...

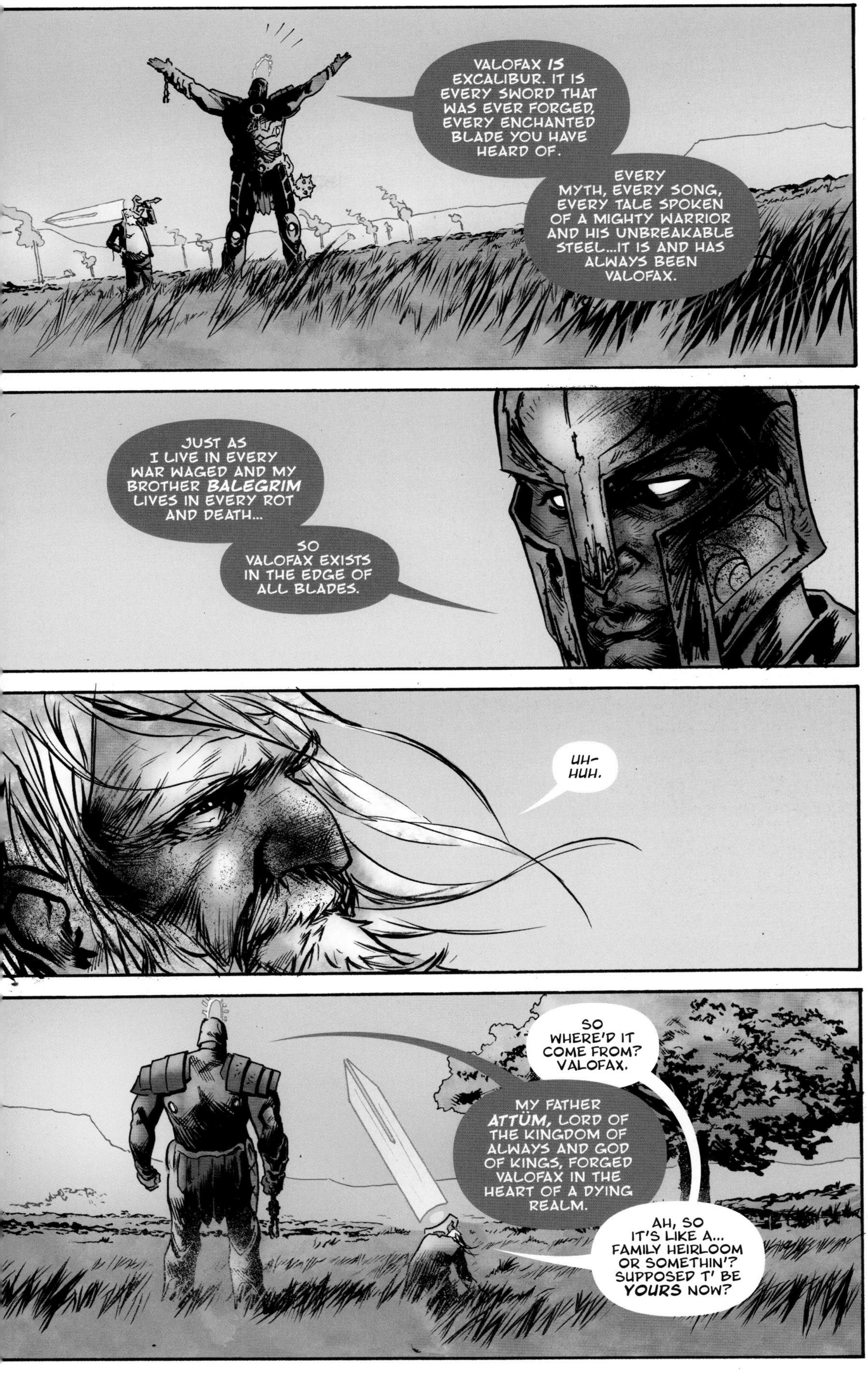
VALOFAX IS EXCALIBUR. IT IS EVERY SWORD THAT WAS EVER FORGED, EVERY ENCHANTED BLADE YOU HAVE HEARD OF.
EVERY MYTH, EVERY SONG, EVERY TALE SPOKEN OF A MIGHTY WARRIOR AND HIS UNBREAKABLE STEEL...IT IS AND HAS ALWAYS BEEN VALOFAX.
JUST AS I LIVE IN EVERY WAR WAGED AND MY BROTHER BALEGRIM LIVES IN EVERY ROT AND DEATH...
SO VALOFAX EXISTS IN THE EDGE OF ALL BLADES.
UH-HUH.
SO WHERE'D IT COME FROM? VALOFAX.
MY FATHER ATTÜM, LORD OF THE KINGDOM OF ALWAYS AND GOD OF KINGS, FORGED VALOFAX IN THE HEART OF A DYING REALM.
AH, SO IT'S LIKE A... FAMILY HEIRLOOM OR SOMETHIN'? SUPPOSED T' BE YOURS NOW?

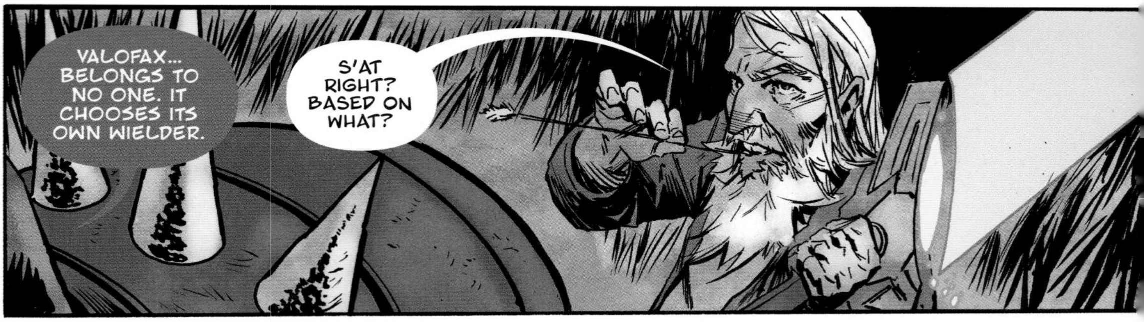
VALOFAX... BELONGS TO NO ONE. IT CHOOSES ITS OWN WIELDER.
S'AT RIGHT? BASED ON WHAT?

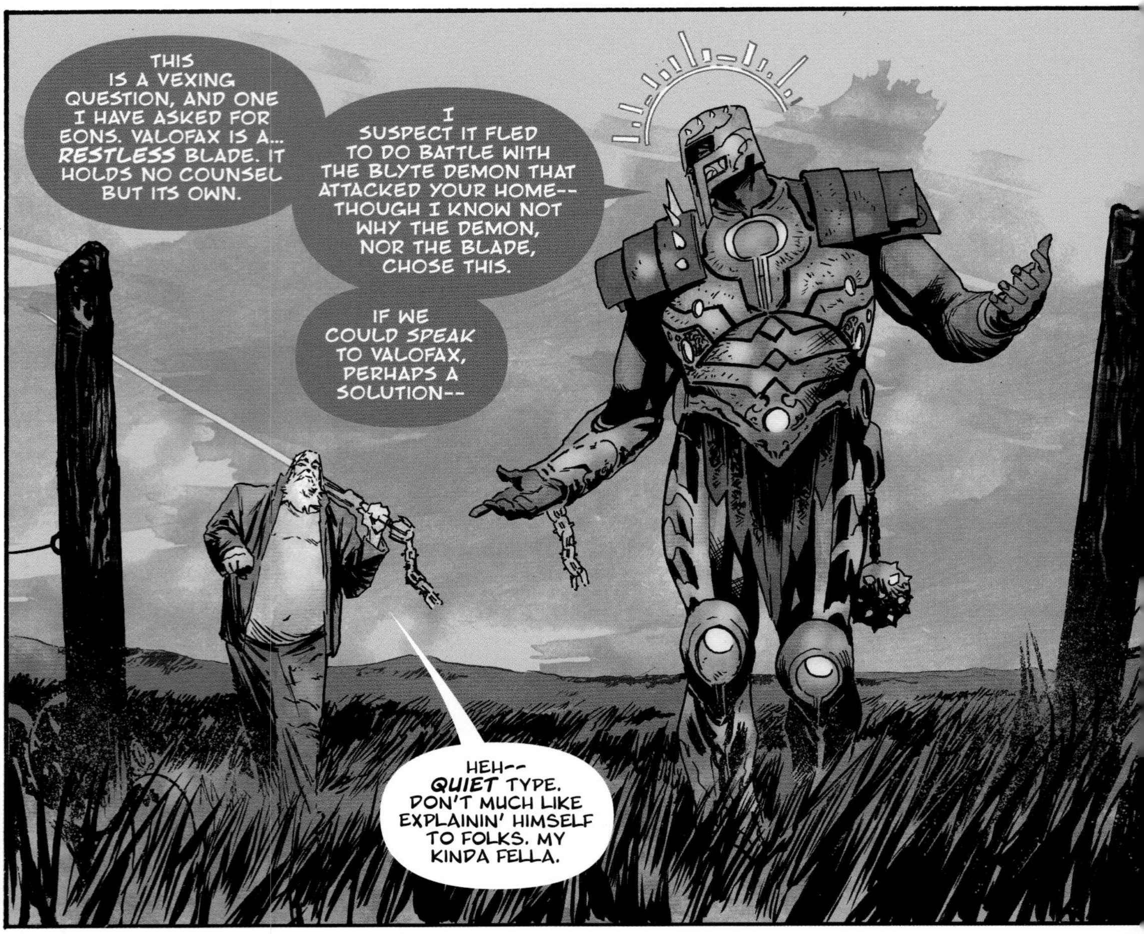
THIS IS A VEXING QUESTION, AND ONE I HAVE ASKED FOR EONS. VALOFAX IS A... RESTLESS BLADE. IT HOLDS NO COUNSEL BUT ITS OWN.
I SUSPECT IT FLED TO DO BATTLE WITH THE BLYTE DEMON THAT ATTACKED YOUR HOME-- THOUGH I KNOW NOT WHY THE DEMON, NOR THE BLADE, CHOSE THIS.
IF WE COULD SPEAK TO VALOFAX, PERHAPS A SOLUTION--
HEH-- QUIET TYPE. DON'T MUCH LIKE EXPLAININ' HIMSELF TO FOLKS. MY KINDA FELLA.

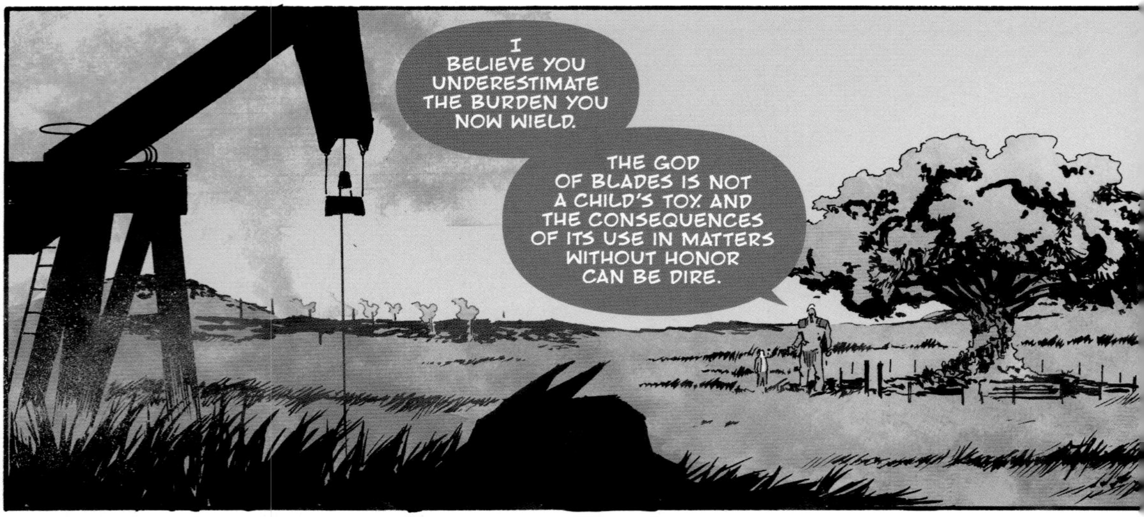
I BELIEVE YOU UNDERESTIMATE THE BURDEN YOU NOW WIELD.
THE GOD OF BLADES IS NOT A CHILD'S TOY. AND THE CONSEQUENCES OF ITS USE IN MATTERS WITHOUT HONOR CAN BE DIRE.

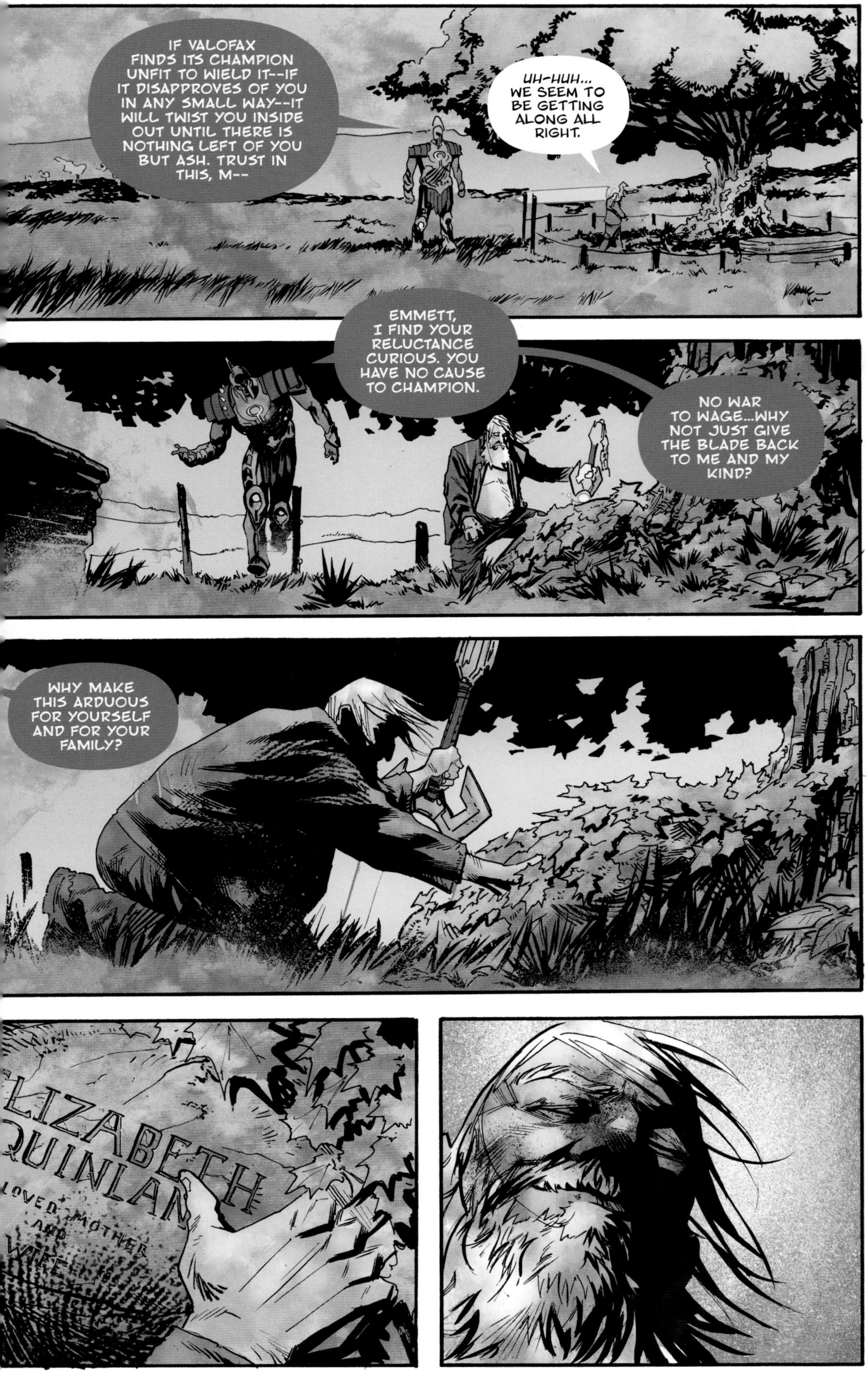
IF VALOFAX FINDS ITS CHAMPION UNFIT TO WIELD IT--IF IT DISAPPROVES OF YOU IN ANY SMALL WAY--IT WILL TWIST YOU INSIDE OUT UNTIL THERE IS NOTHING LEFT OF YOU BUT ASH. TRUST IN THIS, M--
UH-HUH... WE SEEM TO BE GETTING ALONG ALL RIGHT.
EMMETT, I FIND YOUR RELUCTANCE CURIOUS. YOU HAVE NO CAUSE TO CHAMPION.
NO WAR TO WAGE...WHY NOT JUST GIVE THE BLADE BACK TO ME AND MY KIND?
WHY MAKE THIS ARDUOUS FOR YOURSELF AND FOR YOUR FAMILY?
LIZABETH
QUINLAN
LOVED MOTHER
AND
WIFE

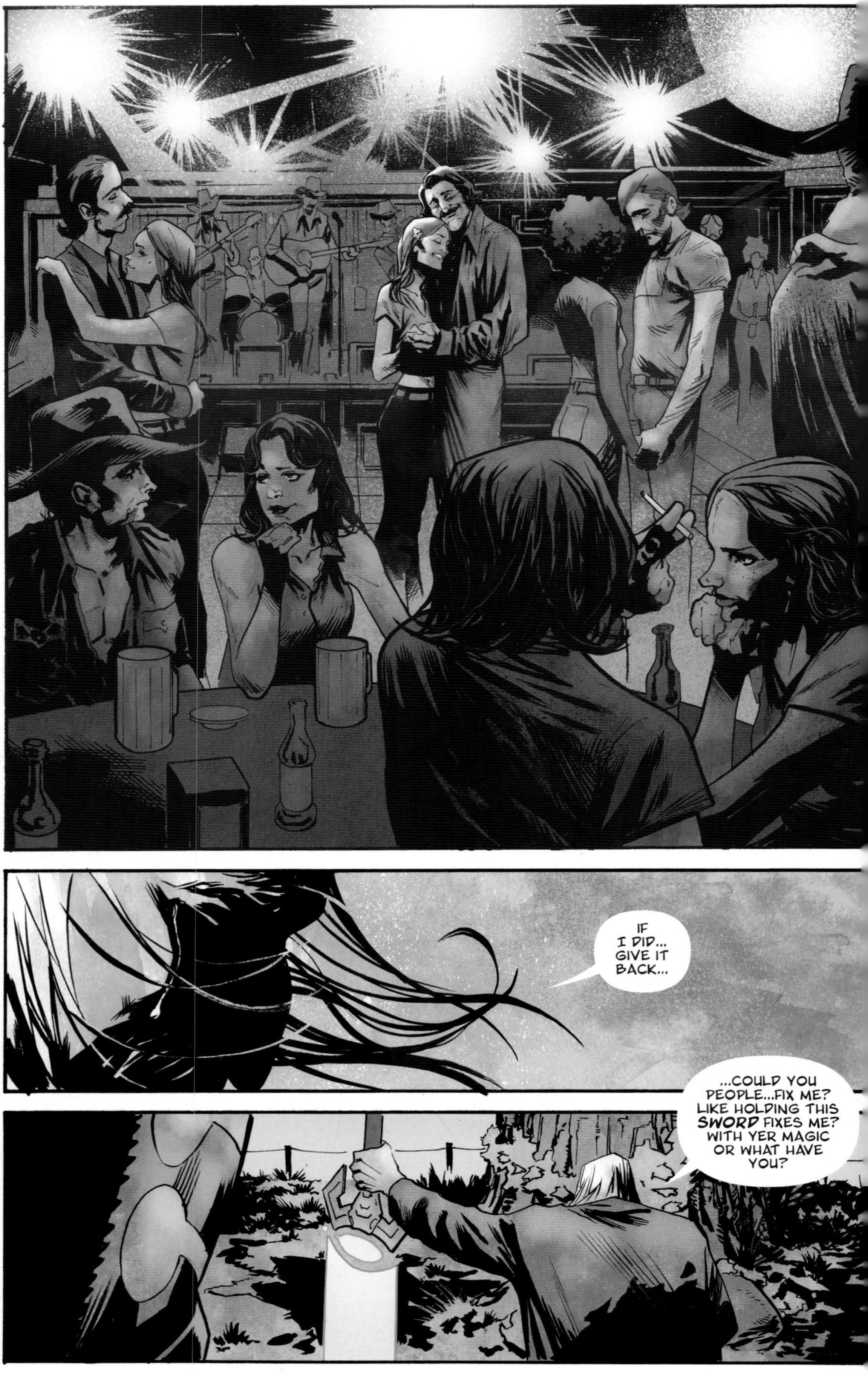
IF I DID... GIVE IT BACK...
...COULD YOU PEOPLE...FIX ME? LIKE HOLDING THIS **SWORD** FIXES ME? WITH YER MAGIC OR WHAT HAVE YOU?

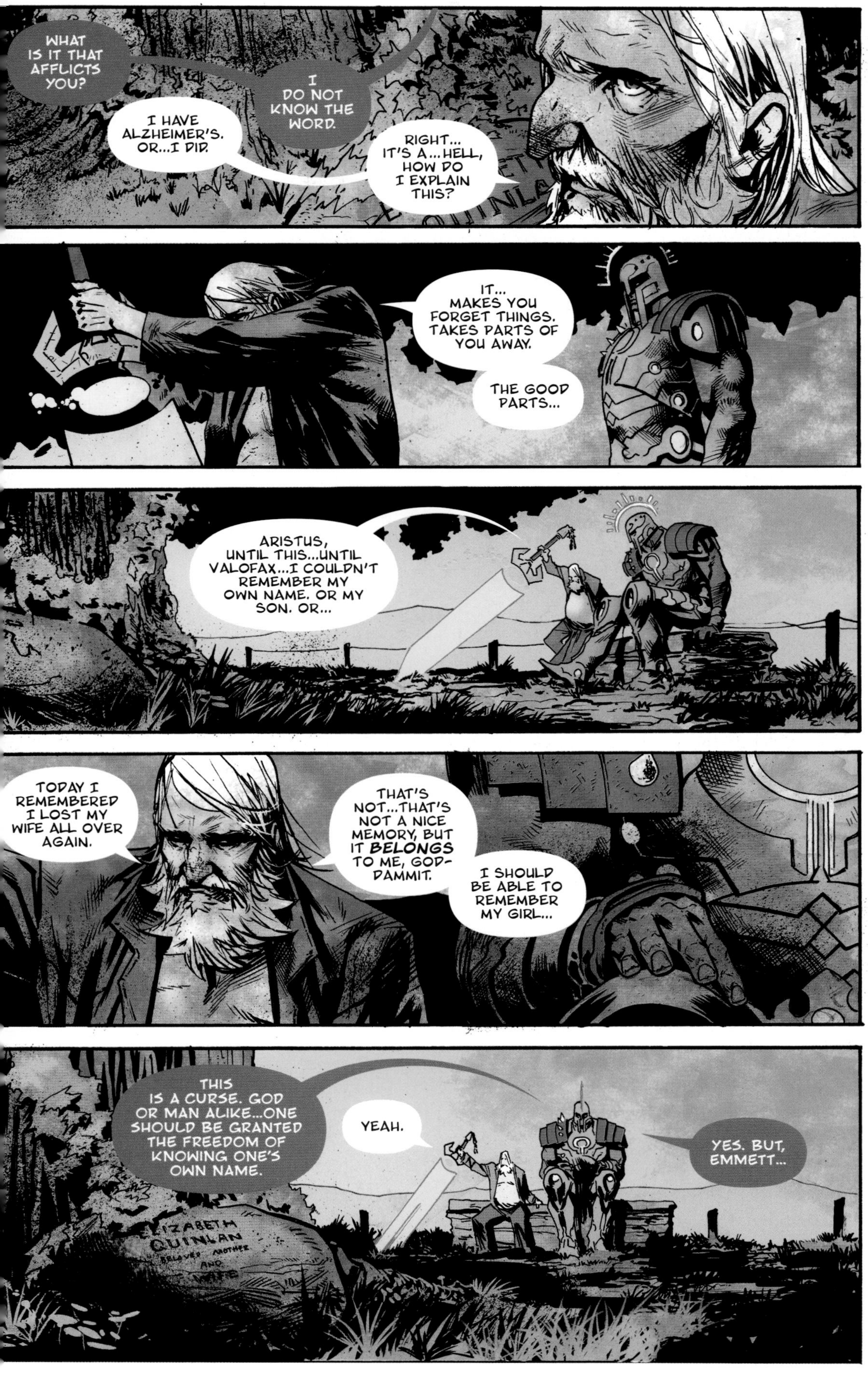
WHAT IS IT THAT AFFLICTS YOU?
I DO NOT KNOW THE WORD.
I HAVE ALZHEIMER'S. OR...I DID.
RIGHT... IT'S A...HELL, HOW DO I EXPLAIN THIS?
IT... MAKES YOU FORGET THINGS. TAKES PARTS OF YOU AWAY.
THE GOOD PARTS...
ARISTUS, UNTIL THIS...UNTIL VALOFAX...I COULDN'T REMEMBER MY OWN NAME. OR MY SON. OR...
TODAY I REMEMBERED I LOST MY WIFE ALL OVER AGAIN.
THAT'S NOT...THAT'S NOT A NICE MEMORY, BUT IT BELONGS TO ME, GOD-DAMMIT.
I SHOULD BE ABLE TO REMEMBER MY GIRL...
THIS IS A CURSE. GOD OR MAN ALIKE...ONE SHOULD BE GRANTED THE FREEDOM OF KNOWING ONE'S OWN NAME.
YEAH.
YES. BUT, EMMETT...
ELIZABETH QUINLAN BELOVED MOTHER AND WIFE

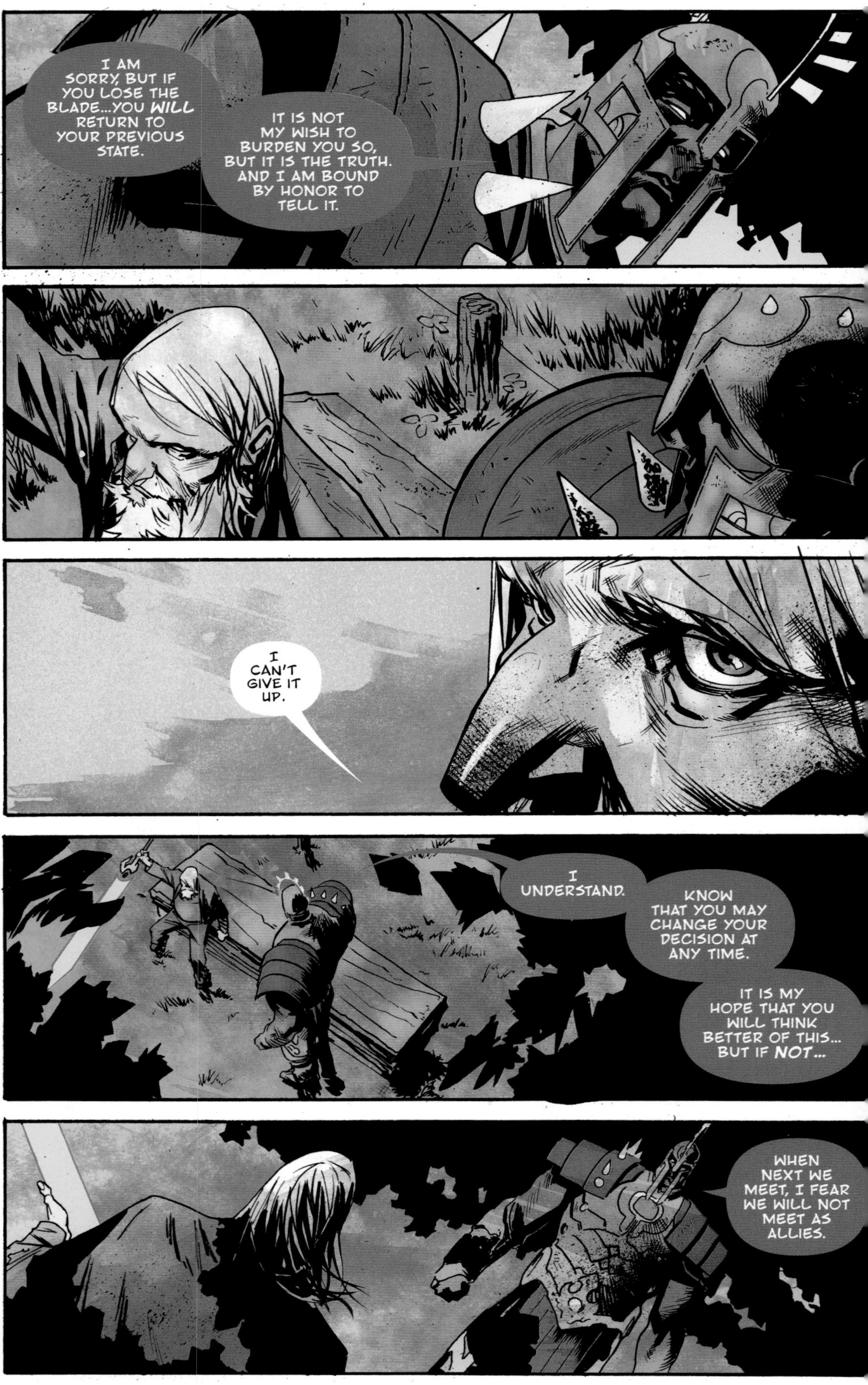
I AM SORRY, BUT IF YOU LOSE THE BLADE...YOU WILL RETURN TO YOUR PREVIOUS STATE.
IT IS NOT MY WISH TO BURDEN YOU SO, BUT IT IS THE TRUTH. AND I AM BOUND BY HONOR TO TELL IT.
I CAN'T GIVE IT UP.
I UNDERSTAND.
KNOW THAT YOU MAY CHANGE YOUR DECISION AT ANY TIME.
IT IS MY HOPE THAT YOU WILL THINK BETTER OF THIS... BUT IF NOT...
WHEN NEXT WE MEET, I FEAR WE WILL NOT MEET AS ALLIES.

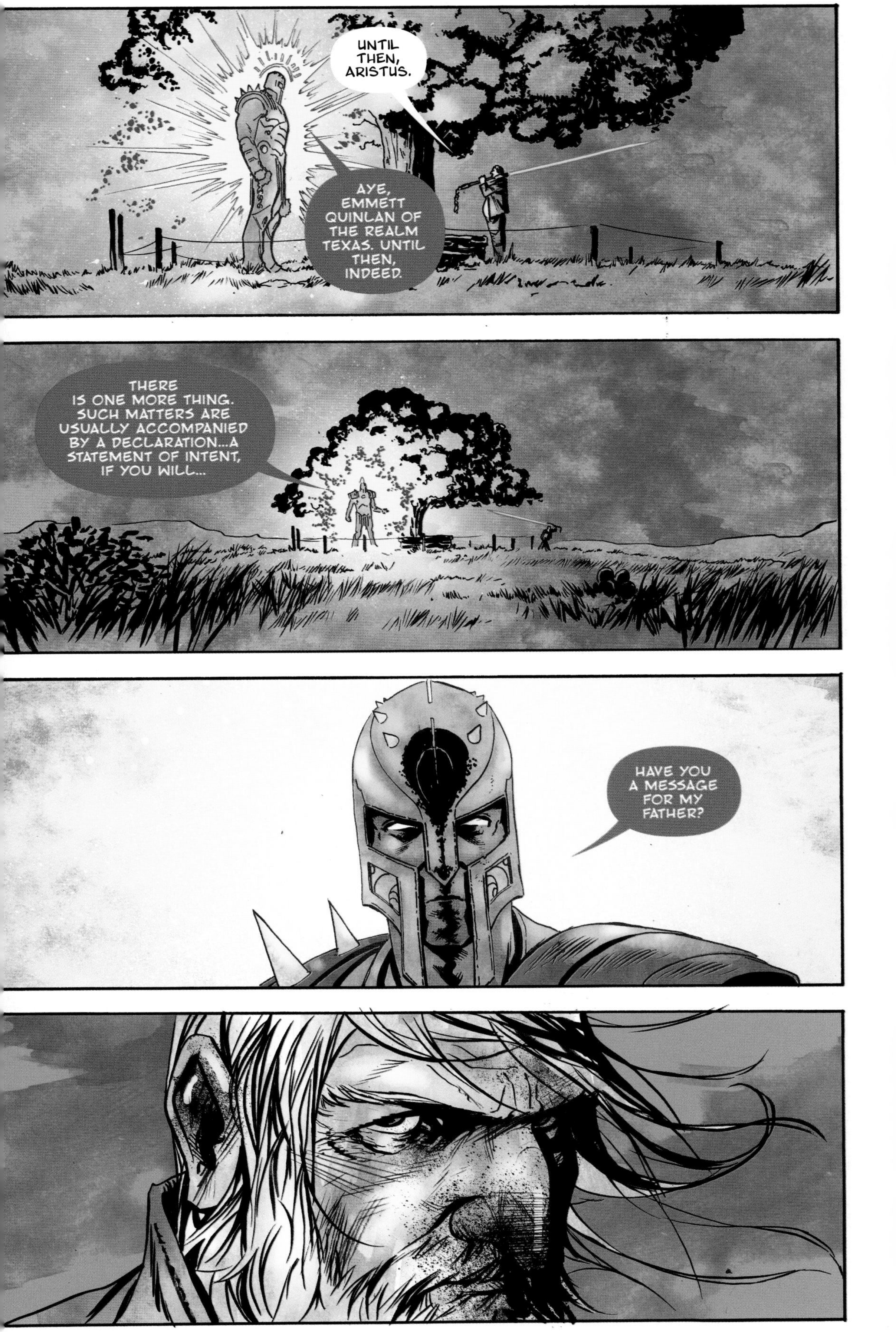
UNTIL THEN, ARISTUS.
AYE, EMMETT QUINLAN OF THE REALM TEXAS. UNTIL THEN, INDEED.
THERE IS ONE MORE THING. SUCH MATTERS ARE USUALLY ACCOMPANIED BY A DECLARATION...A STATEMENT OF INTENT, IF YOU WILL...
HAVE YOU A MESSAGE FOR MY FATHER?

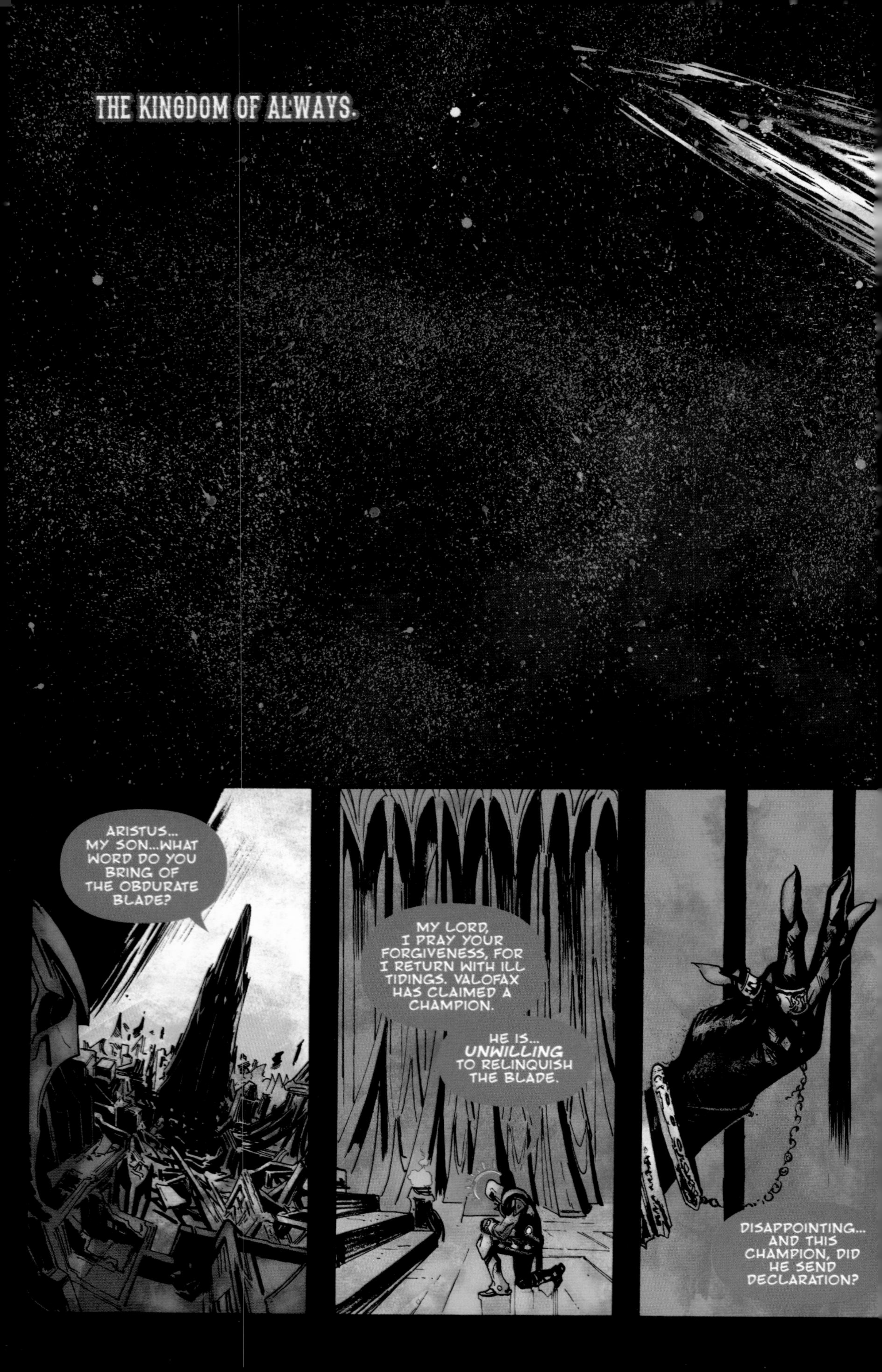
THE KINGDOM OF ALWAYS.
ARISTUS... MY SON...WHAT WORD DO YOU BRING OF THE OBDURATE BLADE?
MY LORD, I PRAY YOUR FORGIVENESS, FOR I RETURN WITH ILL TIDINGS. VALOFAX HAS CLAIMED A CHAMPION.
HE IS... UNWILLING TO RELINQUISH THE BLADE.
DISAPPOINTING... AND THIS CHAMPION, DID HE SEND DECLARATION?

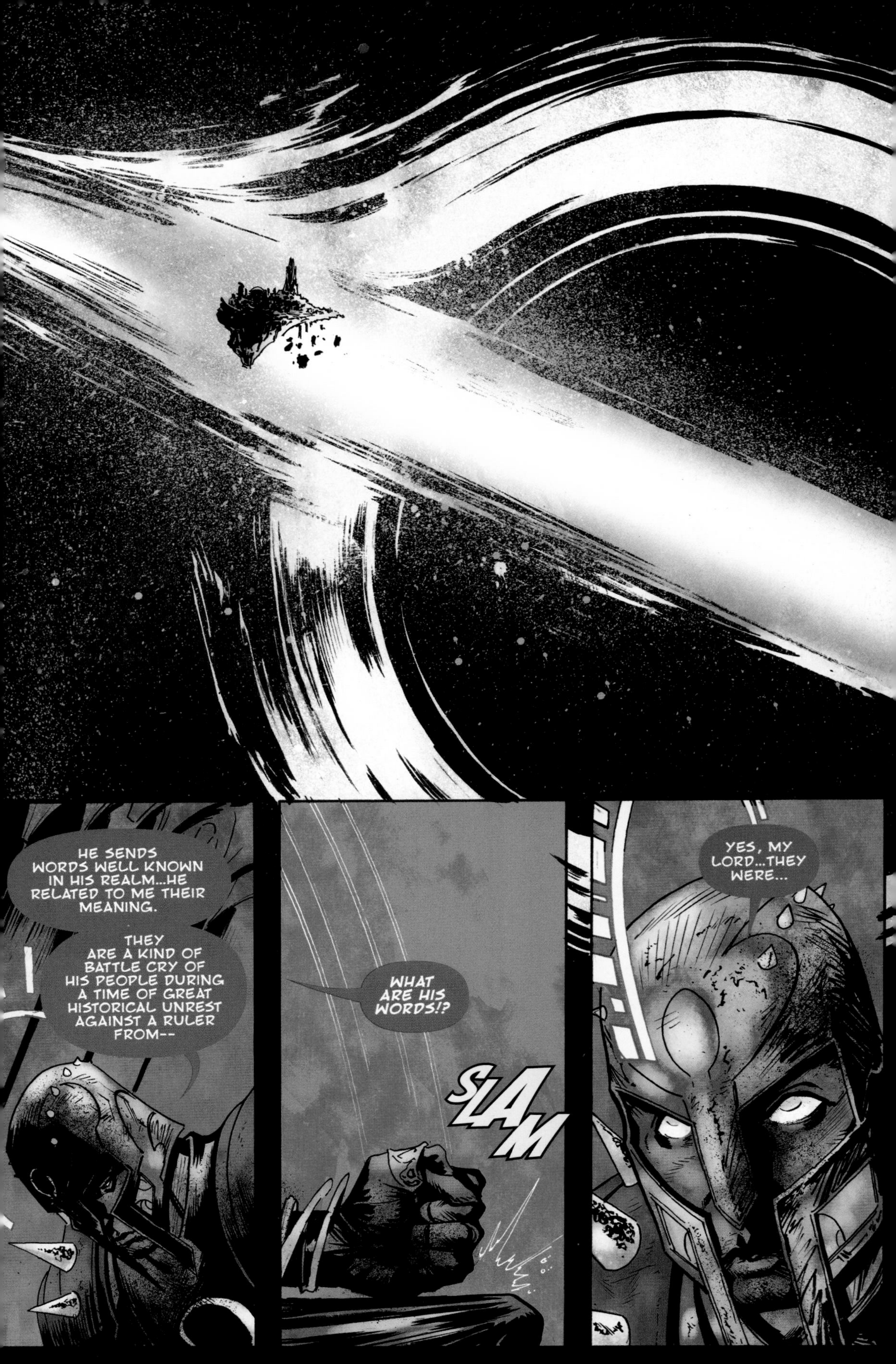
HE SENDS WORDS WELL KNOWN IN HIS REALM...HE RELATED TO ME THEIR MEANING.
THEY ARE A KIND OF BATTLE CRY OF HIS PEOPLE DURING A TIME OF GREAT HISTORICAL UNREST AGAINST A RULER FROM--
WHAT ARE HIS WORDS!?
SLAM
YES, MY LORD...THEY WERE...

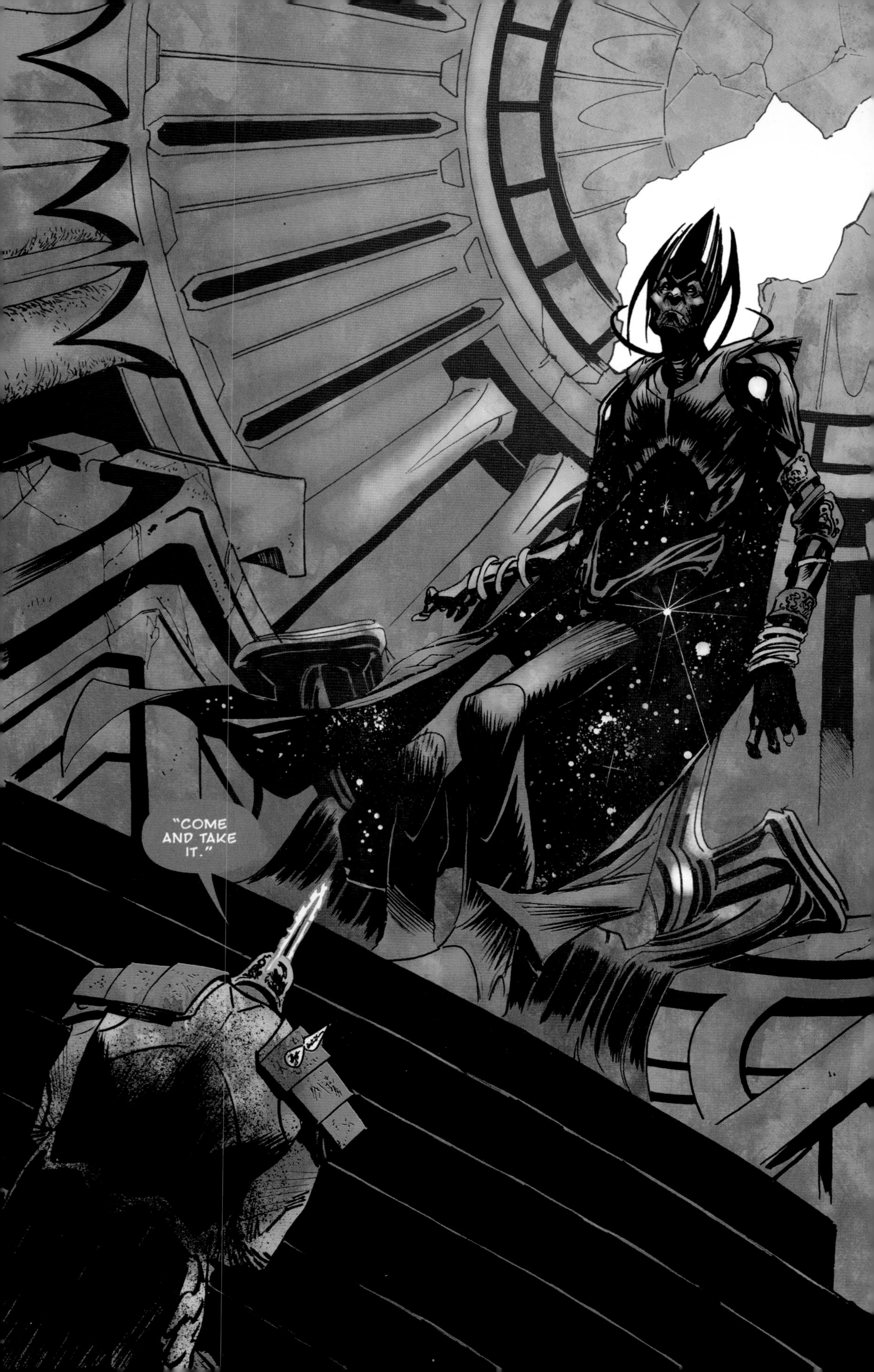
"COME AND TAKE IT."

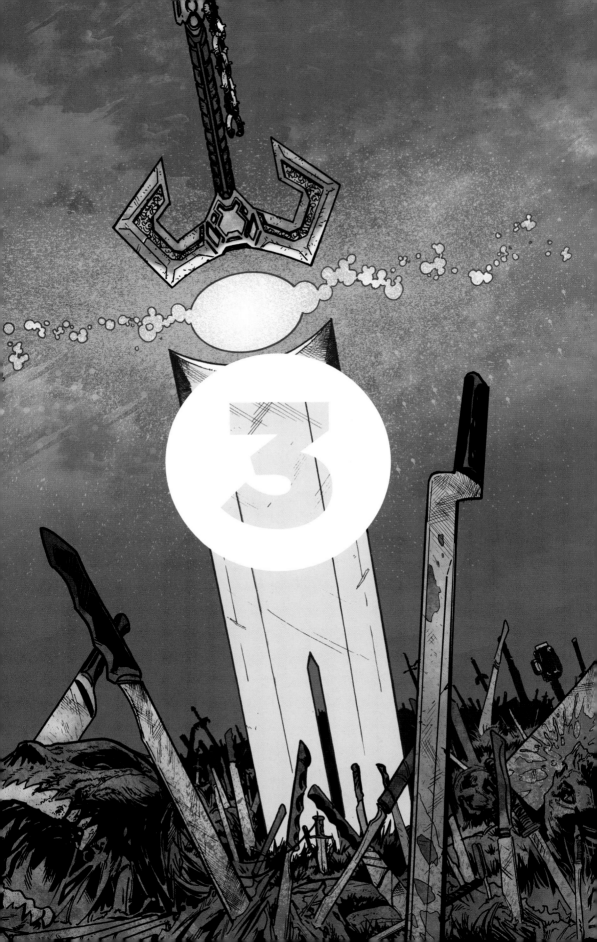

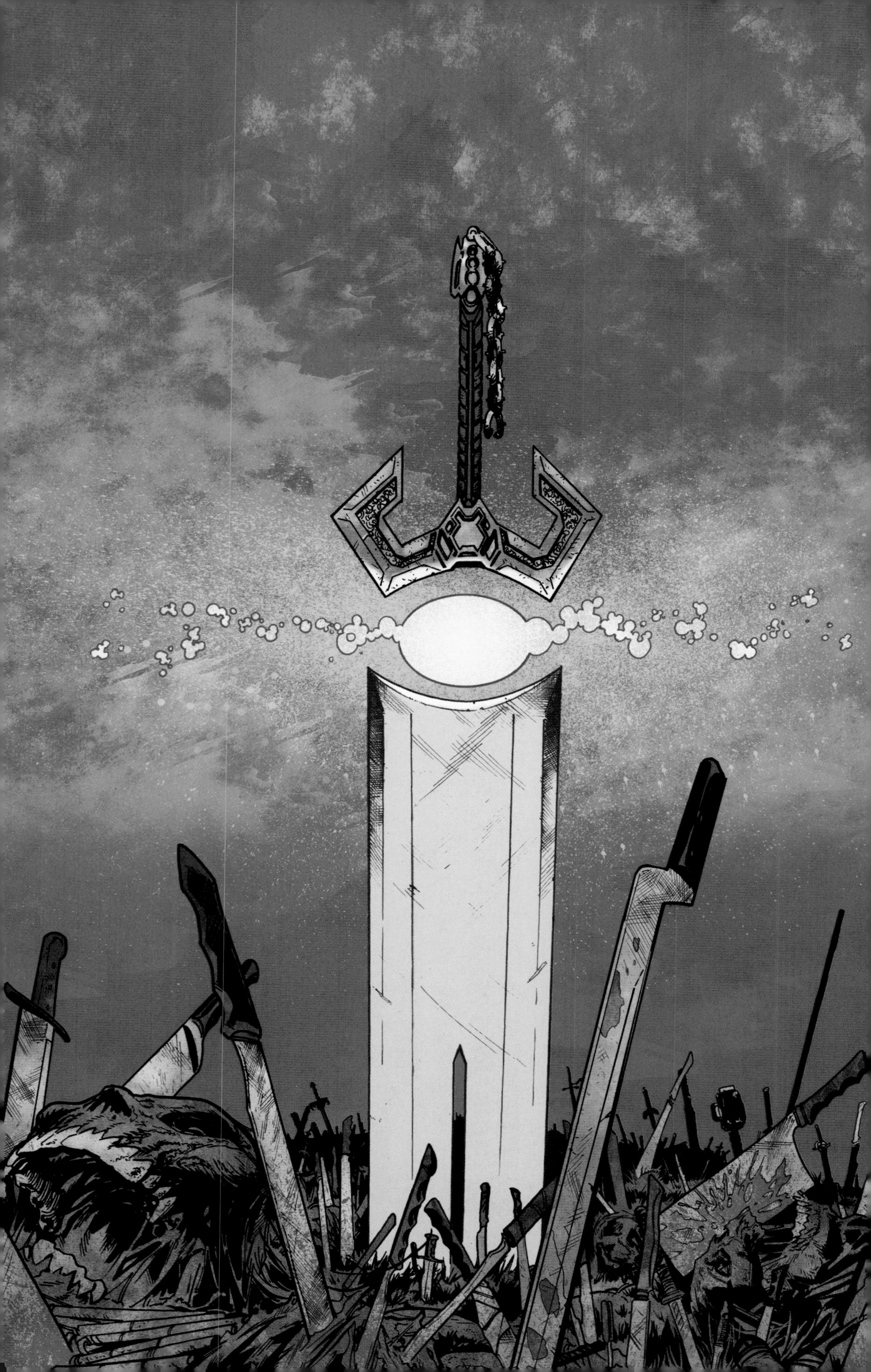

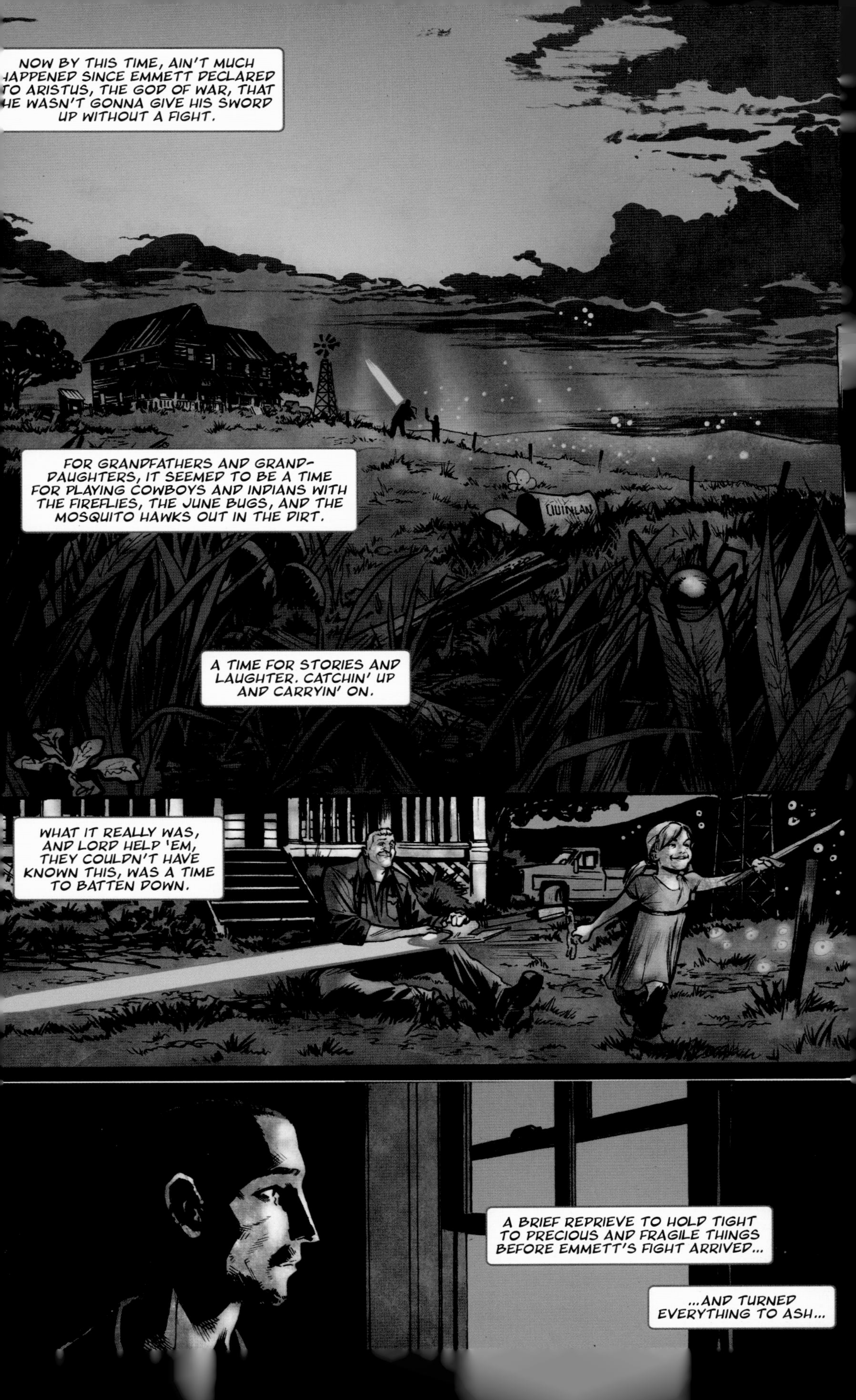
NOW BY THIS TIME, AIN'T MUCH HAPPENED SINCE EMMETT DECLARED TO ARISTUS, THE GOD OF WAR, THAT HE WASN'T GONNA GIVE HIS SWORD UP WITHOUT A FIGHT.
FOR GRANDFATHERS AND GRAND-DAUGHTERS, IT SEEMED TO BE A TIME FOR PLAYING COWBOYS AND INDIANS WITH THE FIREFLIES, THE JUNE BUGS, AND THE MOSQUITO HAWKS OUT IN THE DIRT.
QUINLAN
A TIME FOR STORIES AND LAUGHTER. CATCHIN' UP AND CARRYIN' ON.
WHAT IT REALLY WAS, AND LORD HELP 'EM, THEY COULDN'T HAVE KNOWN THIS, WAS A TIME TO BATTEN DOWN.
A BRIEF REPRIEVE TO HOLD TIGHT TO PRECIOUS AND FRAGILE THINGS BEFORE EMMETT'S FIGHT ARRIVED...
...AND TURNED EVERYTHING TO ASH...

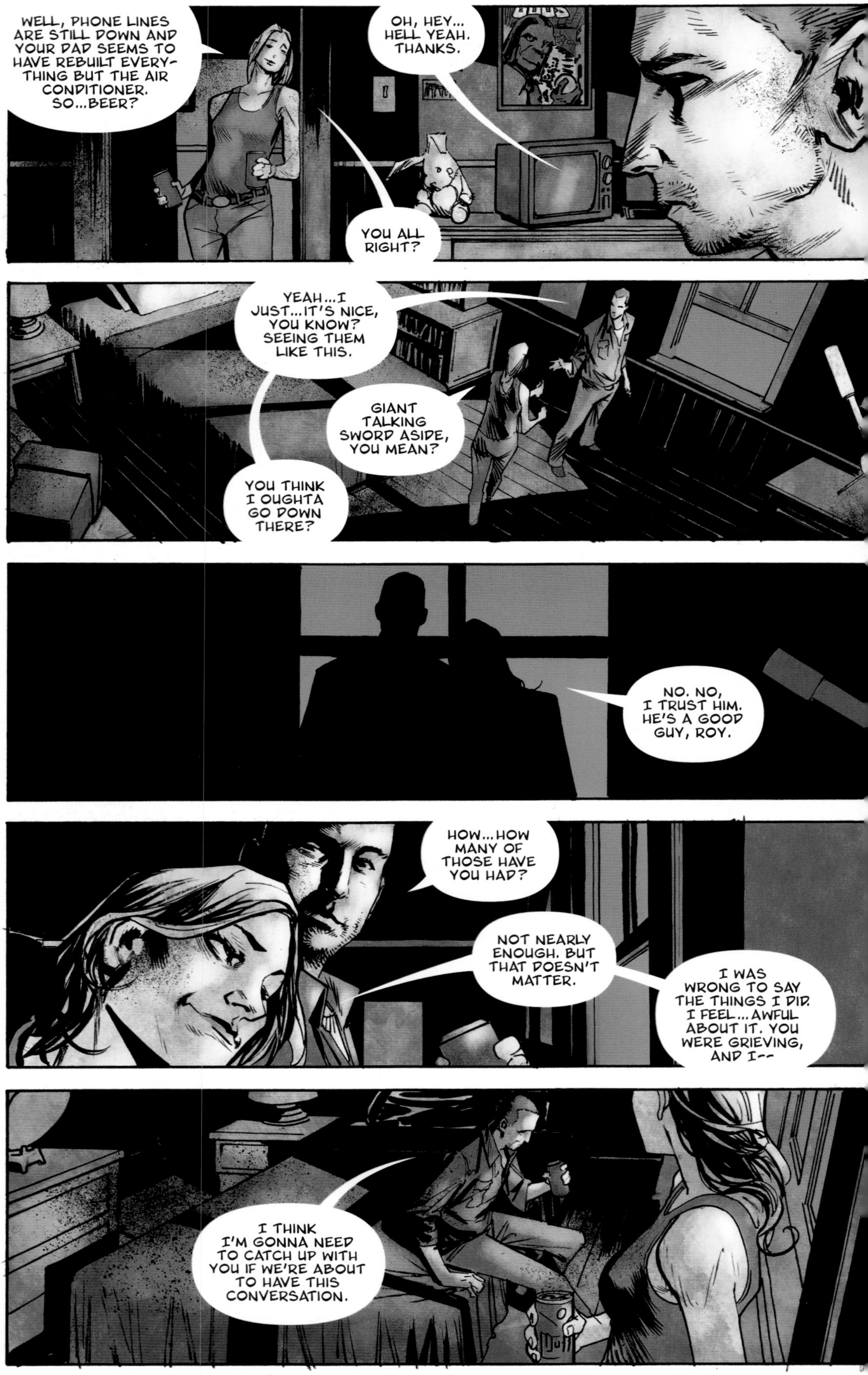
WELL, PHONE LINES ARE STILL DOWN AND YOUR DAD SEEMS TO HAVE REBUILT EVERYTHING BUT THE AIR CONDITIONER. SO...BEER?
OH, HEY... HELL YEAH. THANKS.
YOU ALL RIGHT?
YEAH...I JUST...IT'S NICE, YOU KNOW? SEEING THEM LIKE THIS.
GIANT TALKING SWORD ASIDE, YOU MEAN?
YOU THINK I OUGHTA GO DOWN THERE?
NO. NO, I TRUST HIM. HE'S A GOOD GUY, ROY.
HOW...HOW MANY OF THOSE HAVE YOU HAD?
NOT NEARLY ENOUGH. BUT THAT DOESN'T MATTER.
I WAS WRONG TO SAY THE THINGS I DID. I FEEL...AWFUL ABOUT IT. YOU WERE GRIEVING, AND I--
I THINK I'M GONNA NEED TO CATCH UP WITH YOU IF WE'RE ABOUT TO HAVE THIS CONVERSATION.

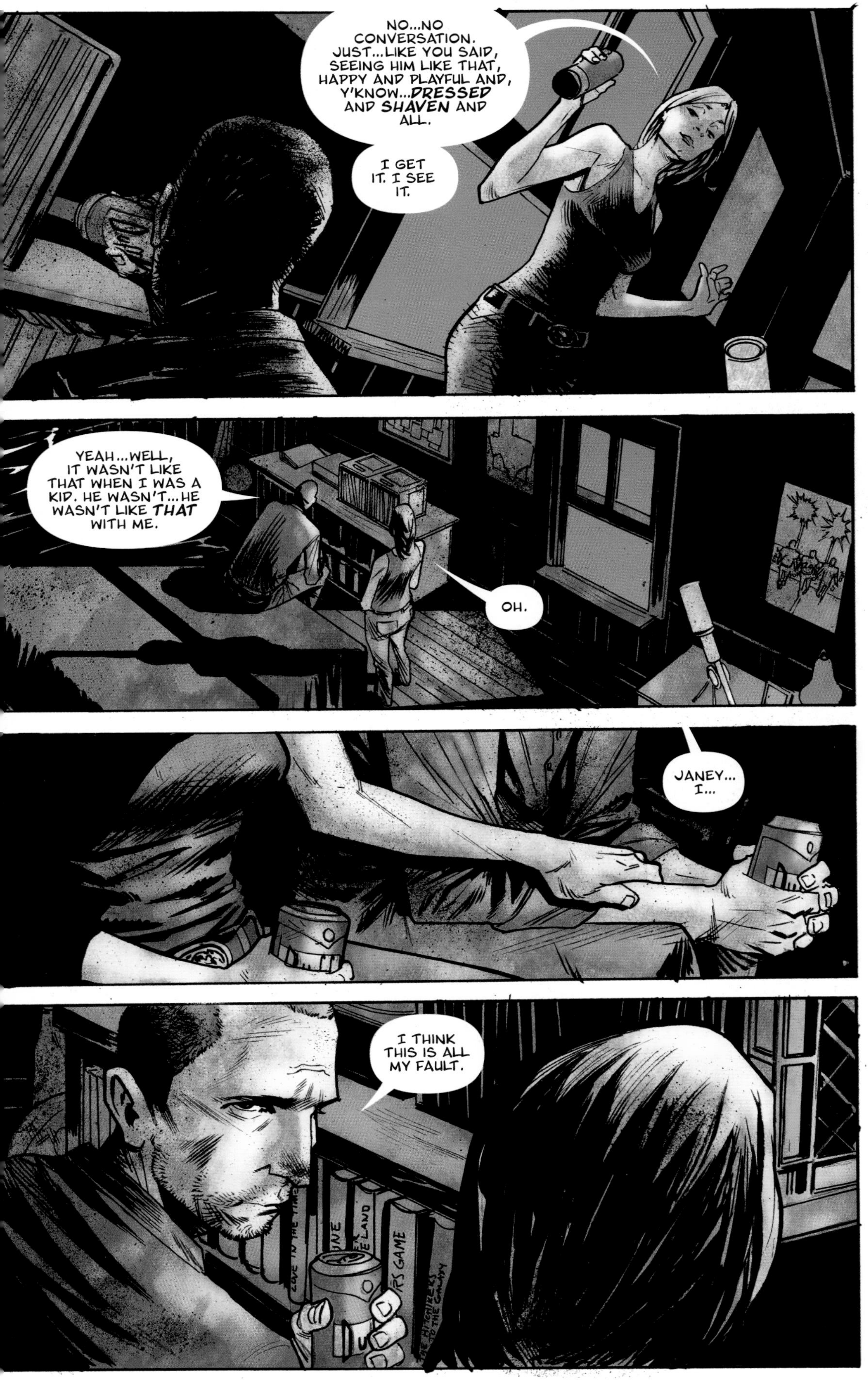
NO...NO CONVERSATION. JUST...LIKE YOU SAID, SEEING HIM LIKE THAT, HAPPY AND PLAYFUL AND, Y'KNOW...DRESSED AND SHAVEN AND ALL.
I GET IT. I SEE IT.
YEAH...WELL, IT WASN'T LIKE THAT WHEN I WAS A KID. HE WASN'T...HE WASN'T LIKE THAT WITH ME.
OH.
JANEY... I...
I THINK THIS IS ALL MY FAULT.

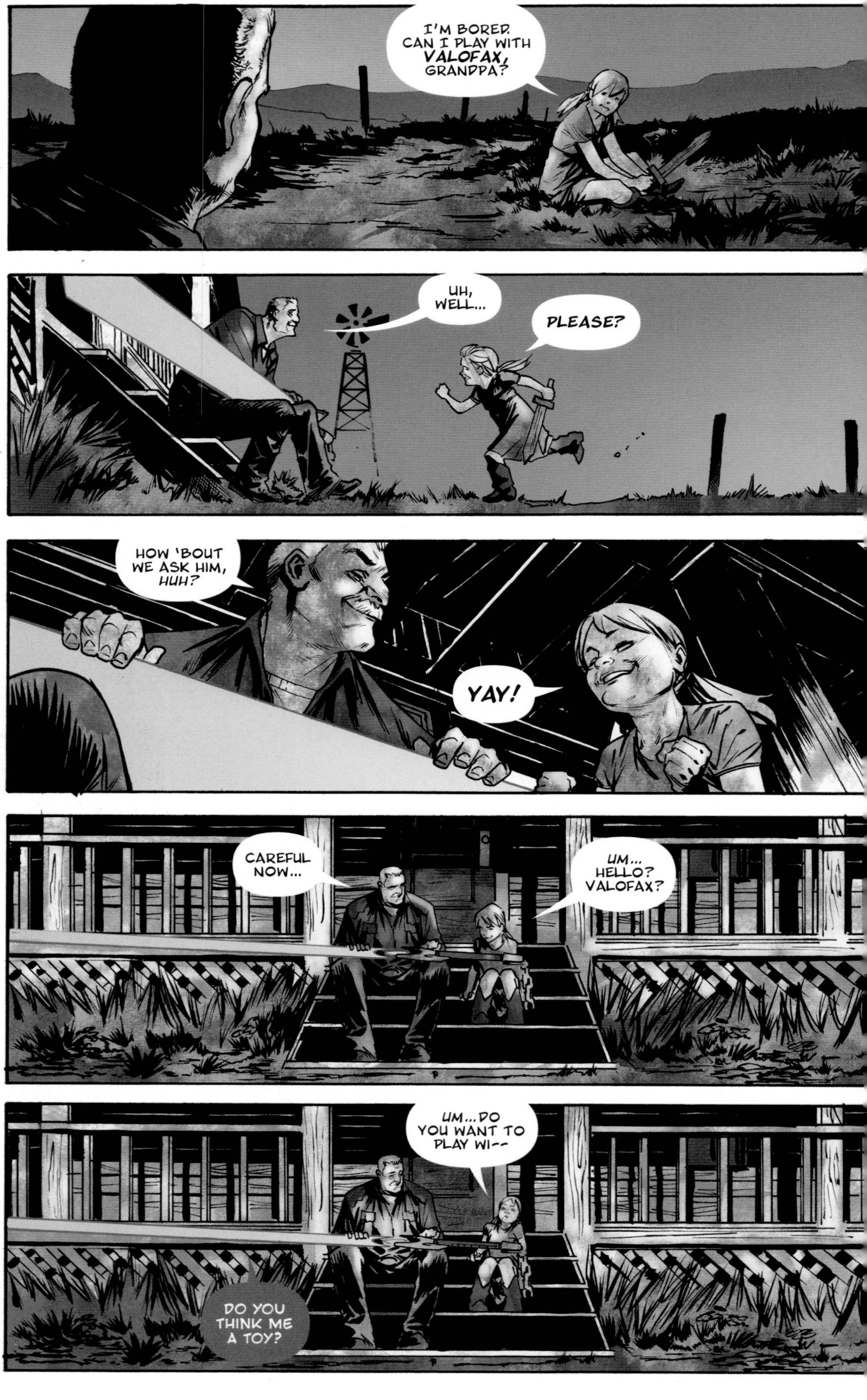
I'M BORED. CAN I PLAY WITH VALOFAX, GRANDPA?
UH, WELL...
PLEASE?
HOW 'BOUT WE ASK HIM, HUH?
YAY!
CAREFUL NOW...
UM... HELLO? VALOFAX?
UM...DO YOU WANT TO PLAY WI--
DO YOU THINK ME A TOY?

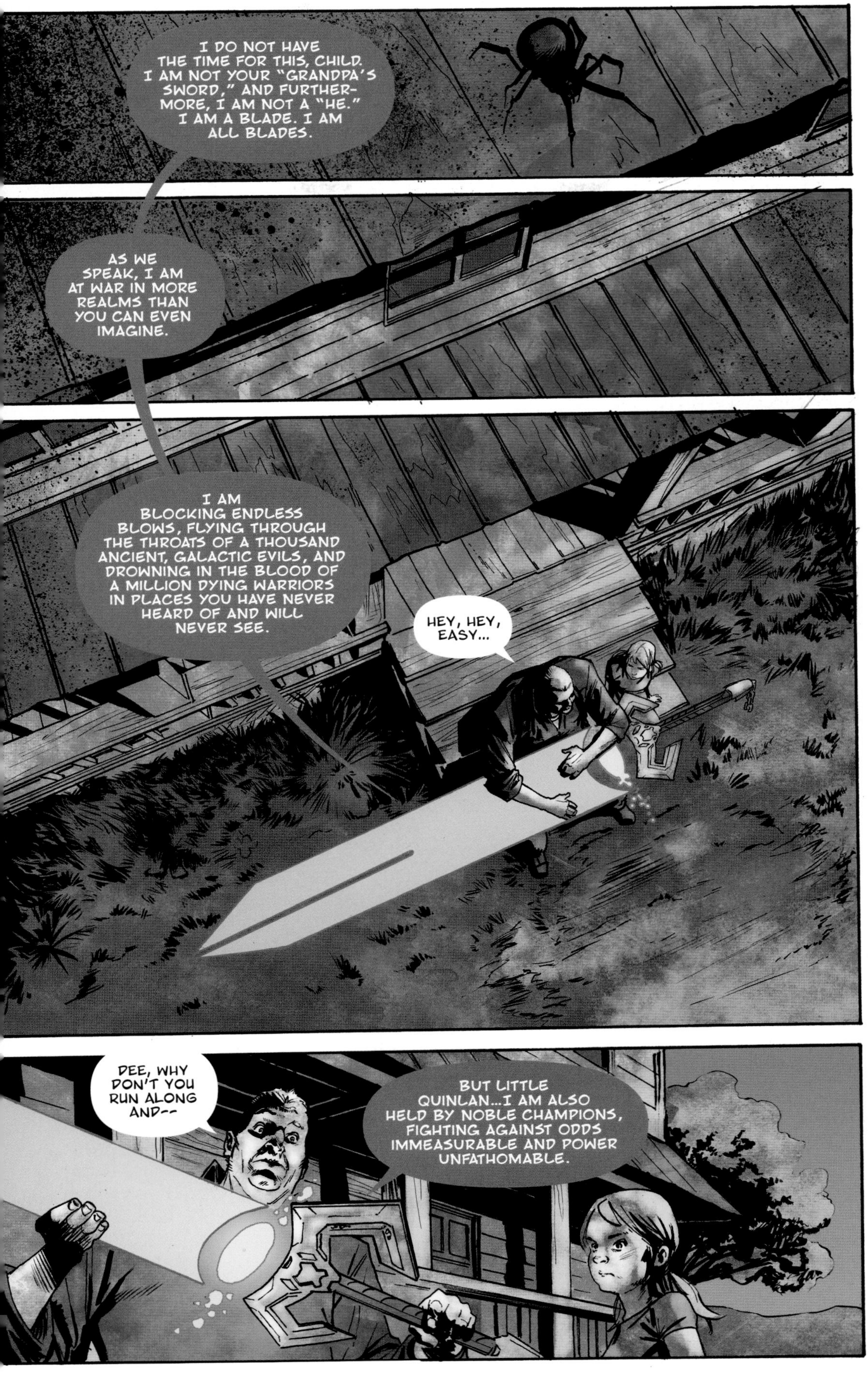
I DO NOT HAVE THE TIME FOR THIS, CHILD. I AM NOT YOUR "GRANDPA'S SWORD," AND FURTHER-MORE, I AM NOT A "HE." I AM A BLADE. I AM ALL BLADES.
AS WE SPEAK, I AM AT WAR IN MORE REALMS THAN YOU CAN EVEN IMAGINE.
I AM BLOCKING ENDLESS BLOWS, FLYING THROUGH THE THROATS OF A THOUSAND ANCIENT, GALACTIC EVILS, AND DROWNING IN THE BLOOD OF A MILLION DYING WARRIORS IN PLACES YOU HAVE NEVER HEARD OF AND WILL NEVER SEE.
HEY, HEY, EASY...
DEE, WHY DON'T YOU RUN ALONG AND--
BUT LITTLE QUINLAN...I AM ALSO HELD BY NOBLE CHAMPIONS, FIGHTING AGAINST ODDS IMMEASURABLE AND POWER UNFATHOMABLE.

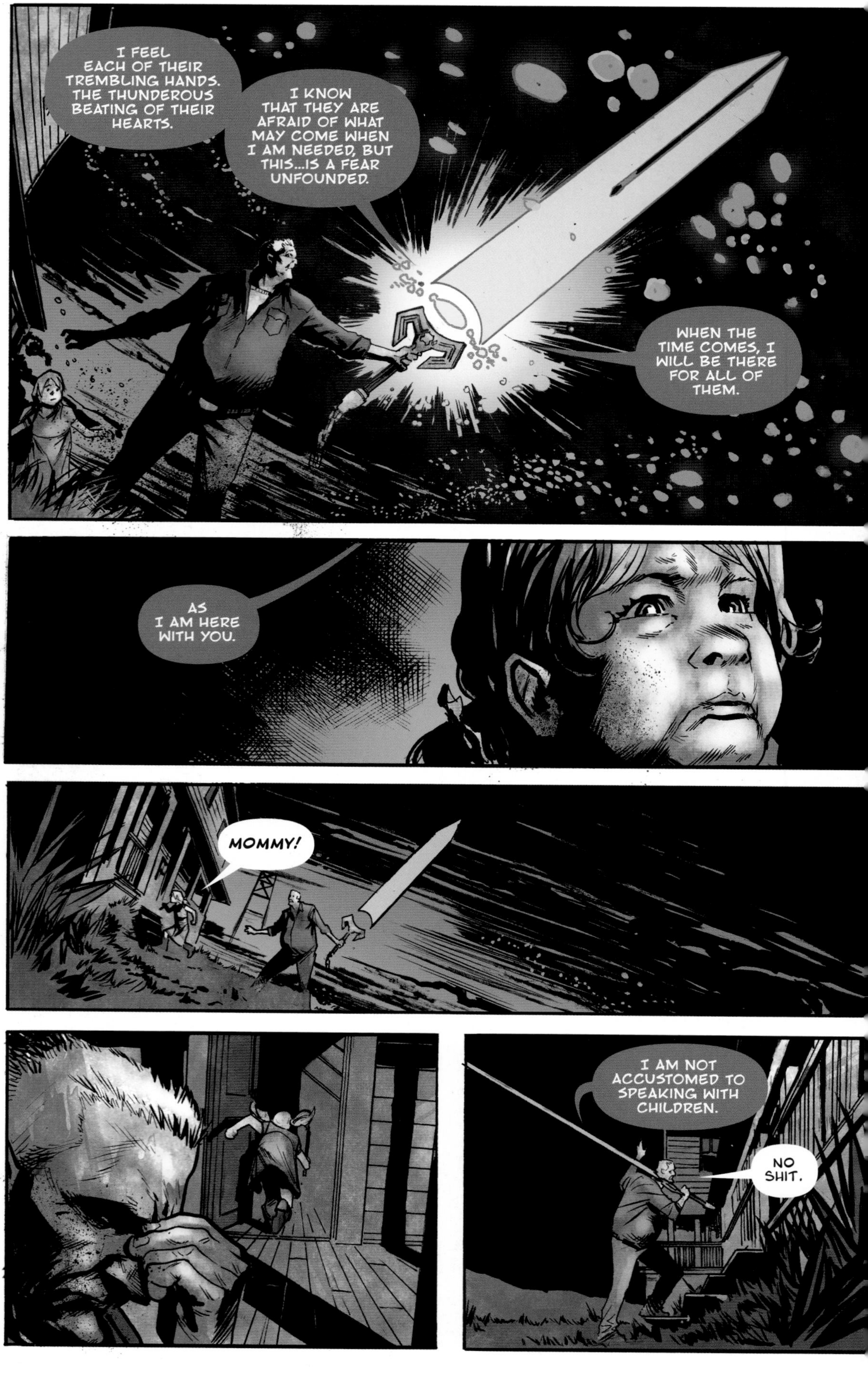
I FEEL EACH OF THEIR TREMBLING HANDS. THE THUNDEROUS BEATING OF THEIR HEARTS.
I KNOW THAT THEY ARE AFRAID OF WHAT MAY COME WHEN I AM NEEDED, BUT THIS...IS A FEAR UNFOUNDED.
WHEN THE TIME COMES, I WILL BE THERE FOR ALL OF THEM.
AS I AM HERE WITH YOU.
MOMMY!
I AM NOT ACCUSTOMED TO SPEAKING WITH CHILDREN.
NO SHIT.

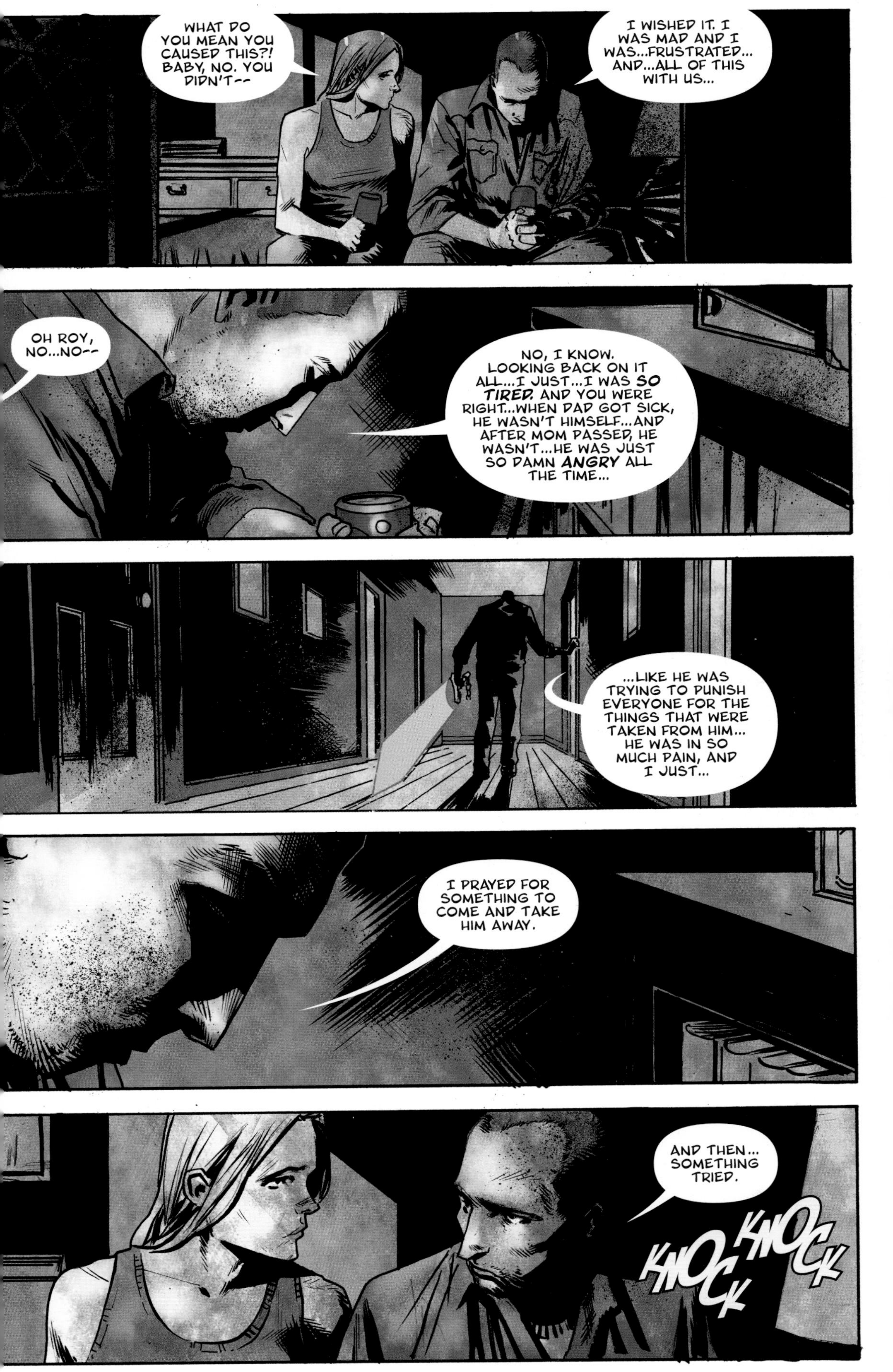
WHAT DO YOU MEAN YOU CAUSED THIS?! BABY, NO. YOU DIDN'T--
I WISHED IT. I WAS MAD AND I WAS...FRUSTRATED... AND...ALL OF THIS WITH US...
OH ROY, NO...NO--
NO, I KNOW. LOOKING BACK ON IT ALL...I JUST...I WAS SO TIRED. AND YOU WERE RIGHT...WHEN DAD GOT SICK, HE WASN'T HIMSELF...AND AFTER MOM PASSED, HE WASN'T...HE WAS JUST SO DAMN ANGRY ALL THE TIME...
...LIKE HE WAS TRYING TO PUNISH EVERYONE FOR THE THINGS THAT WERE TAKEN FROM HIM... HE WAS IN SO MUCH PAIN, AND I JUST...
I PRAYED FOR SOMETHING TO COME AND TAKE HIM AWAY.
AND THEN... SOMETHING TRIED.
KNOCK KNOCK

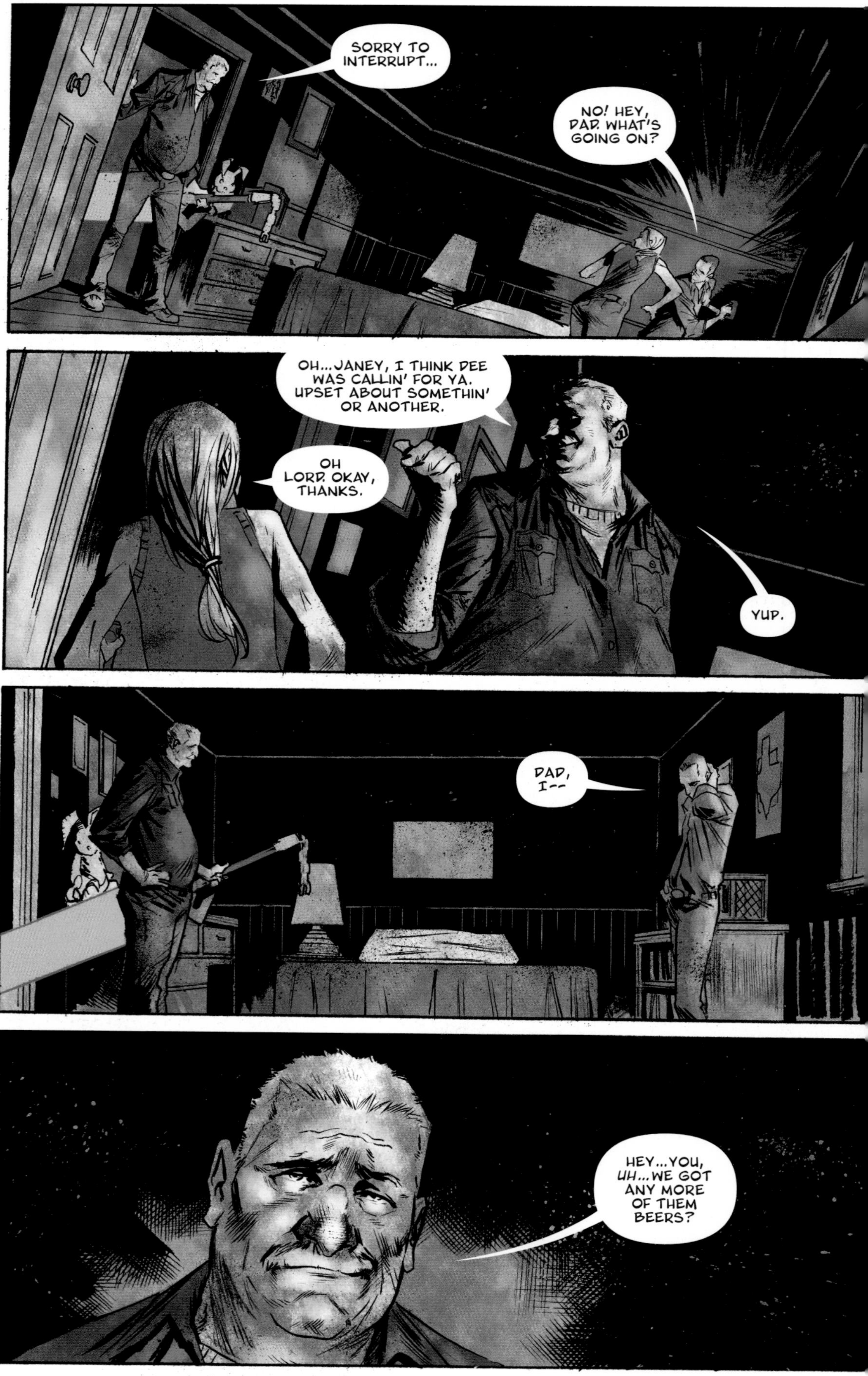
SORRY TO INTERRUPT...
NO! HEY, DAD. WHAT'S GOING ON?
OH...JANEY, I THINK DEE WAS CALLIN' FOR YA. UPSET ABOUT SOMETHIN' OR ANOTHER.
OH LORD. OKAY, THANKS.
YUP.
DAD, I--
HEY...YOU, UH...WE GOT ANY MORE OF THEM BEERS?

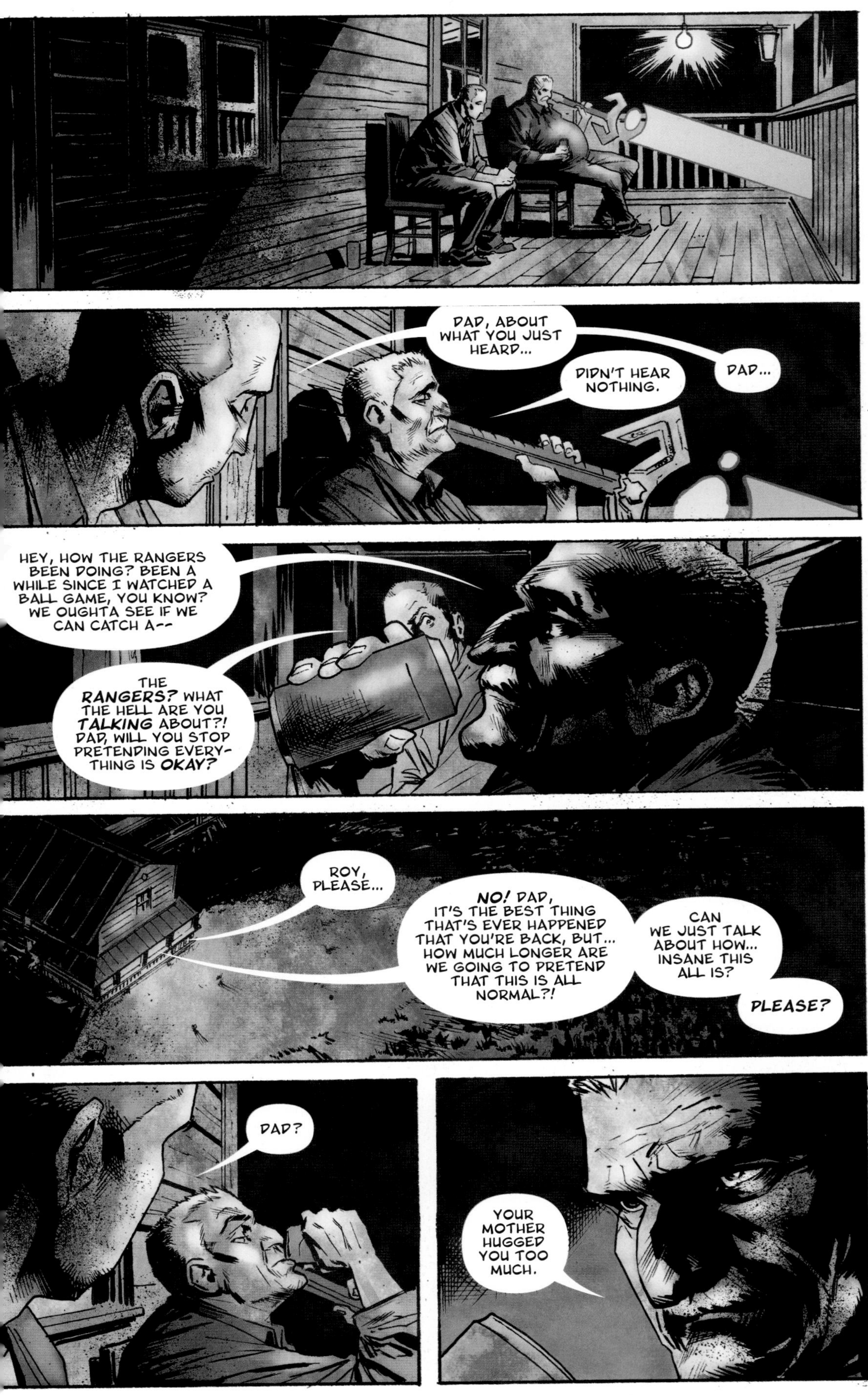
DAD, ABOUT WHAT YOU JUST HEARD...
DAD...
DIDN'T HEAR NOTHING.
HEY, HOW THE RANGERS BEEN DOING? BEEN A WHILE SINCE I WATCHED A BALL GAME, YOU KNOW? WE OUGHTA SEE IF WE CAN CATCH A--
THE RANGERS? WHAT THE HELL ARE YOU TALKING ABOUT?! DAD, WILL YOU STOP PRETENDING EVERY-THING IS OKAY?
ROY, PLEASE...
NO! DAD, IT'S THE BEST THING THAT'S EVER HAPPENED THAT YOU'RE BACK, BUT... HOW MUCH LONGER ARE WE GOING TO PRETEND THAT THIS IS ALL NORMAL?!
CAN WE JUST TALK ABOUT HOW... INSANE THIS ALL IS?
PLEASE?
DAD?
YOUR MOTHER HUGGED YOU TOO MUCH.

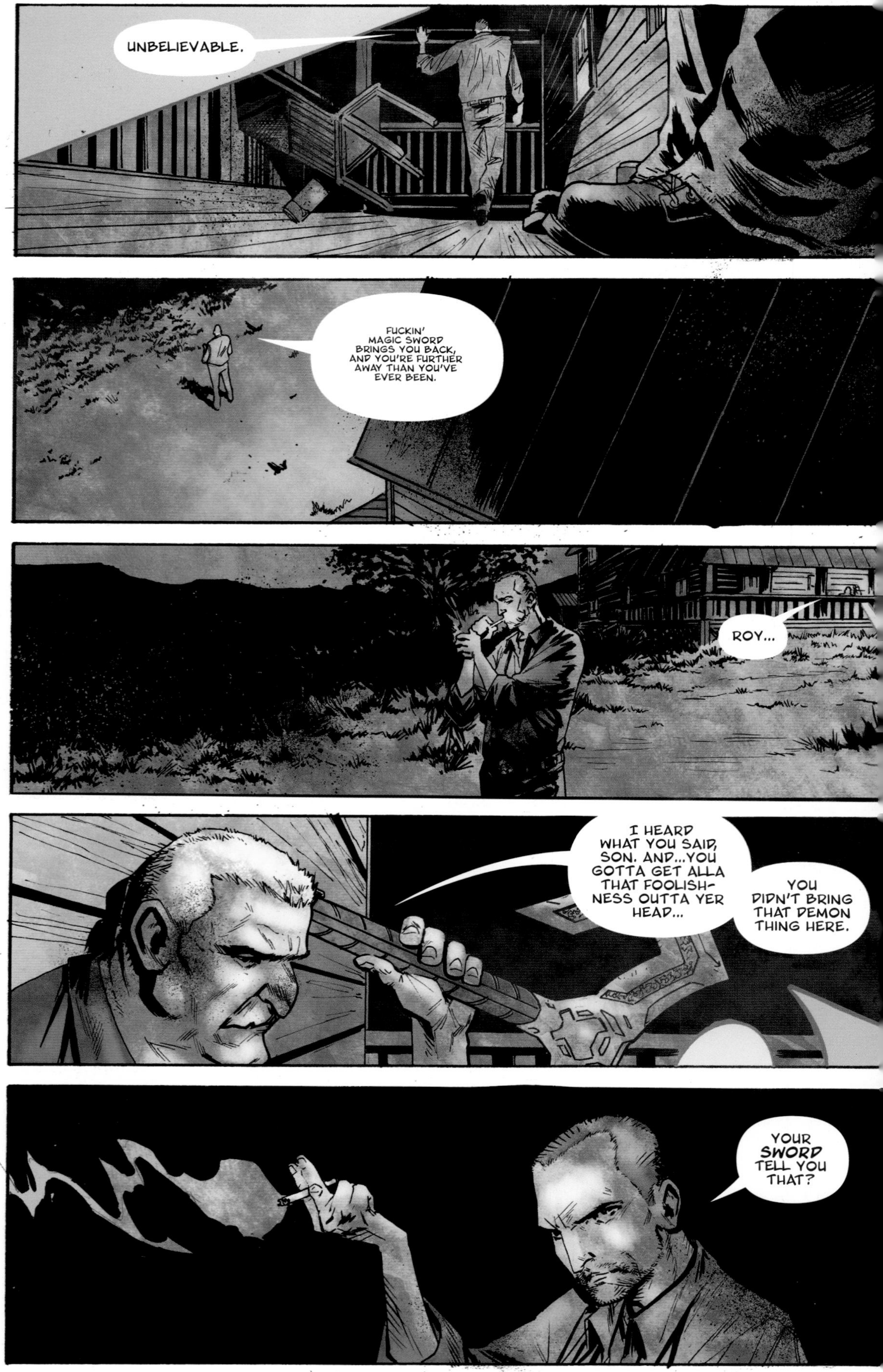
UNBELIEVABLE.
FUCKIN' MAGIC SWORD BRINGS YOU BACK, AND YOU'RE FURTHER AWAY THAN YOU'VE EVER BEEN.
ROY...
I HEARD WHAT YOU SAID, SON. AND...YOU GOTTA GET ALLA THAT FOOLISHNESS OUTTA YER HEAD...
YOU DIDN'T BRING THAT DEMON THING HERE.
YOUR **SWORD** TELL YOU THAT?

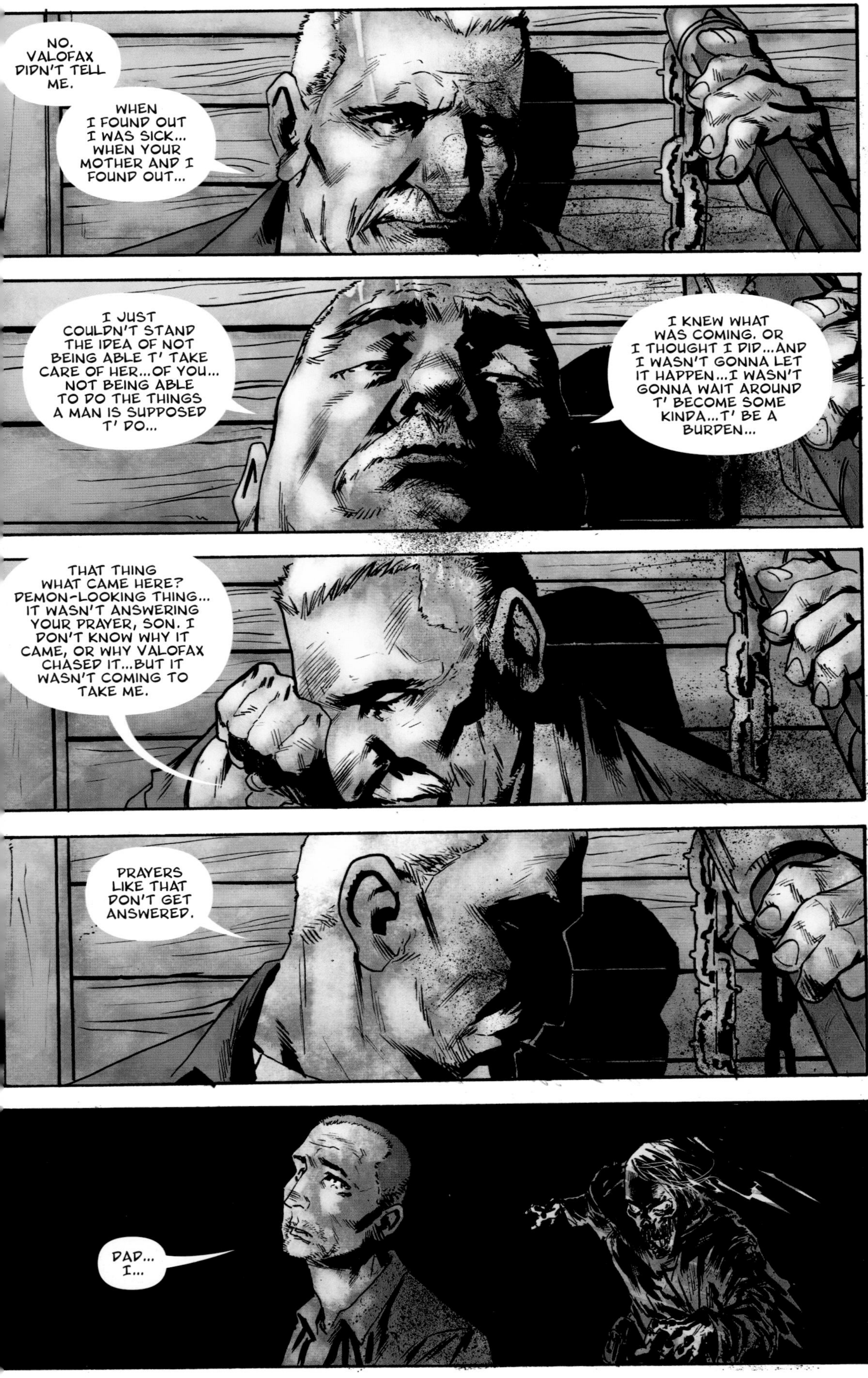
NO. VALOFAX DIDN'T TELL ME.
WHEN I FOUND OUT I WAS SICK... WHEN YOUR MOTHER AND I FOUND OUT...
I JUST COULDN'T STAND THE IDEA OF NOT BEING ABLE T' TAKE CARE OF HER...OF YOU... NOT BEING ABLE TO DO THE THINGS A MAN IS SUPPOSED T' DO...
I KNEW WHAT WAS COMING. OR I THOUGHT I DID...AND I WASN'T GONNA LET IT HAPPEN...I WASN'T GONNA WAIT AROUND T' BECOME SOME KINDA...T' BE A BURDEN...
THAT THING WHAT CAME HERE? DEMON-LOOKING THING... IT WASN'T ANSWERING YOUR PRAYER, SON. I DON'T KNOW WHY IT CAME, OR WHY VALOFAX CHASED IT...BUT IT WASN'T COMING TO TAKE ME.
PRAYERS LIKE THAT DON'T GET ANSWERED.
DAD... I...

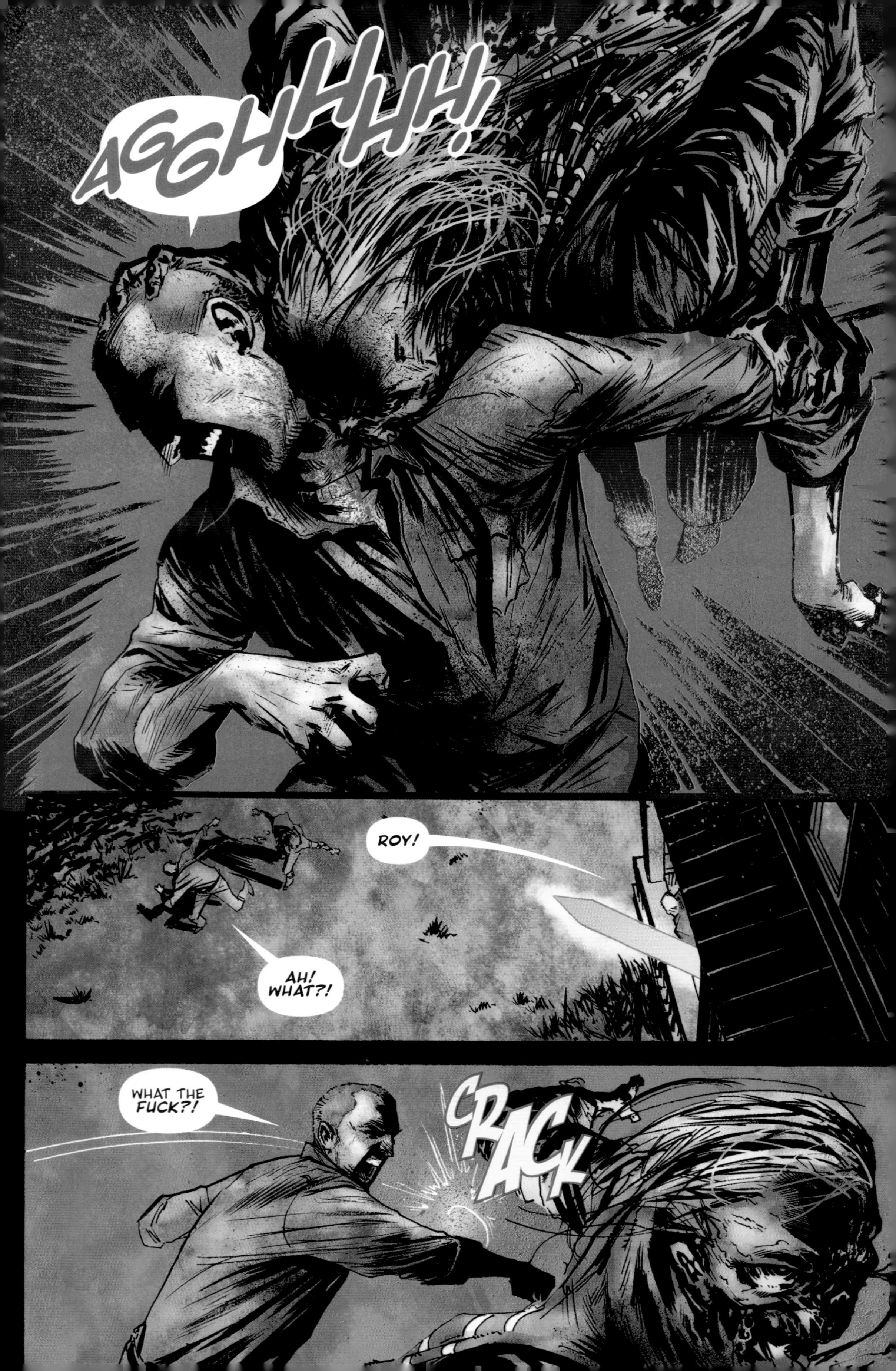
AGGHHHHH!
ROY!
AH! WHAT?!
WHAT THE FUCK?!
CRACK

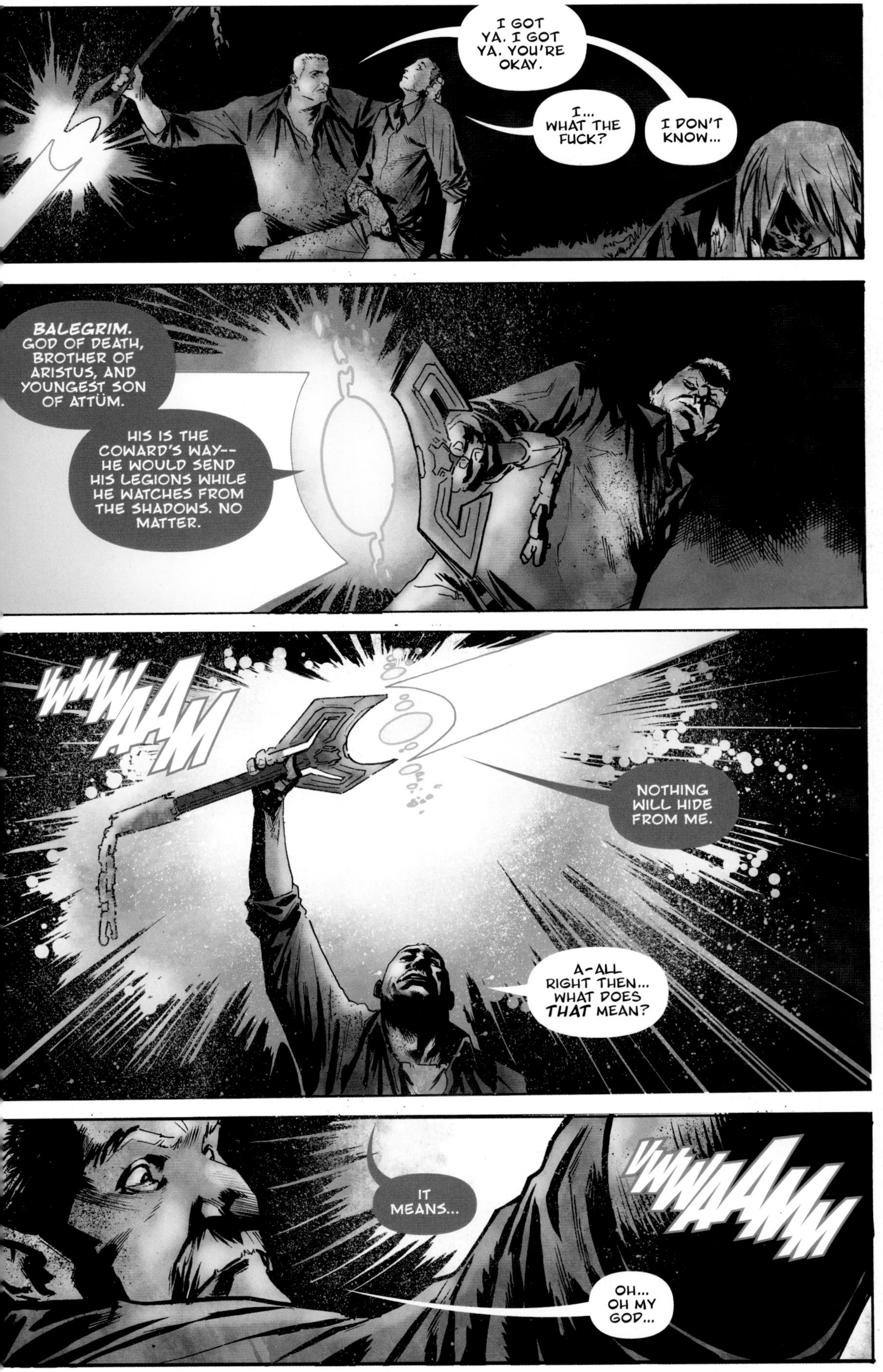
I GOT YA. I GOT YA. YOU'RE OKAY.
I... WHAT THE FUCK?
I DON'T KNOW...
BALEGRIM. GOD OF DEATH, BROTHER OF ARISTUS, AND YOUNGEST SON OF ATTÜM.
HIS IS THE COWARD'S WAY-- HE WOULD SEND HIS LEGIONS WHILE HE WATCHES FROM THE SHADOWS. NO MATTER.
VVVWAAM
NOTHING WILL HIDE FROM ME.
A-ALL RIGHT THEN... WHAT DOES THAT MEAN?
IT MEANS...
VVVWAAAMM
OH... OH MY GOD...

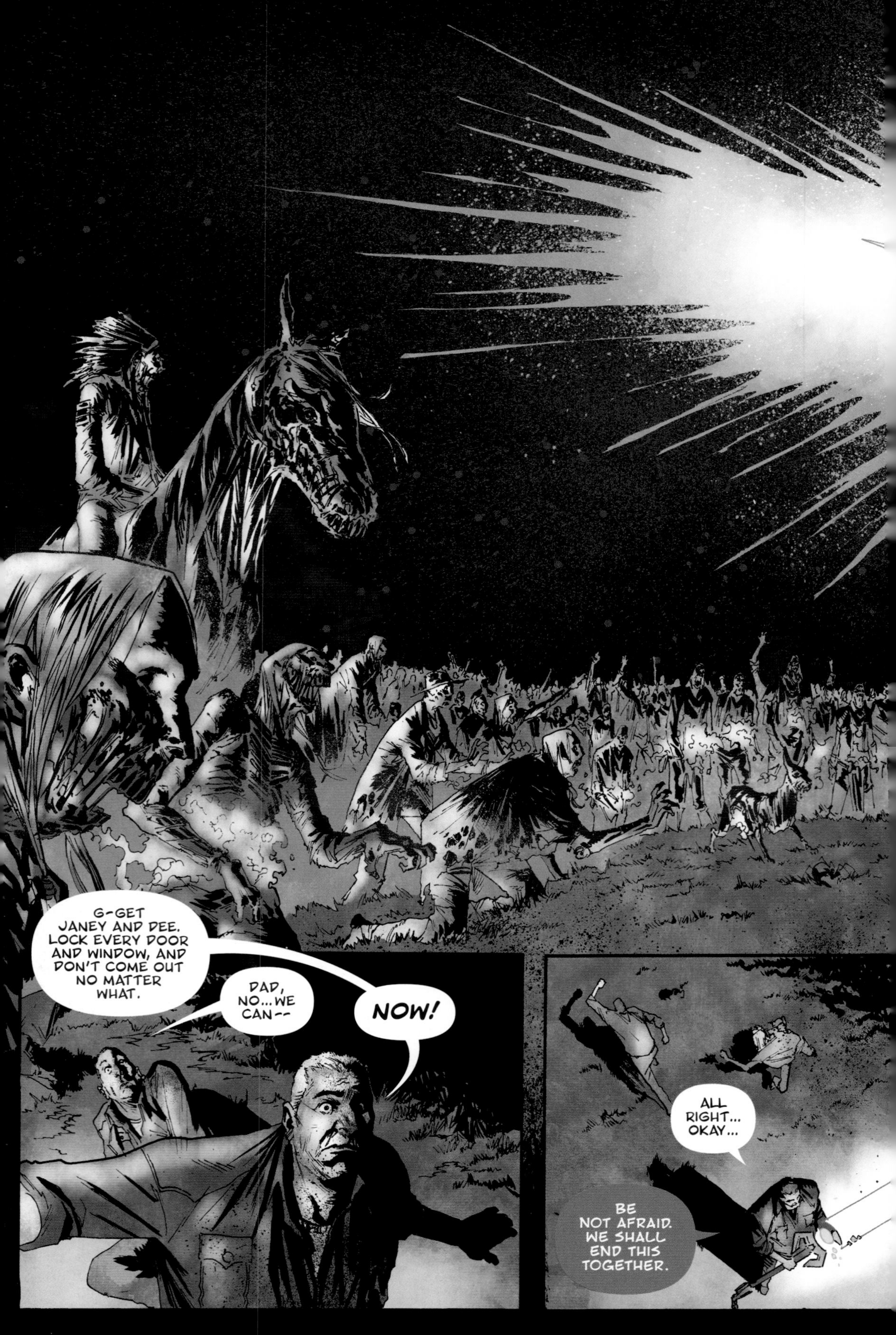
G-GET JANEY AND DEE. LOCK EVERY DOOR AND WINDOW, AND DON'T COME OUT NO MATTER WHAT.
DAD, NO... WE CAN--
NOW!
ALL RIGHT... OKAY...
BE NOT AFRAID. WE SHALL END THIS TOGETHER.

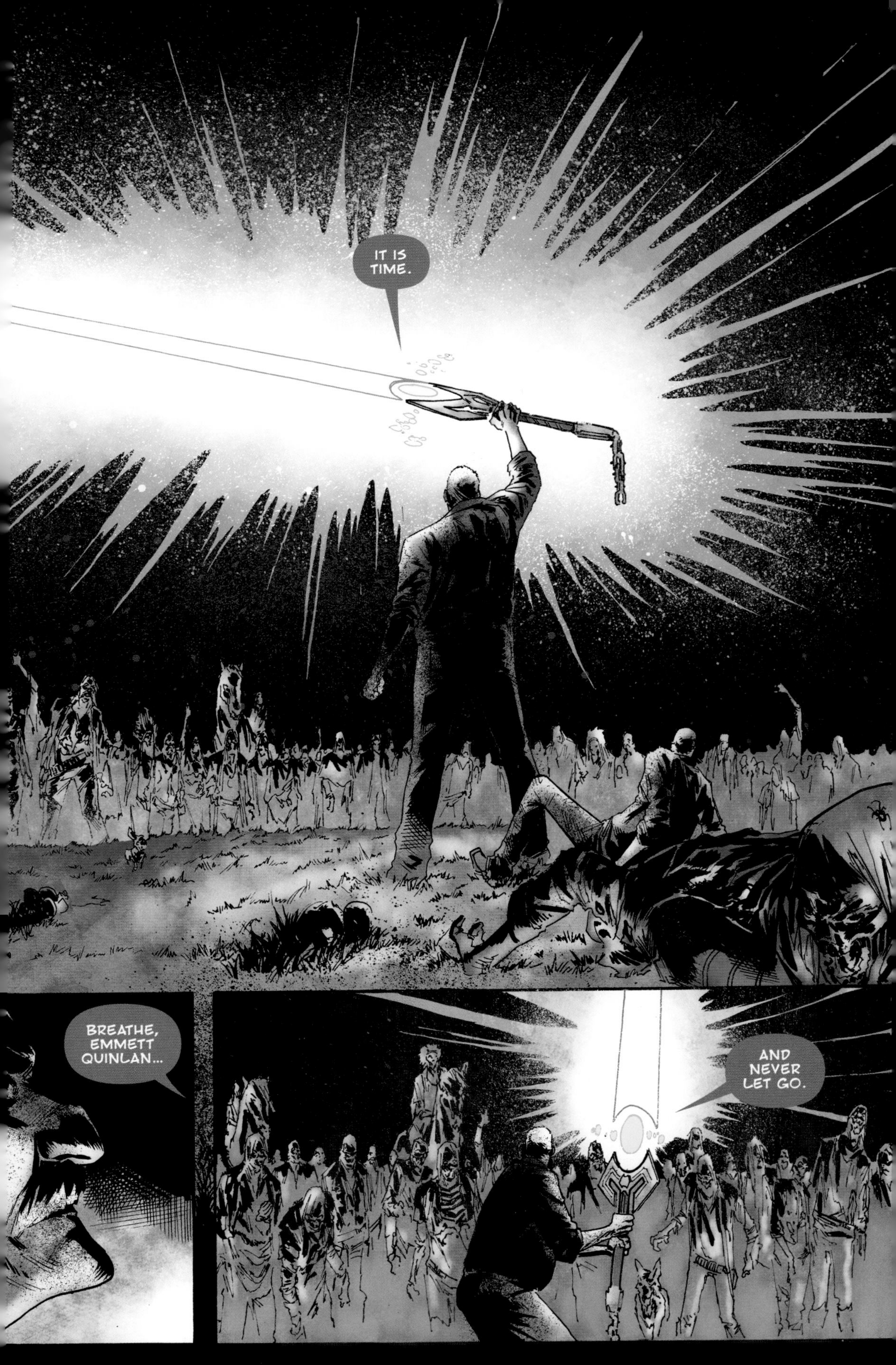
IT IS TIME.
BREATHE, EMMETT QUINLAN...
AND NEVER LET GO.

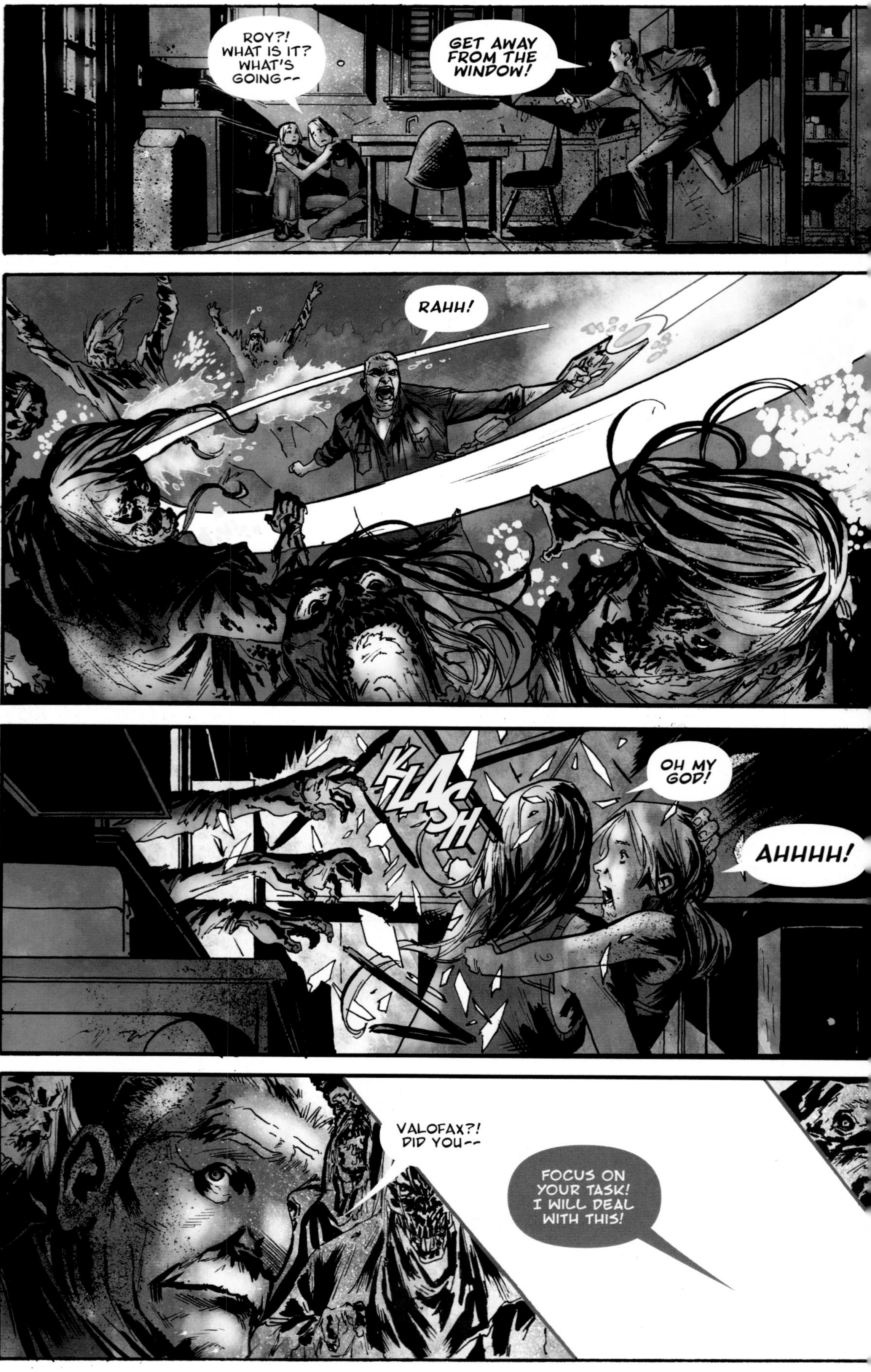
ROY?! WHAT IS IT? WHAT'S GOING--
GET AWAY FROM THE WINDOW!
RAHH!
KLASH
OH MY GOD!
AHHHH!
VALOFAX?! DID YOU--
FOCUS ON YOUR TASK! I WILL DEAL WITH THIS!

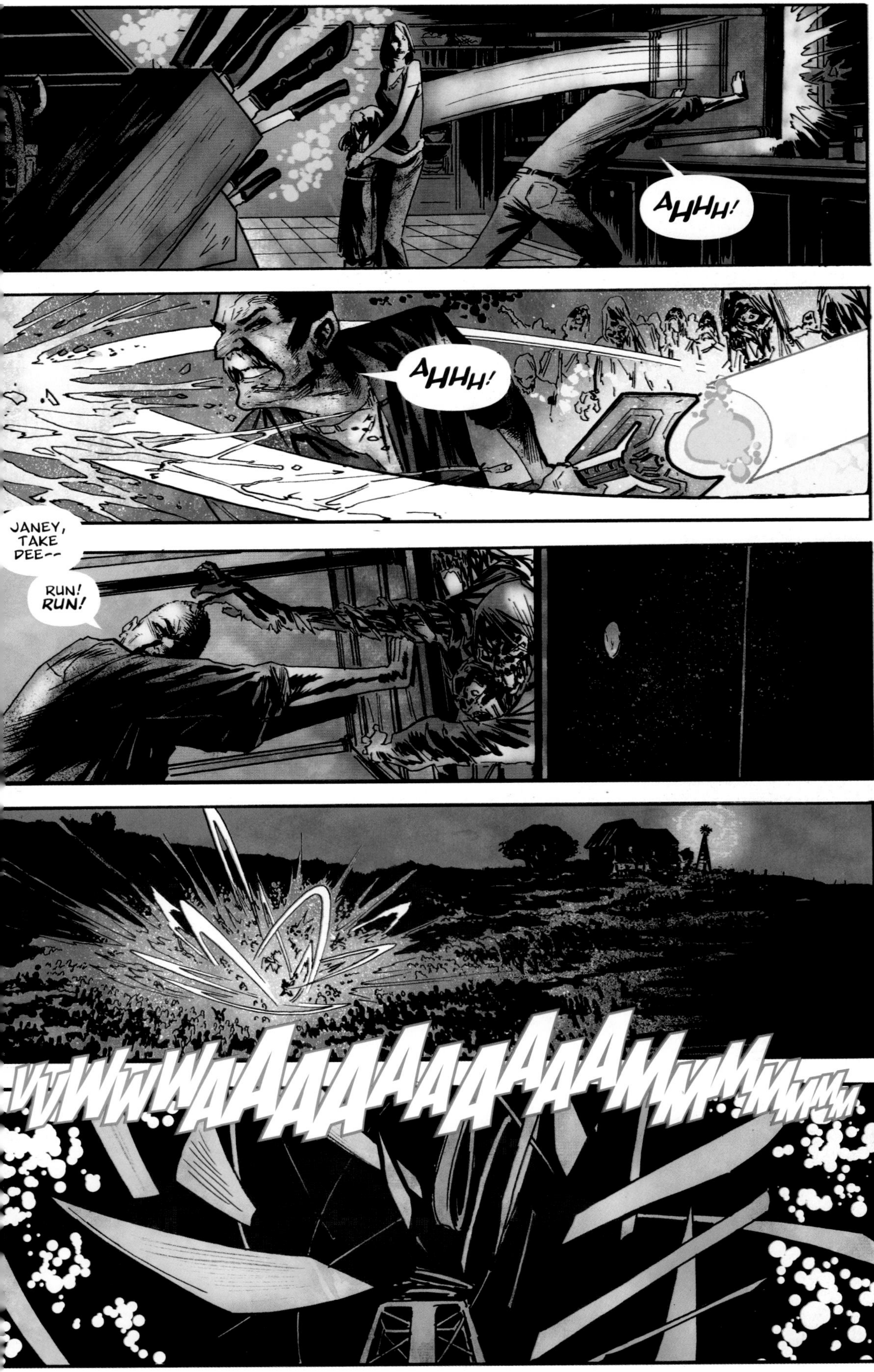
AHHH!
AHHH!
JANEY, TAKE DEE--
RUN! RUN!
VTWWWAAAAAAAAAAMMMMMMM

BOOM

VVWWWAAAAAAAAAAMMMMMMM

SHUNK

SHUNK

SHUNK

SHUNK

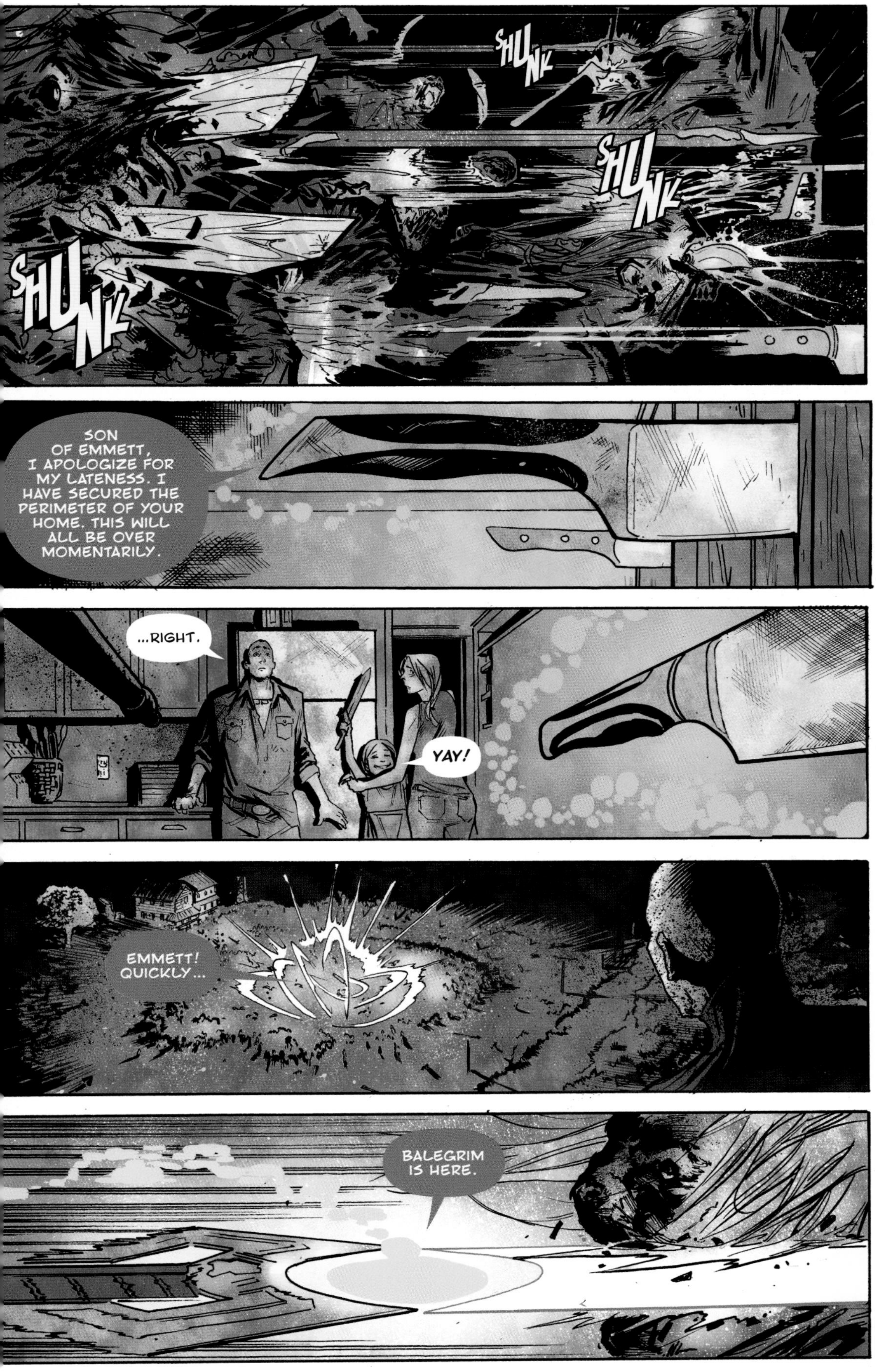
SHUNK
SHUNK
SHUNK
SON OF EMMETT, I APOLOGIZE FOR MY LATENESS. I HAVE SECURED THE PERIMETER OF YOUR HOME. THIS WILL ALL BE OVER MOMENTARILY.
...RIGHT.
YAY!
EMMETT! QUICKLY...
BALEGRIM IS HERE.

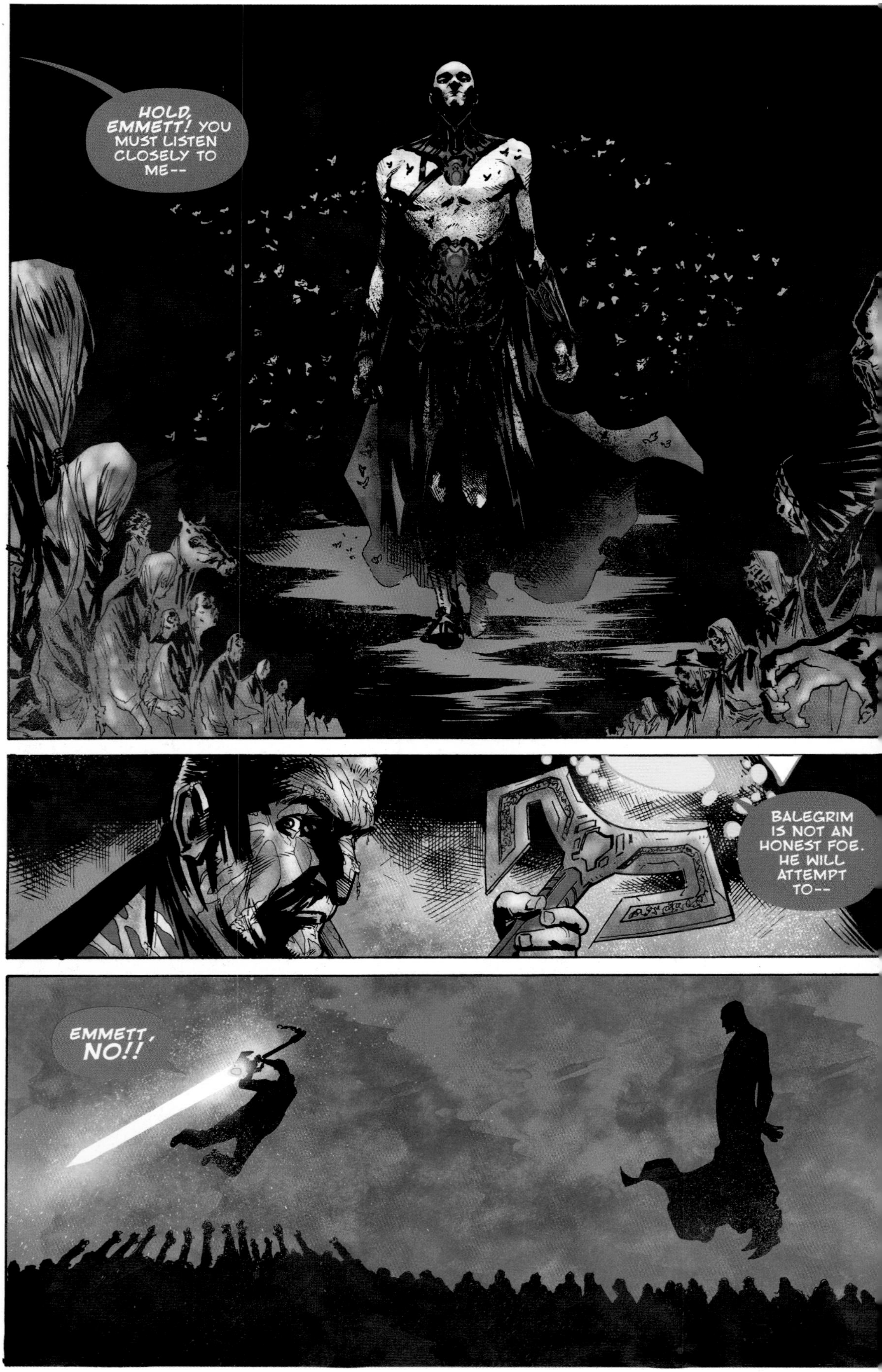
HOLD, EMMETT! YOU MUST LISTEN CLOSELY TO ME--
BALEGRIM IS NOT AN HONEST FOE. HE WILL ATTEMPT TO--
EMMETT, NO!!

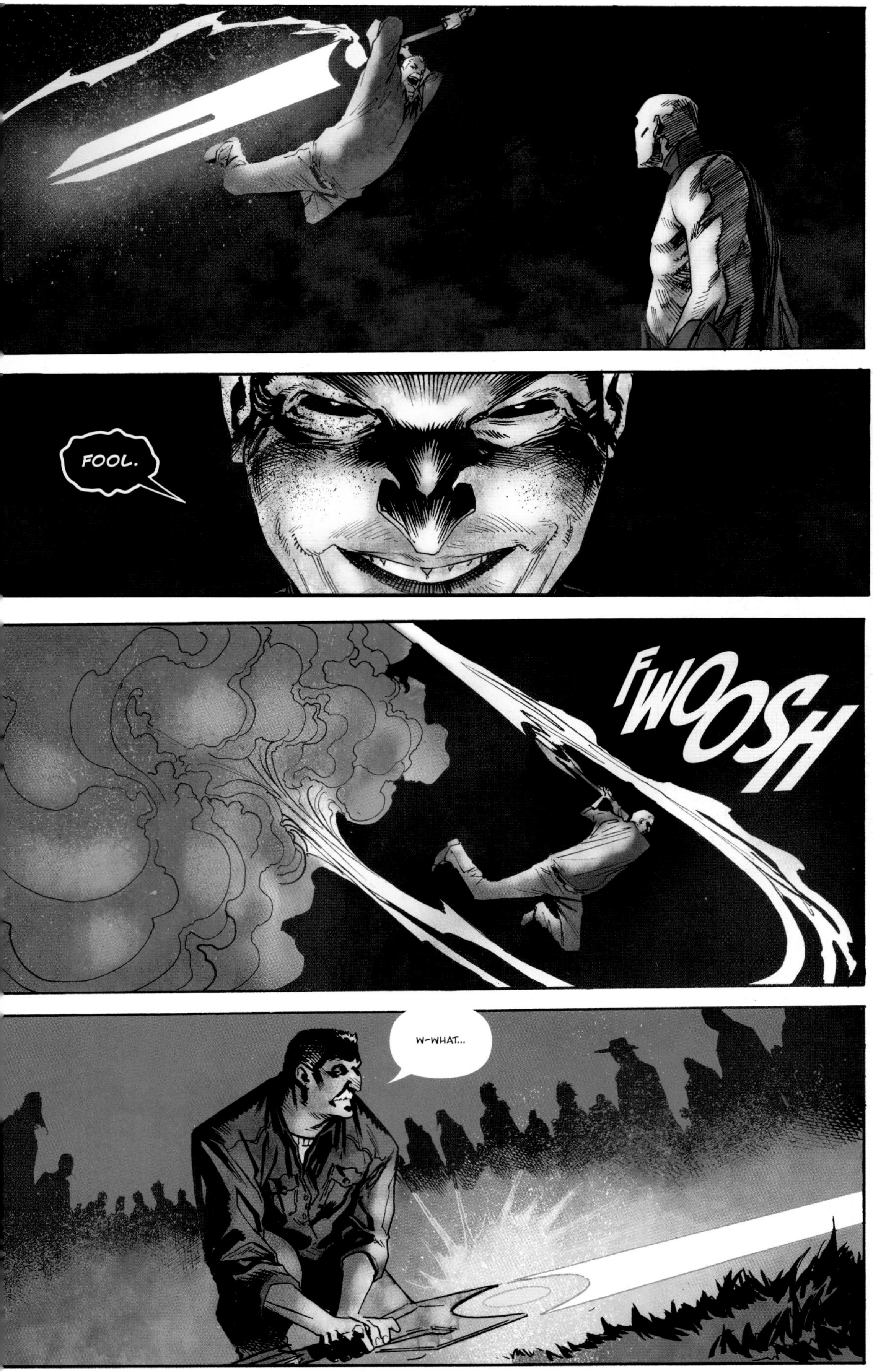
FOOL.
FWOOSH
W-WHAT...

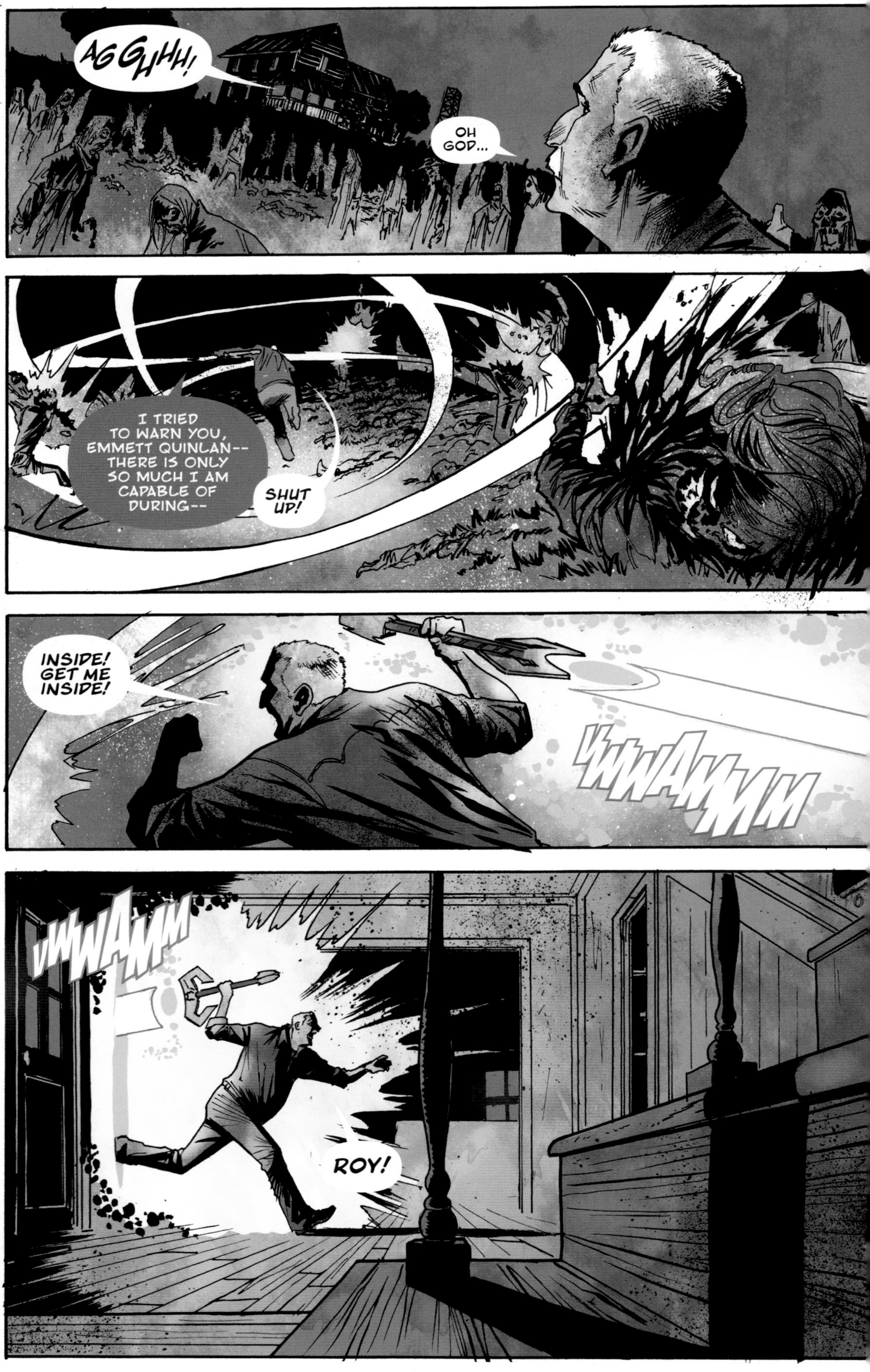
AGGHHH!
OH GOD...
I TRIED TO WARN YOU, EMMETT QUINLAN-- THERE IS ONLY SO MUCH I AM CAPABLE OF DURING--
SHUT UP!
INSIDE! GET ME INSIDE!
VWWAMMM
VWWAMM
ROY!

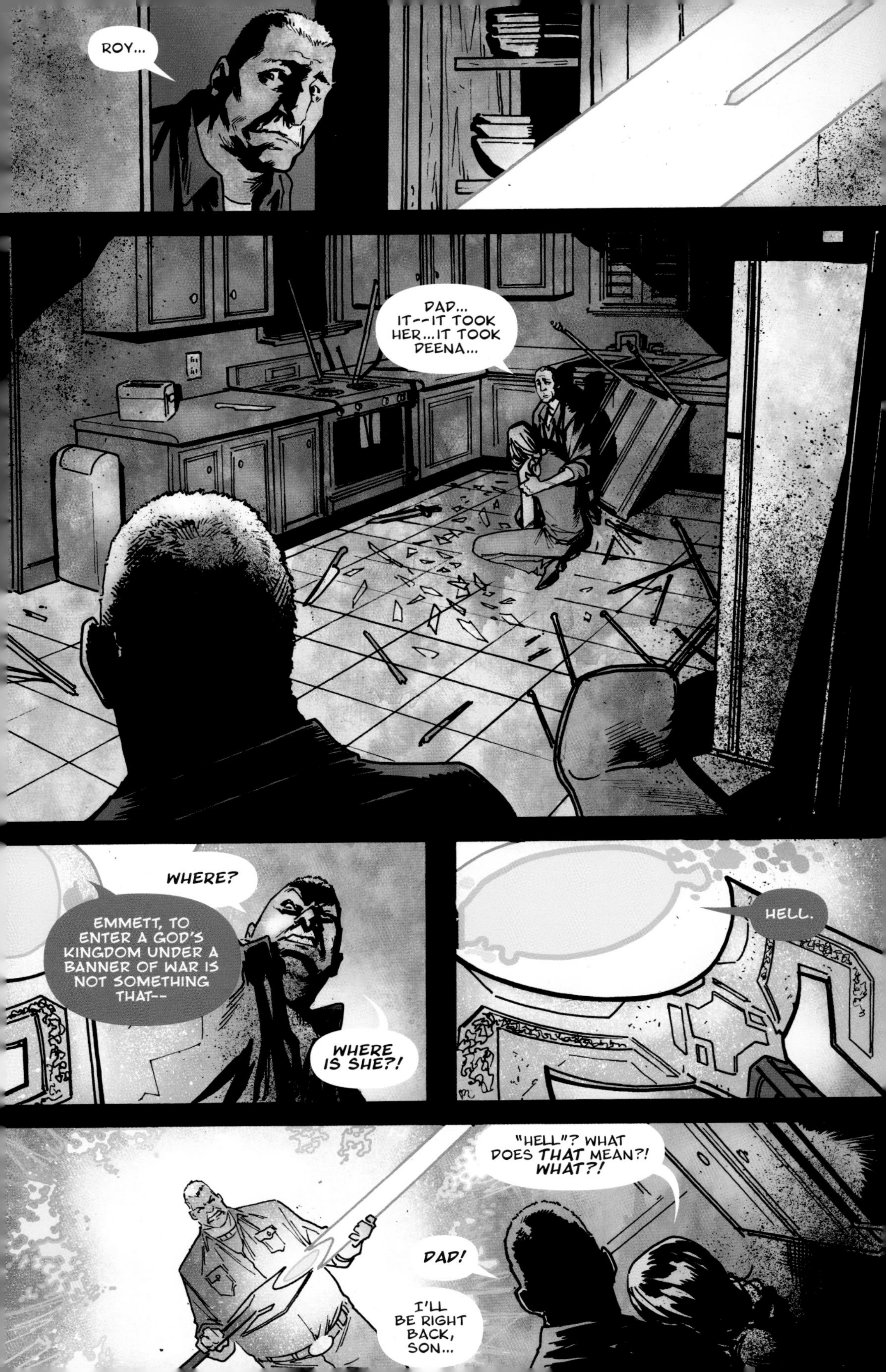
ROY...
DAD... IT--IT TOOK HER...IT TOOK DEENA...
WHERE?
EMMETT, TO ENTER A GOD'S KINGDOM UNDER A BANNER OF WAR IS NOT SOMETHING THAT--
WHERE IS SHE?!
HELL.
"HELL"? WHAT DOES THAT MEAN?! WHAT?!
DAD!
I'LL BE RIGHT BACK, SON...

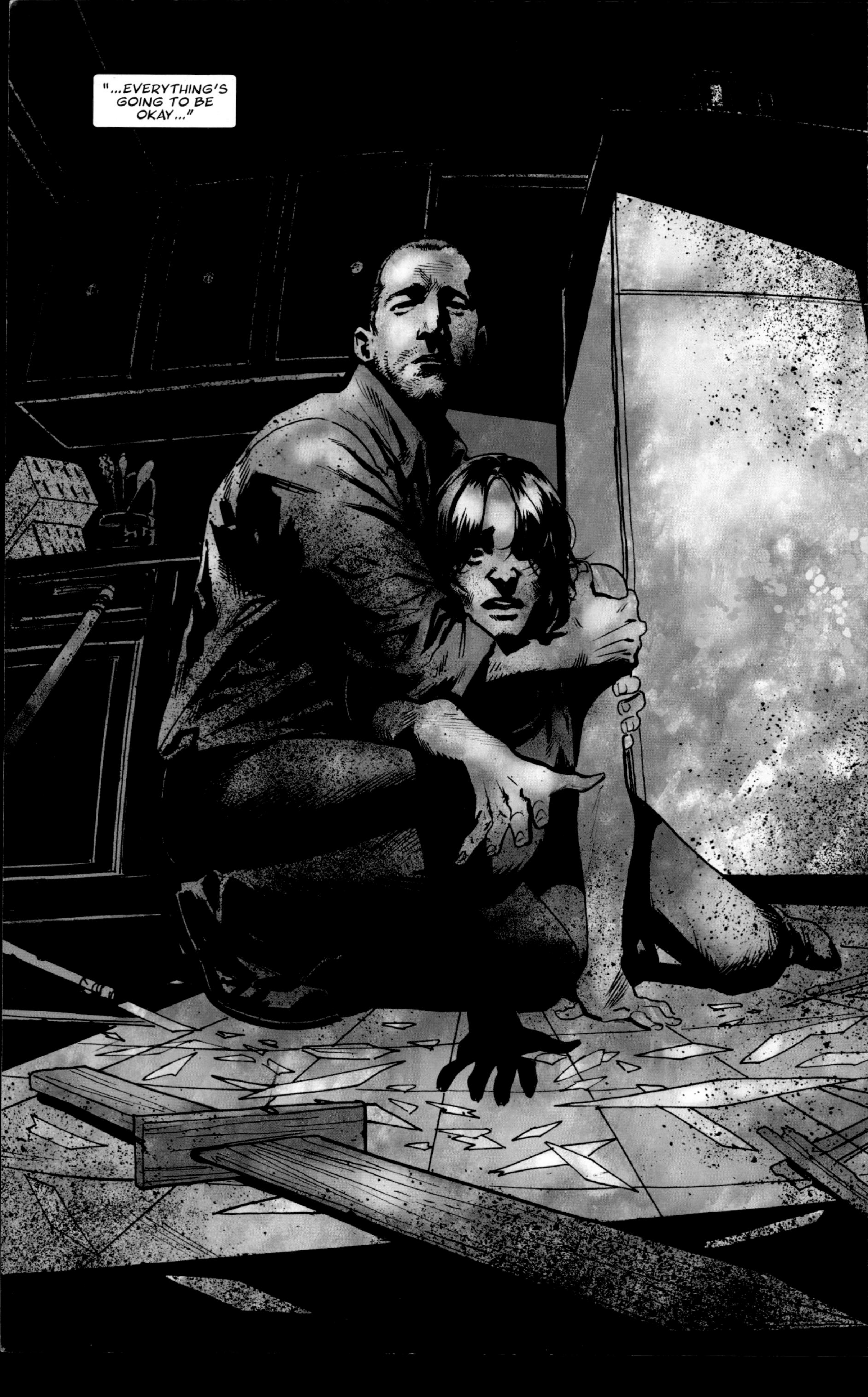
"...EVERYTHING'S GOING TO BE OKAY..."

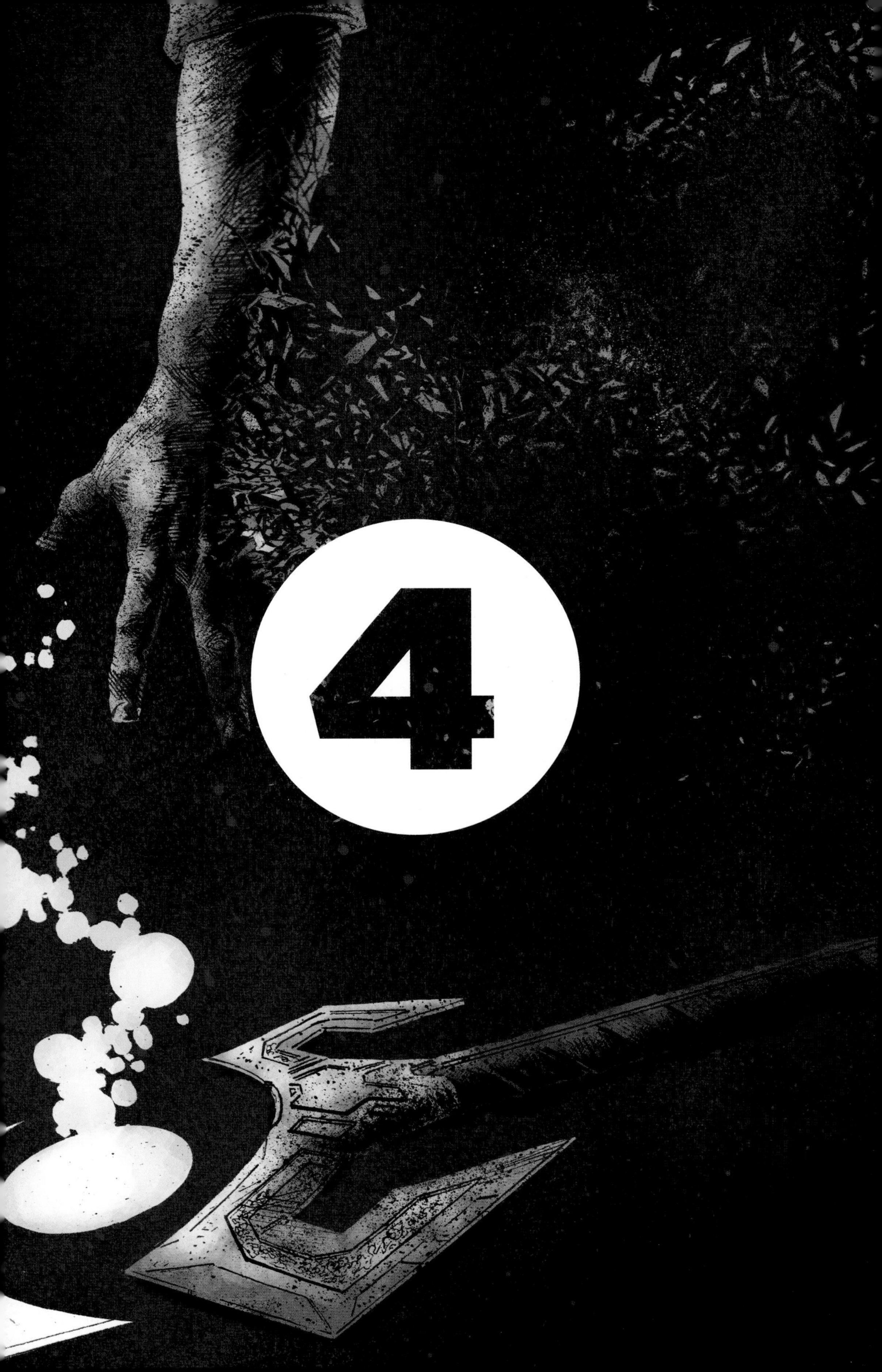
4

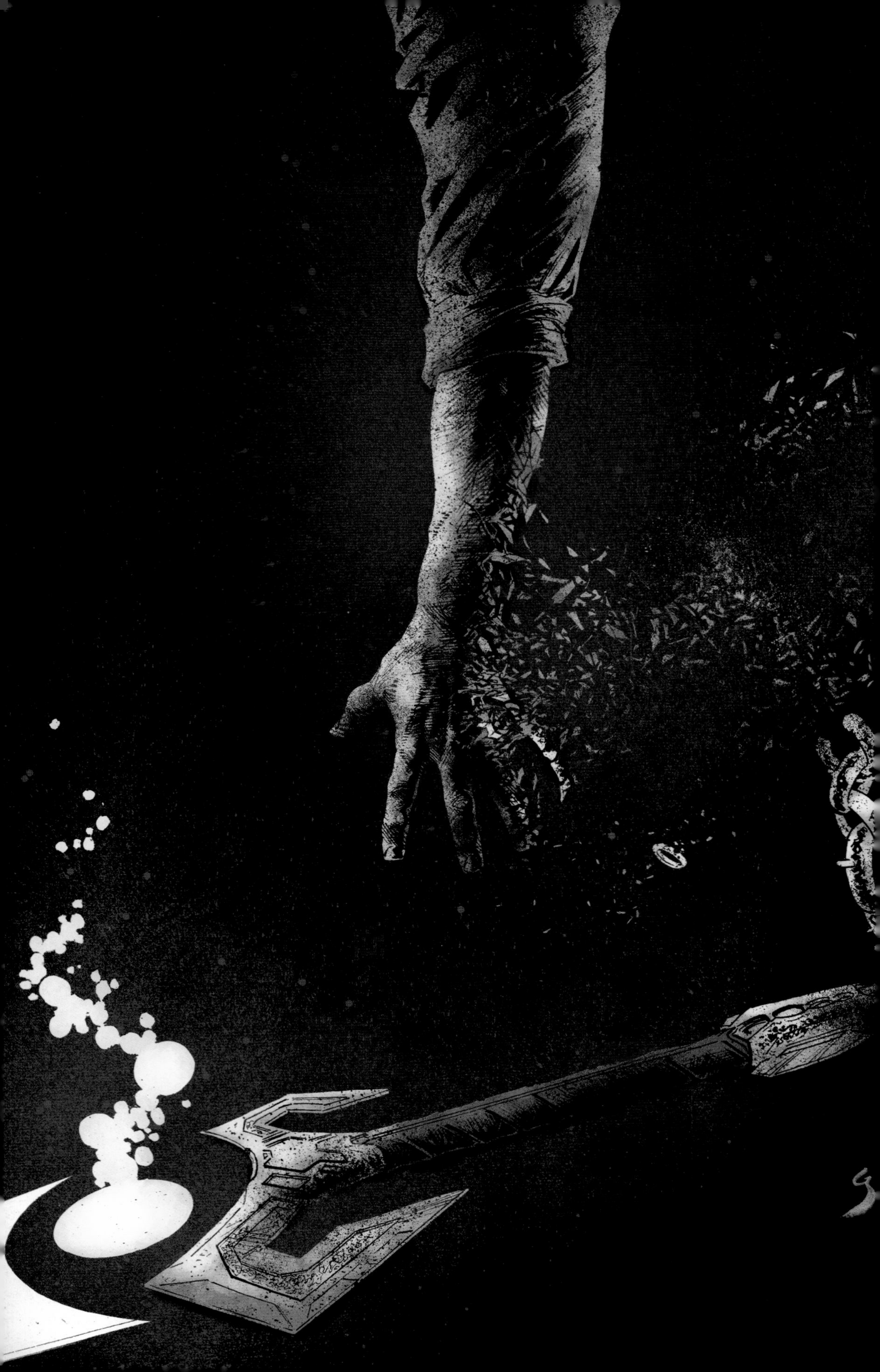

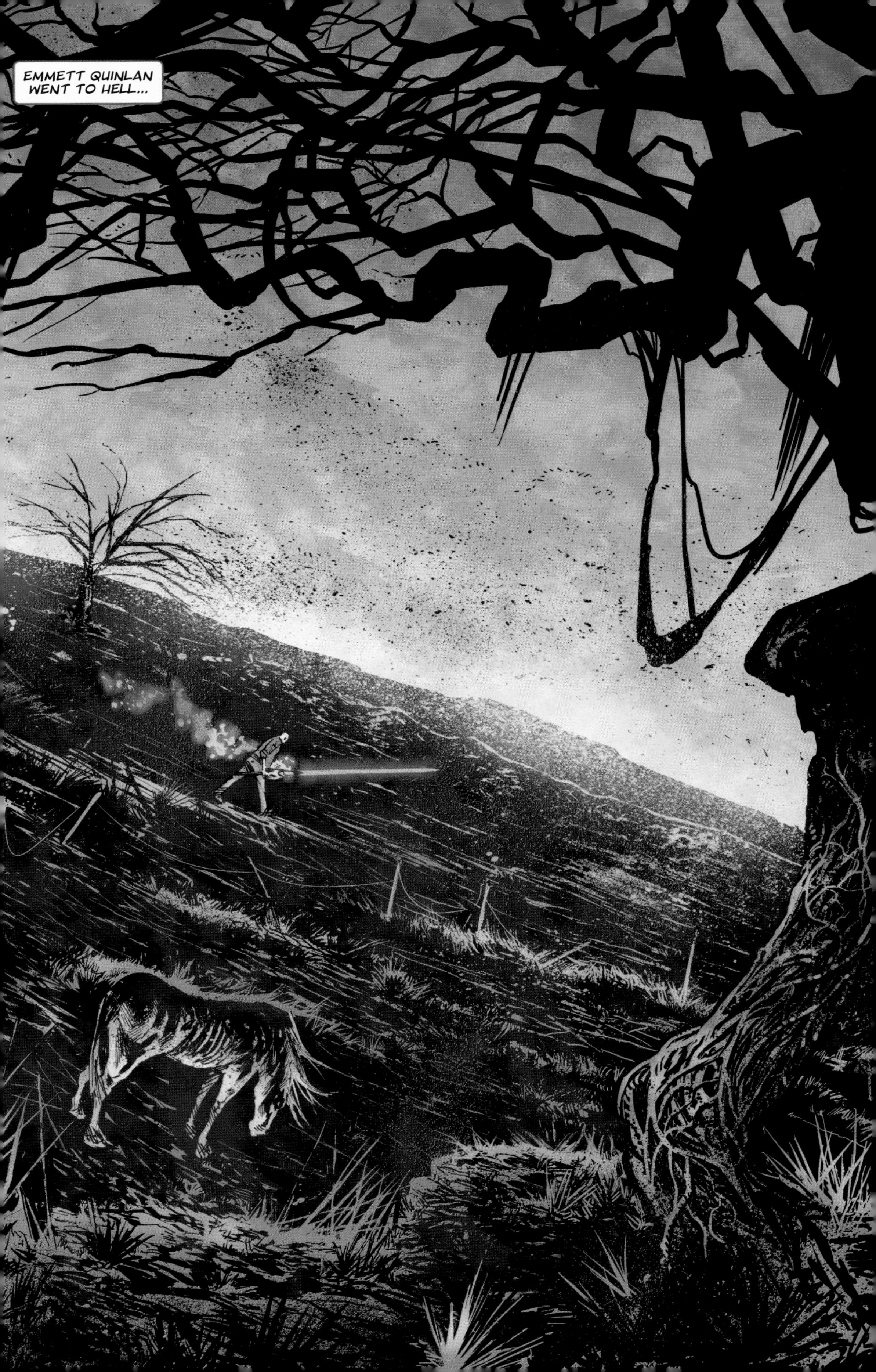
EMMETT QUINLAN WENT TO HELL...

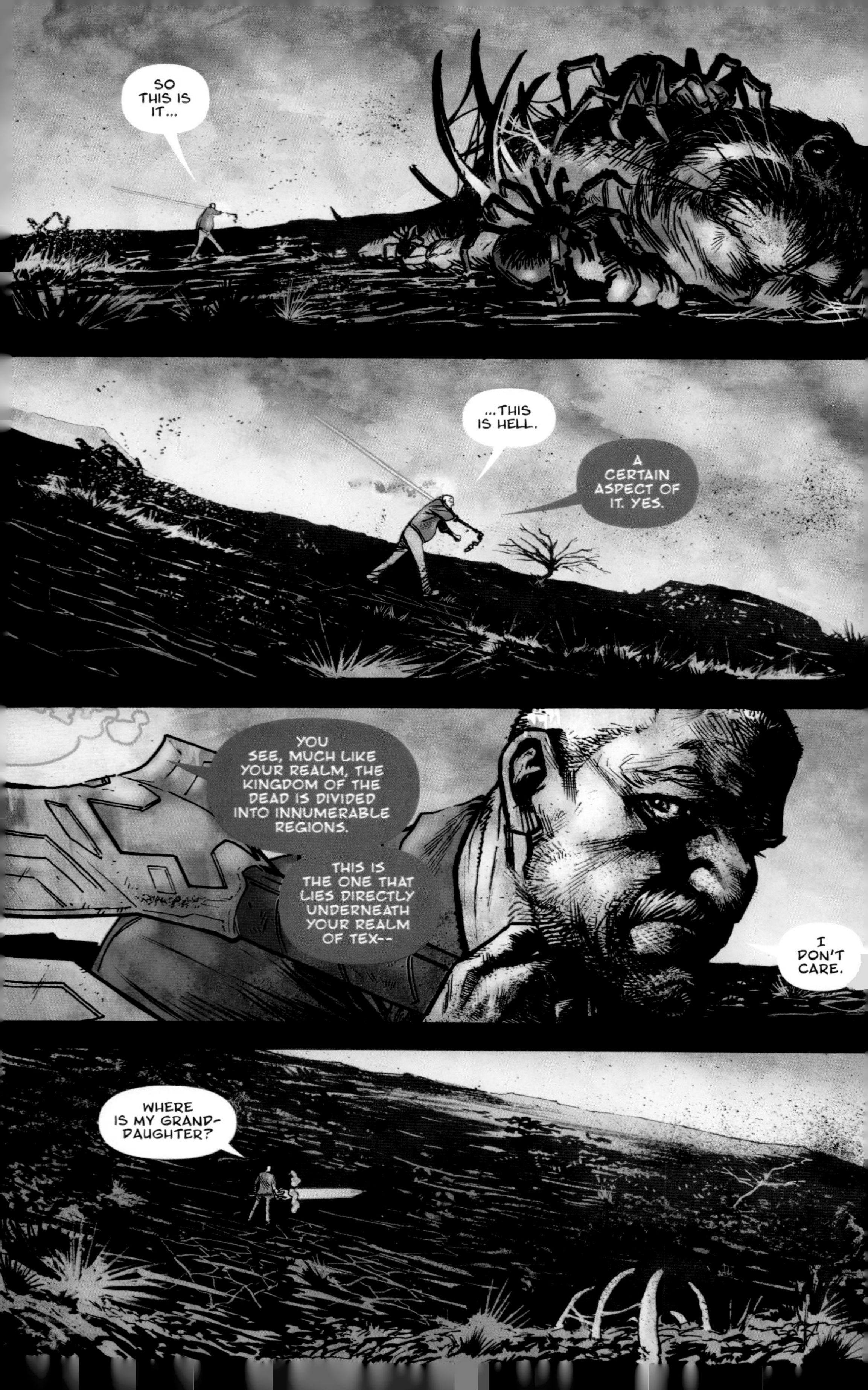
SO THIS IS IT...
...THIS IS HELL.
A CERTAIN ASPECT OF IT. YES.
YOU SEE, MUCH LIKE YOUR REALM, THE KINGDOM OF THE DEAD IS DIVIDED INTO INNUMERABLE REGIONS.
THIS IS THE ONE THAT LIES DIRECTLY UNDERNEATH YOUR REALM OF TEX--
I DON'T CARE.
WHERE IS MY GRAND-DAUGHTER?

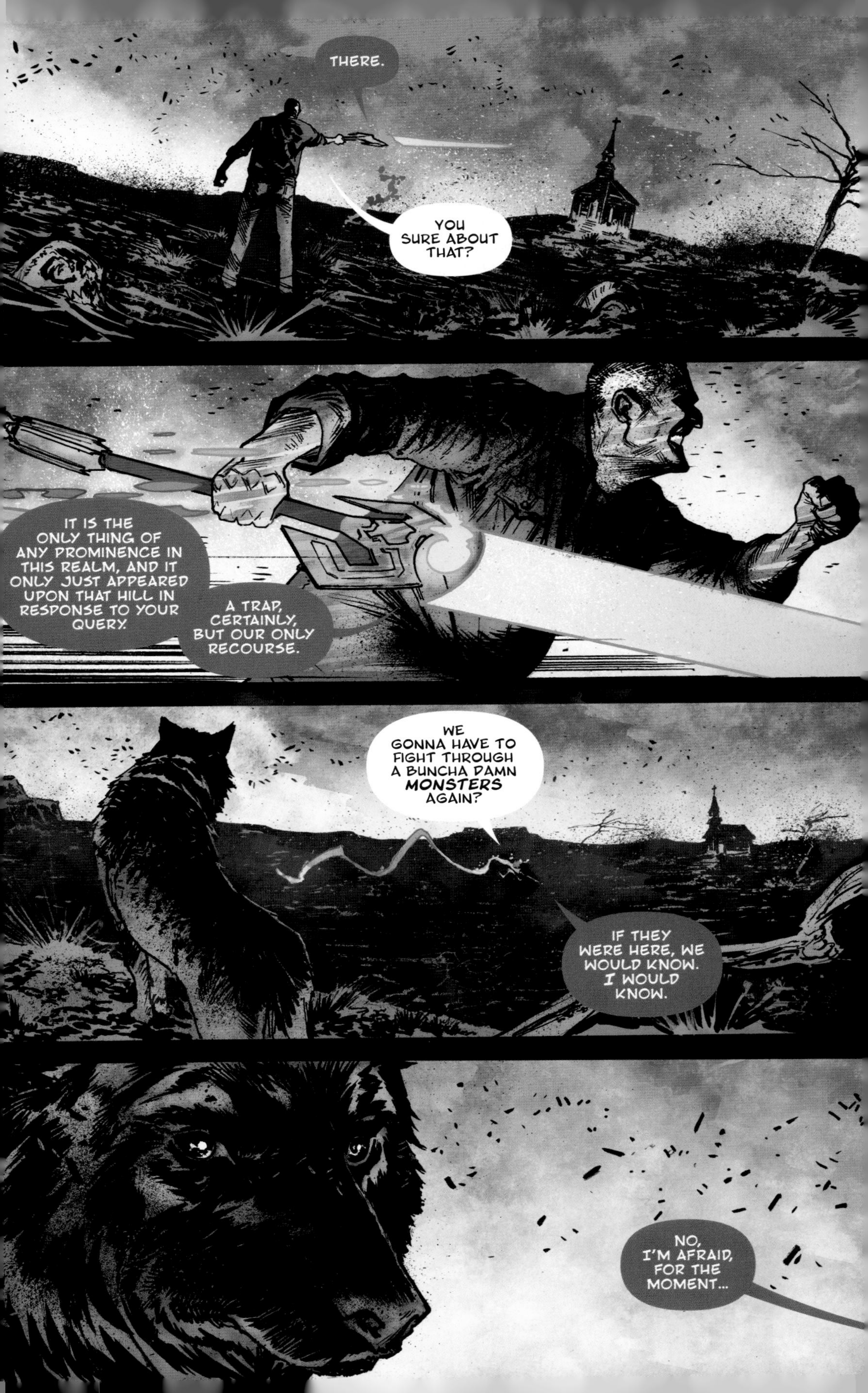
THERE.
YOU SURE ABOUT THAT?
IT IS THE ONLY THING OF ANY PROMINENCE IN THIS REALM, AND IT ONLY JUST APPEARED UPON THAT HILL IN RESPONSE TO YOUR QUERY.
A TRAP, CERTAINLY, BUT OUR ONLY RECOURSE.
WE GONNA HAVE TO FIGHT THROUGH A BUNCHA DAMN MONSTERS AGAIN?
IF THEY WERE HERE, WE WOULD KNOW. I WOULD KNOW.
NO, I'M AFRAID, FOR THE MOMENT...

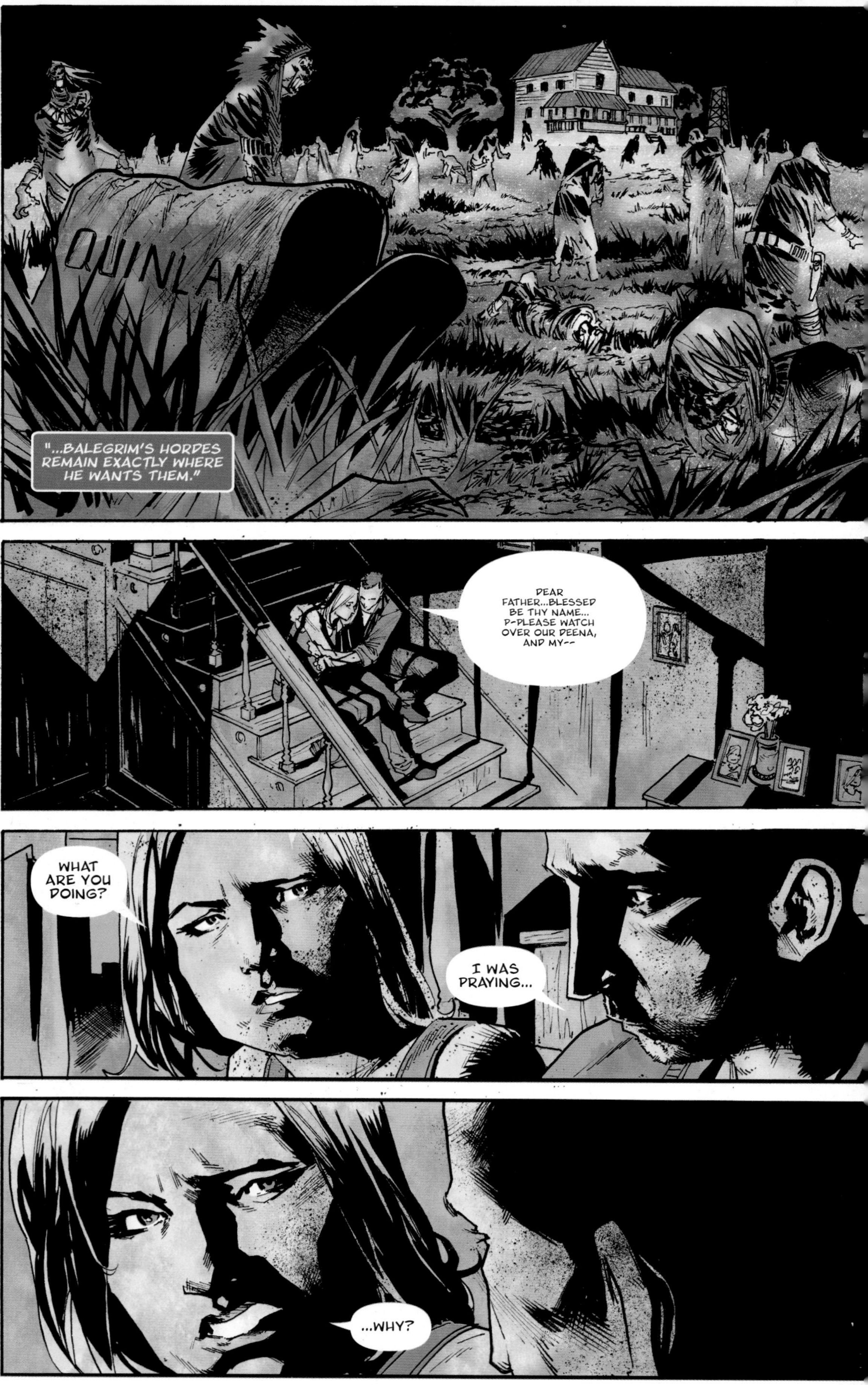
QUINLAN
"...BALEGRIM'S HORDES REMAIN EXACTLY WHERE HE WANTS THEM."
DEAR FATHER...BLESSED BE THY NAME... P-PLEASE WATCH OVER OUR DEENA, AND MY--
WHAT ARE YOU DOING?
I WAS PRAYING...
...WHY?

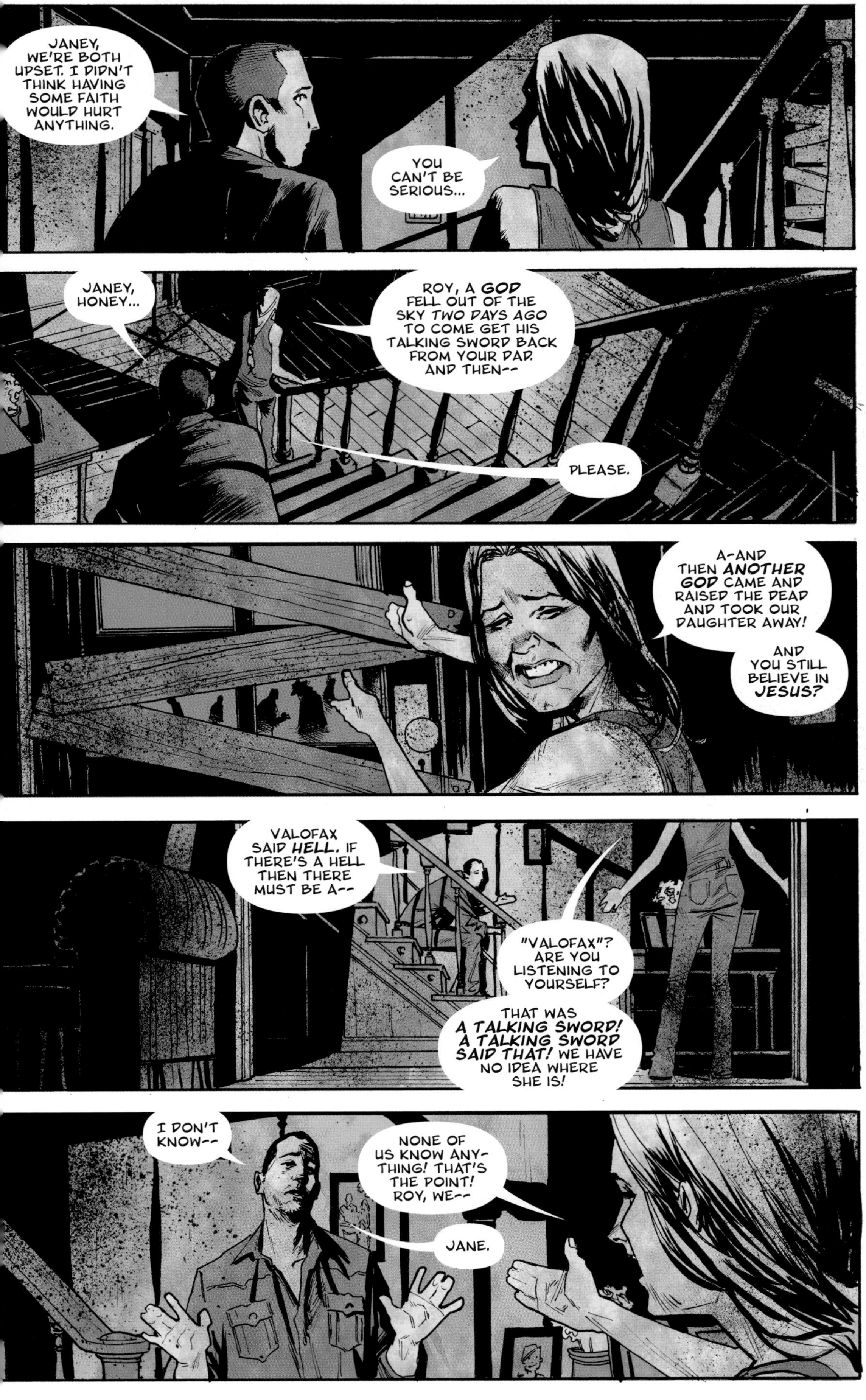
JANEY, WE'RE BOTH UPSET. I DIDN'T THINK HAVING SOME FAITH WOULD HURT ANYTHING.
YOU CAN'T BE SERIOUS...
JANEY, HONEY...
ROY, A **GOD** FELL OUT OF THE SKY *TWO DAYS AGO* TO COME GET HIS TALKING SWORD BACK FROM YOUR DAD. AND THEN--
PLEASE.
A-AND THEN **ANOTHER GOD** CAME AND RAISED THE DEAD AND TOOK OUR DAUGHTER AWAY!
AND YOU STILL BELIEVE IN ***JESUS?***
VALOFAX SAID **HELL.** IF THERE'S A HELL THEN THERE MUST BE A--
"VALOFAX"? ARE YOU LISTENING TO YOURSELF?
THAT WAS ***A TALKING SWORD! A TALKING SWORD SAID THAT!*** WE HAVE NO IDEA WHERE SHE IS!
I DON'T KNOW--
NONE OF US KNOW ANYTHING! THAT'S THE POINT! ROY, WE--
JANE.

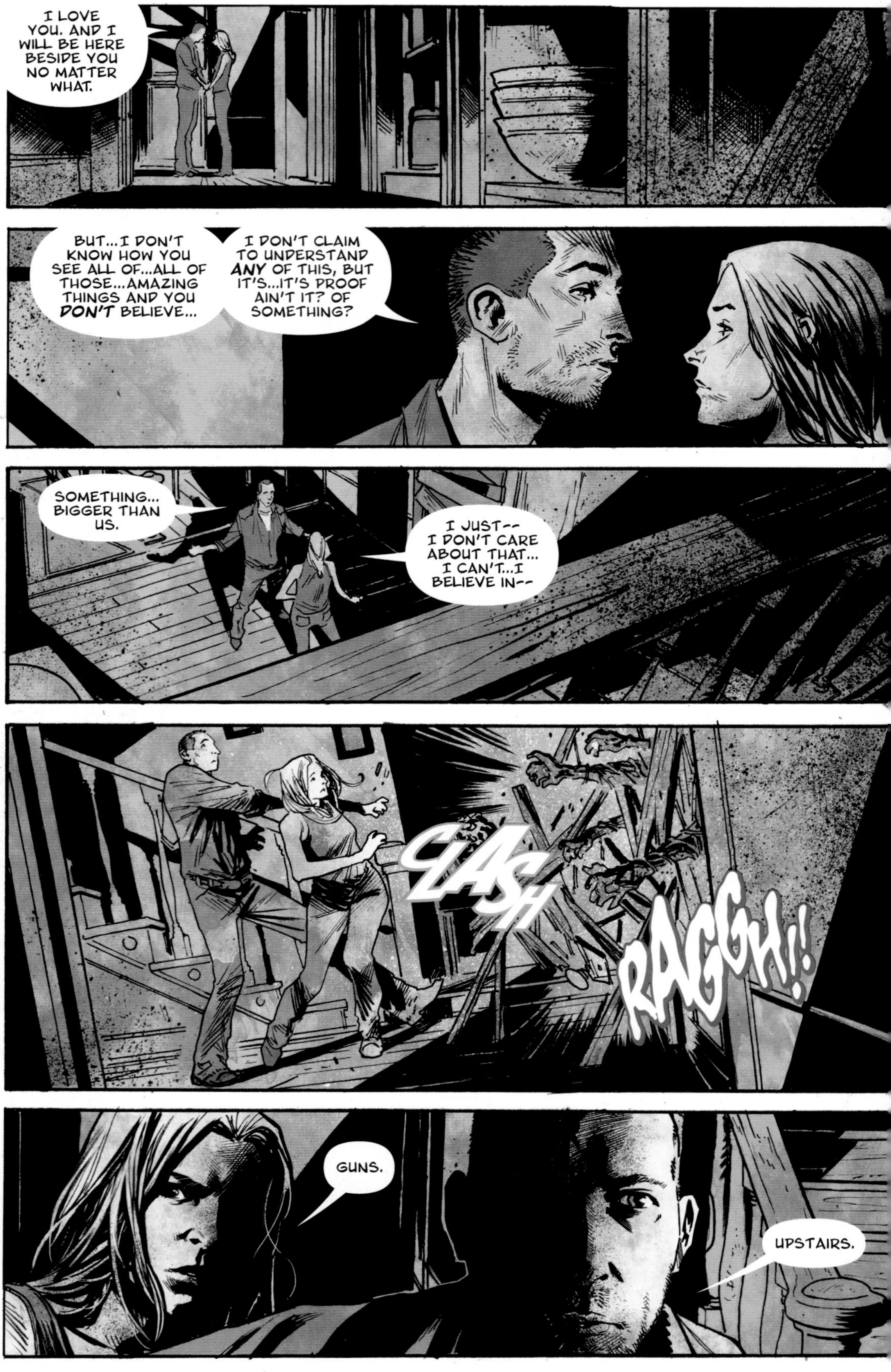
I LOVE YOU. AND I WILL BE HERE BESIDE YOU NO MATTER WHAT.
BUT...I DON'T KNOW HOW YOU SEE ALL OF...ALL OF THOSE...AMAZING THINGS AND YOU DON'T BELIEVE...
I DON'T CLAIM TO UNDERSTAND ANY OF THIS, BUT IT'S...IT'S PROOF AIN'T IT? OF SOMETHING?
SOMETHING... BIGGER THAN US.
I JUST-- I DON'T CARE ABOUT THAT... I CAN'T...I BELIEVE IN--
CLASH
RAGGH!!
GUNS.
UPSTAIRS.

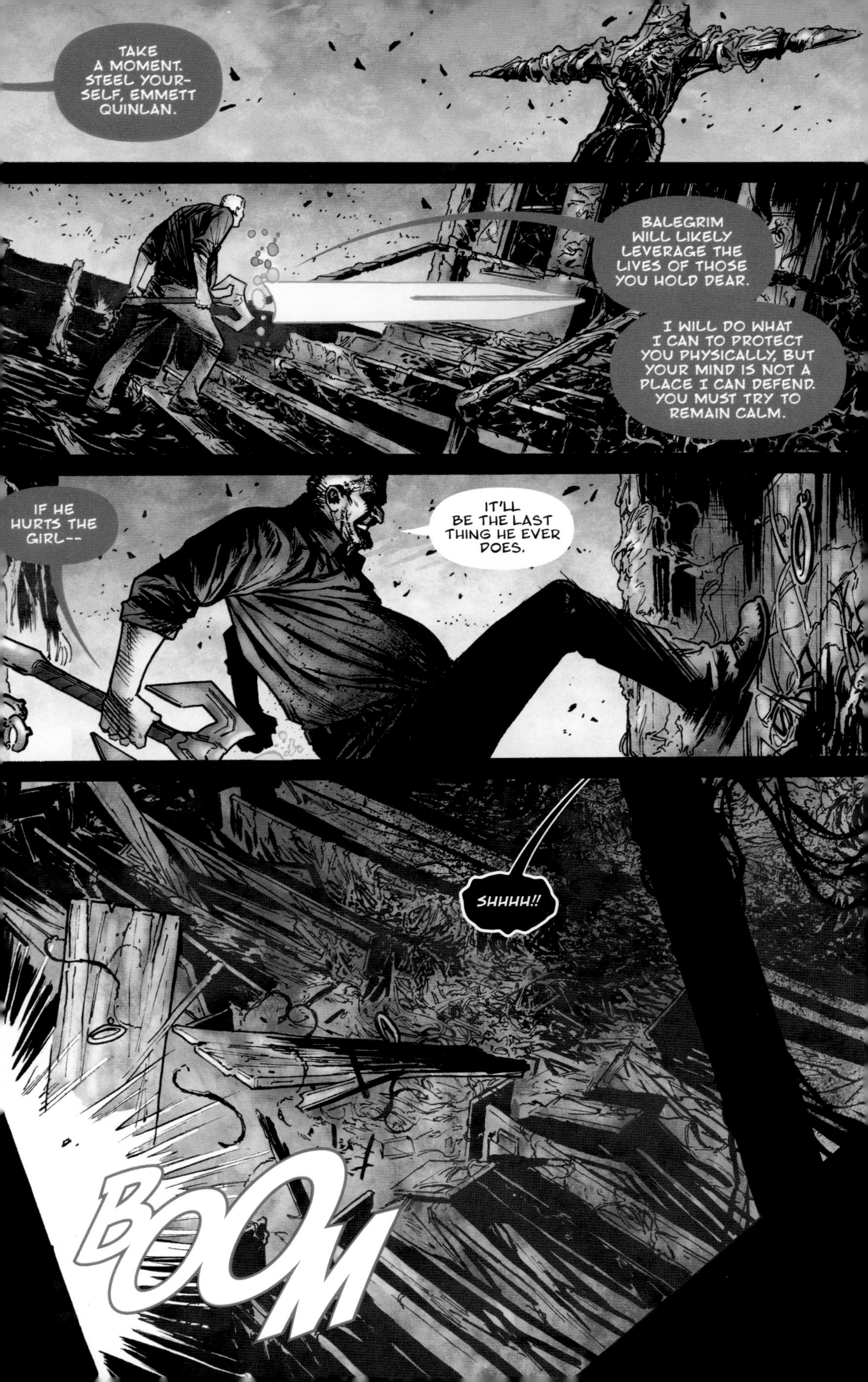
TAKE A MOMENT. STEEL YOURSELF, EMMETT QUINLAN.
BALEGRIM WILL LIKELY LEVERAGE THE LIVES OF THOSE YOU HOLD DEAR.
I WILL DO WHAT I CAN TO PROTECT YOU PHYSICALLY, BUT YOUR MIND IS NOT A PLACE I CAN DEFEND. YOU MUST TRY TO REMAIN CALM.
IF HE HURTS THE GIRL--
IT'LL BE THE LAST THING HE EVER DOES.
SHHHH!!
BOOM

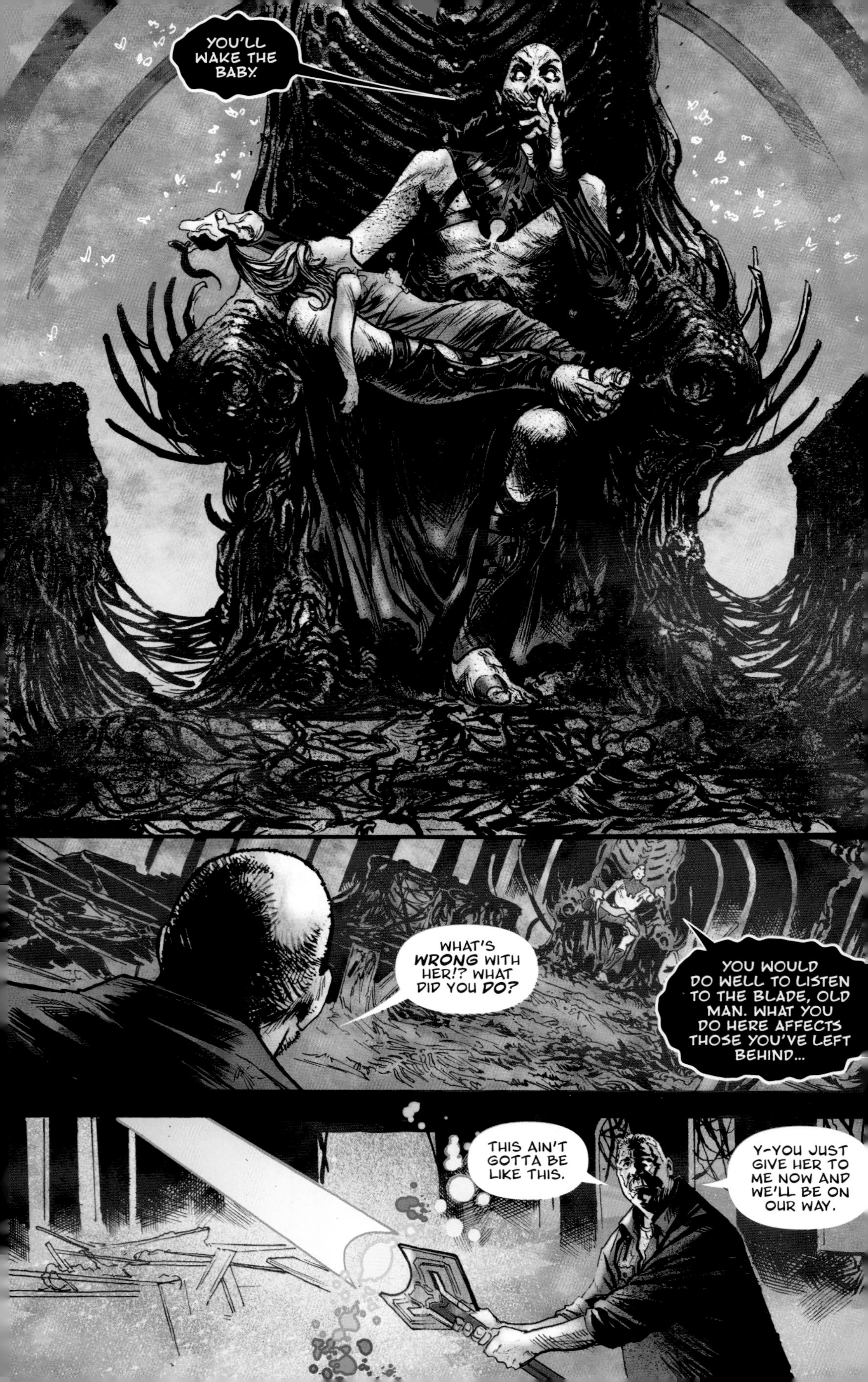
YOU'LL WAKE THE BABY.
WHAT'S **WRONG** WITH HER!? WHAT DID YOU **DO?**
YOU WOULD DO WELL TO LISTEN TO THE BLADE, OLD MAN. WHAT YOU DO HERE AFFECTS THOSE YOU'VE LEFT BEHIND...
THIS AIN'T GOTTA BE LIKE THIS.
Y-YOU JUST GIVE HER TO ME NOW AND WE'LL BE ON OUR WAY.

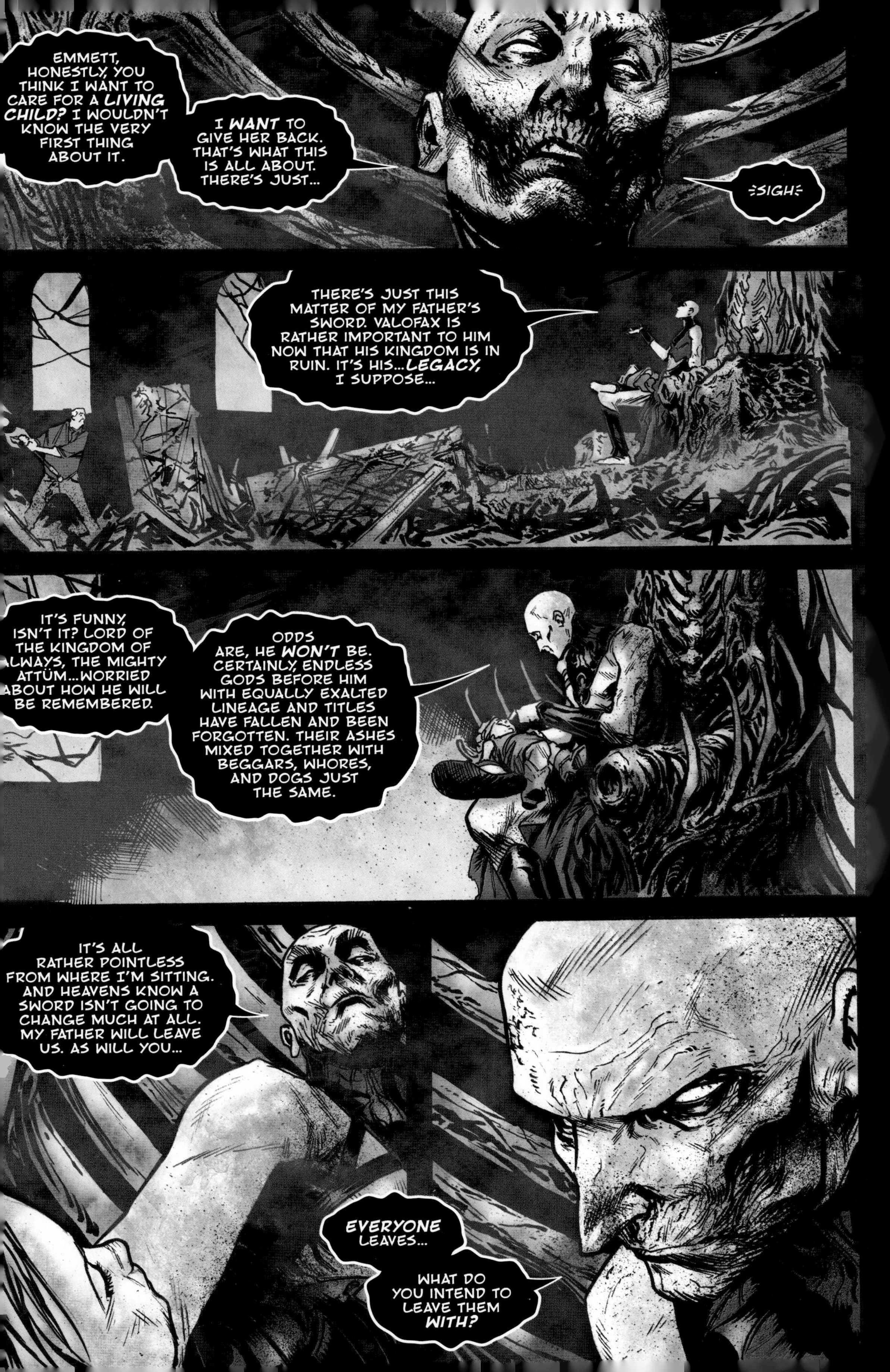
EMMETT, HONESTLY, YOU THINK I WANT TO CARE FOR A LIVING CHILD? I WOULDN'T KNOW THE VERY FIRST THING ABOUT IT.
I WANT TO GIVE HER BACK. THAT'S WHAT THIS IS ALL ABOUT. THERE'S JUST...
=SIGH=
THERE'S JUST THIS MATTER OF MY FATHER'S SWORD. VALOFAX IS RATHER IMPORTANT TO HIM NOW THAT HIS KINGDOM IS IN RUIN. IT'S HIS...LEGACY, I SUPPOSE...
IT'S FUNNY, ISN'T IT? LORD OF THE KINGDOM OF ALWAYS, THE MIGHTY ATTÜM...WORRIED ABOUT HOW HE WILL BE REMEMBERED.
ODDS ARE, HE WON'T BE. CERTAINLY, ENDLESS GODS BEFORE HIM WITH EQUALLY EXALTED LINEAGE AND TITLES HAVE FALLEN AND BEEN FORGOTTEN. THEIR ASHES MIXED TOGETHER WITH BEGGARS, WHORES, AND DOGS JUST THE SAME.
IT'S ALL RATHER POINTLESS FROM WHERE I'M SITTING. AND HEAVENS KNOW A SWORD ISN'T GOING TO CHANGE MUCH AT ALL. MY FATHER WILL LEAVE US. AS WILL YOU...
EVERYONE LEAVES...
WHAT DO YOU INTEND TO LEAVE THEM WITH?

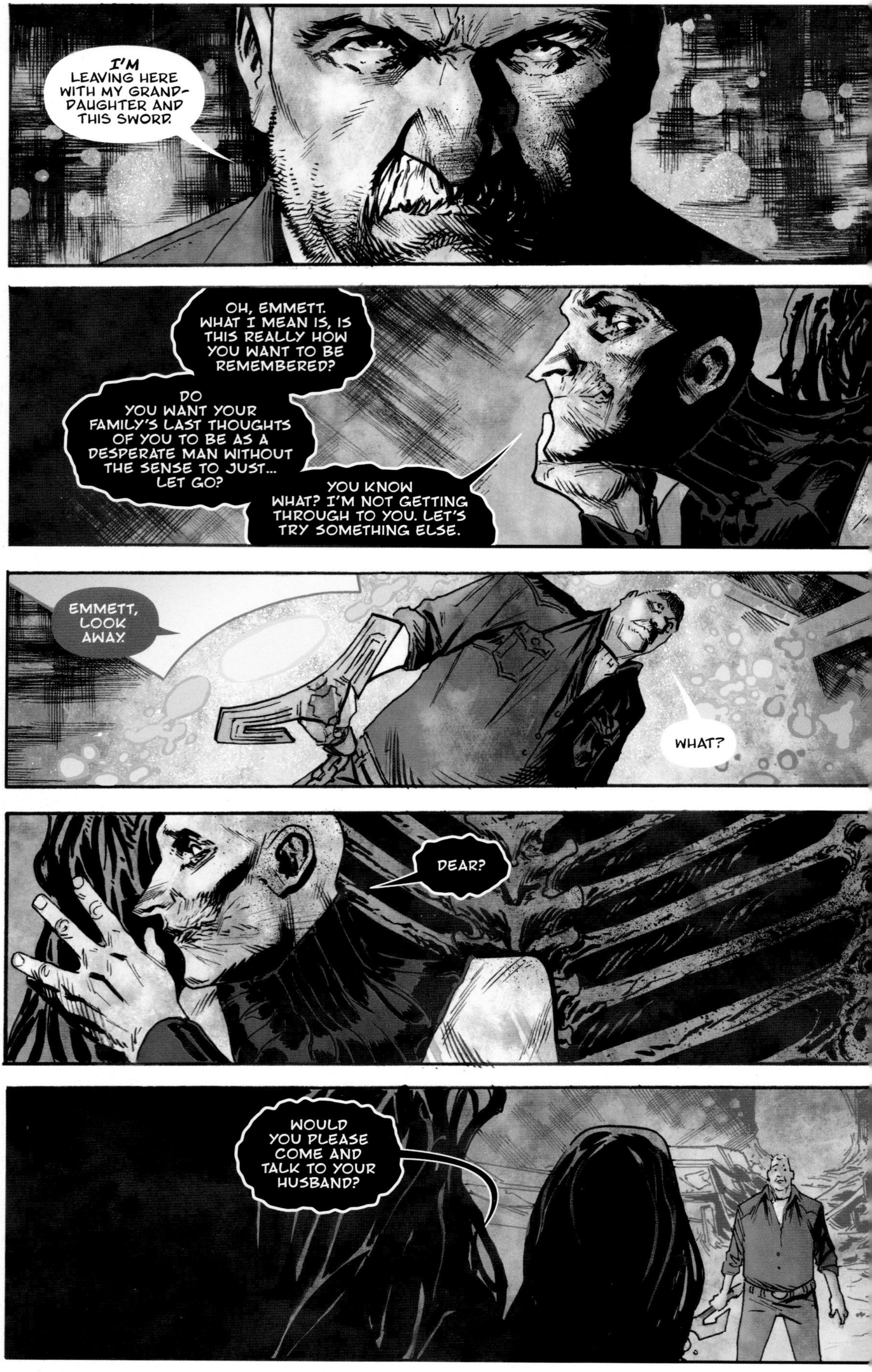
I'M LEAVING HERE WITH MY GRAND-DAUGHTER AND THIS SWORD.
OH, EMMETT. WHAT I MEAN IS, IS THIS REALLY HOW YOU WANT TO BE REMEMBERED?
DO YOU WANT YOUR FAMILY'S LAST THOUGHTS OF YOU TO BE AS A DESPERATE MAN WITHOUT THE SENSE TO JUST... LET GO?
YOU KNOW WHAT? I'M NOT GETTING THROUGH TO YOU. LET'S TRY SOMETHING ELSE.
EMMETT, LOOK AWAY.
WHAT?
DEAR?
WOULD YOU PLEASE COME AND TALK TO YOUR HUSBAND?

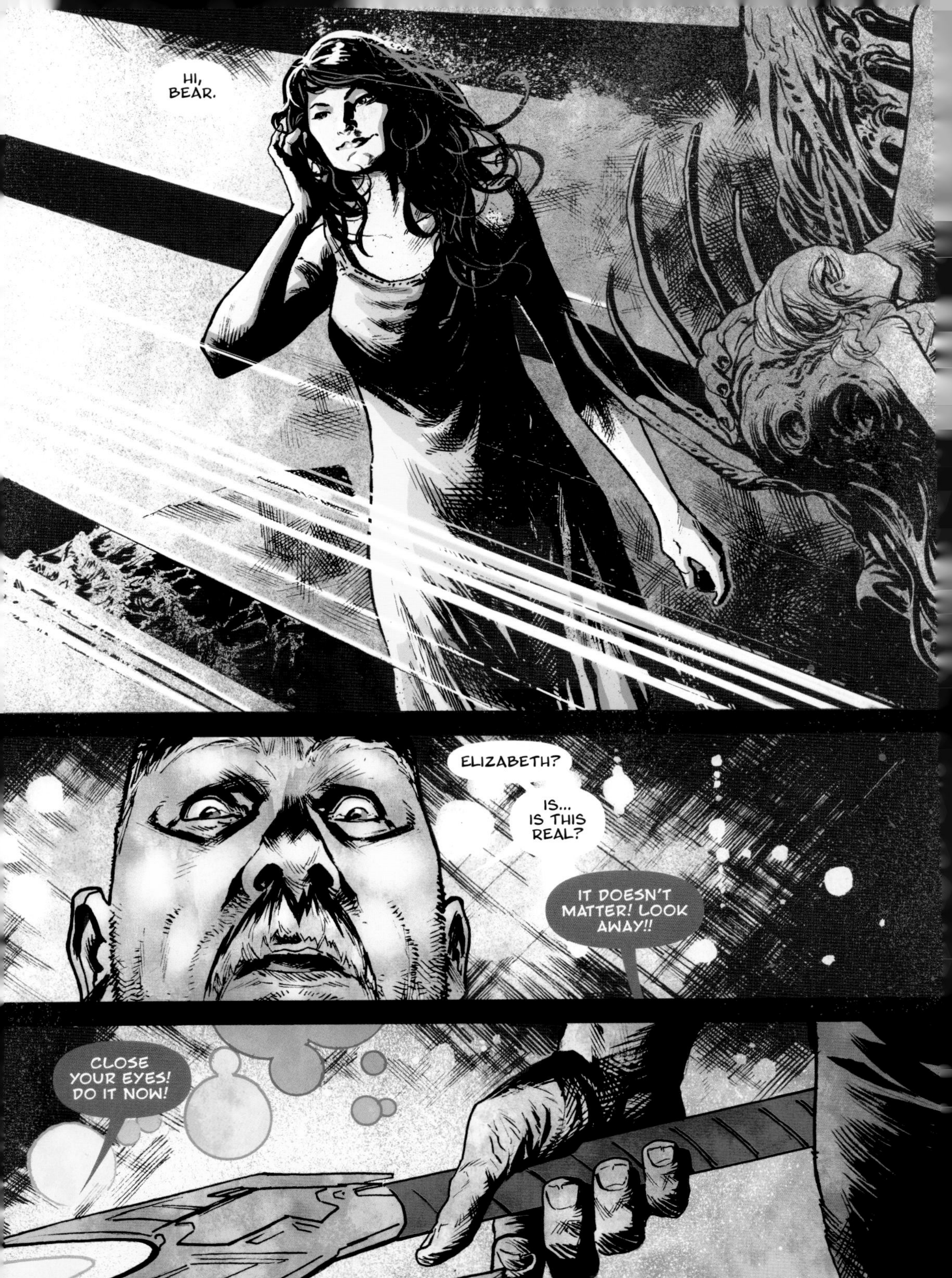
HI, BEAR.
ELIZABETH?
IS... IS THIS REAL?
IT DOESN'T MATTER! LOOK AWAY!!
CLOSE YOUR EYES! DO IT NOW!

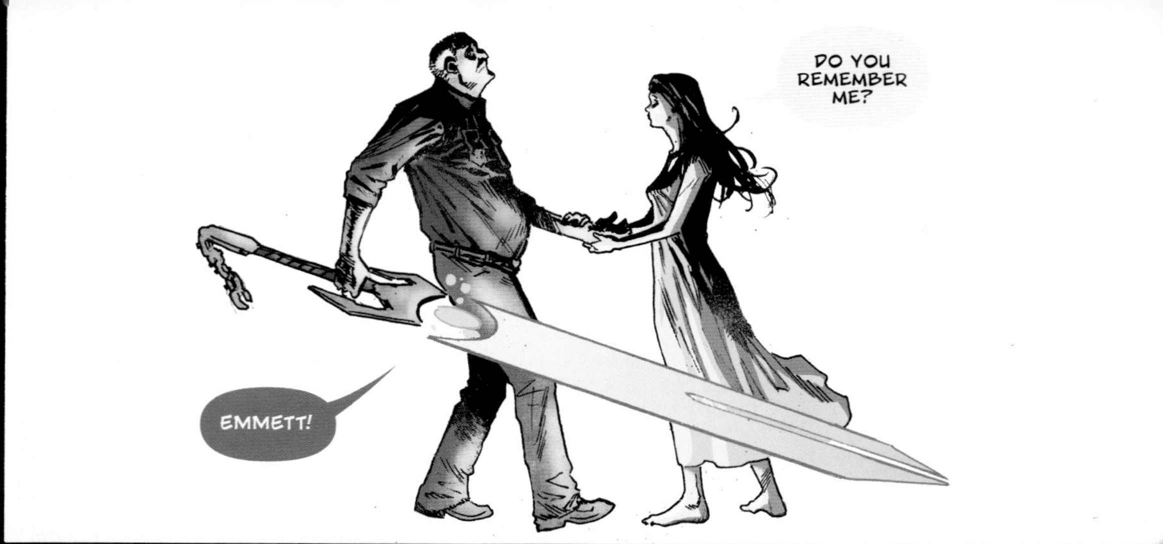
DO YOU REMEMBER ME?
EMMETT!
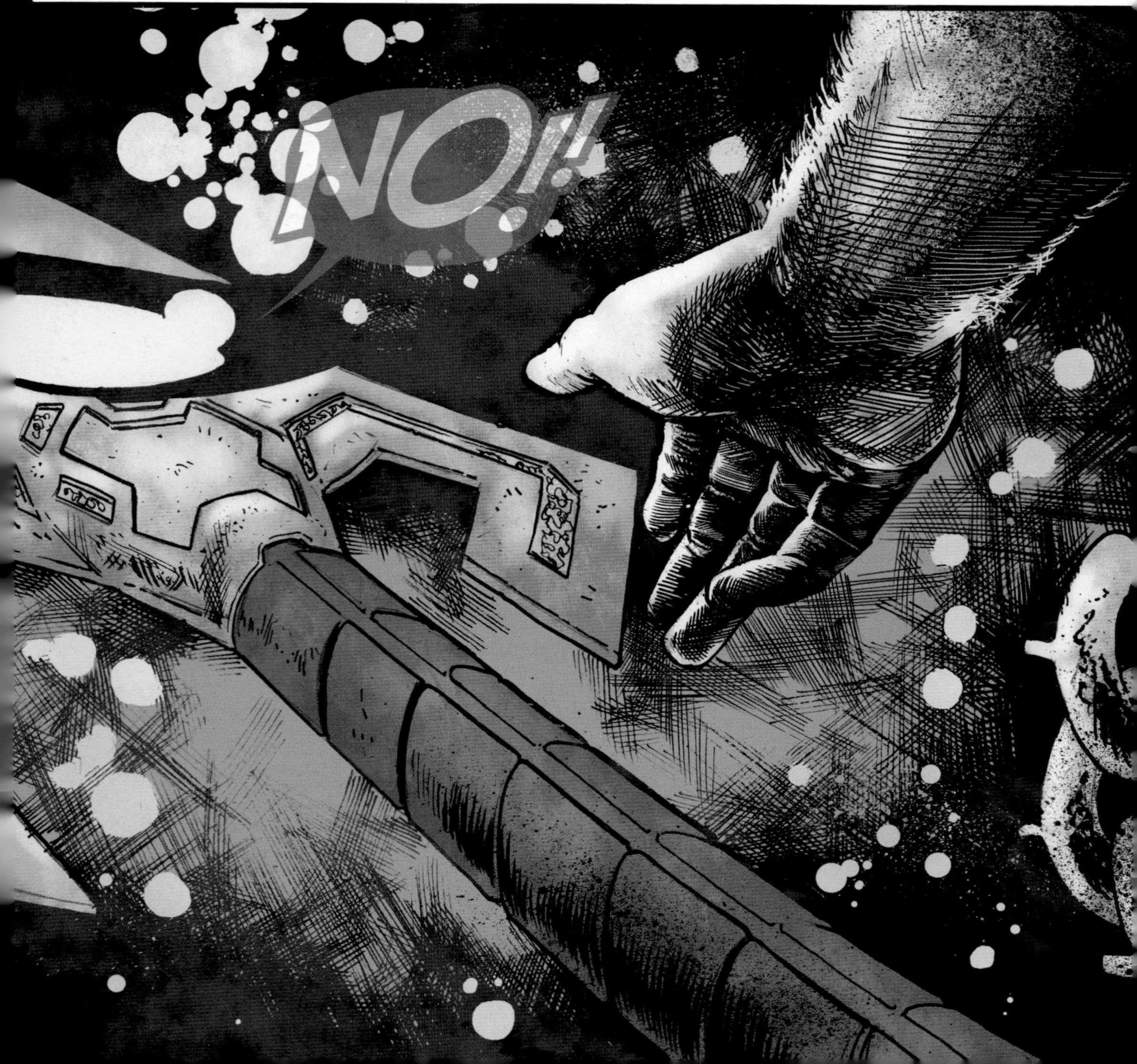
NO!!

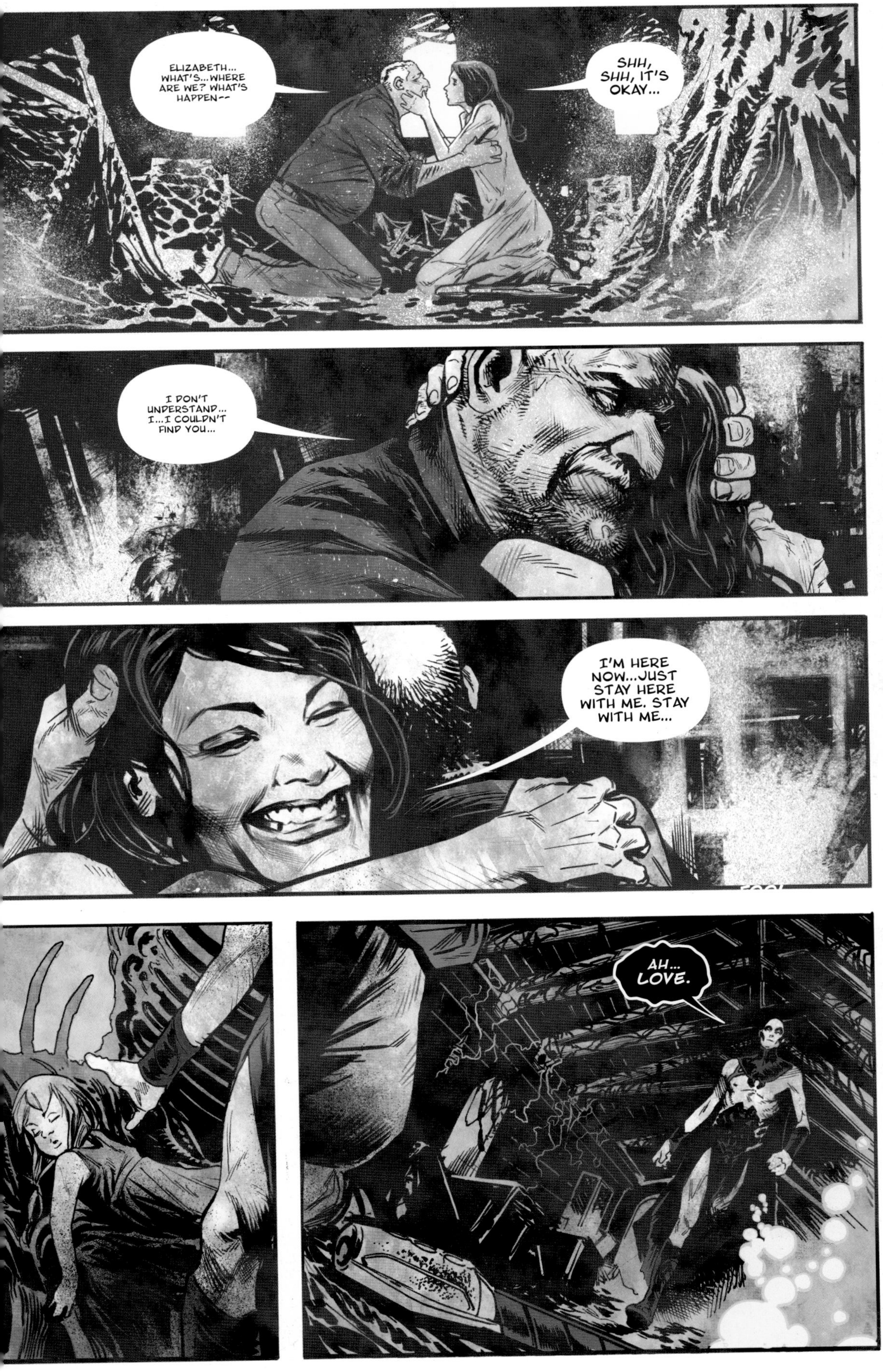
ELIZABETH... WHAT'S...WHERE ARE WE? WHAT'S HAPPEN--
SHH, SHH, IT'S OKAY...
I DON'T UNDERSTAND... I...I COULDN'T FIND YOU...
I'M HERE NOW...JUST STAY HERE WITH ME. STAY WITH ME...
AH... LOVE.

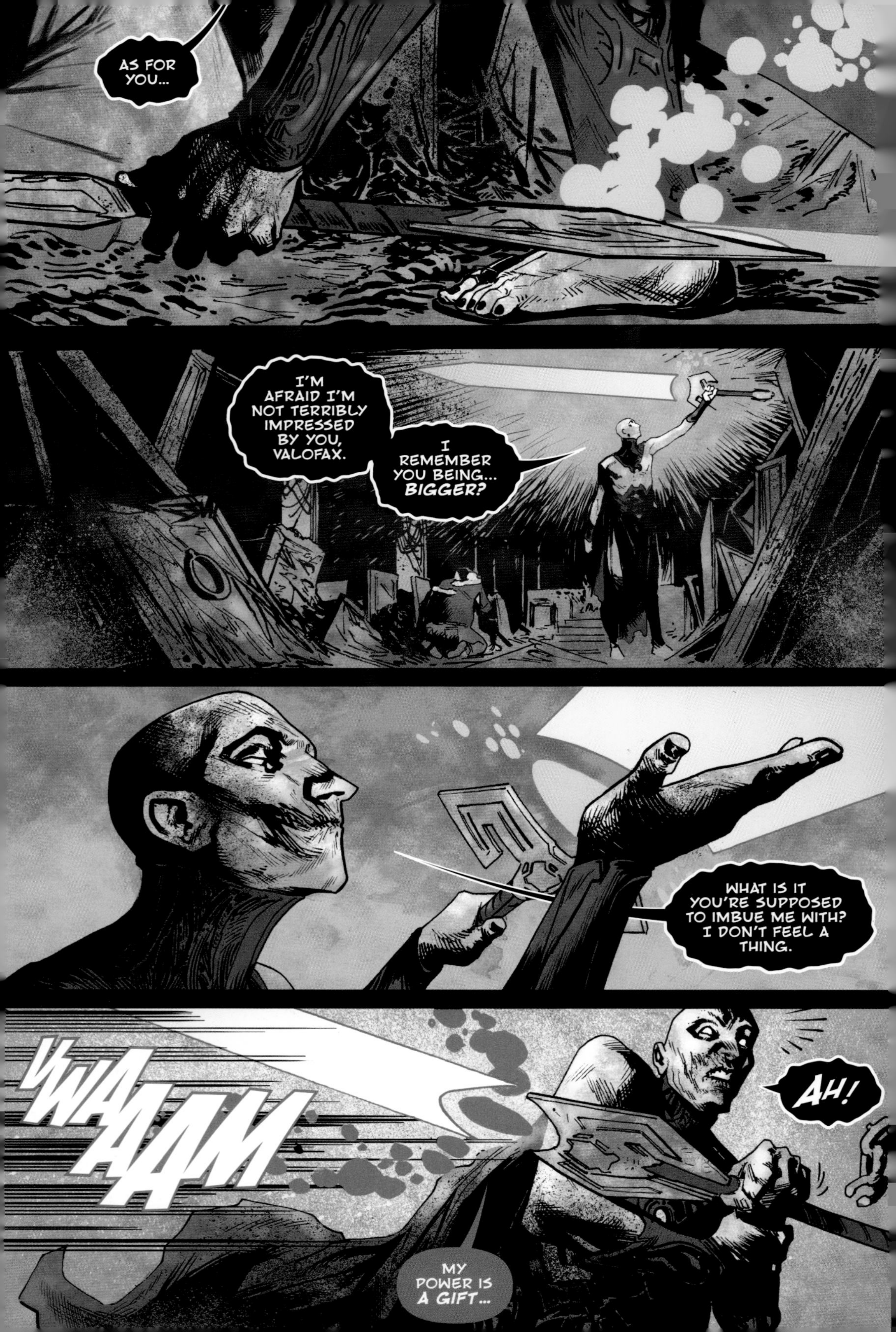
AS FOR YOU...
I'M AFRAID I'M NOT TERRIBLY IMPRESSED BY YOU, VALOFAX.
I REMEMBER YOU BEING... *BIGGER?*
WHAT IS IT YOU'RE SUPPOSED TO IMBUE ME WITH? I DON'T FEEL A THING.
VWAAAAM
AH!
MY POWER IS A *GIFT*...

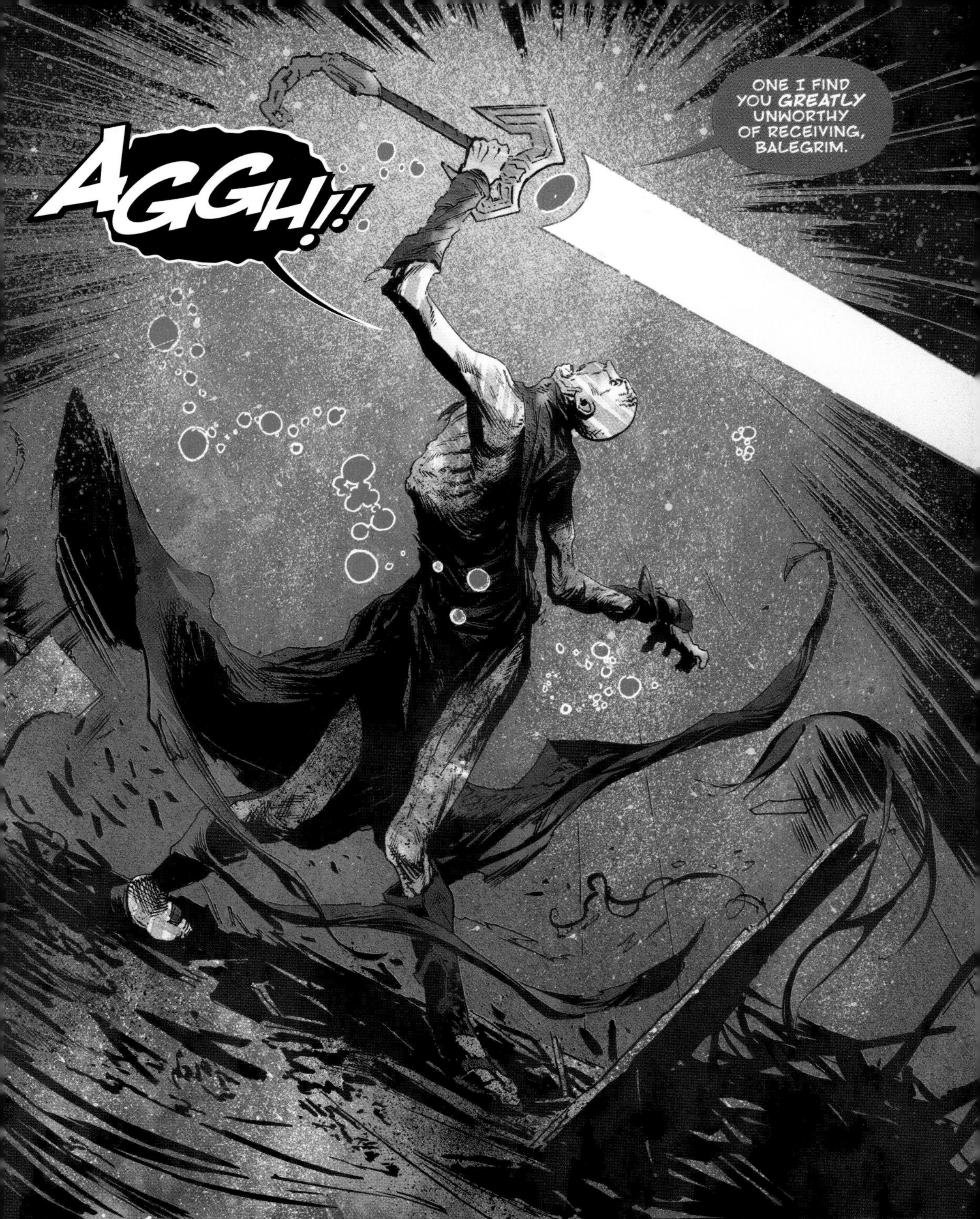
AGGH!!
ONE I FIND YOU GREATLY UNWORTHY OF RECEIVING, BALEGRIM.

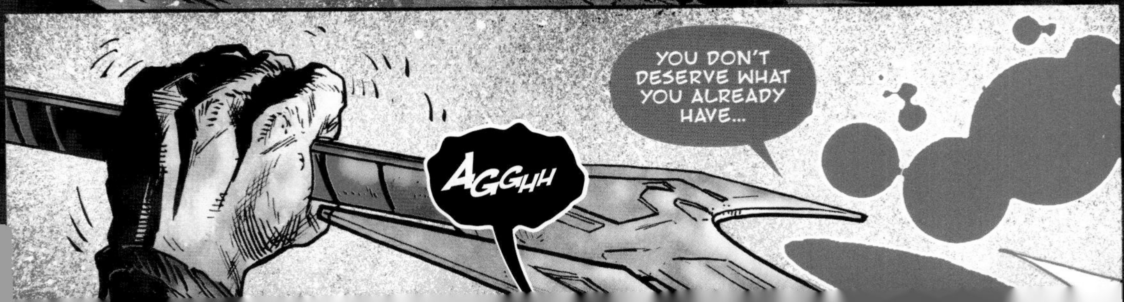
YOU DON'T DESERVE WHAT YOU ALREADY HAVE...
AGGHH

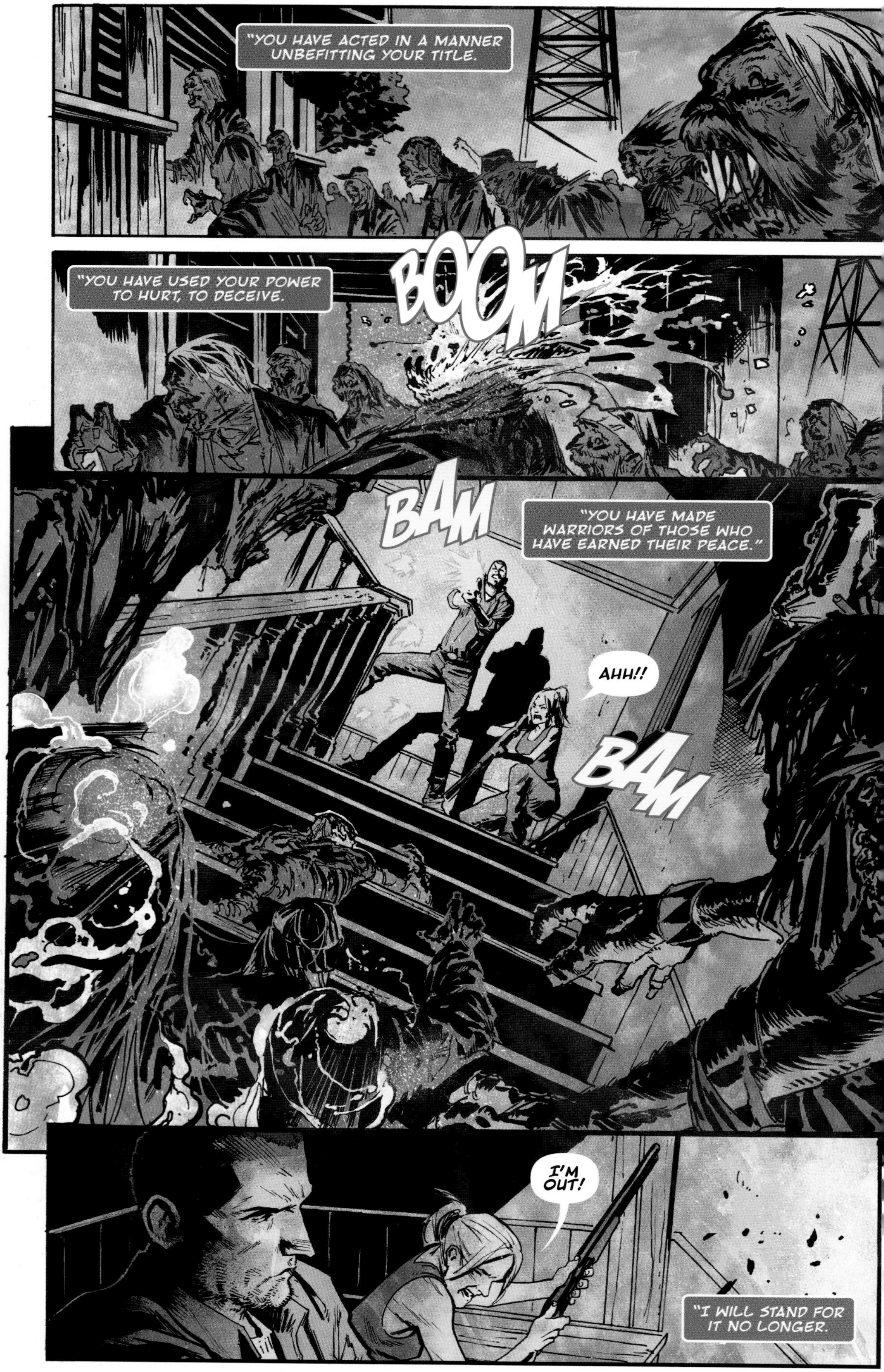
"YOU HAVE ACTED IN A MANNER UNBEFITTING YOUR TITLE.
"YOU HAVE USED YOUR POWER TO HURT, TO DECEIVE.
BOOM
BAM
"YOU HAVE MADE WARRIORS OF THOSE WHO HAVE EARNED THEIR PEACE."
AHH!!
BAM
I'M OUT!
"I WILL STAND FOR IT NO LONGER.

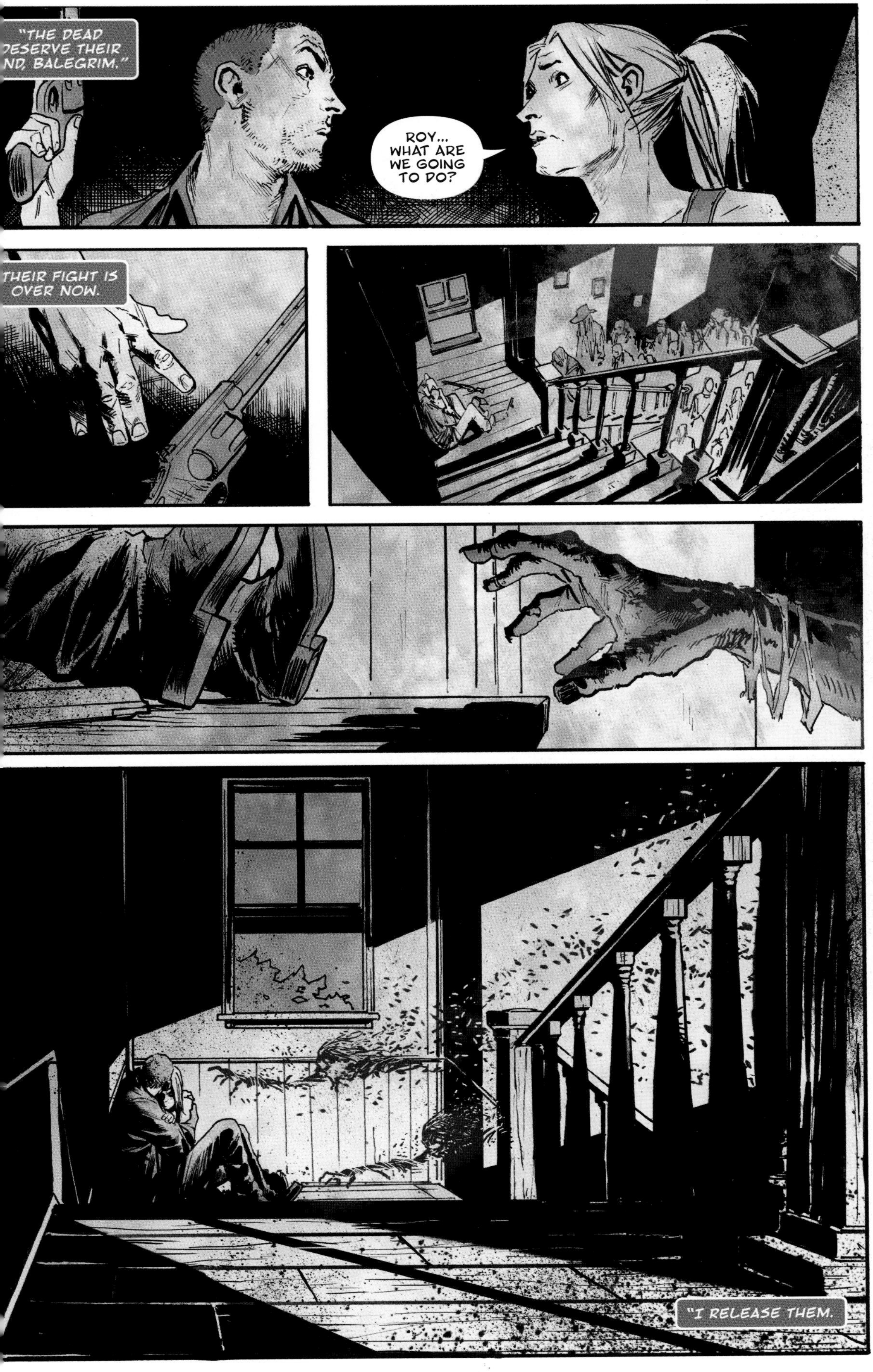
"THE DEAD
DESERVE THEIR
ND, BALEGRIM."
ROY... WHAT ARE WE GOING TO DO?
THEIR FIGHT IS OVER NOW.
"I RELEASE THEM.

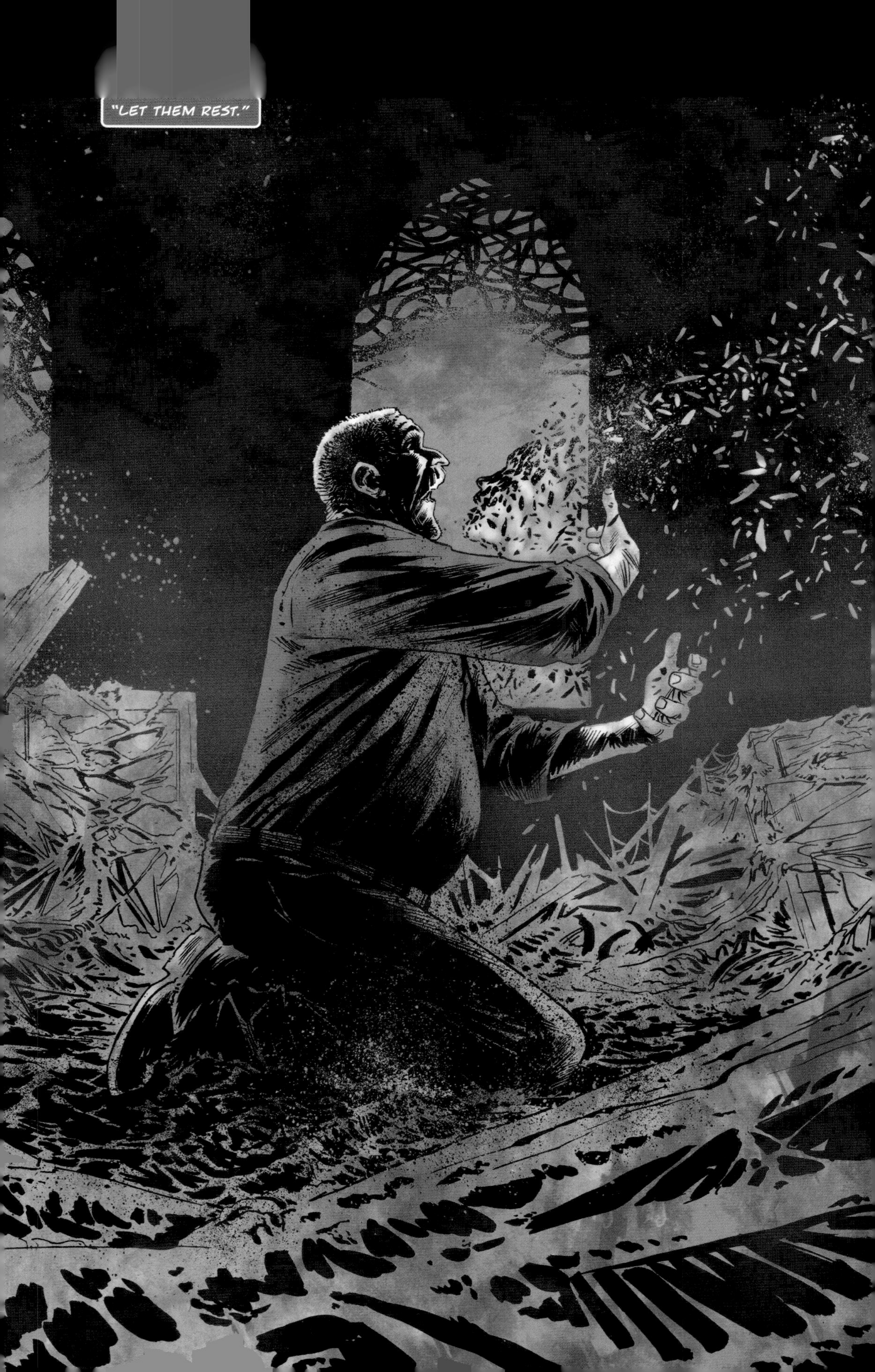
"LET THEM REST."

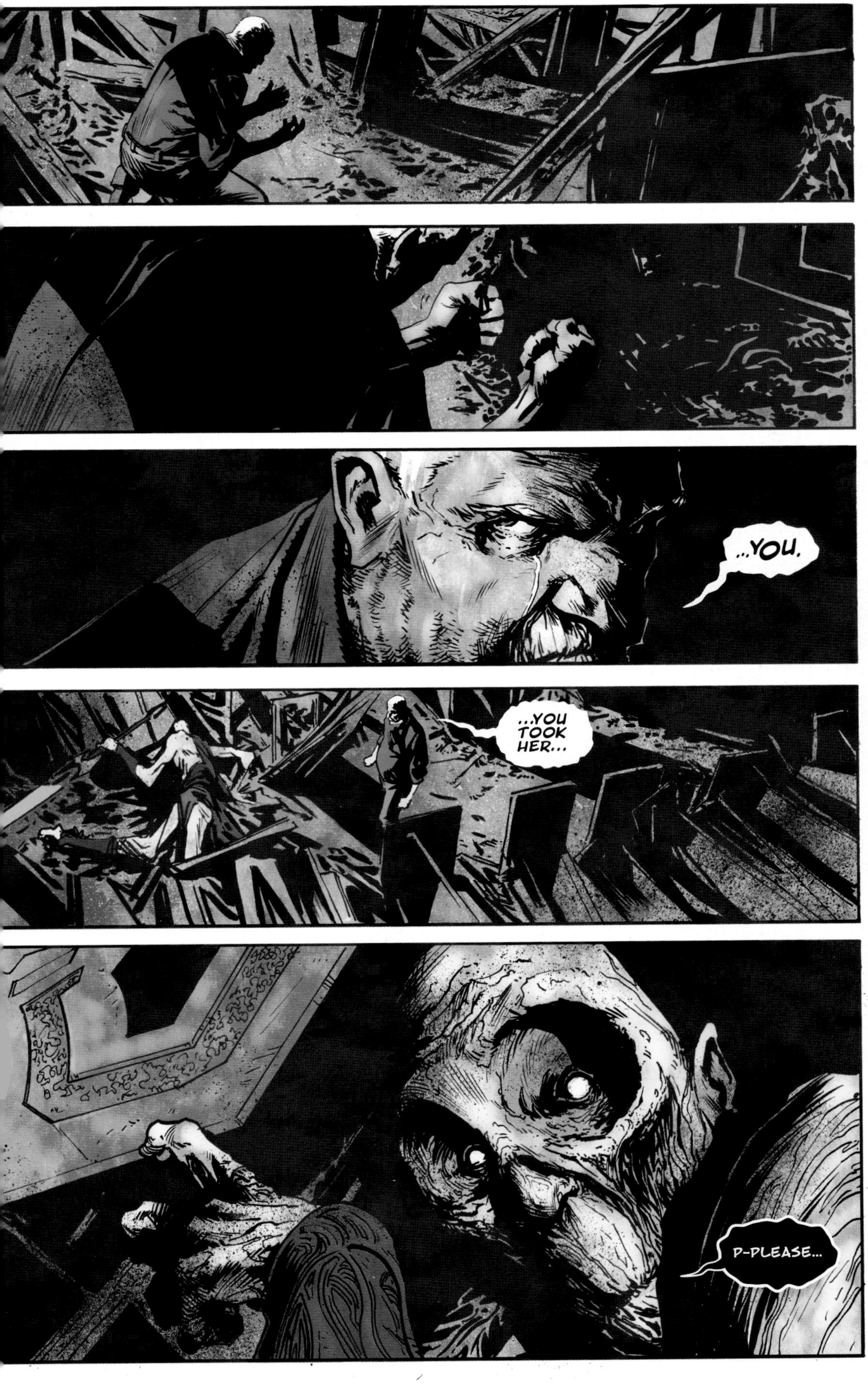
...YOU.
...YOU TOOK HER...
D-PLEASE...

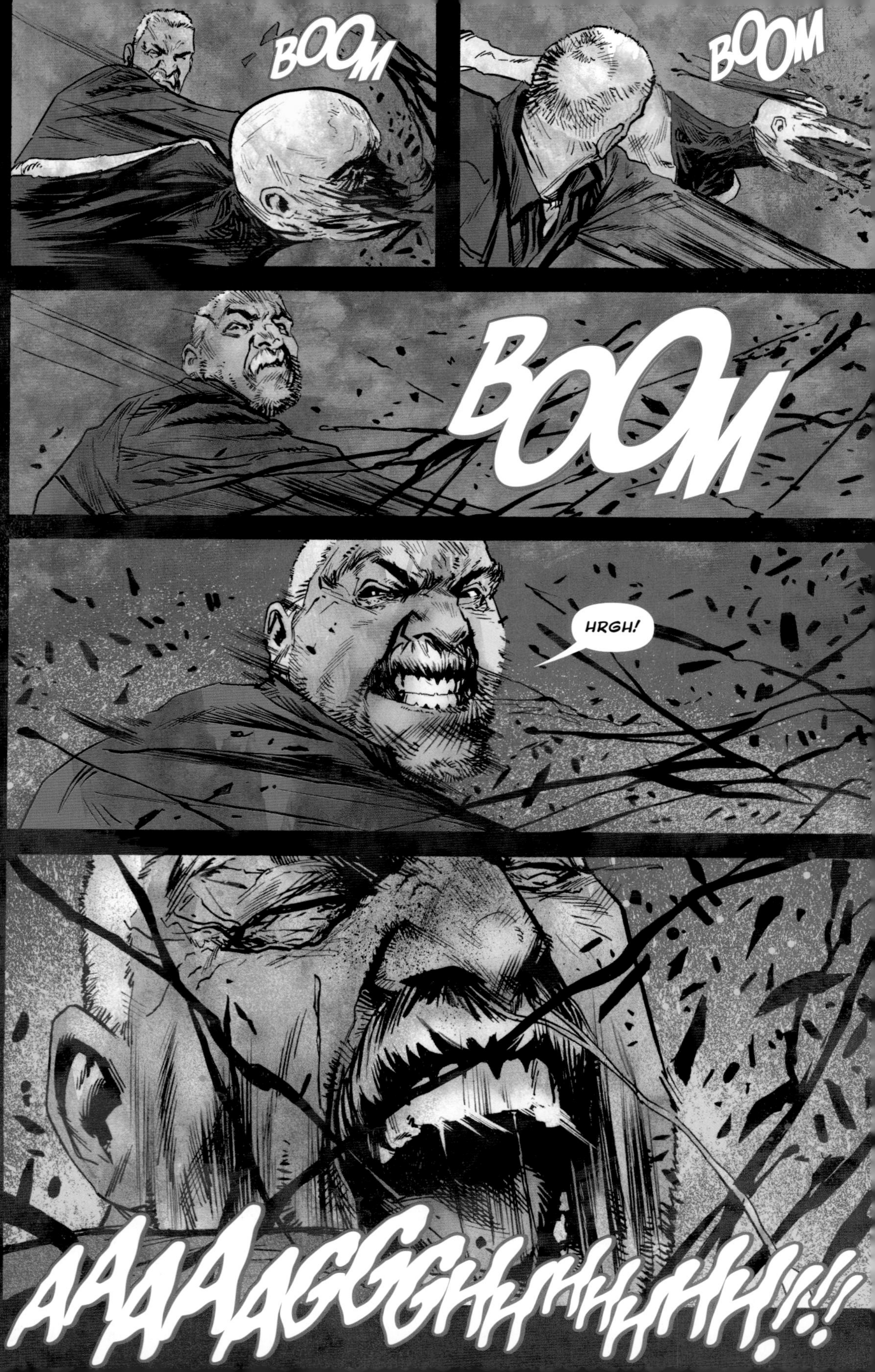
BOOM
BOOM
BOOM
HRGH!
AAAAAGGGHHHHHHHH!!!

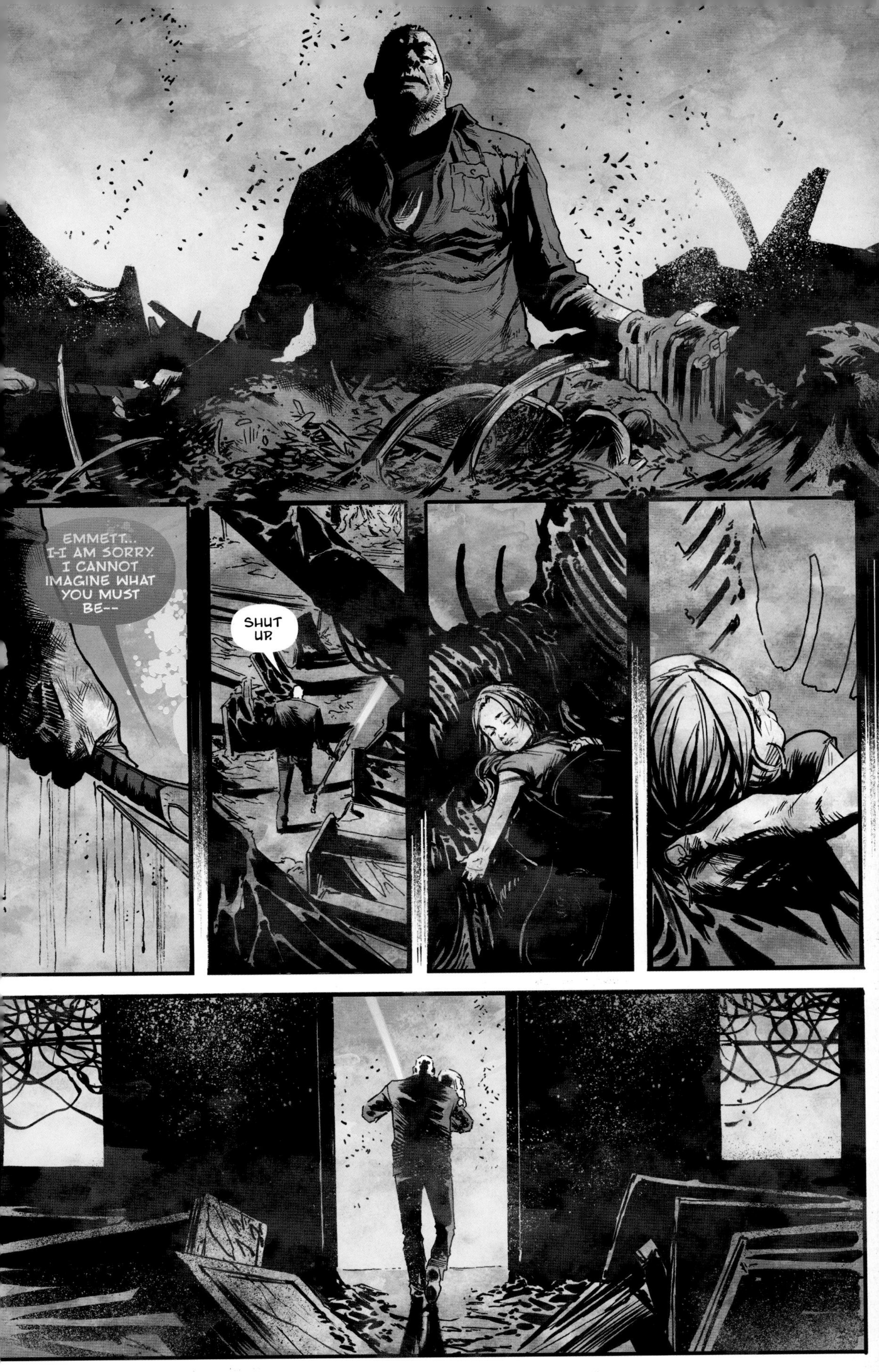
EMMETT... I-I AM SORRY. I CANNOT IMAGINE WHAT YOU MUST BE--
SHUT UP.

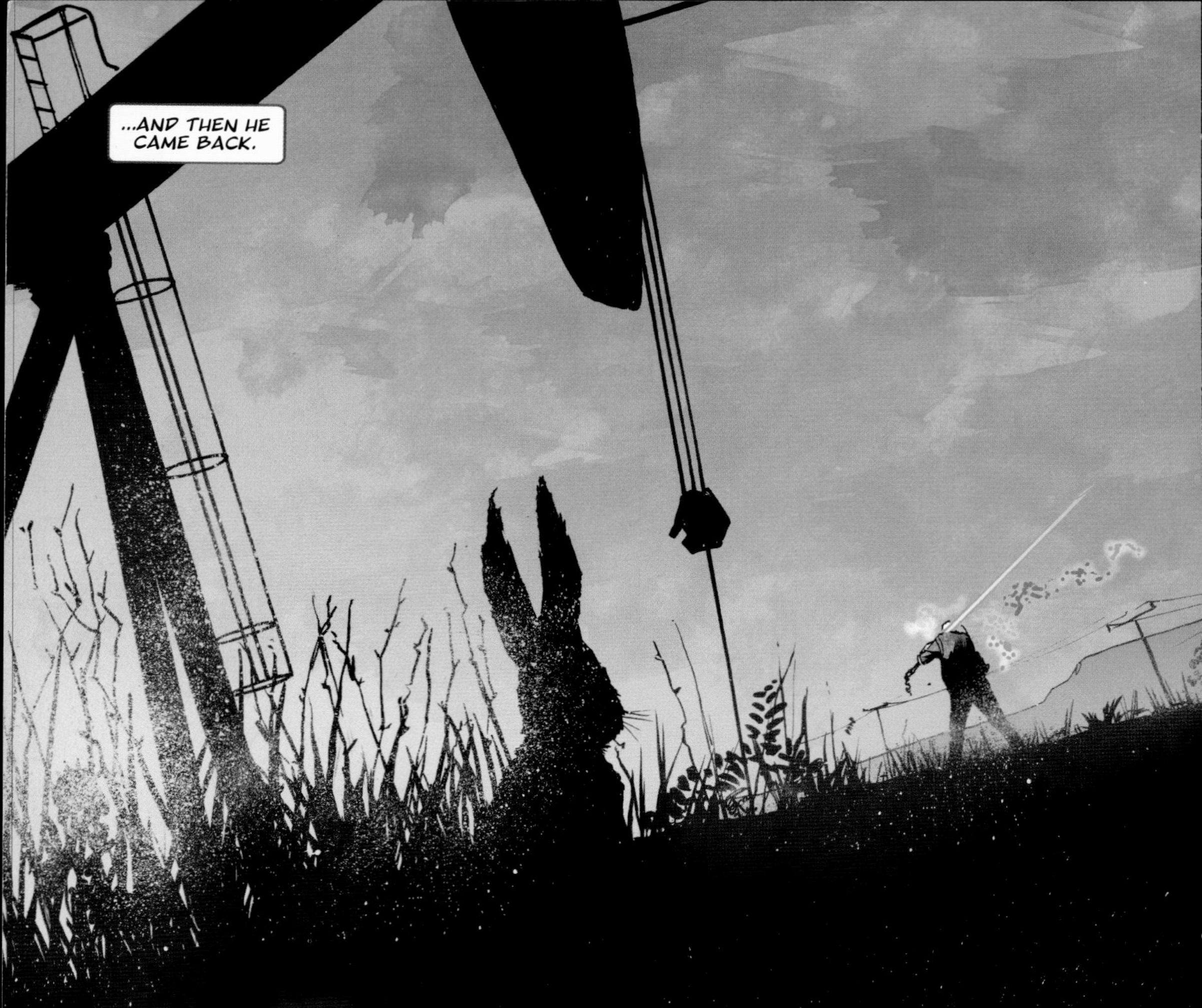
...AND THEN HE
CAME BACK.
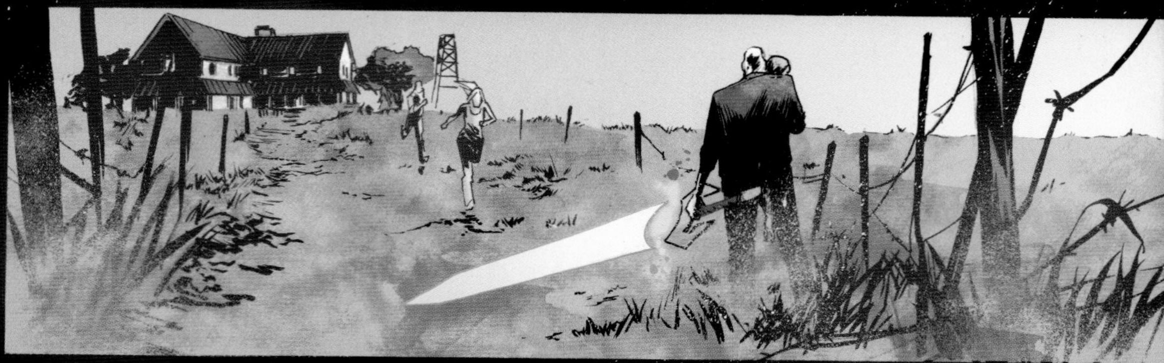
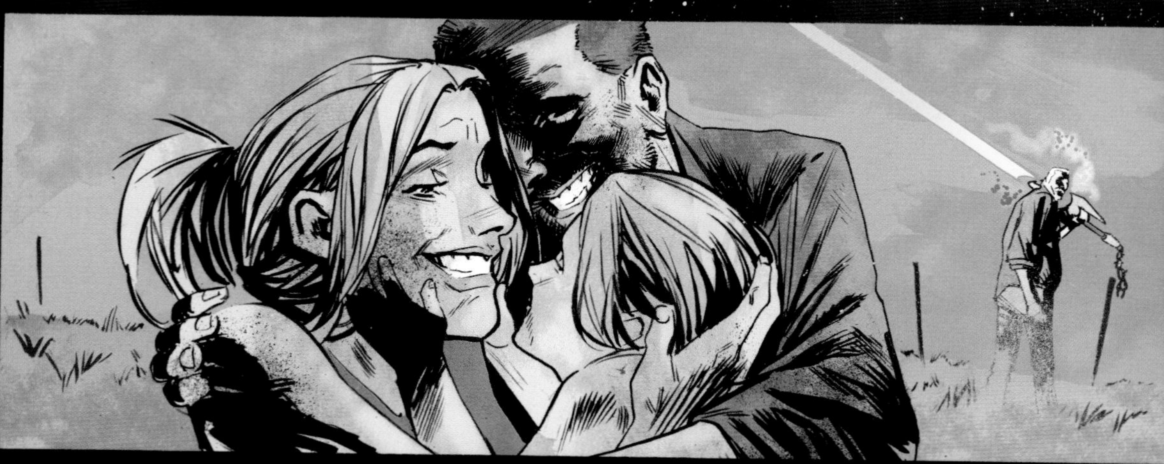

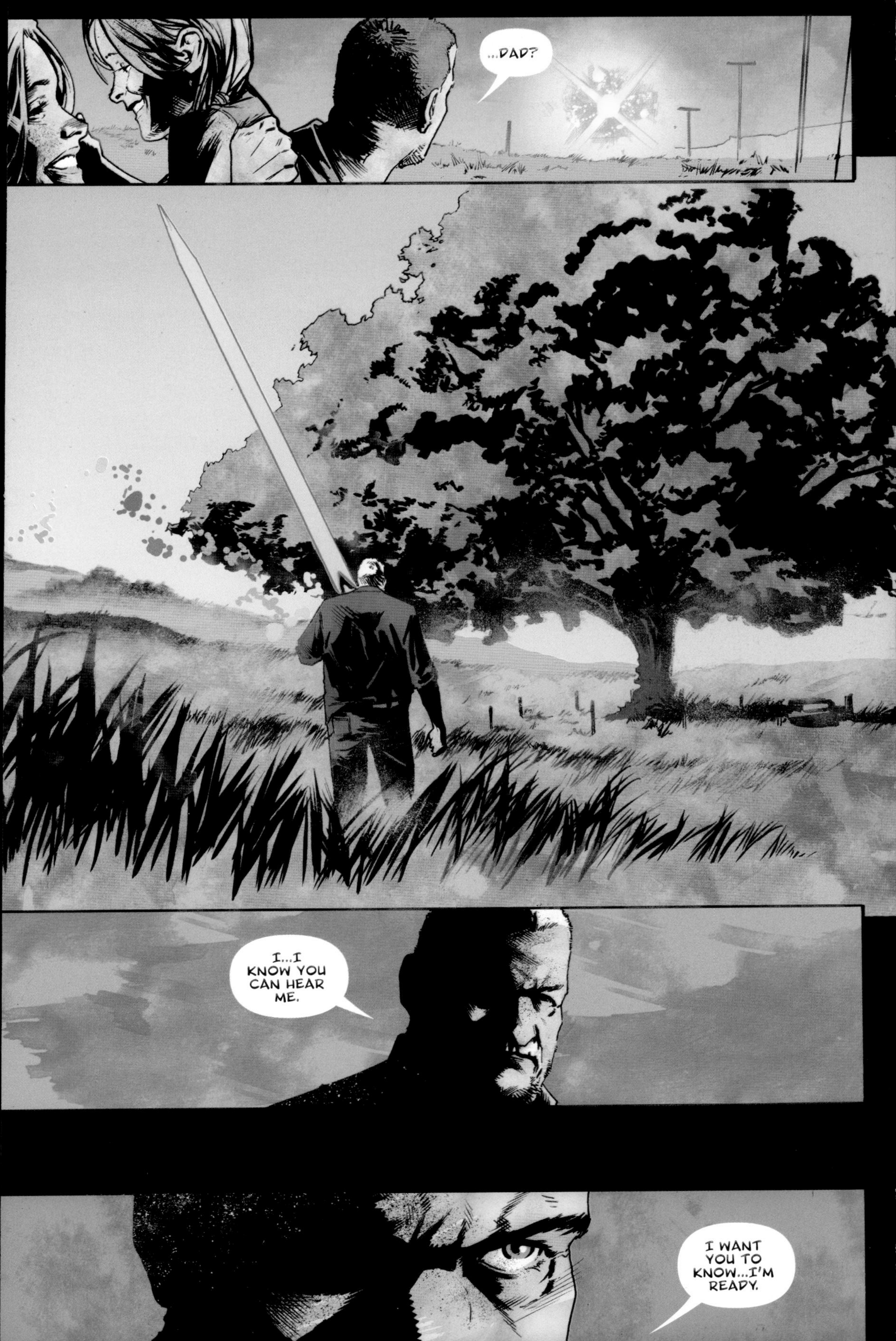
...DAD?
I...I KNOW YOU CAN HEAR ME.
I WANT YOU TO KNOW...I'M READY.

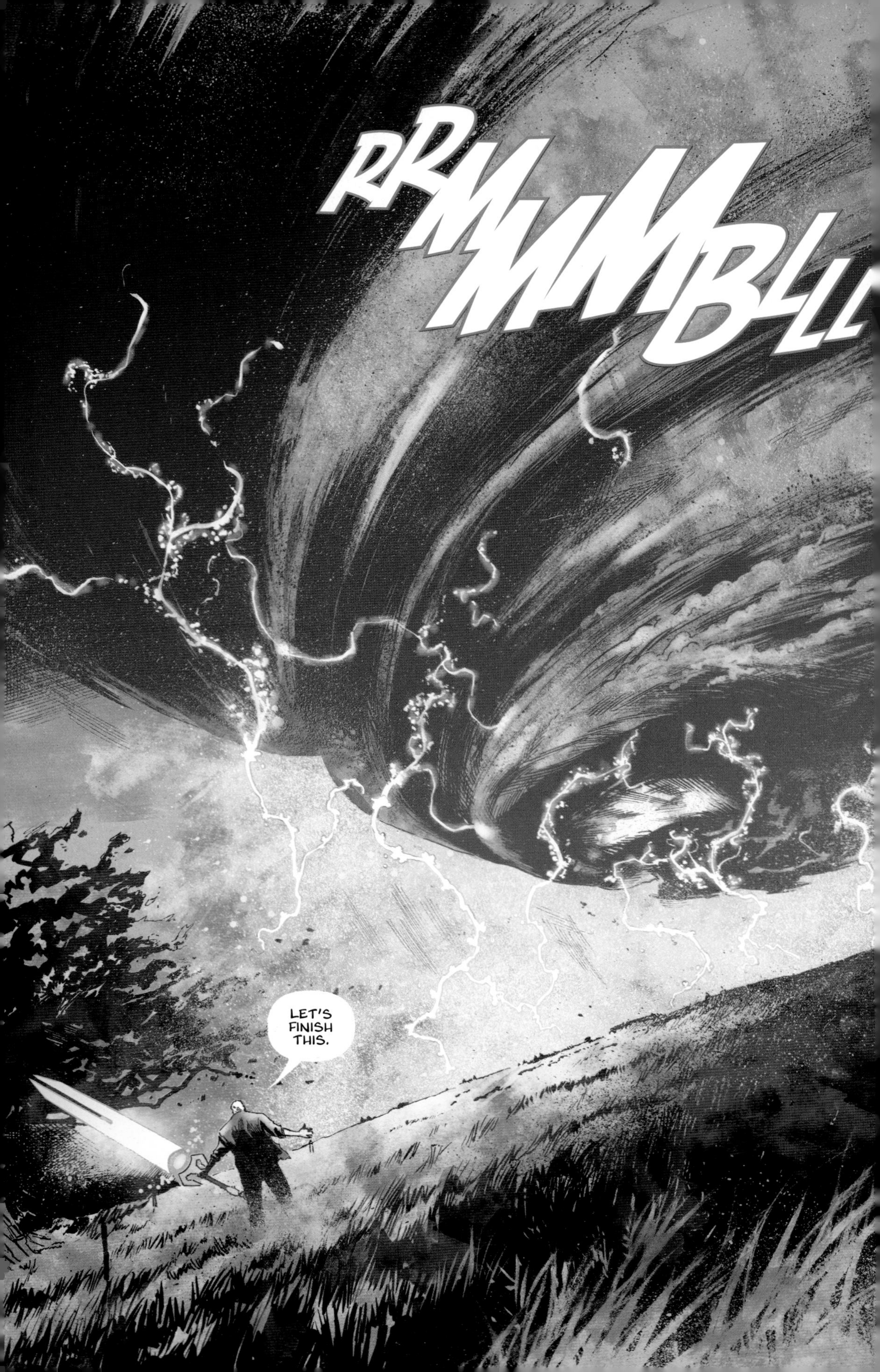
RRMMMBLL
LET'S FINISH THIS.

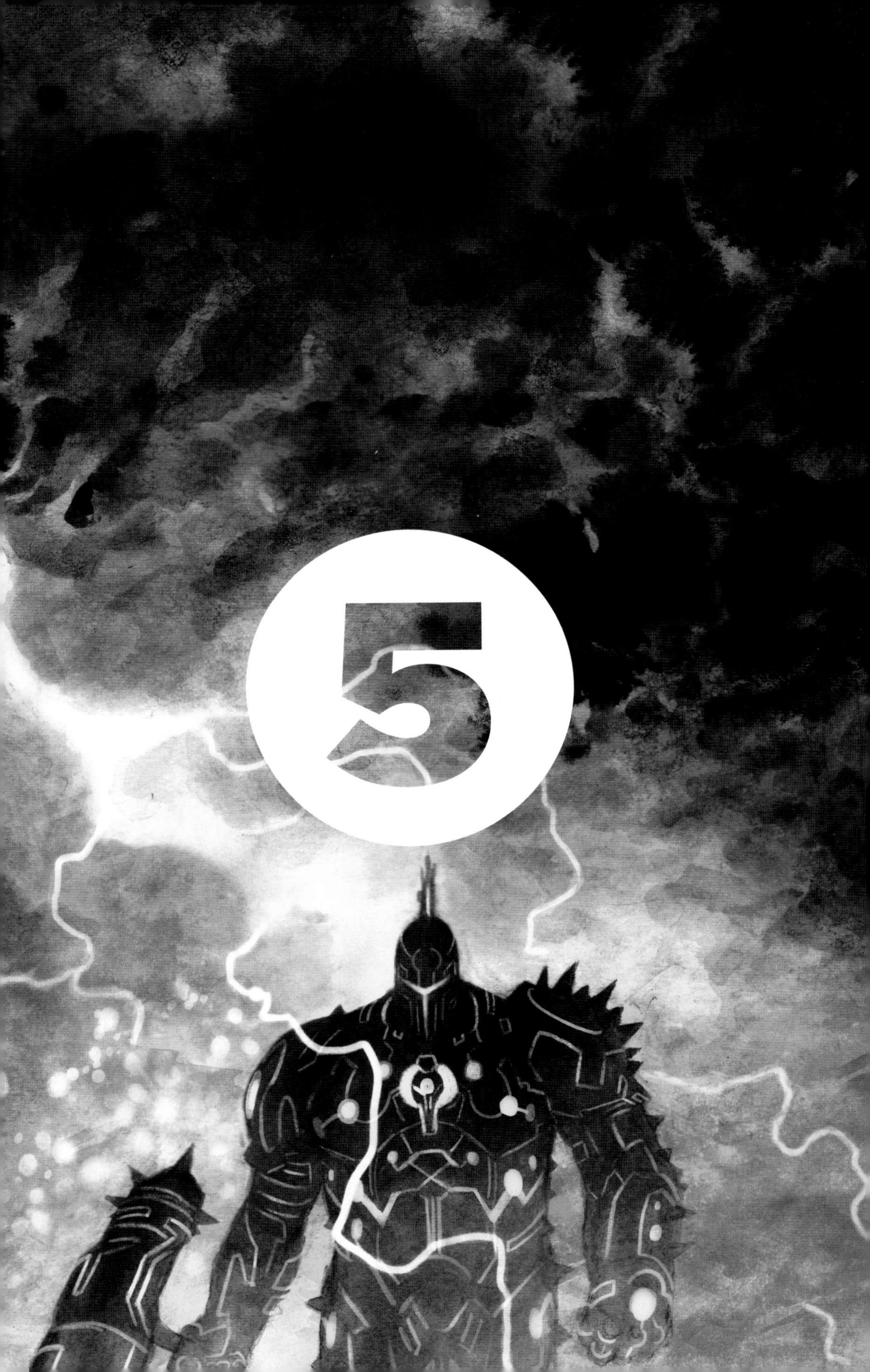
5

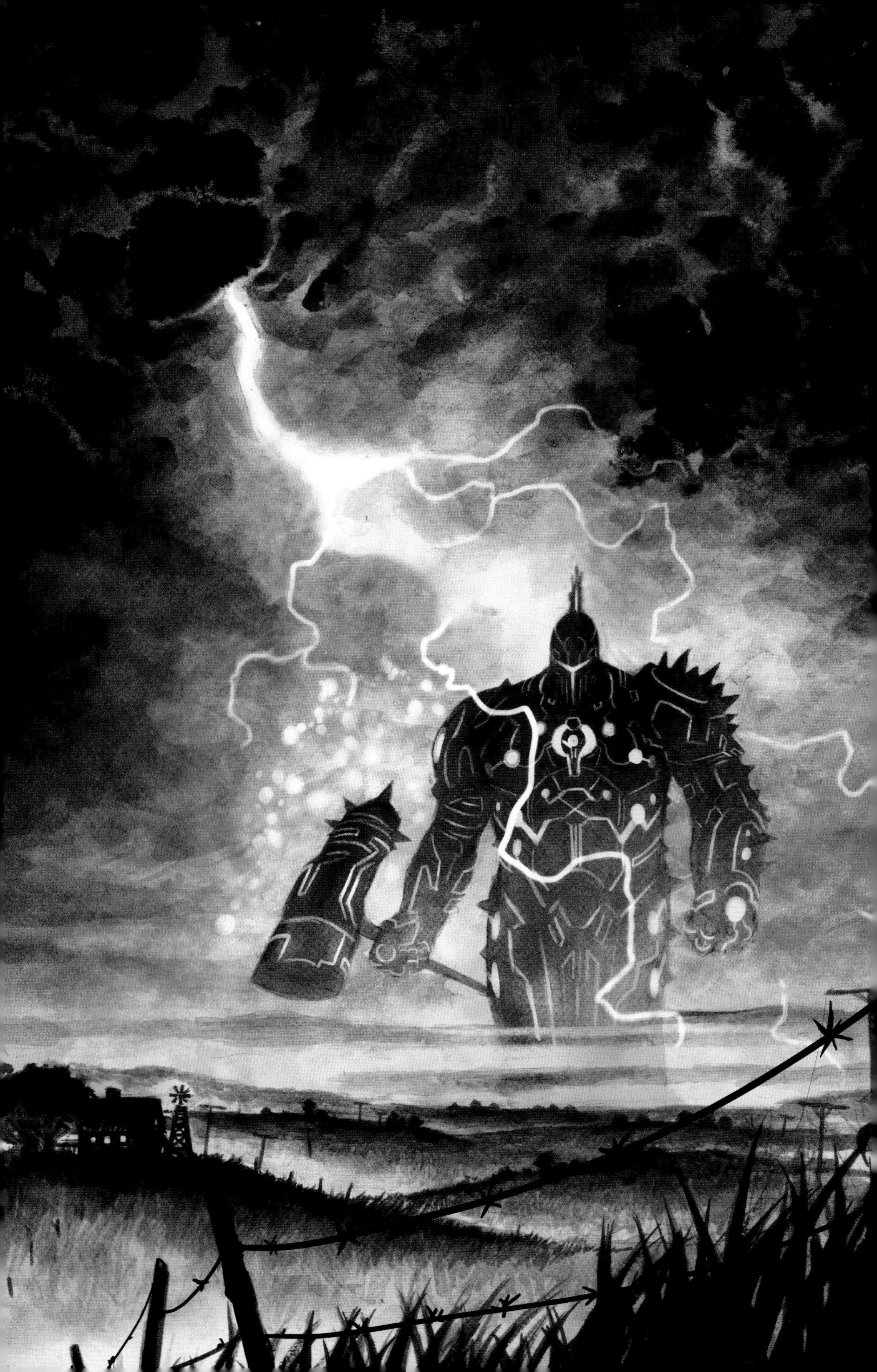

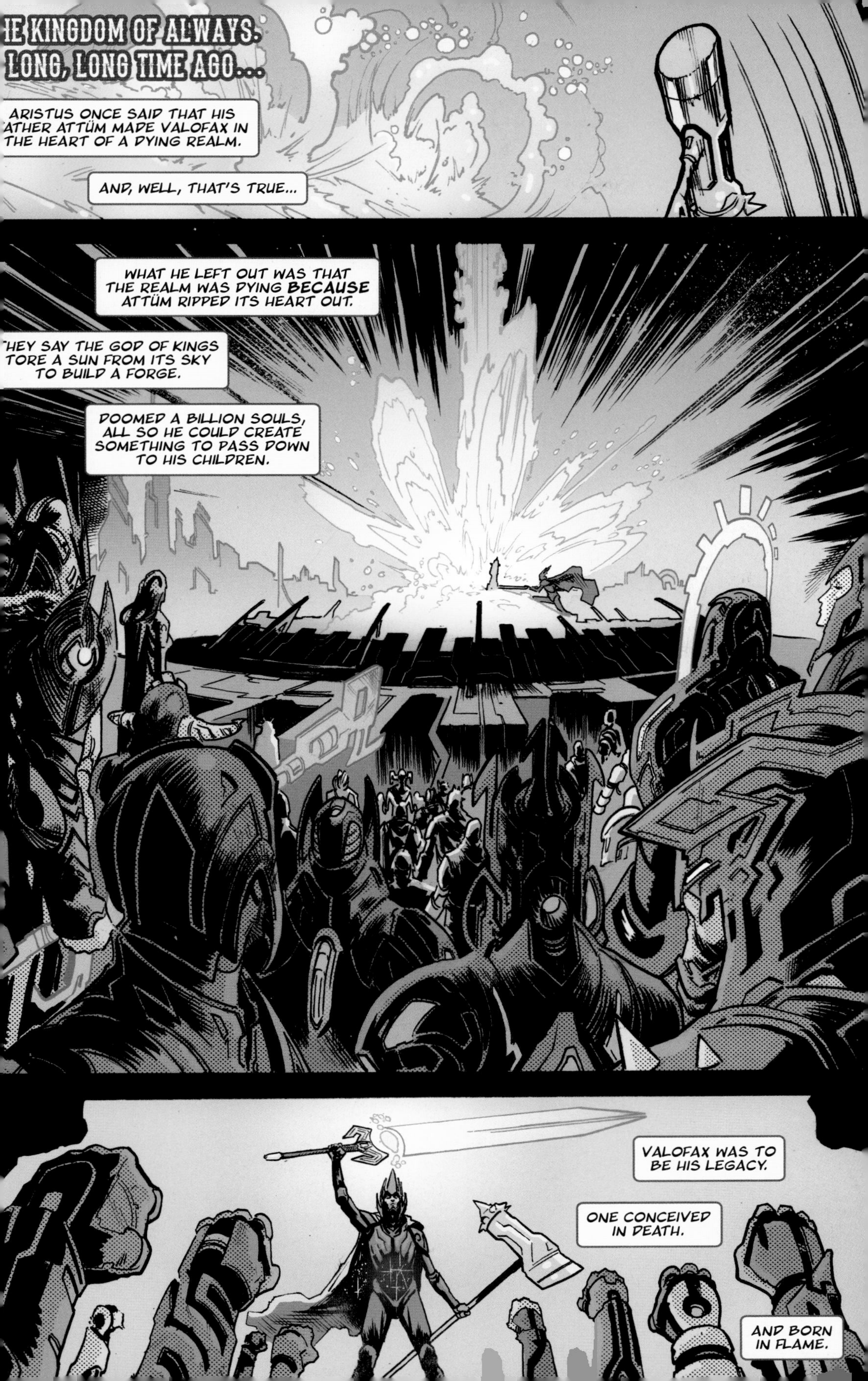

HE KINGDOM OF ALWAYS. LONG, LONG TIME AGO...
ARISTUS ONCE SAID THAT HIS ATHER ATTÜM MADE VALOFAX IN THE HEART OF A DYING REALM.
AND, WELL, THAT'S TRUE...
WHAT HE LEFT OUT WAS THAT THE REALM WAS DYING BECAUSE ATTÜM RIPPED ITS HEART OUT.
HEY SAY THE GOD OF KINGS TORE A SUN FROM ITS SKY TO BUILD A FORGE.
DOOMED A BILLION SOULS, ALL SO HE COULD CREATE SOMETHING TO PASS DOWN TO HIS CHILDREN.
VALOFAX WAS TO BE HIS LEGACY.
ONE CONCEIVED IN DEATH.
AND BORN IN FLAME.

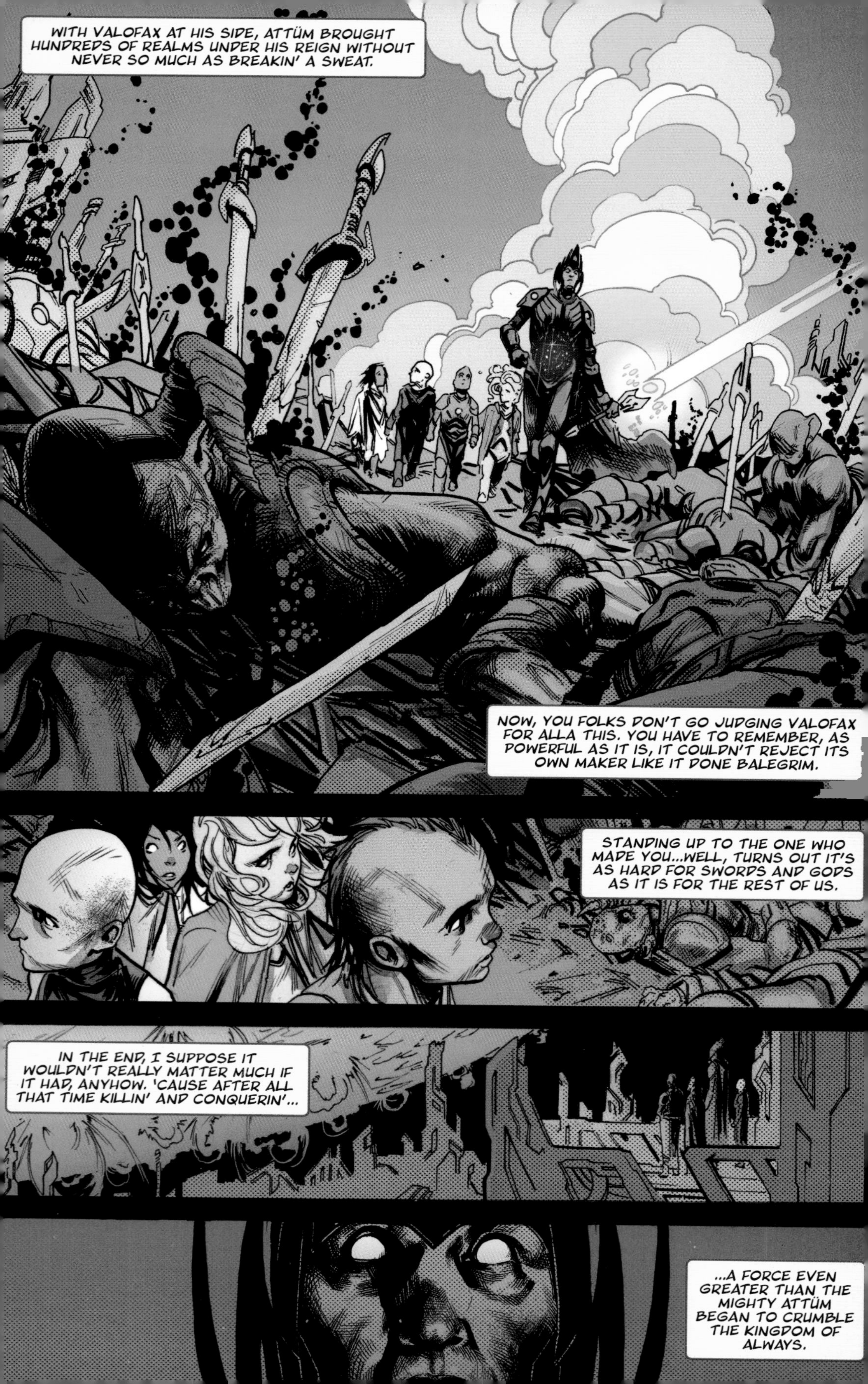
WITH VALOFAX AT HIS SIDE, ATTÜM BROUGHT HUNDREDS OF REALMS UNDER HIS REIGN WITHOUT NEVER SO MUCH AS BREAKIN' A SWEAT.
NOW, YOU FOLKS DON'T GO JUDGING VALOFAX FOR ALLA THIS. YOU HAVE TO REMEMBER, AS POWERFUL AS IT IS, IT COULDN'T REJECT ITS OWN MAKER LIKE IT DONE BALEGRIM.
STANDING UP TO THE ONE WHO MADE YOU...WELL, TURNS OUT IT'S AS HARD FOR SWORDS AND GODS AS IT IS FOR THE REST OF US.
IN THE END, I SUPPOSE IT WOULDN'T REALLY MATTER MUCH IF IT HAD, ANYHOW. 'CAUSE AFTER ALL THAT TIME KILLIN' AND CONQUERIN'...
...A FORCE EVEN GREATER THAN THE MIGHTY ATTÜM BEGAN TO CRUMBLE THE KINGDOM OF ALWAYS.

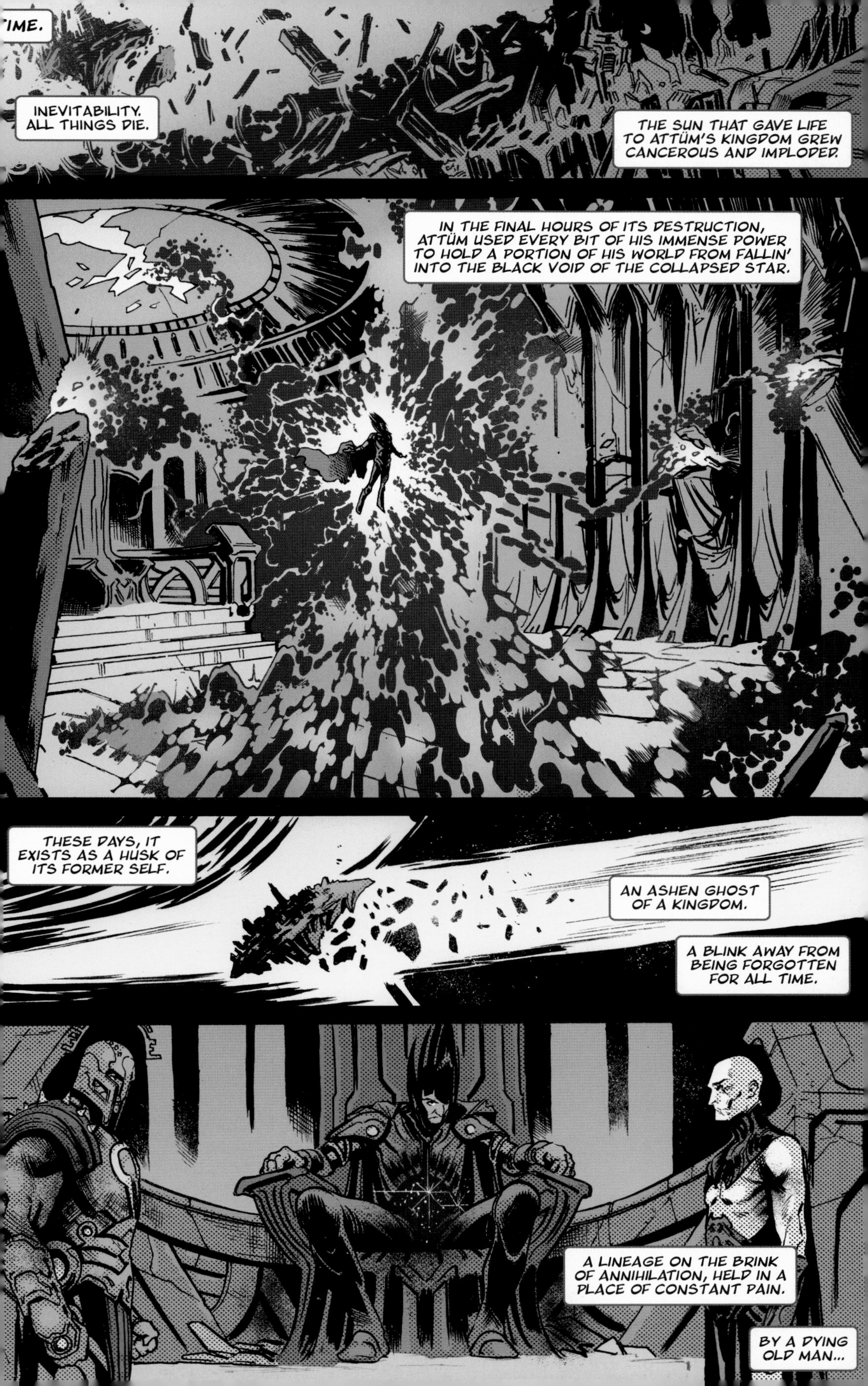
TIME.
INEVITABILITY. ALL THINGS DIE.
THE SUN THAT GAVE LIFE TO ATTÜM'S KINGDOM GREW CANCEROUS AND IMPLODED.
IN THE FINAL HOURS OF ITS DESTRUCTION, ATTÜM USED EVERY BIT OF HIS IMMENSE POWER TO HOLD A PORTION OF HIS WORLD FROM FALLIN' INTO THE BLACK VOID OF THE COLLAPSED STAR.
THESE DAYS, IT EXISTS AS A HUSK OF ITS FORMER SELF.
AN ASHEN GHOST OF A KINGDOM.
A BLINK AWAY FROM BEING FORGOTTEN FOR ALL TIME.
A LINEAGE ON THE BRINK OF ANNIHILATION, HELD IN A PLACE OF CONSTANT PAIN.
BY A DYING OLD MAN...

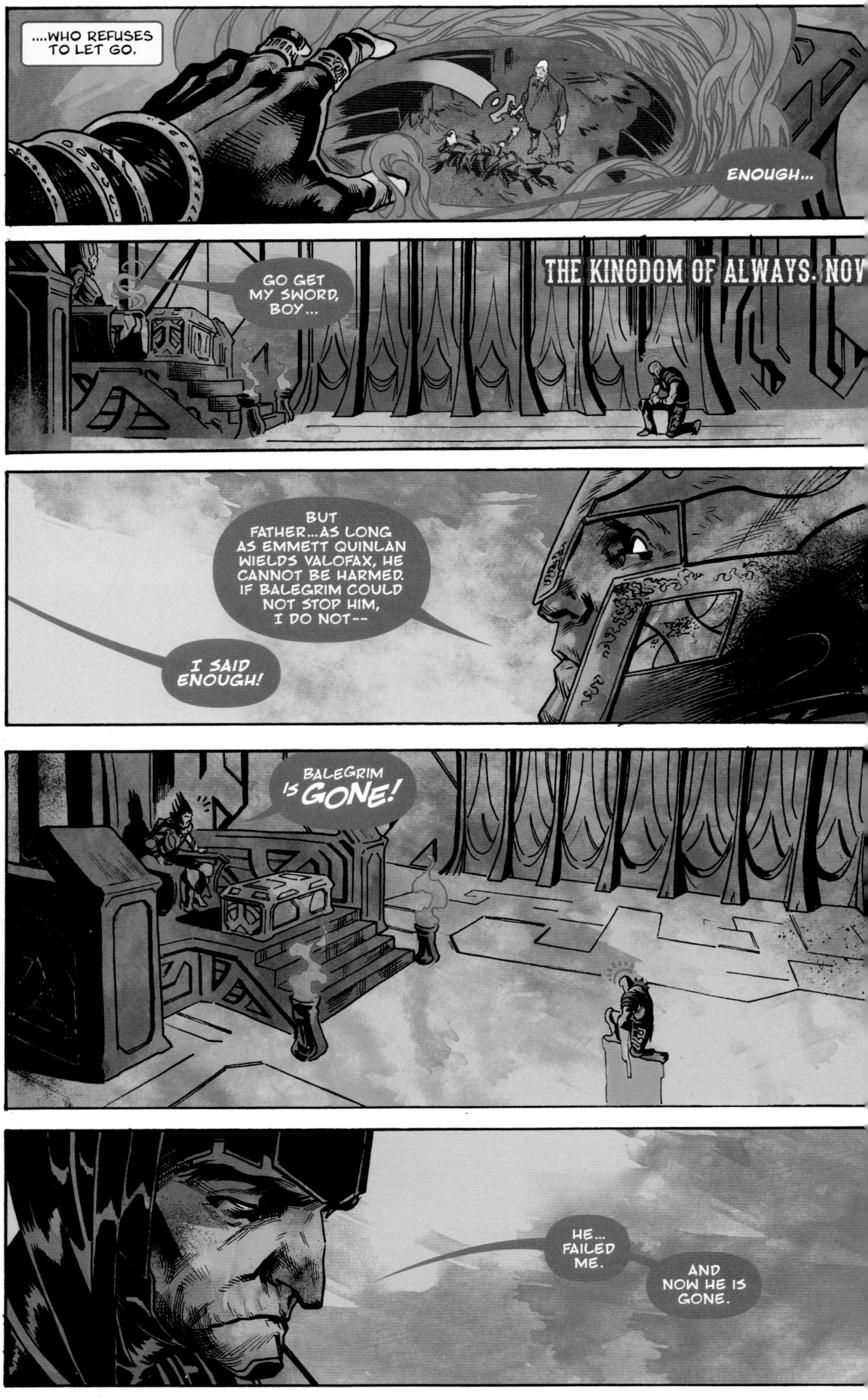

....WHO REFUSES TO LET GO.
ENOUGH...
GO GET MY SWORD, BOY...
THE KINGDOM OF ALWAYS. NOW
BUT FATHER...AS LONG AS EMMETT QUINLAN WIELDS VALOFAX, HE CANNOT BE HARMED. IF BALEGRIM COULD NOT STOP HIM, I DO NOT--
I SAID ENOUGH!
BALEGRIM IS GONE!
HE... FAILED ME.
AND NOW HE IS GONE.

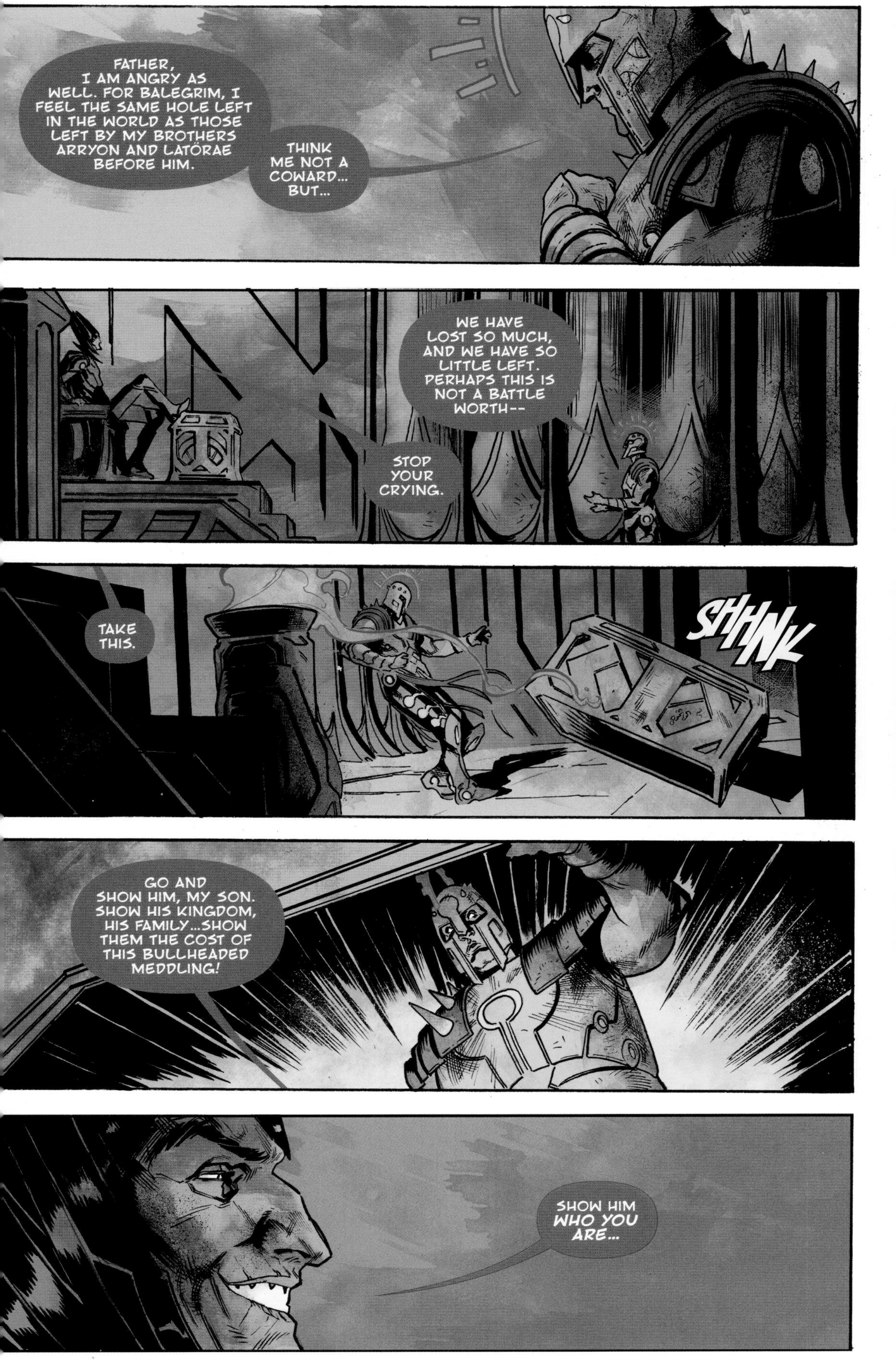

FATHER, I AM ANGRY AS WELL. FOR BALEGRIM, I FEEL THE SAME HOLE LEFT IN THE WORLD AS THOSE LEFT BY MY BROTHERS ARRYON AND LATÖRAE BEFORE HIM.
THINK ME NOT A COWARD... BUT...
WE HAVE LOST SO MUCH, AND WE HAVE SO LITTLE LEFT. PERHAPS THIS IS NOT A BATTLE WORTH--
STOP YOUR CRYING.
TAKE THIS.
SHHNK
GO AND SHOW HIM, MY SON. SHOW HIS KINGDOM, HIS FAMILY...SHOW THEM THE COST OF THIS BULLHEADED MEDDLING!
SHOW HIM WHO YOU ARE...

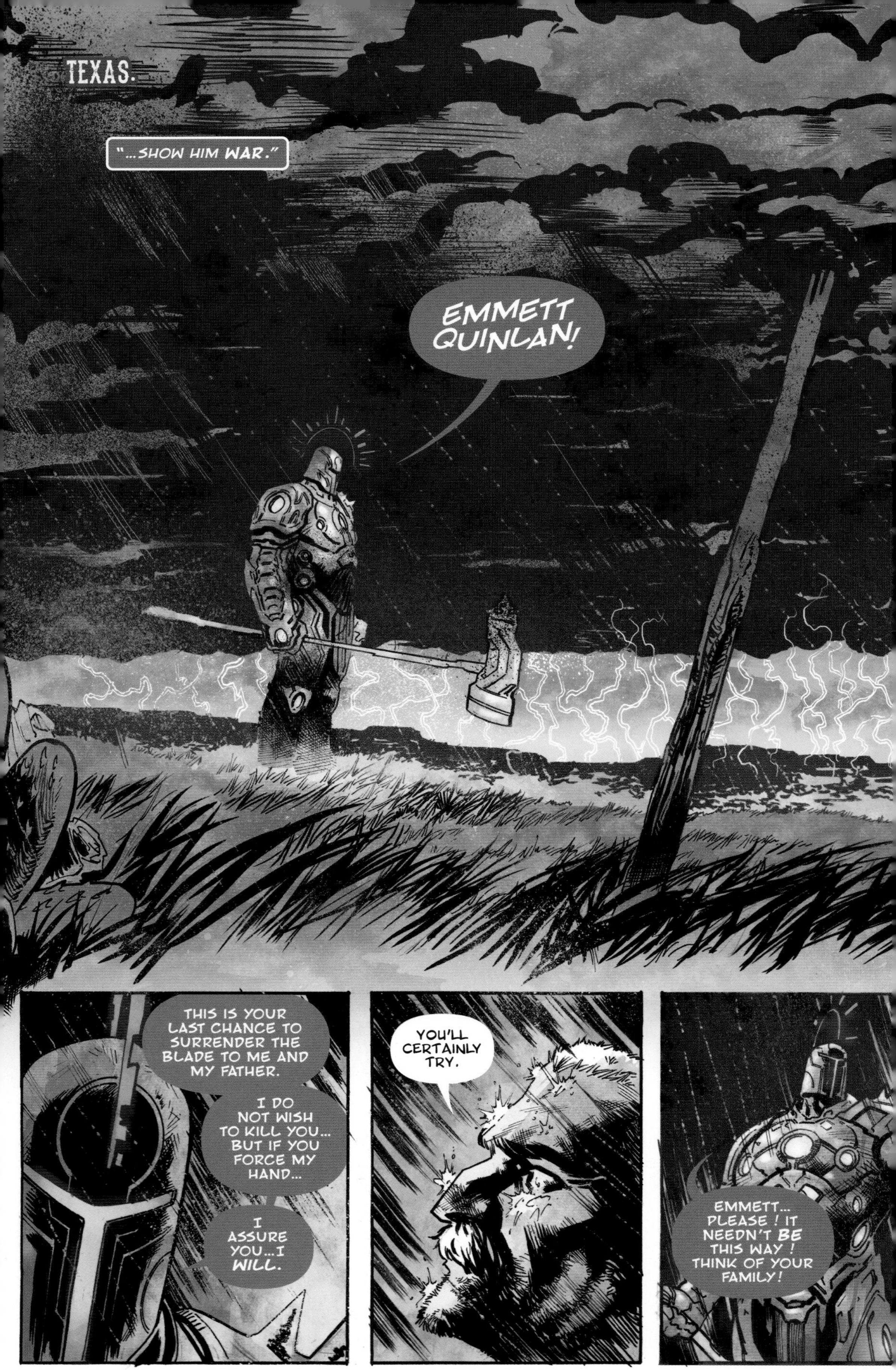
TEXAS.
"...SHOW HIM WAR."
EMMETT QUINLAN!
THIS IS YOUR LAST CHANCE TO SURRENDER THE BLADE TO ME AND MY FATHER.
I DO NOT WISH TO KILL YOU... BUT IF YOU FORCE MY HAND...
I ASSURE YOU...I WILL.
YOU'LL CERTAINLY TRY.
EMMETT... PLEASE! IT NEEDN'T BE THIS WAY! THINK OF YOUR FAMILY!

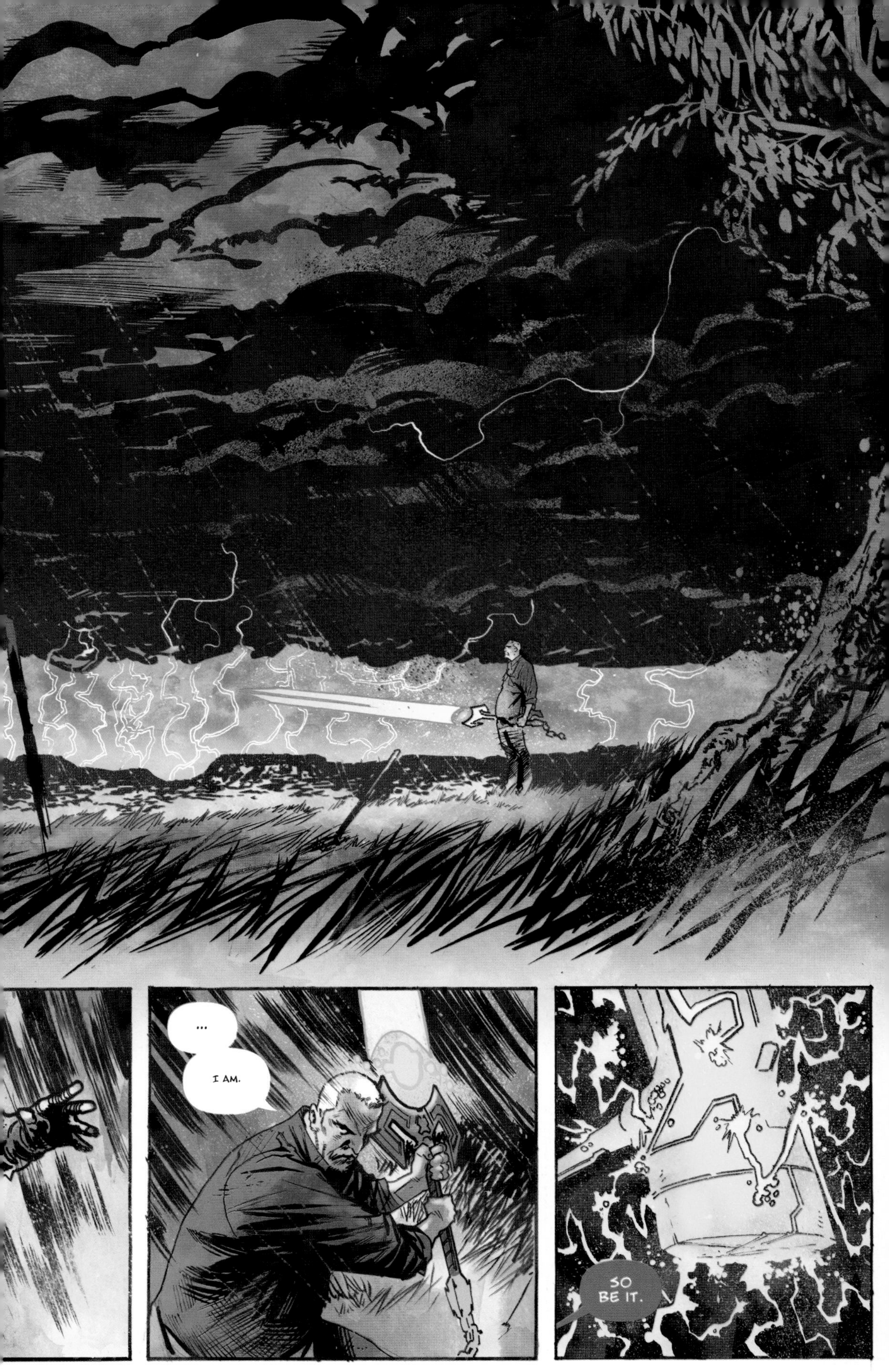
...
I AM.
SO BE IT.

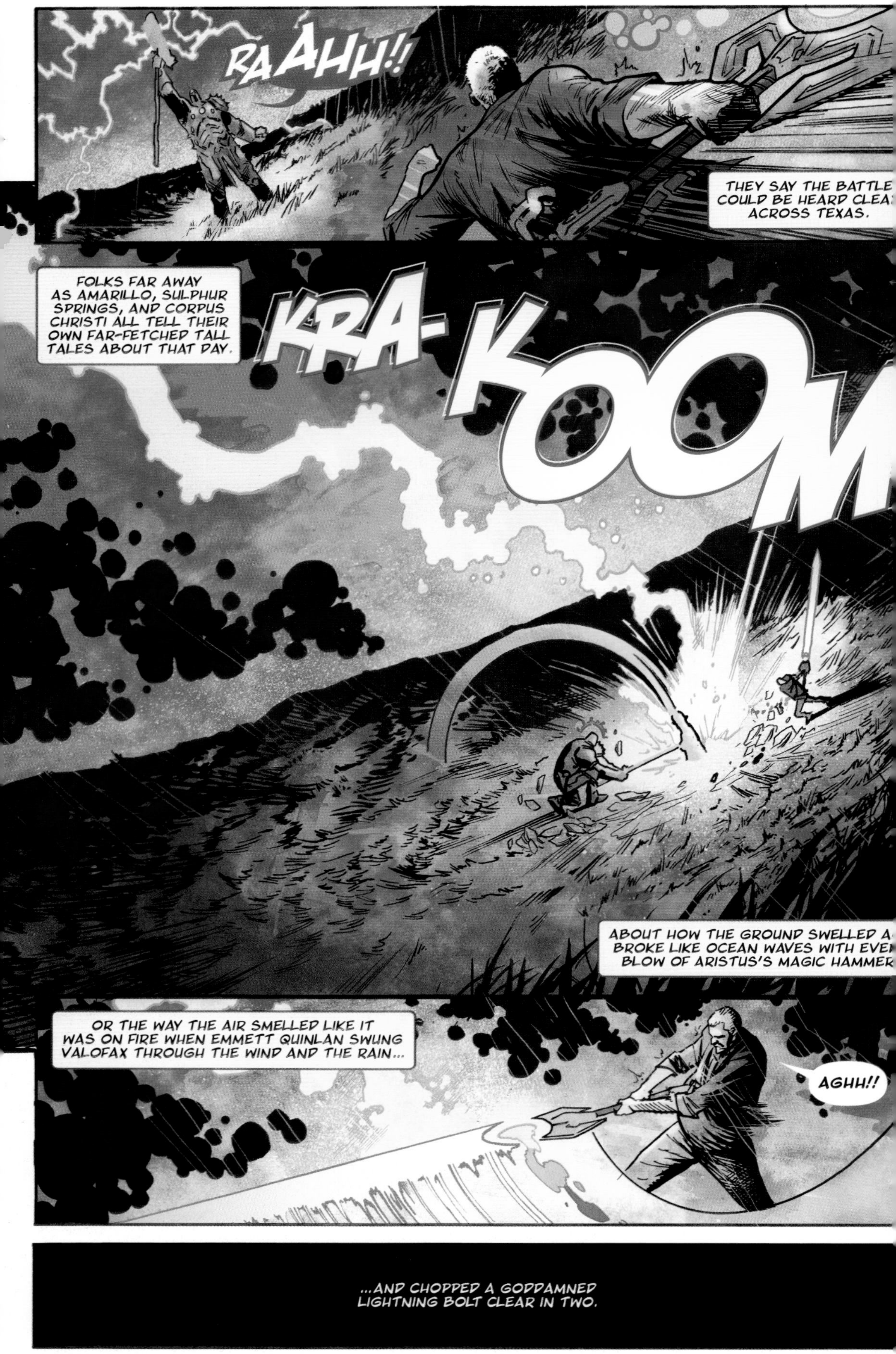
RAAHH!!
THEY SAY THE BATTLE COULD BE HEARD CLEA ACROSS TEXAS.
FOLKS FAR AWAY AS AMARILLO, SULPHUR SPRINGS, AND CORPUS CHRISTI ALL TELL THEIR OWN FAR-FETCHED TALL TALES ABOUT THAT DAY.
KRA-KOOM
ABOUT HOW THE GROUND SWELLED A BROKE LIKE OCEAN WAVES WITH EVE BLOW OF ARISTUS'S MAGIC HAMMER
OR THE WAY THE AIR SMELLED LIKE IT WAS ON FIRE WHEN EMMETT QUINLAN SWUNG VALOFAX THROUGH THE WIND AND THE RAIN...
AGHH!!
...AND CHOPPED A GODDAMNED LIGHTNING BOLT CLEAR IN TWO.

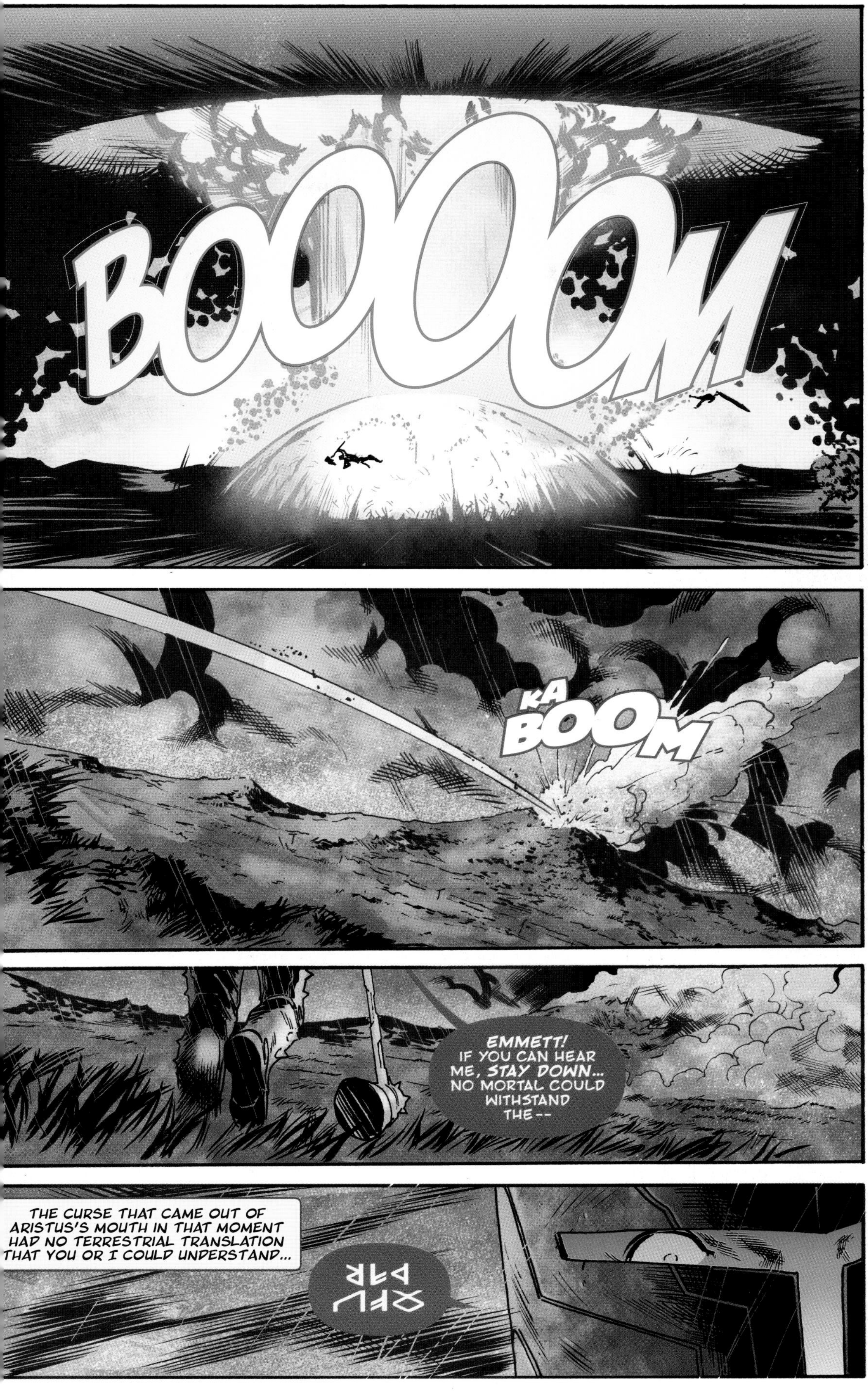
BOOOOM
KA BOOM
EMMETT! IF YOU CAN HEAR ME, STAY DOWN... NO MORTAL COULD WITHSTAND THE--
THE CURSE THAT CAME OUT OF ARISTUS'S MOUTH IN THAT MOMENT HAD NO TERRESTRIAL TRANSLATION THAT YOU OR I COULD UNDERSTAND...

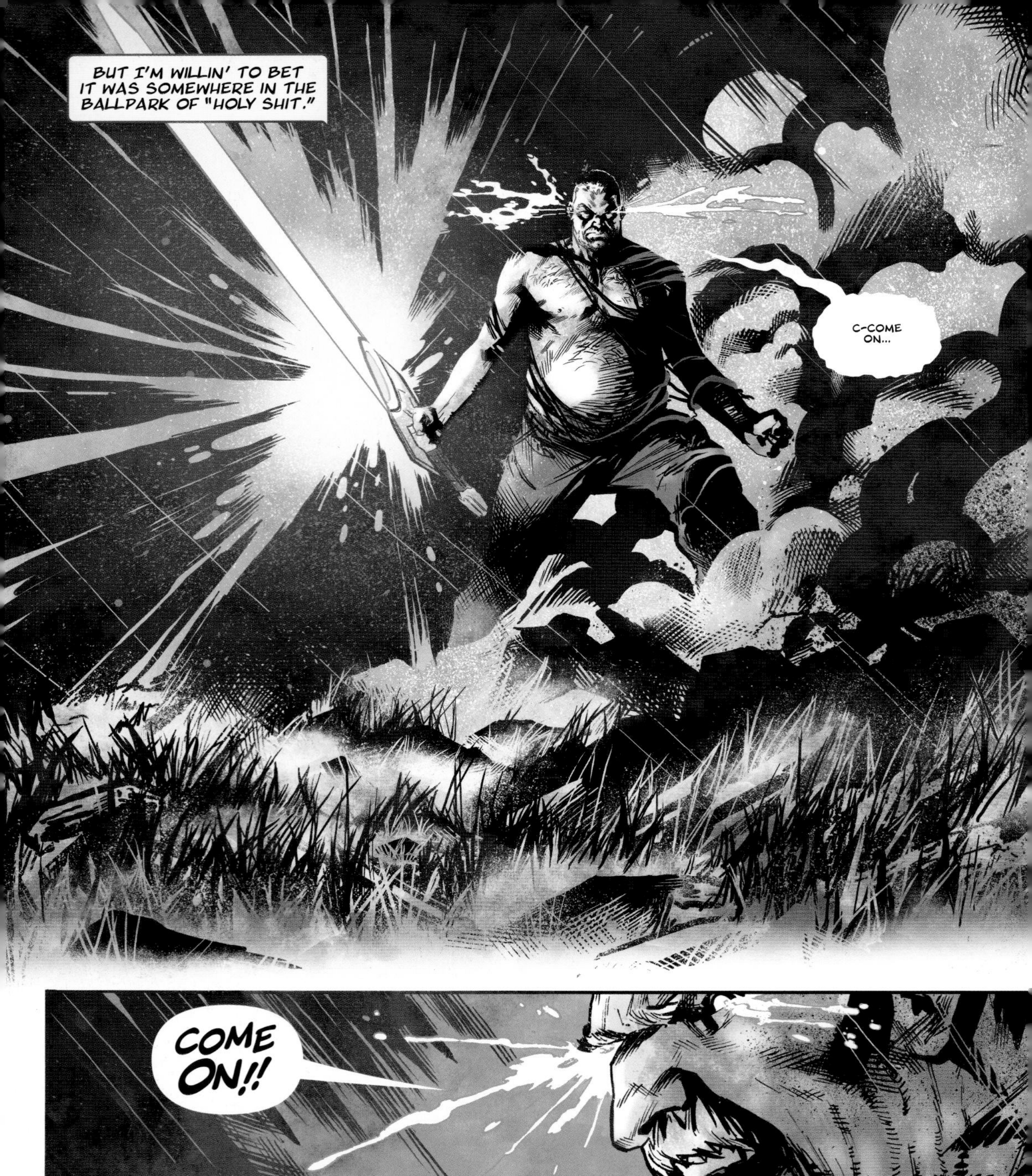
BUT I'M WILLIN' TO BET IT WAS SOMEWHERE IN THE BALLPARK OF "HOLY SHIT."
C-COME ON...
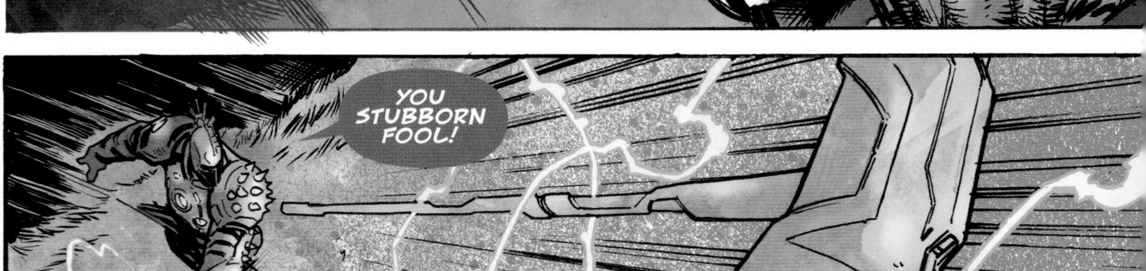
COME ON!!
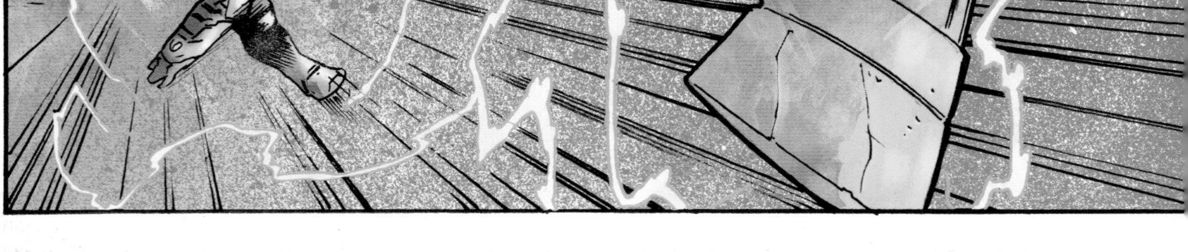
YOU STUBBORN FOOL!

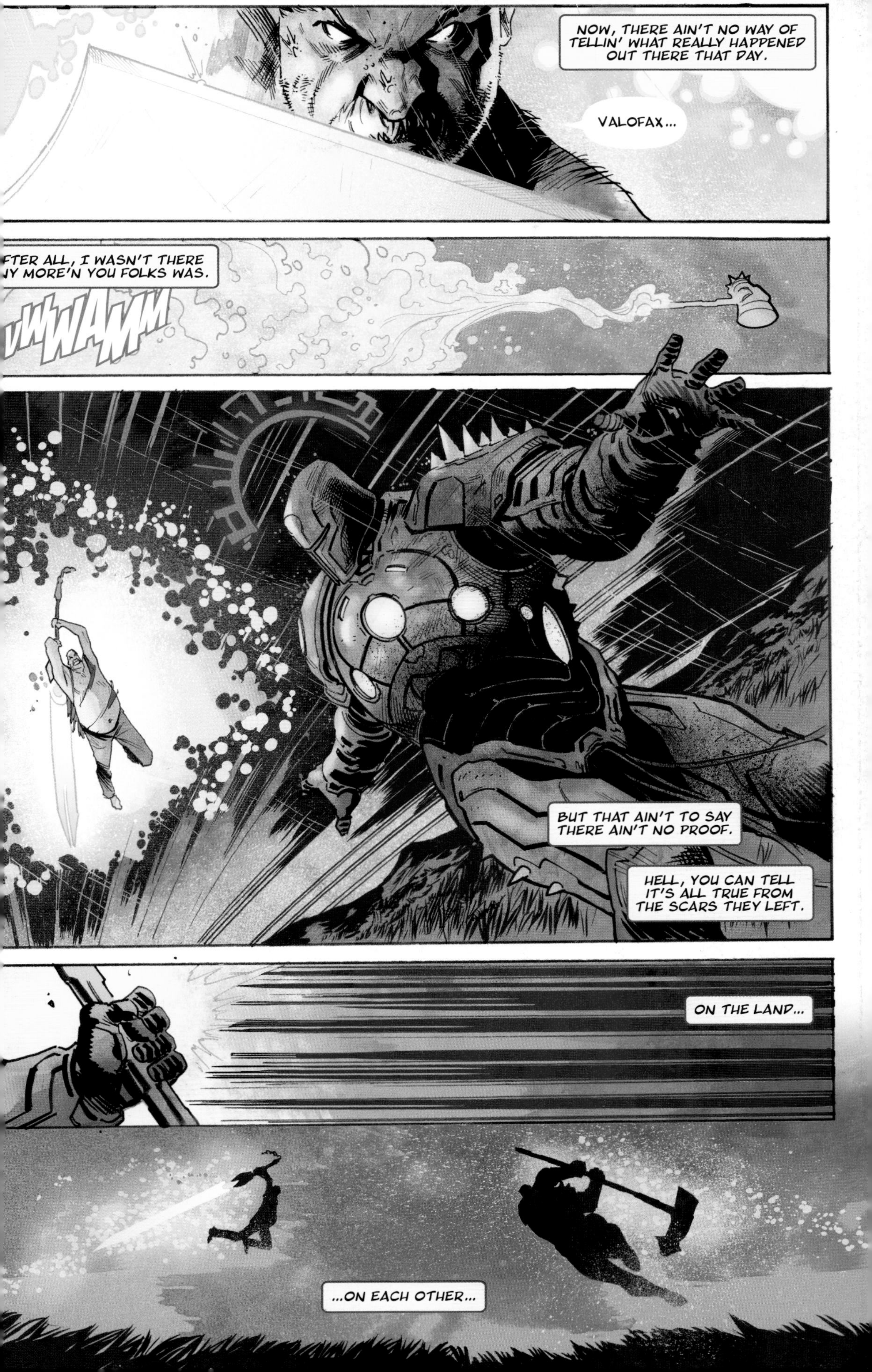
NOW, THERE AIN'T NO WAY OF TELLIN' WHAT REALLY HAPPENED OUT THERE THAT DAY.
VALOFAX...
FTER ALL, I WASN'T THERE NY MORE'N YOU FOLKS WAS.
VWWAMM
BUT THAT AIN'T TO SAY THERE AIN'T NO PROOF.
HELL, YOU CAN TELL IT'S ALL TRUE FROM THE SCARS THEY LEFT.
ON THE LAND...
...ON EACH OTHER...

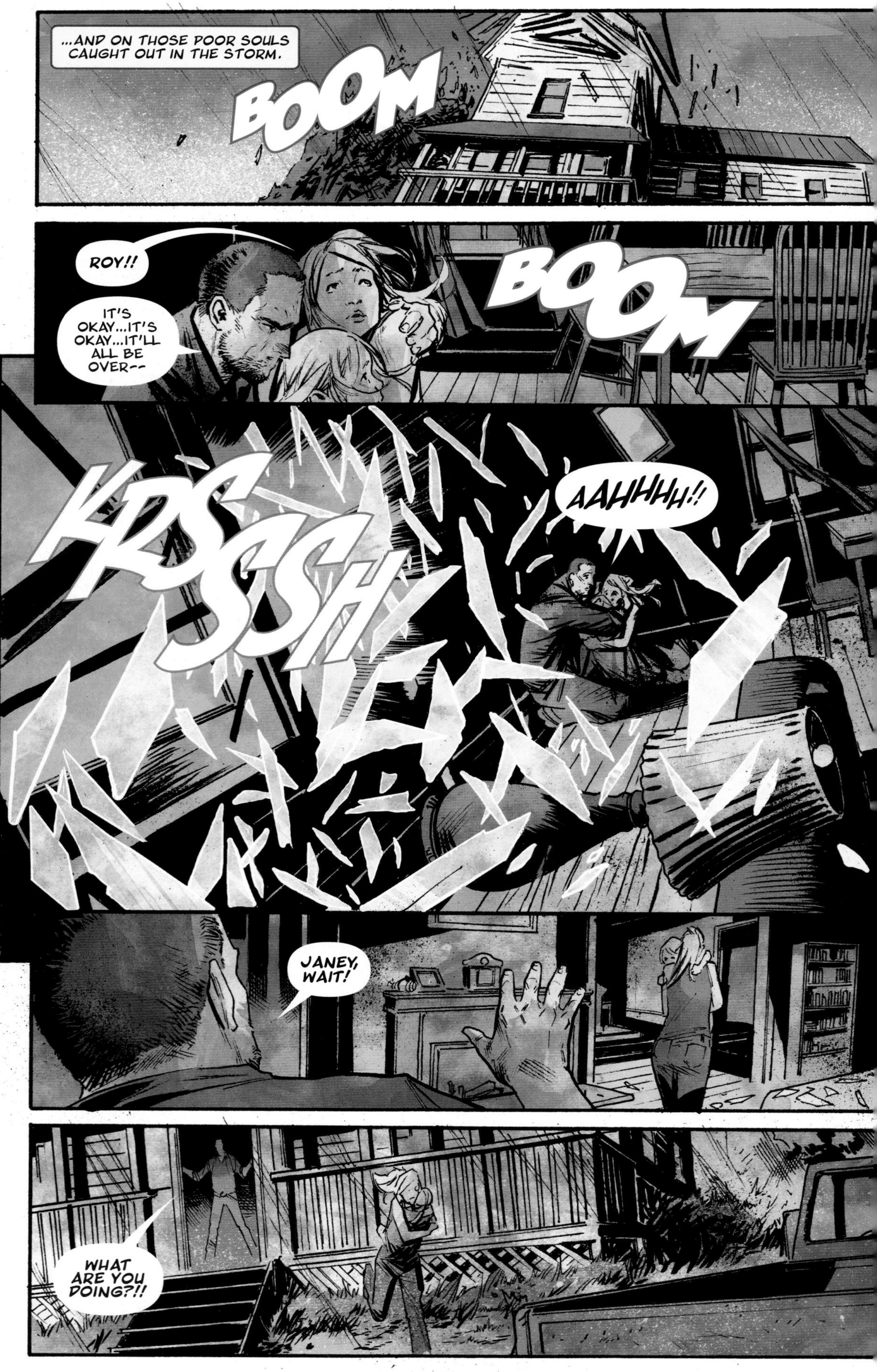
...AND ON THOSE POOR SOULS CAUGHT OUT IN THE STORM.
BOOM
ROY!!
IT'S OKAY...IT'S OKAY...IT'LL ALL BE OVER--
BOOM
KRSSSH
AAHHHH!!
JANEY, WAIT!
WHAT ARE YOU DOING?!!

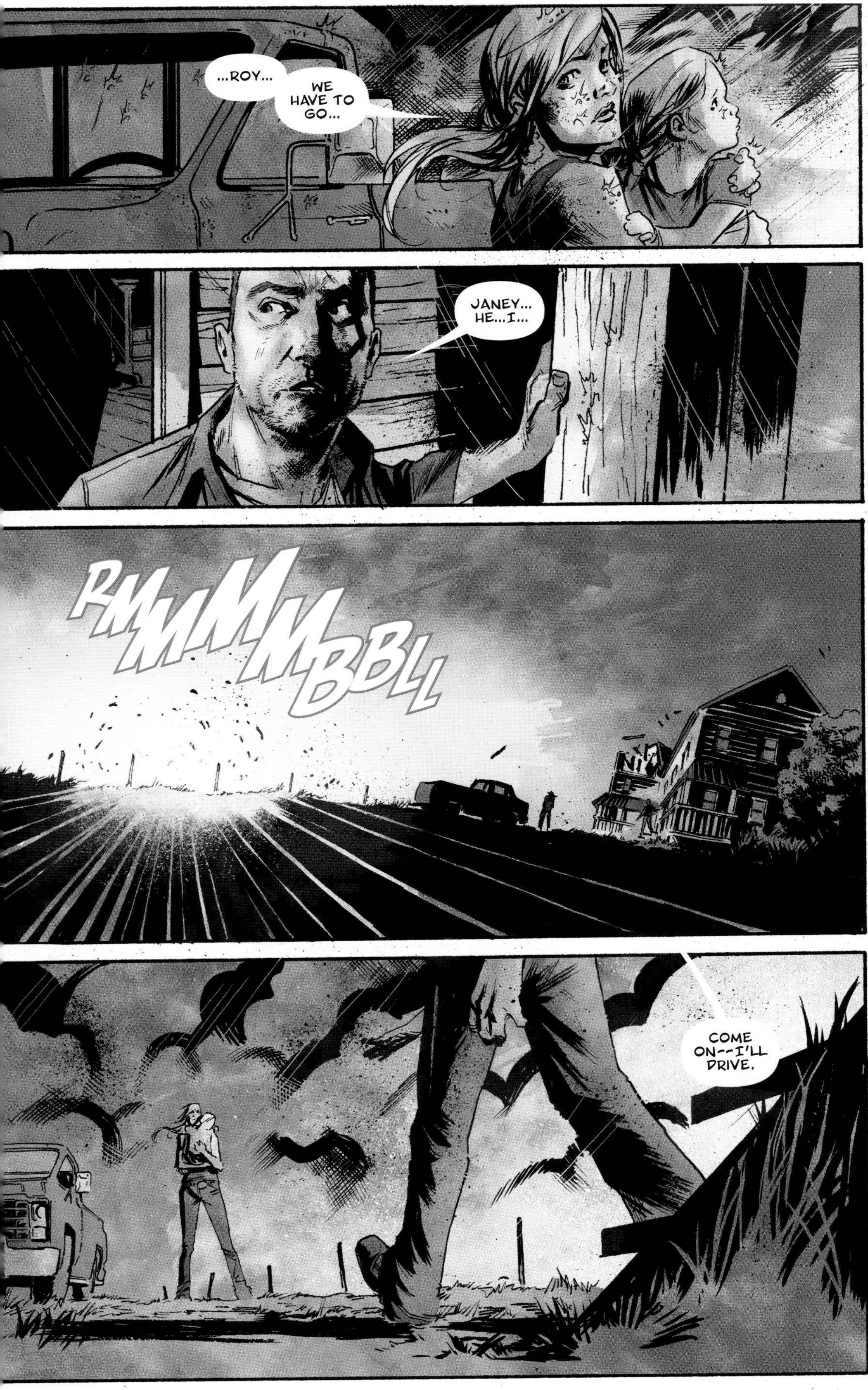
...ROY...
WE HAVE TO GO...
JANEY... HE...I...
RMMMMMBBLL
COME ON--I'LL DRIVE.

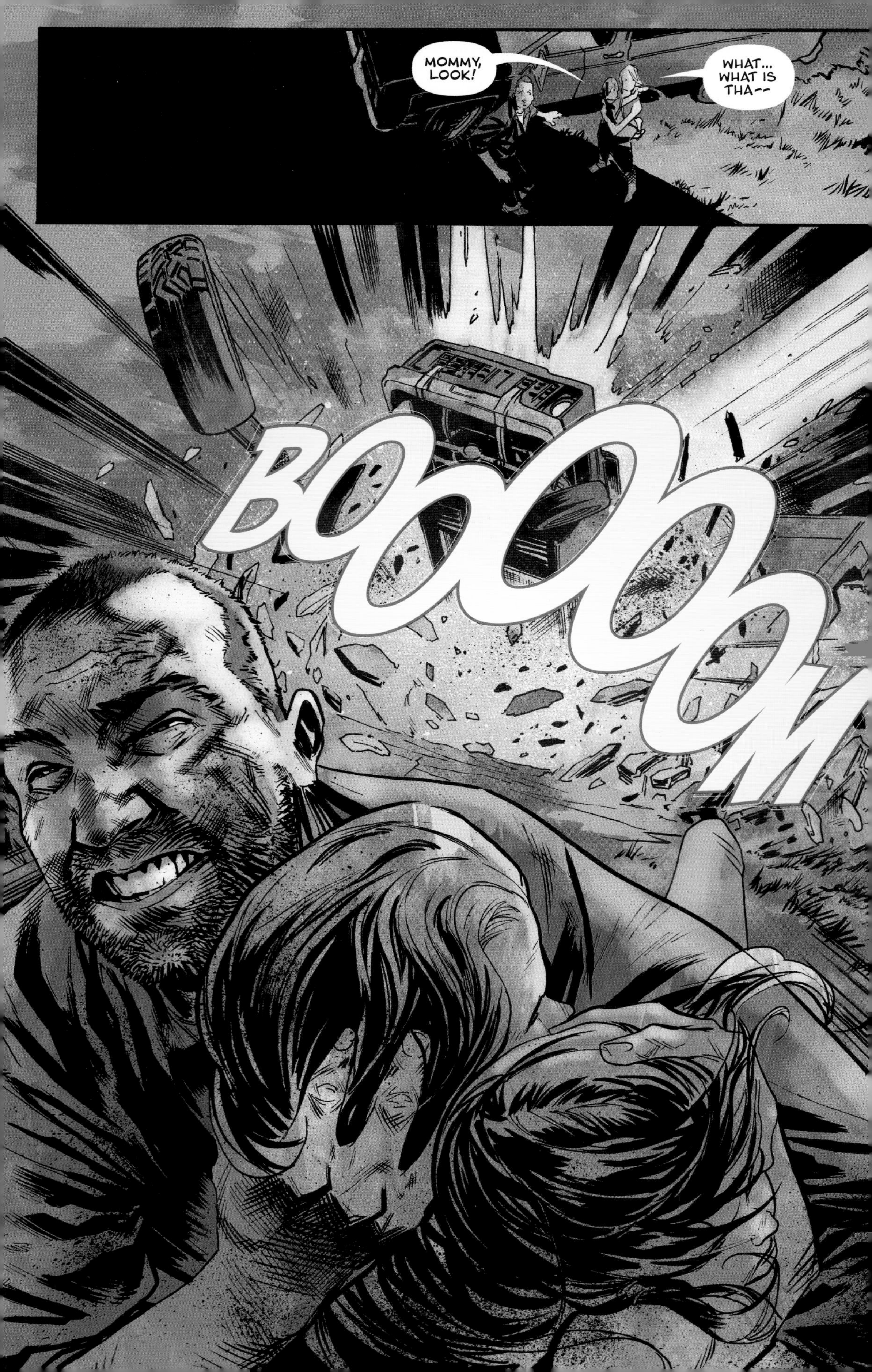
MOMMY, LOOK!
WHAT... WHAT IS THA--
BOOOOOM

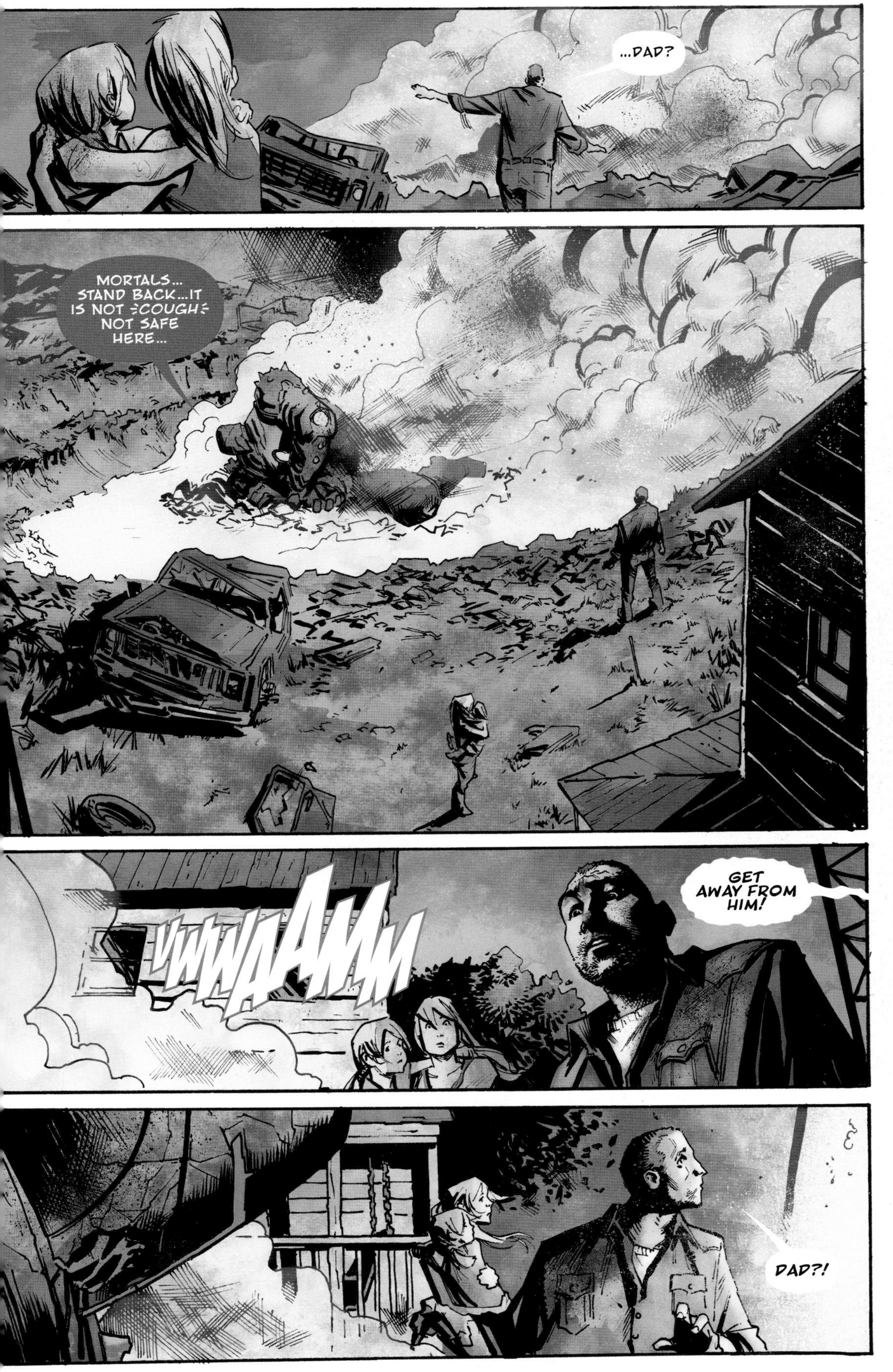
...DAD?
MORTALS... STAND BACK...IT IS NOT =COUGH= NOT SAFE HERE...
VWWAAMM
GET AWAY FROM HIM!
DAD?!

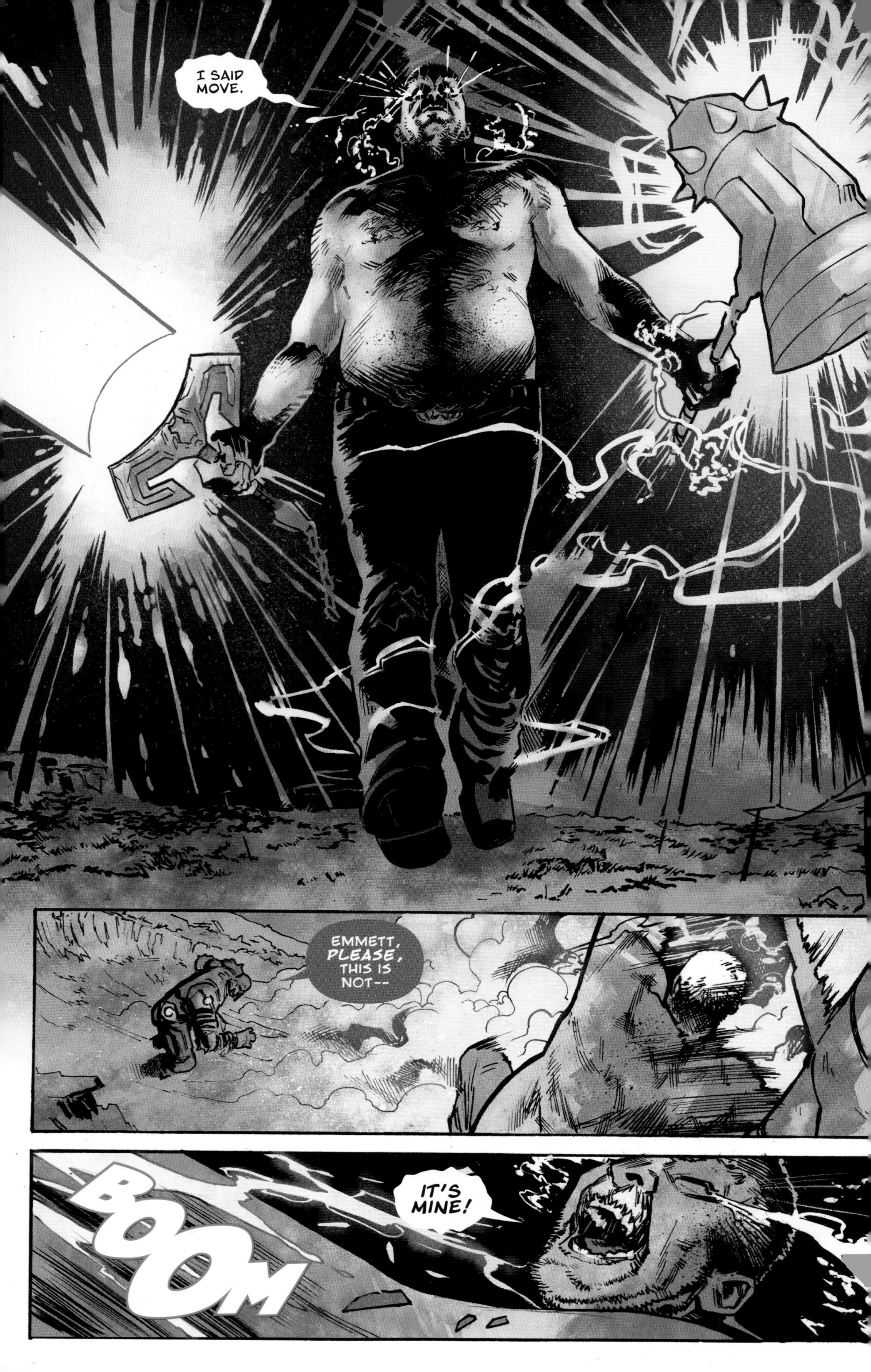
I SAID MOVE.
EMMETT, PLEASE, THIS IS NOT--
BOOM
IT'S MINE!

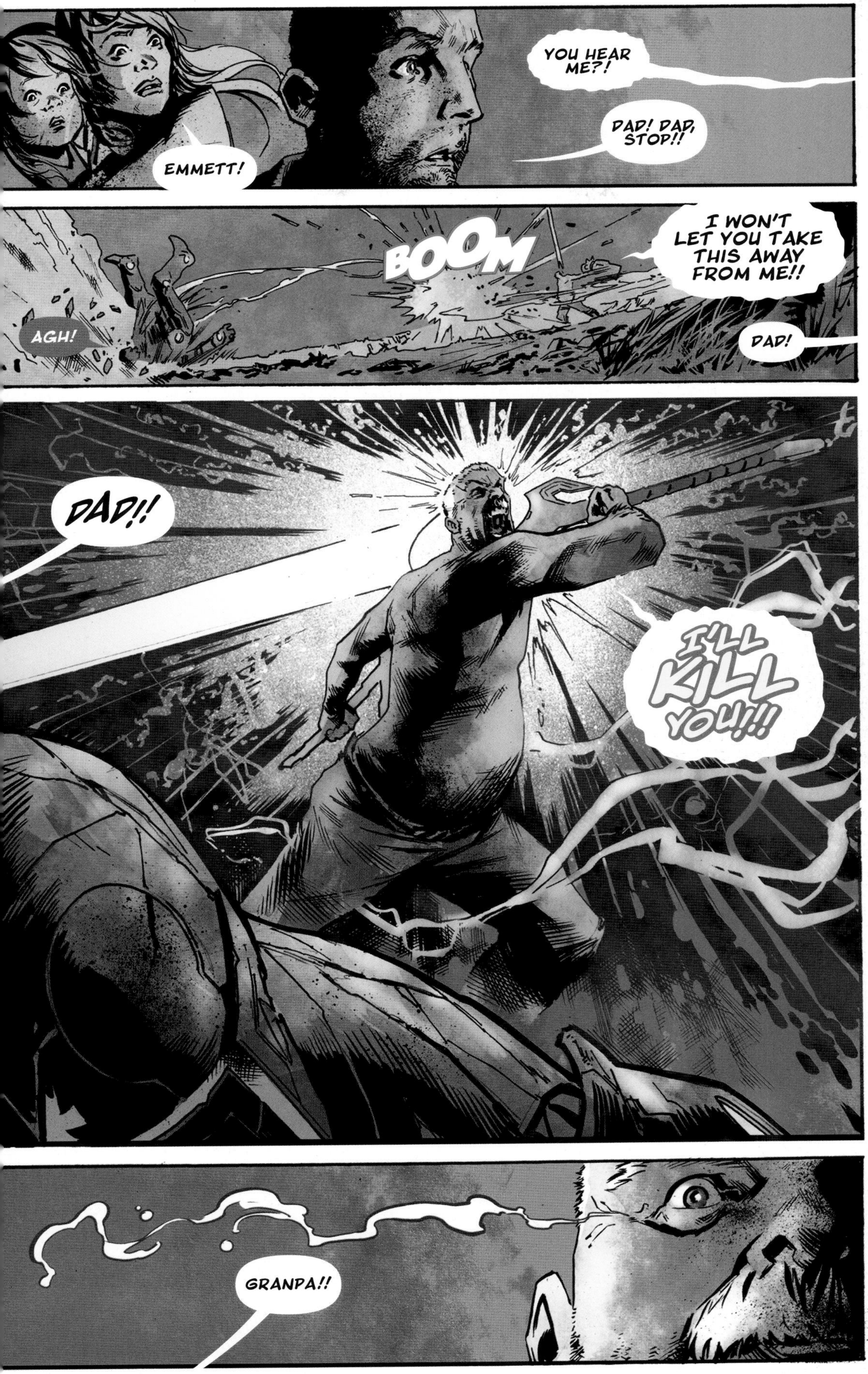
YOU HEAR ME?!
EMMETT!
DAD! DAD, STOP!!
I WON'T LET YOU TAKE THIS AWAY FROM ME!!
BOOM
AGH!
DAD!
DAD!!
I'LL KILL YOU!!!
GRANPA!!

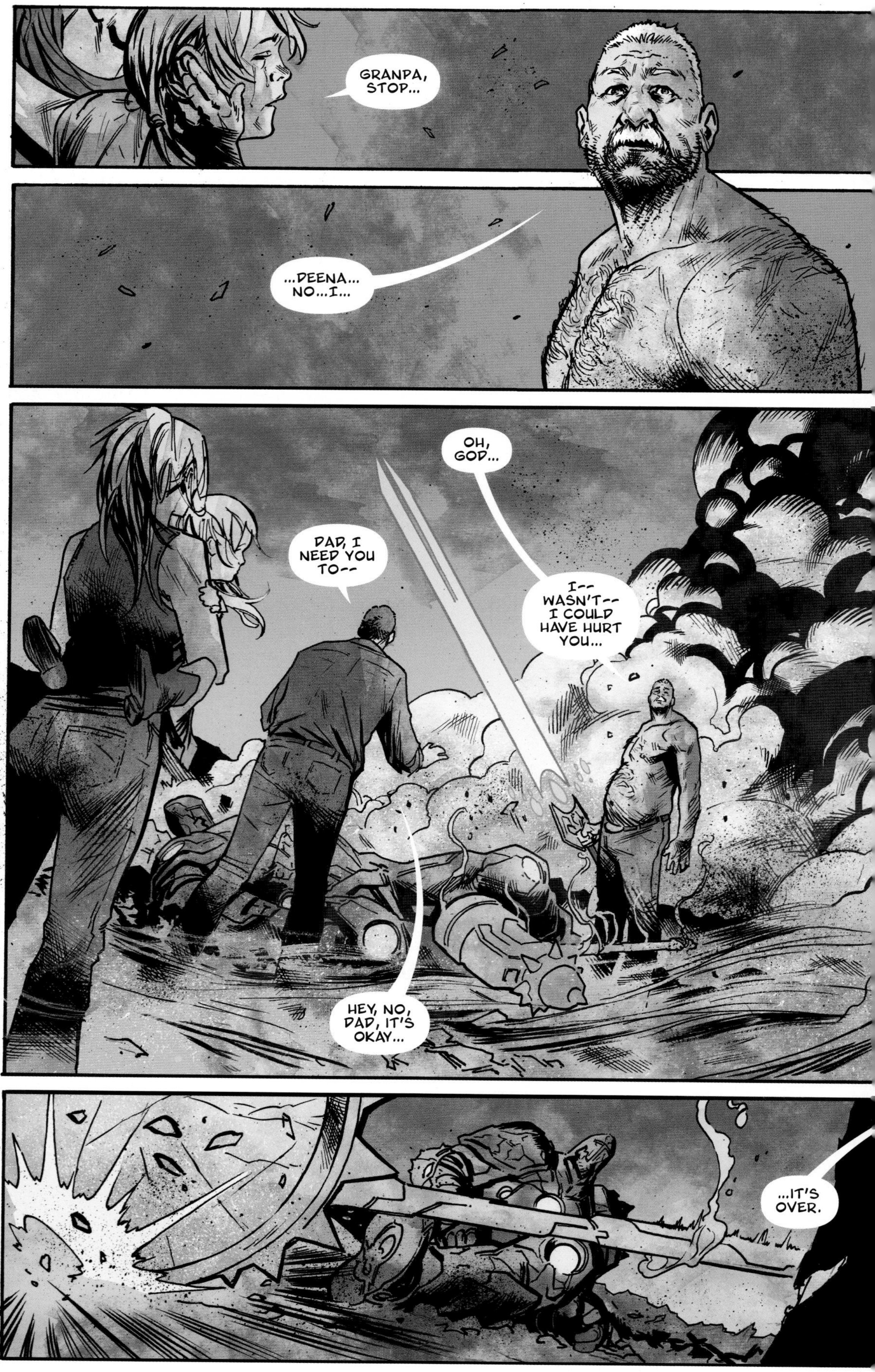
GRANPA, STOP...
...DEENA... NO...I...
OH, GOD...
DAD, I NEED YOU TO--
I-- WASN'T-- I COULD HAVE HURT YOU...
HEY, NO, DAD, IT'S OKAY...
...IT'S OVER.

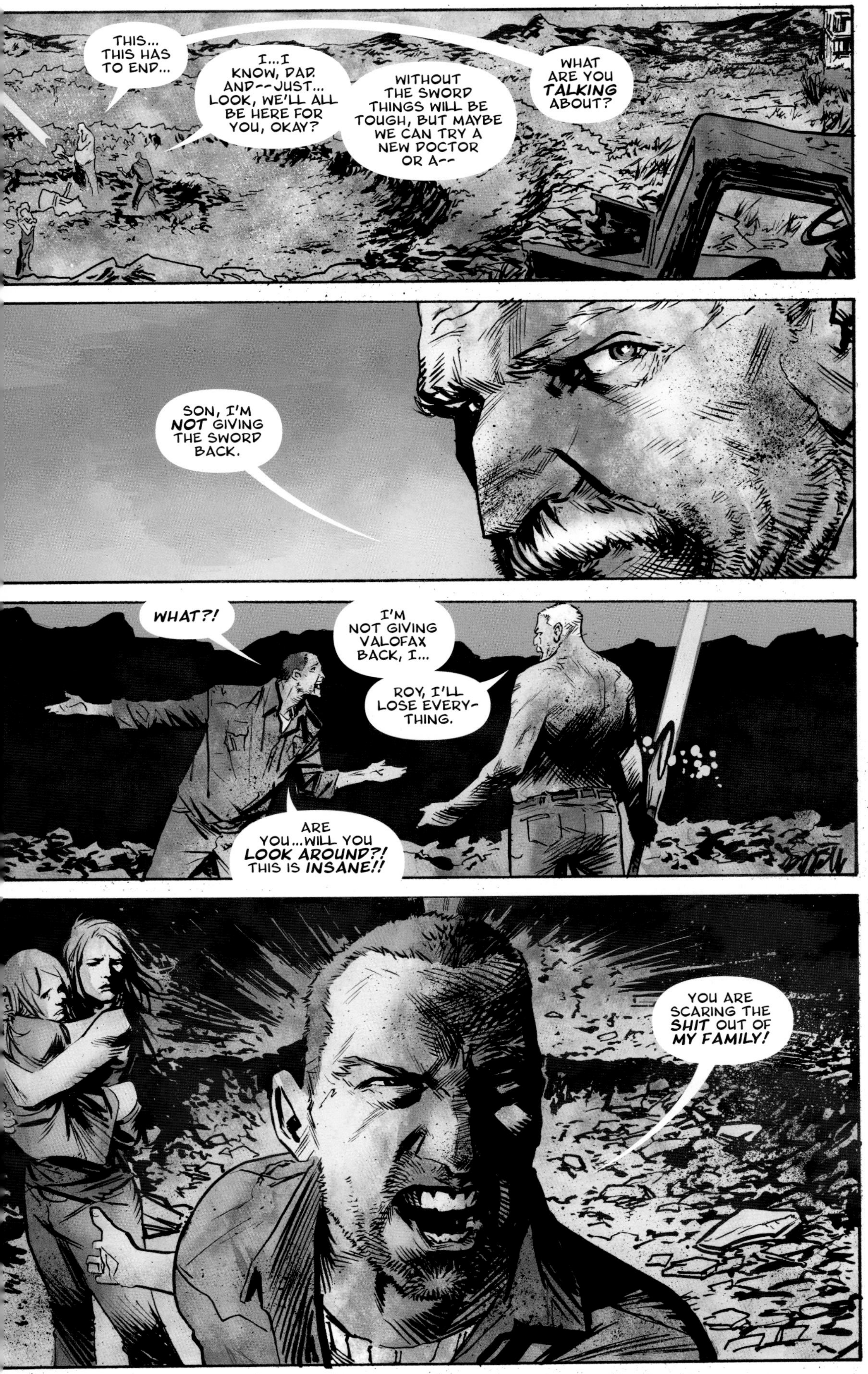
THIS... THIS HAS TO END...
I...I KNOW, DAD. AND--JUST... LOOK, WE'LL ALL BE HERE FOR YOU, OKAY?
WITHOUT THE SWORD THINGS WILL BE TOUGH, BUT MAYBE WE CAN TRY A NEW DOCTOR OR A--
WHAT ARE YOU **TALKING** ABOUT?
SON, I'M **NOT** GIVING THE SWORD BACK.
WHAT?!
I'M NOT GIVING VALOFAX BACK, I...
ROY, I'LL LOSE EVERY-THING.
ARE YOU...WILL YOU **LOOK AROUND?!** THIS IS **INSANE!!**
YOU ARE SCARING THE **SHIT** OUT OF **MY FAMILY!**

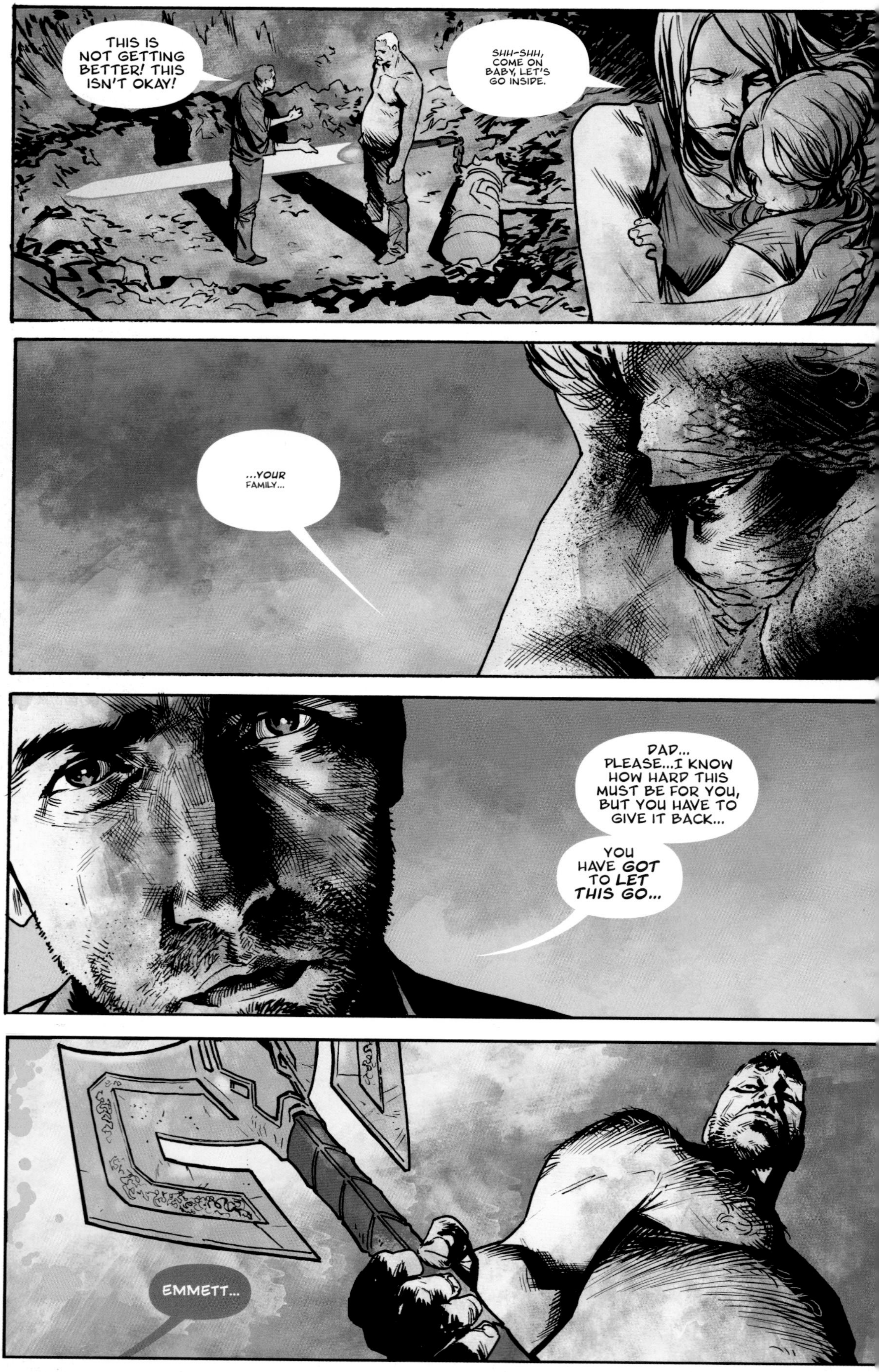
THIS IS NOT GETTING BETTER! THIS ISN'T OKAY!
SHH-SHH, COME ON BABY, LET'S GO INSIDE.
...YOUR FAMILY...
DAD... PLEASE...I KNOW HOW HARD THIS MUST BE FOR YOU, BUT YOU HAVE TO GIVE IT BACK...
YOU HAVE GOT TO LET THIS GO...
EMMETT...

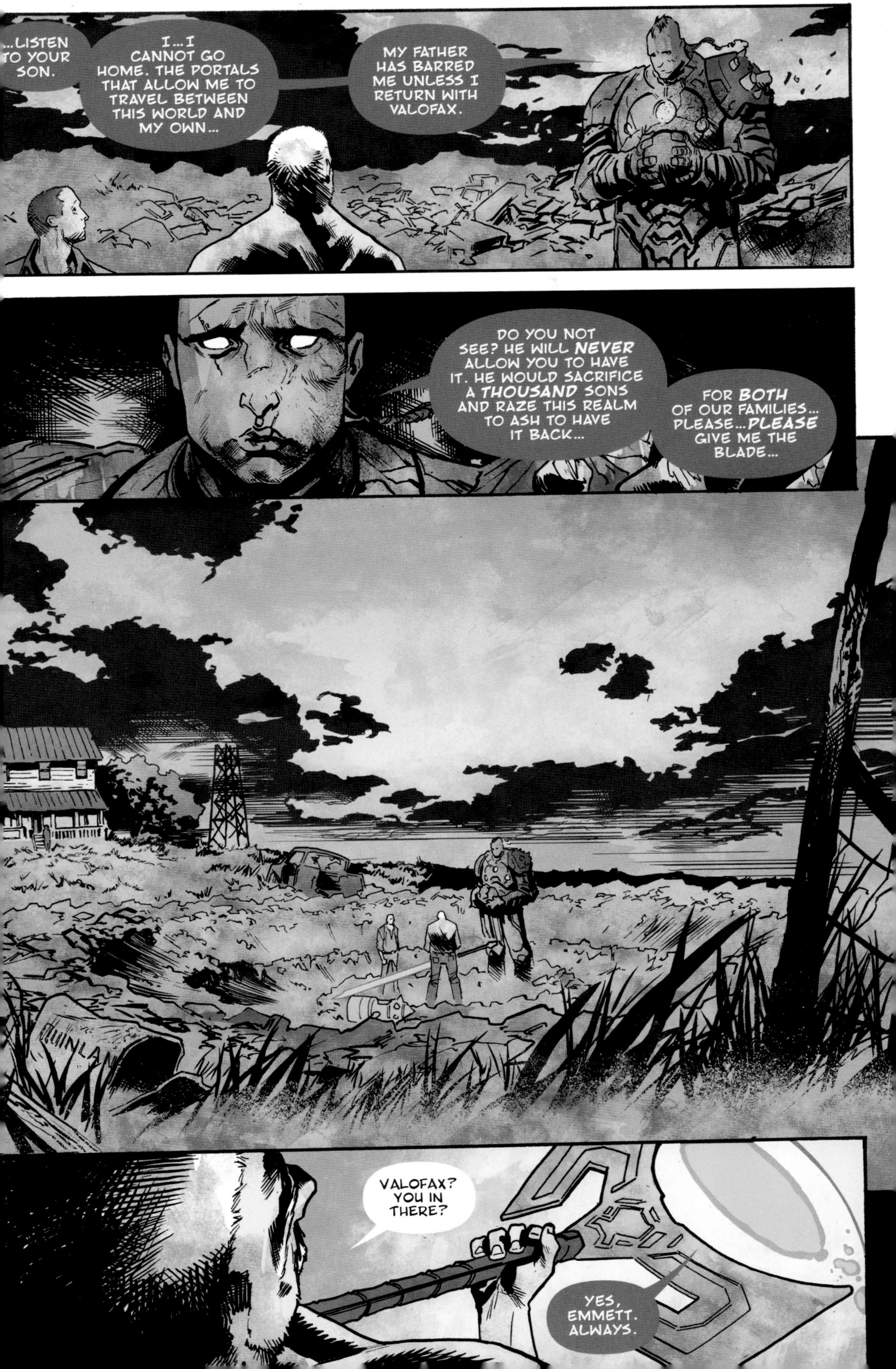
...LISTEN TO YOUR SON.
I...I CANNOT GO HOME. THE PORTALS THAT ALLOW ME TO TRAVEL BETWEEN THIS WORLD AND MY OWN...
MY FATHER HAS BARRED ME UNLESS I RETURN WITH VALOFAX.
DO YOU NOT SEE? HE WILL NEVER ALLOW YOU TO HAVE IT. HE WOULD SACRIFICE A THOUSAND SONS AND RAZE THIS REALM TO ASH TO HAVE IT BACK...
FOR BOTH OF OUR FAMILIES... PLEASE...PLEASE GIVE ME THE BLADE...
VALOFAX? YOU IN THERE?
YES, EMMETT. ALWAYS.

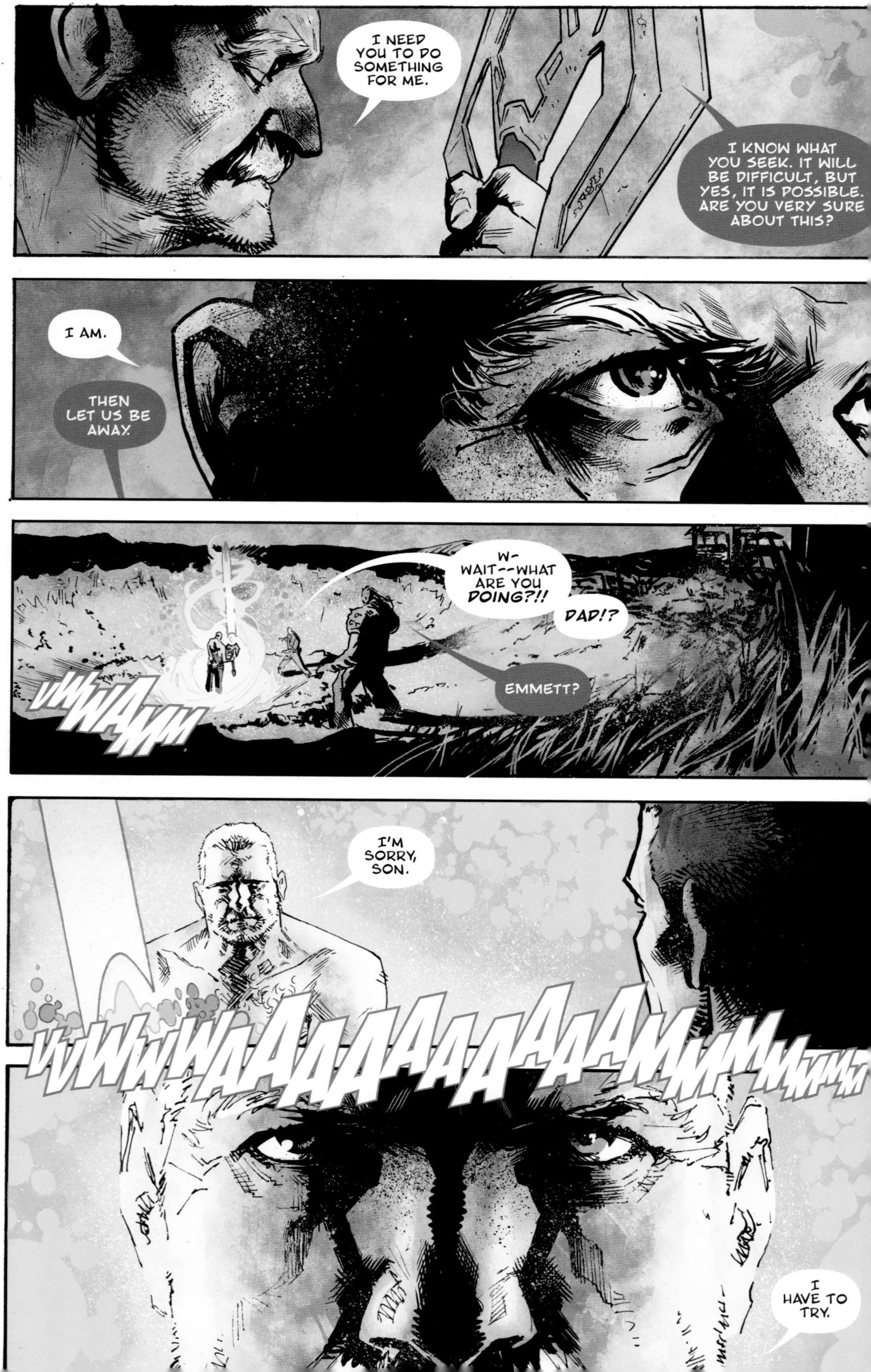
I NEED YOU TO DO SOMETHING FOR ME.
I KNOW WHAT YOU SEEK. IT WILL BE DIFFICULT, BUT YES, IT IS POSSIBLE. ARE YOU VERY SURE ABOUT THIS?
I AM.
THEN LET US BE AWAY.
W-WAIT--WHAT ARE YOU DOING?!!
DAD!?
EMMETT?
VWWAMM
I'M SORRY, SON.
VVWWWAAAAAAAAAAAAMMMMMMMMM
I HAVE TO TRY.

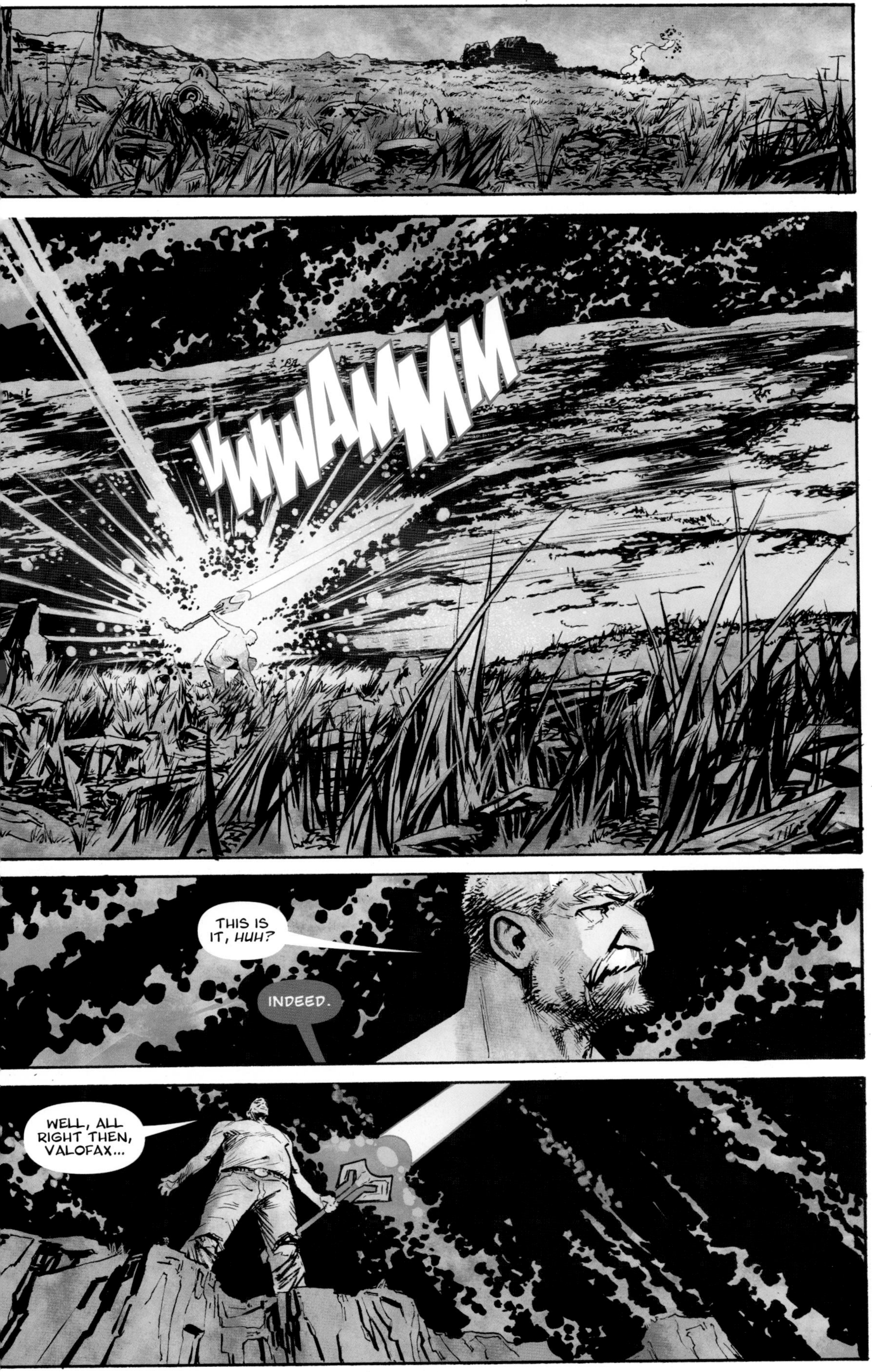
VWWAMMMM
THIS IS IT, HUH?
INDEED.
WELL, ALL RIGHT THEN, VALOFAX...

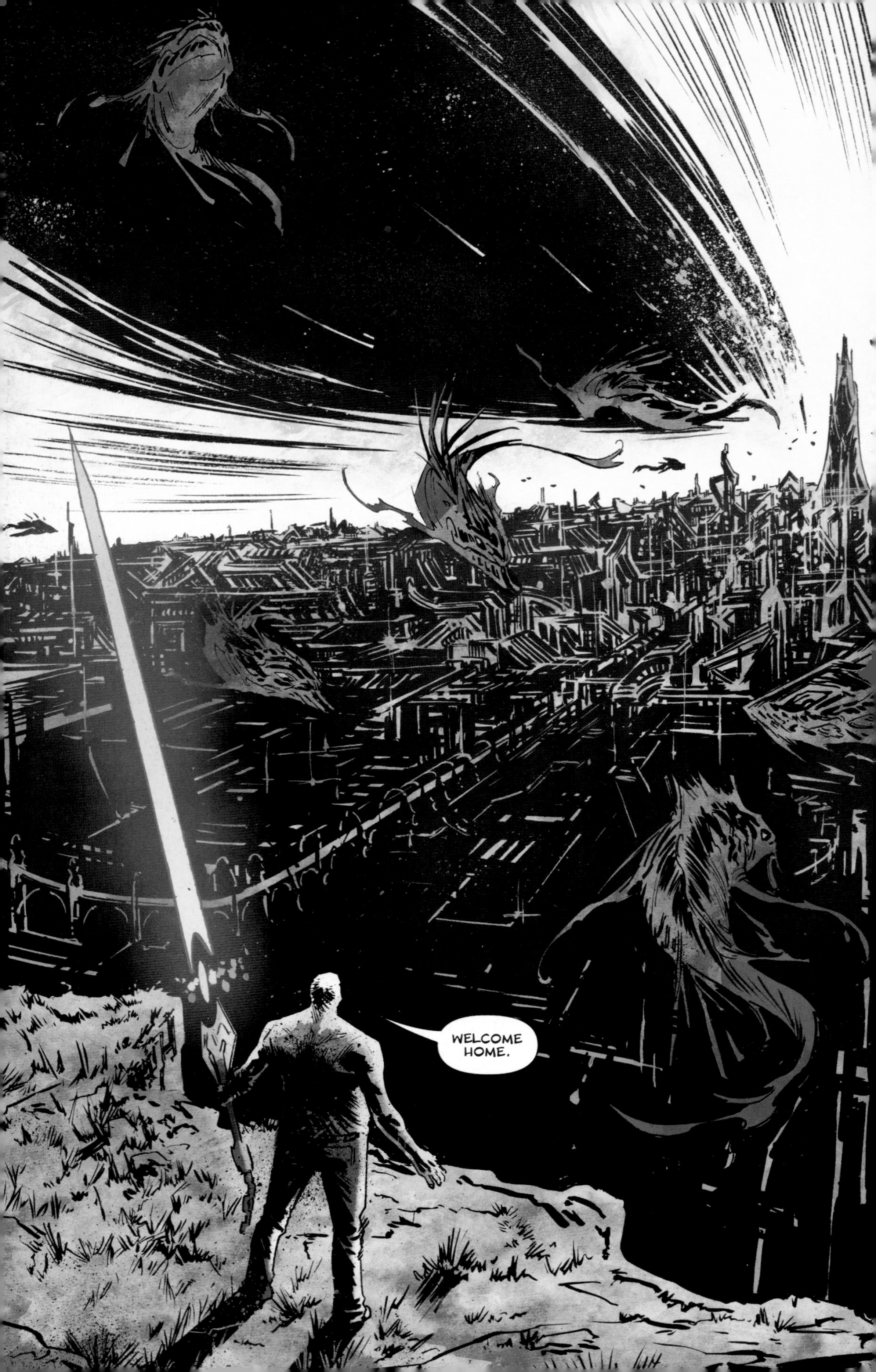
WELCOME HOME.

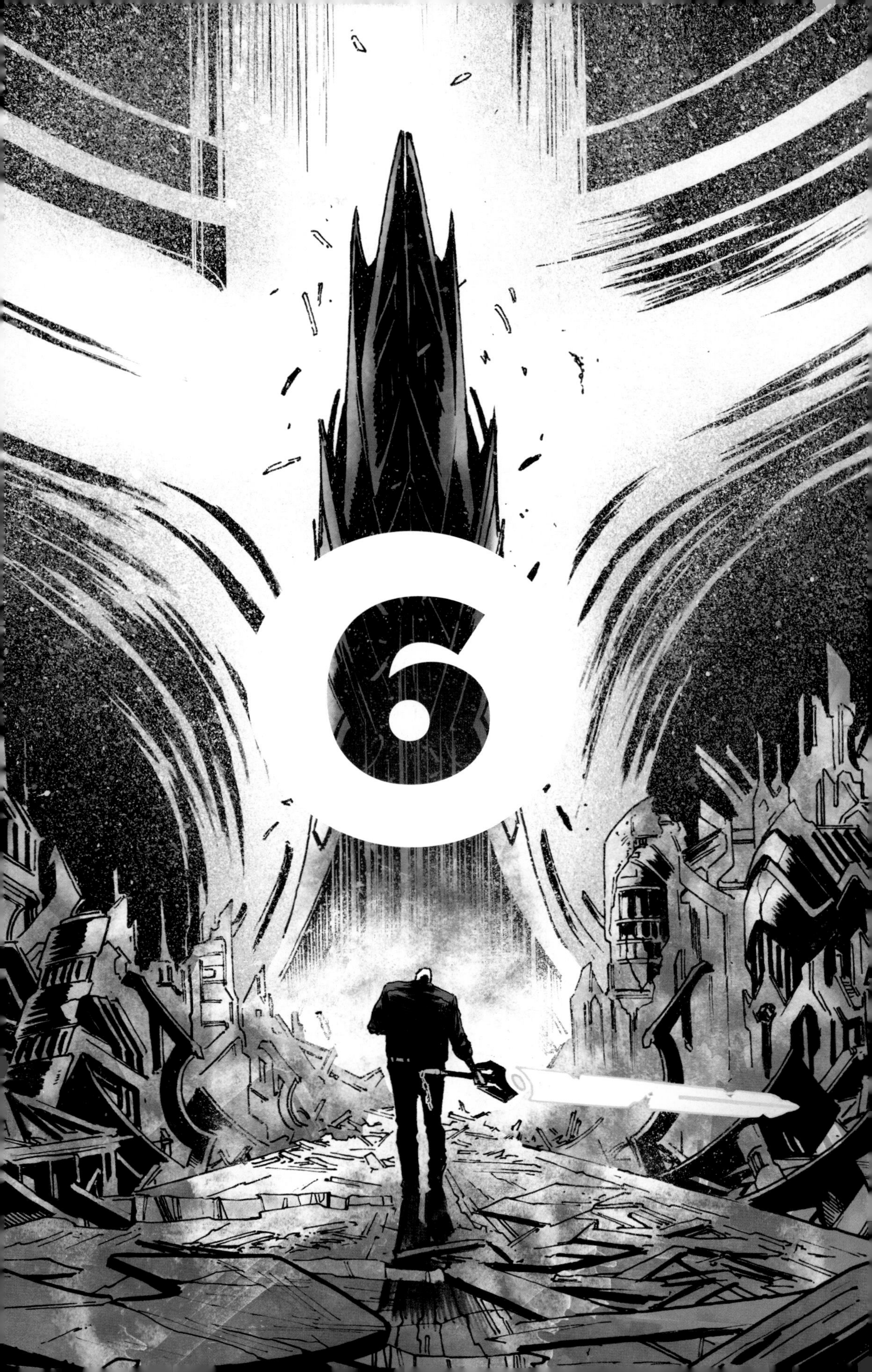
6

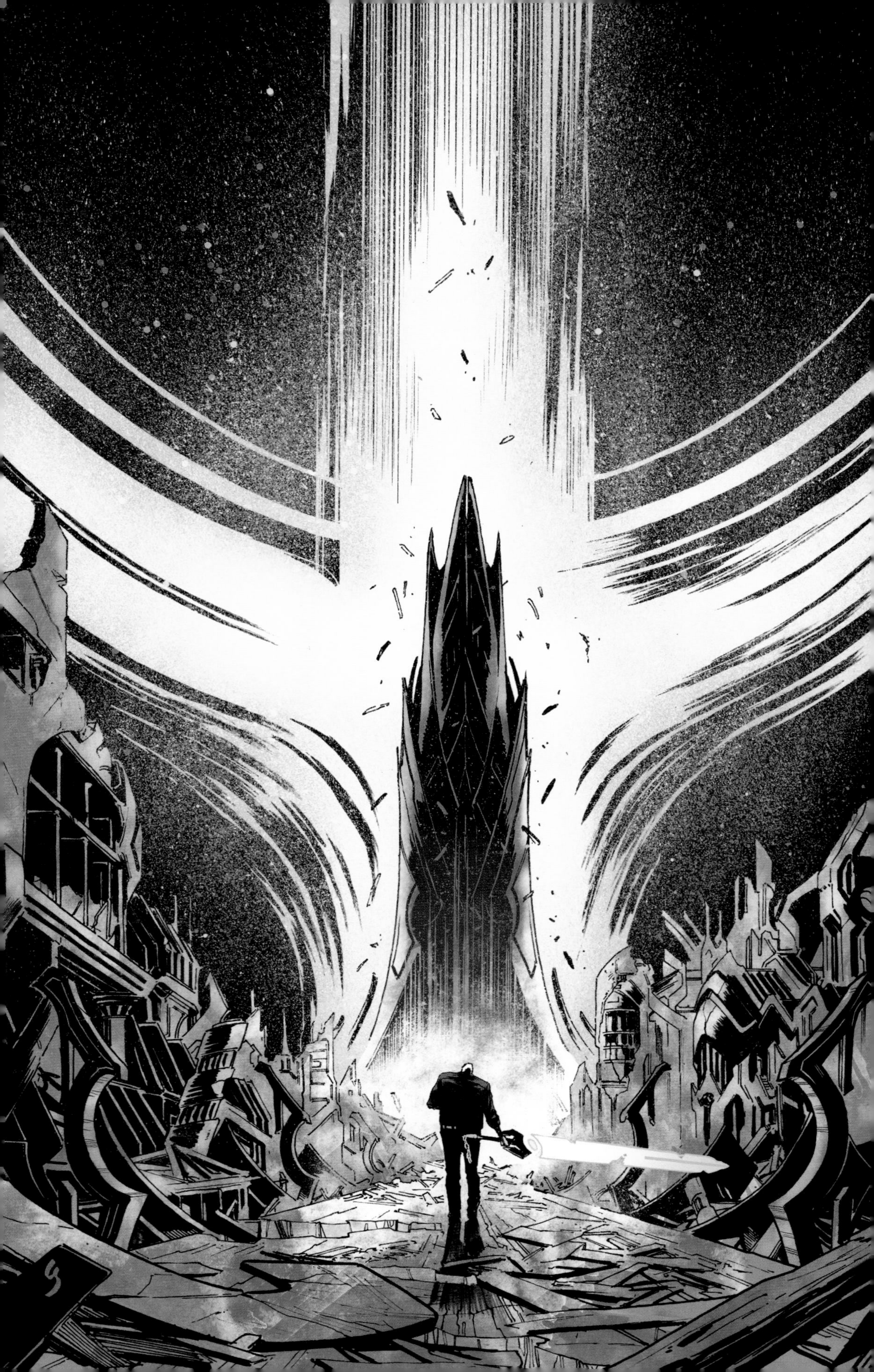

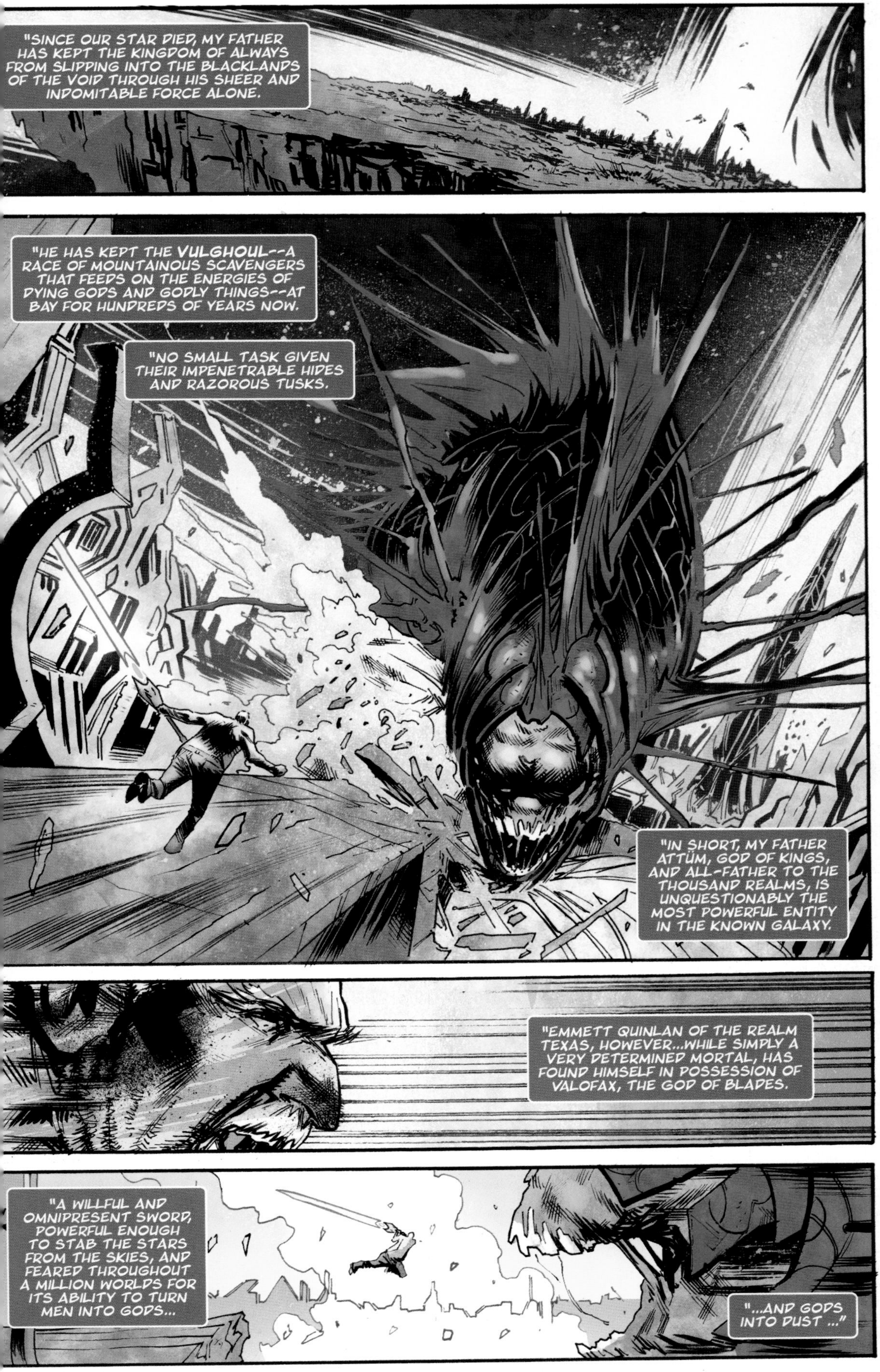
"SINCE OUR STAR DIED, MY FATHER HAS KEPT THE KINGDOM OF ALWAYS FROM SLIPPING INTO THE BLACKLANDS OF THE VOID THROUGH HIS SHEER AND INDOMITABLE FORCE ALONE.
"HE HAS KEPT THE VULGHOUL--A RACE OF MOUNTAINOUS SCAVENGERS THAT FEEDS ON THE ENERGIES OF DYING GODS AND GODLY THINGS--AT BAY FOR HUNDREDS OF YEARS NOW.
"NO SMALL TASK GIVEN THEIR IMPENETRABLE HIDES AND RAZOROUS TUSKS.
"IN SHORT, MY FATHER ATTÜM, GOD OF KINGS, AND ALL-FATHER TO THE THOUSAND REALMS, IS UNQUESTIONABLY THE MOST POWERFUL ENTITY IN THE KNOWN GALAXY.
"EMMETT QUINLAN OF THE REALM TEXAS, HOWEVER...WHILE SIMPLY A VERY DETERMINED MORTAL, HAS FOUND HIMSELF IN POSSESSION OF VALOFAX, THE GOD OF BLADES.
"A WILLFUL AND OMNIPRESENT SWORD, POWERFUL ENOUGH TO STAB THE STARS FROM THE SKIES, AND FEARED THROUGHOUT A MILLION WORLDS FOR ITS ABILITY TO TURN MEN INTO GODS...
"...AND GODS INTO DUST ..."

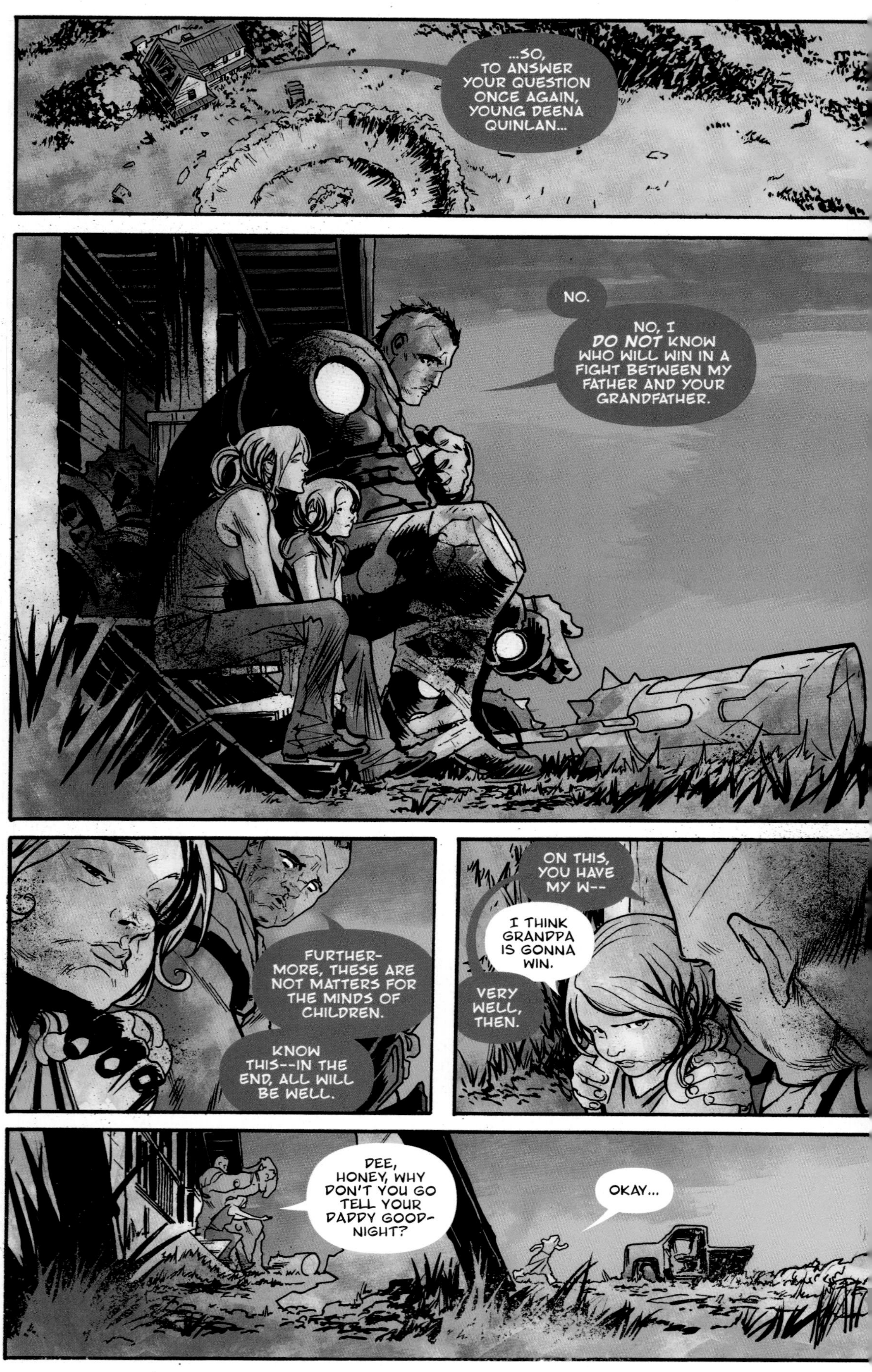
...SO, TO ANSWER YOUR QUESTION ONCE AGAIN, YOUNG DEENA QUINLAN...
NO.
NO, I *DO NOT* KNOW WHO WILL WIN IN A FIGHT BETWEEN MY FATHER AND YOUR GRANDFATHER.
FURTHER-MORE, THESE ARE NOT MATTERS FOR THE MINDS OF CHILDREN.
KNOW THIS--IN THE END, ALL WILL BE WELL.
ON THIS, YOU HAVE MY W--
I THINK GRANDPA IS GONNA WIN.
VERY WELL, THEN.
DEE, HONEY, WHY DON'T YOU GO TELL YOUR DADDY GOOD-NIGHT?
OKAY...

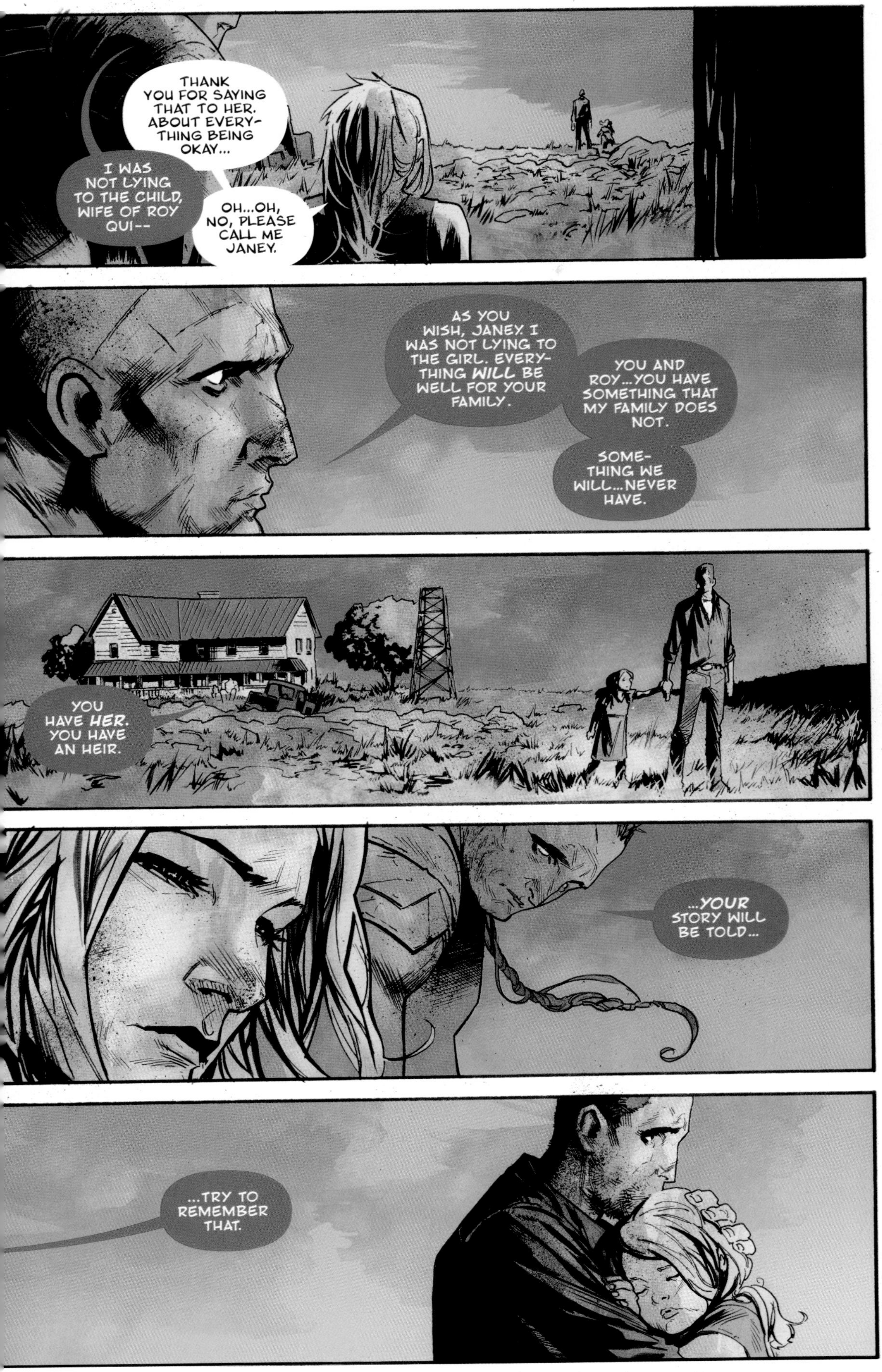
THANK YOU FOR SAYING THAT TO HER. ABOUT EVERY-THING BEING OKAY...
I WAS NOT LYING TO THE CHILD, WIFE OF ROY QUI--
OH...OH, NO, PLEASE CALL ME JANEY.
AS YOU WISH, JANEY. I WAS NOT LYING TO THE GIRL. EVERY-THING WILL BE WELL FOR YOUR FAMILY.
YOU AND ROY...YOU HAVE SOMETHING THAT MY FAMILY DOES NOT.
SOME-THING WE WILL...NEVER HAVE.
YOU HAVE HER. YOU HAVE AN HEIR.
...YOUR STORY WILL BE TOLD...
...TRY TO REMEMBER THAT.

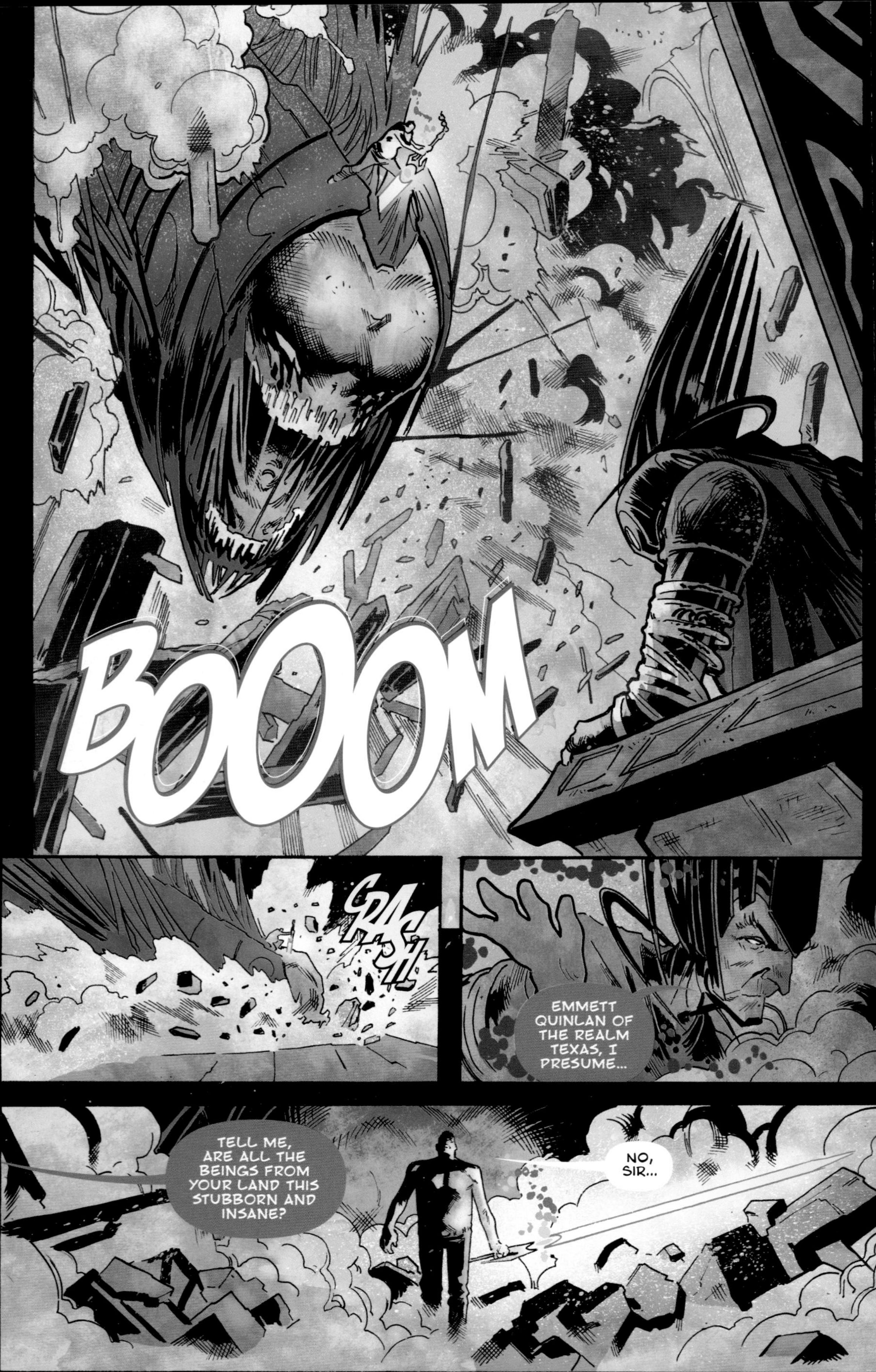
BOOOM
CRACH
EMMETT QUINLAN OF THE REALM TEXAS, I PRESUME...
TELL ME, ARE ALL THE BEINGS FROM YOUR LAND THIS STUBBORN AND INSANE?
NO, SIR...

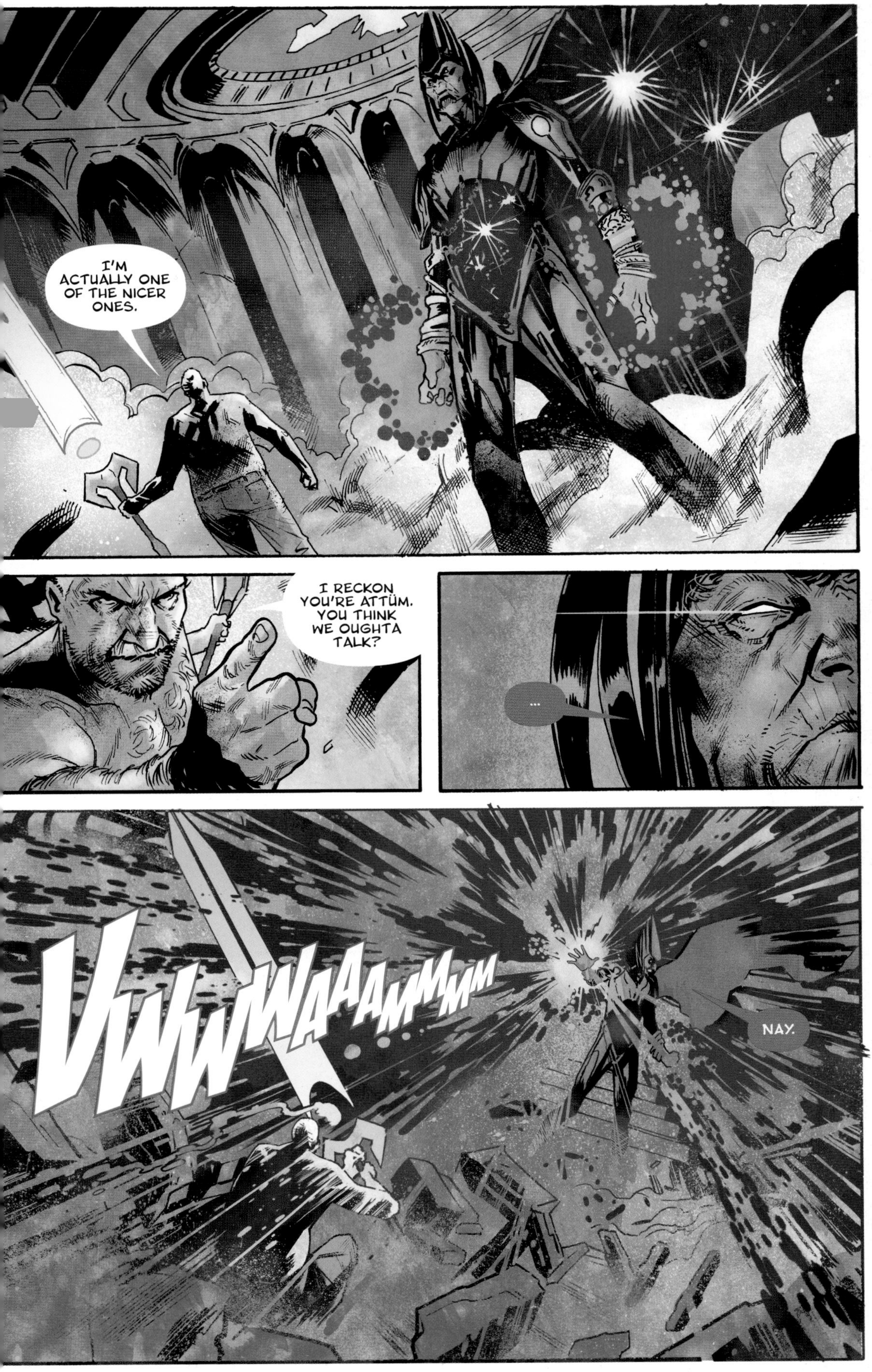
I'M ACTUALLY ONE OF THE NICER ONES.
I RECKON YOU'RE ATTÜM. YOU THINK WE OUGHTA TALK?
...
VWWWAAAAMMMMM
NAY.

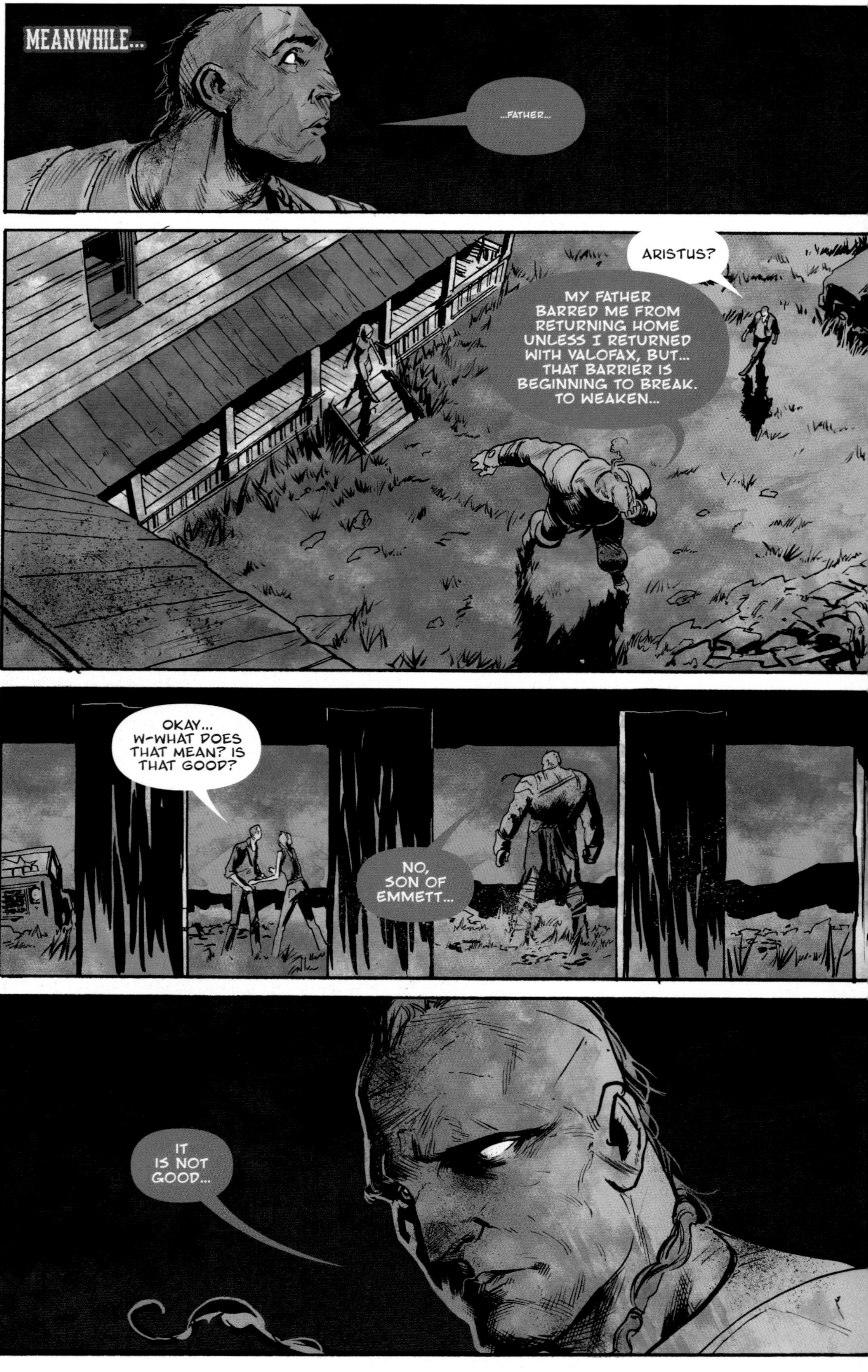
MEANWHILE...
...FATHER...
ARISTUS?
MY FATHER BARRED ME FROM RETURNING HOME UNLESS I RETURNED WITH VALOFAX, BUT... THAT BARRIER IS BEGINNING TO BREAK. TO WEAKEN...
OKAY... W-WHAT DOES THAT MEAN? IS THAT GOOD?
NO, SON OF EMMETT...
IT IS NOT GOOD...

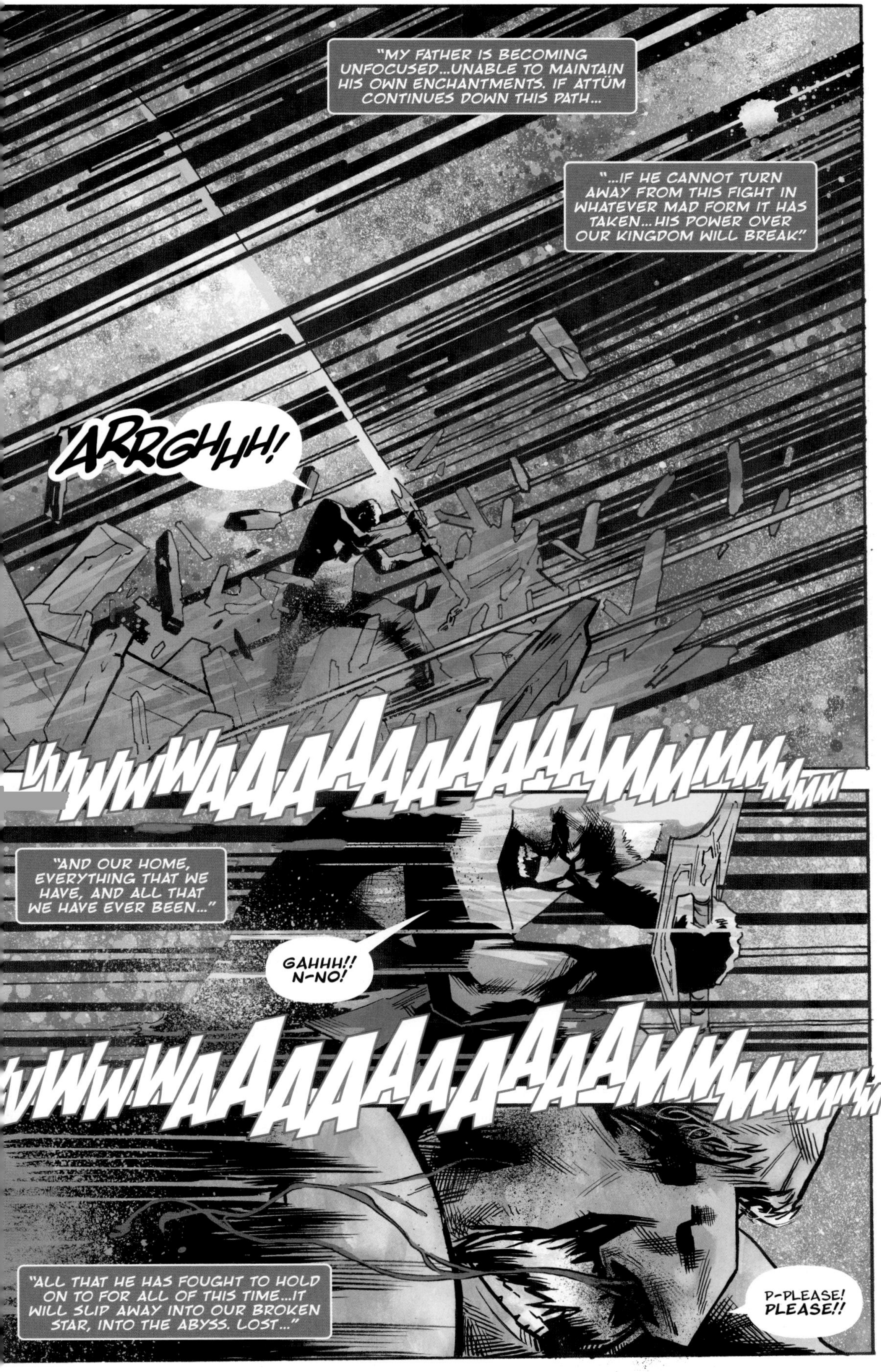
"MY FATHER IS BECOMING UNFOCUSED...UNABLE TO MAINTAIN HIS OWN ENCHANTMENTS. IF ATTÜM CONTINUES DOWN THIS PATH...
"...IF HE CANNOT TURN AWAY FROM THIS FIGHT IN WHATEVER MAD FORM IT HAS TAKEN...HIS POWER OVER OUR KINGDOM WILL BREAK."
ARRGHHH!
VVWWWAAAAAAAAAAMMMMMMM
"AND OUR HOME, EVERYTHING THAT WE HAVE, AND ALL THAT WE HAVE EVER BEEN..."
GAHHH!! N-NO!
VWWWAAAAAAAAAAMMMMMMM
"ALL THAT HE HAS FOUGHT TO HOLD ON TO FOR ALL OF THIS TIME...IT WILL SLIP AWAY INTO OUR BROKEN STAR, INTO THE ABYSS. LOST..."
P-PLEASE! PLEASE!!

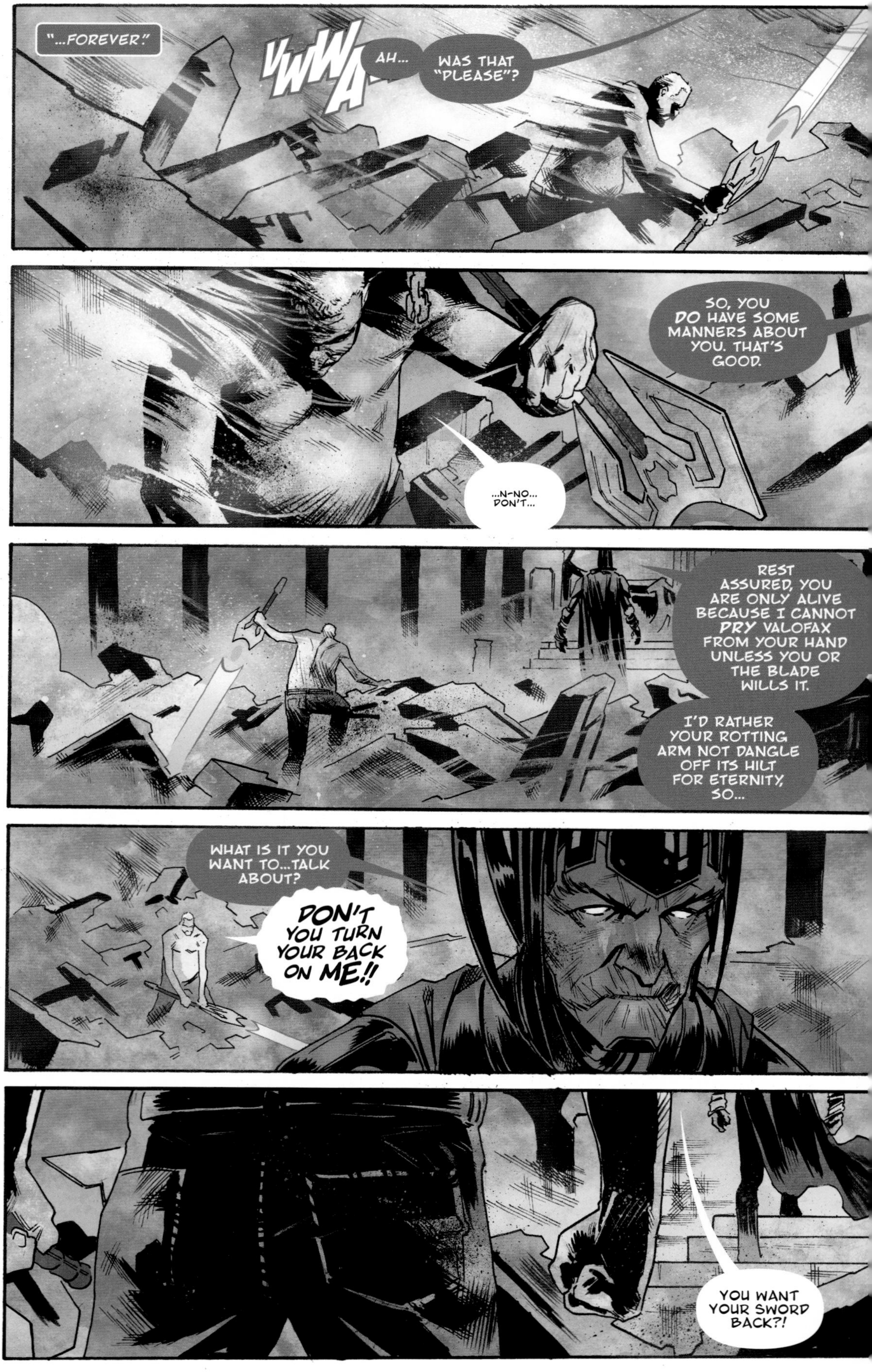
"...FOREVER."
VWWA
AH...
WAS THAT "PLEASE"?
SO, YOU DO HAVE SOME MANNERS ABOUT YOU. THAT'S GOOD.
...N-NO... DON'T...
REST ASSURED, YOU ARE ONLY ALIVE BECAUSE I CANNOT PRY VALOFAX FROM YOUR HAND UNLESS YOU OR THE BLADE WILLS IT.
I'D RATHER YOUR ROTTING ARM NOT DANGLE OFF ITS HILT FOR ETERNITY, SO...
WHAT IS IT YOU WANT TO...TALK ABOUT?
DON'T YOU TURN YOUR BACK ON ME!!
YOU WANT YOUR SWORD BACK?!

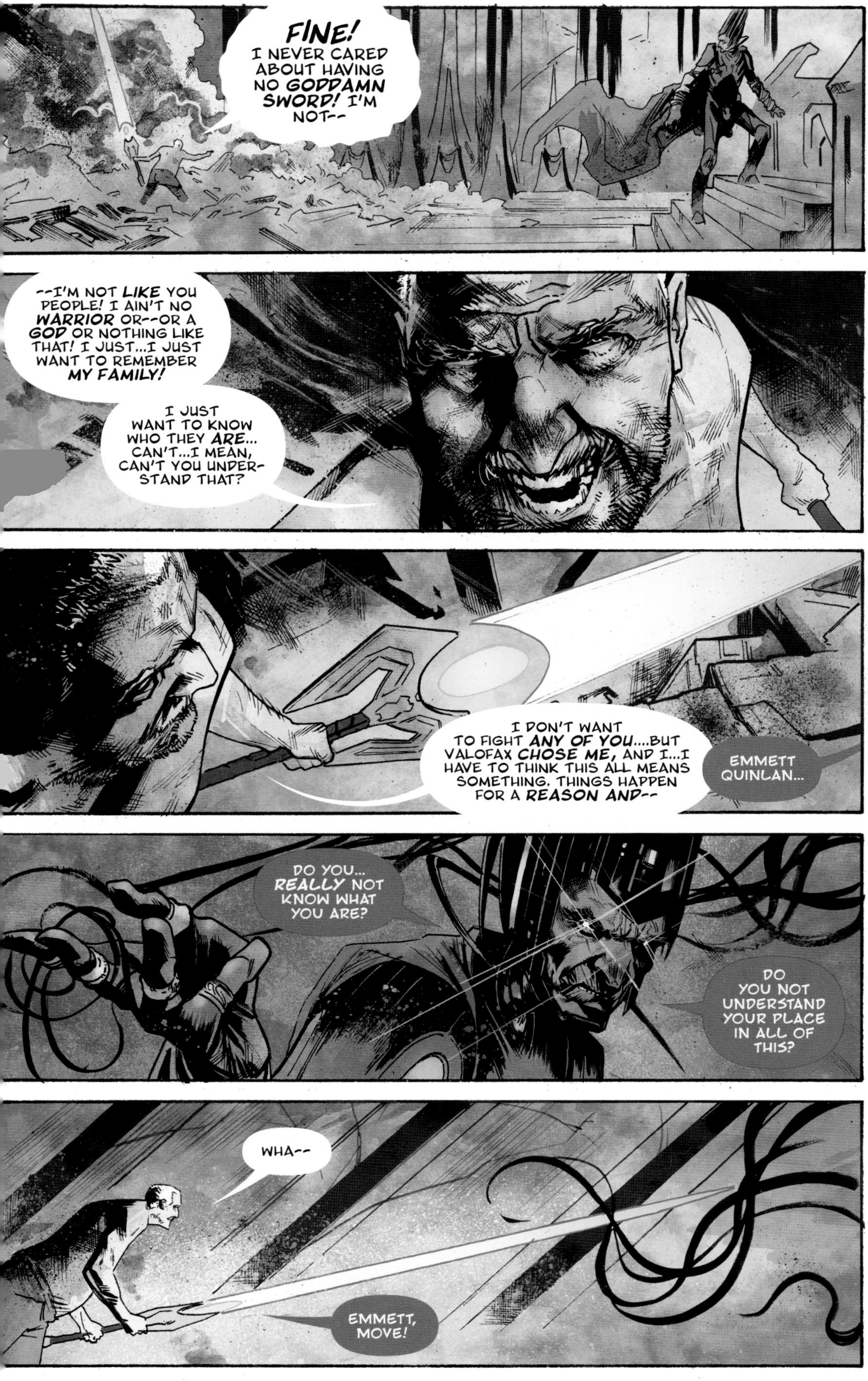
FINE! I NEVER CARED ABOUT HAVING NO GODDAMN SWORD! I'M NOT--
--I'M NOT LIKE YOU PEOPLE! I AIN'T NO WARRIOR OR--OR A GOD OR NOTHING LIKE THAT! I JUST...I JUST WANT TO REMEMBER MY FAMILY!
I JUST WANT TO KNOW WHO THEY ARE... CAN'T...I MEAN, CAN'T YOU UNDERSTAND THAT?
I DON'T WANT TO FIGHT ANY OF YOU....BUT VALOFAX CHOSE ME, AND I...I HAVE TO THINK THIS ALL MEANS SOMETHING. THINGS HAPPEN FOR A REASON AND--
EMMETT QUINLAN...
DO YOU... REALLY NOT KNOW WHAT YOU ARE?
DO YOU NOT UNDERSTAND YOUR PLACE IN ALL OF THIS?
WHA--
EMMETT, MOVE!

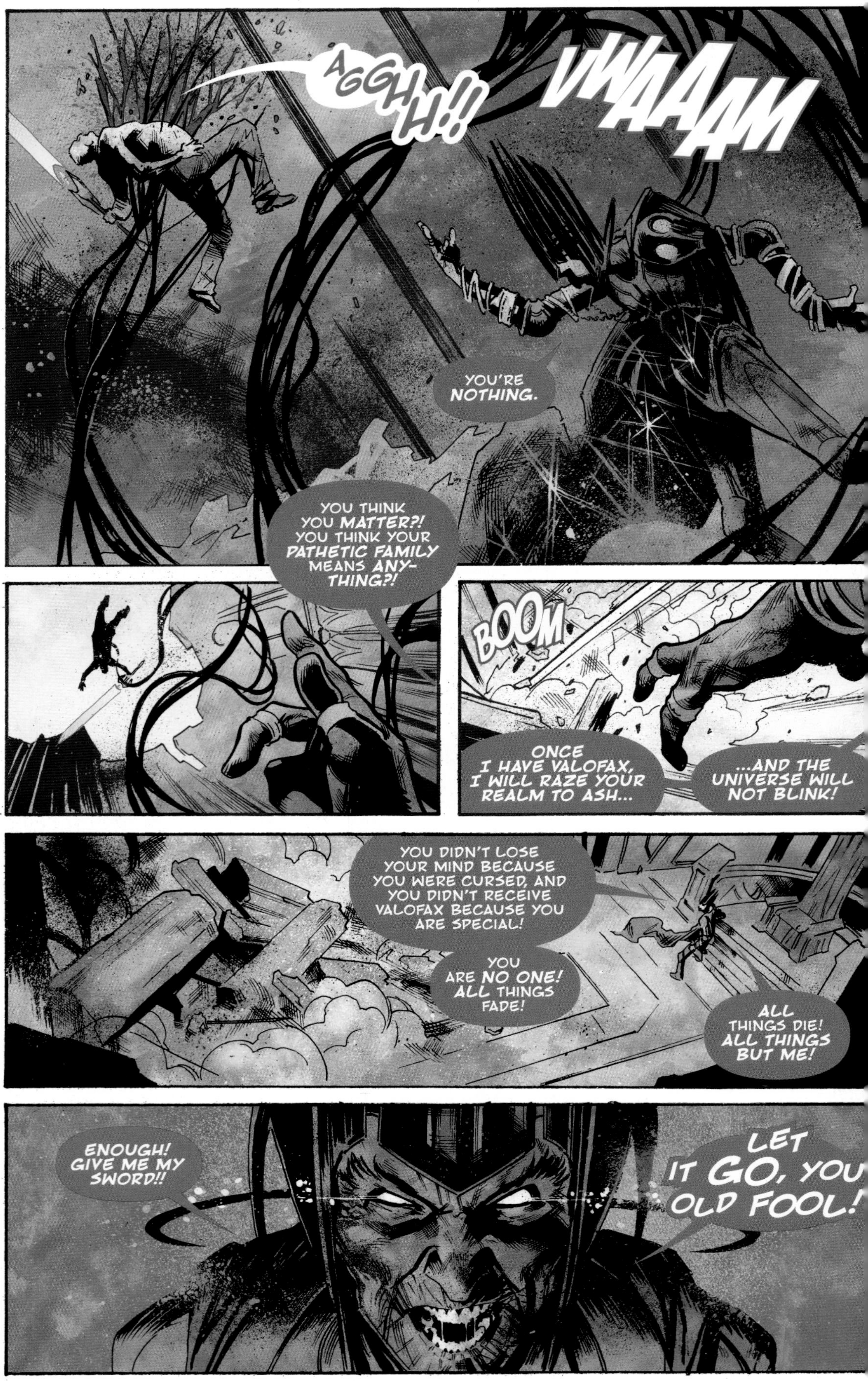
AGGHH!!
VWAAAAM
YOU'RE NOTHING.
YOU THINK YOU MATTER?! YOU THINK YOUR PATHETIC FAMILY MEANS ANY-THING?!
BOOM
ONCE I HAVE VALOFAX, I WILL RAZE YOUR REALM TO ASH...
...AND THE UNIVERSE WILL NOT BLINK!
YOU DIDN'T LOSE YOUR MIND BECAUSE YOU WERE CURSED, AND YOU DIDN'T RECEIVE VALOFAX BECAUSE YOU ARE SPECIAL!
YOU ARE NO ONE! ALL THINGS FADE!
ALL THINGS DIE! ALL THINGS BUT ME!
ENOUGH! GIVE ME MY SWORD!!
LET IT GO, YOU OLD FOOL!

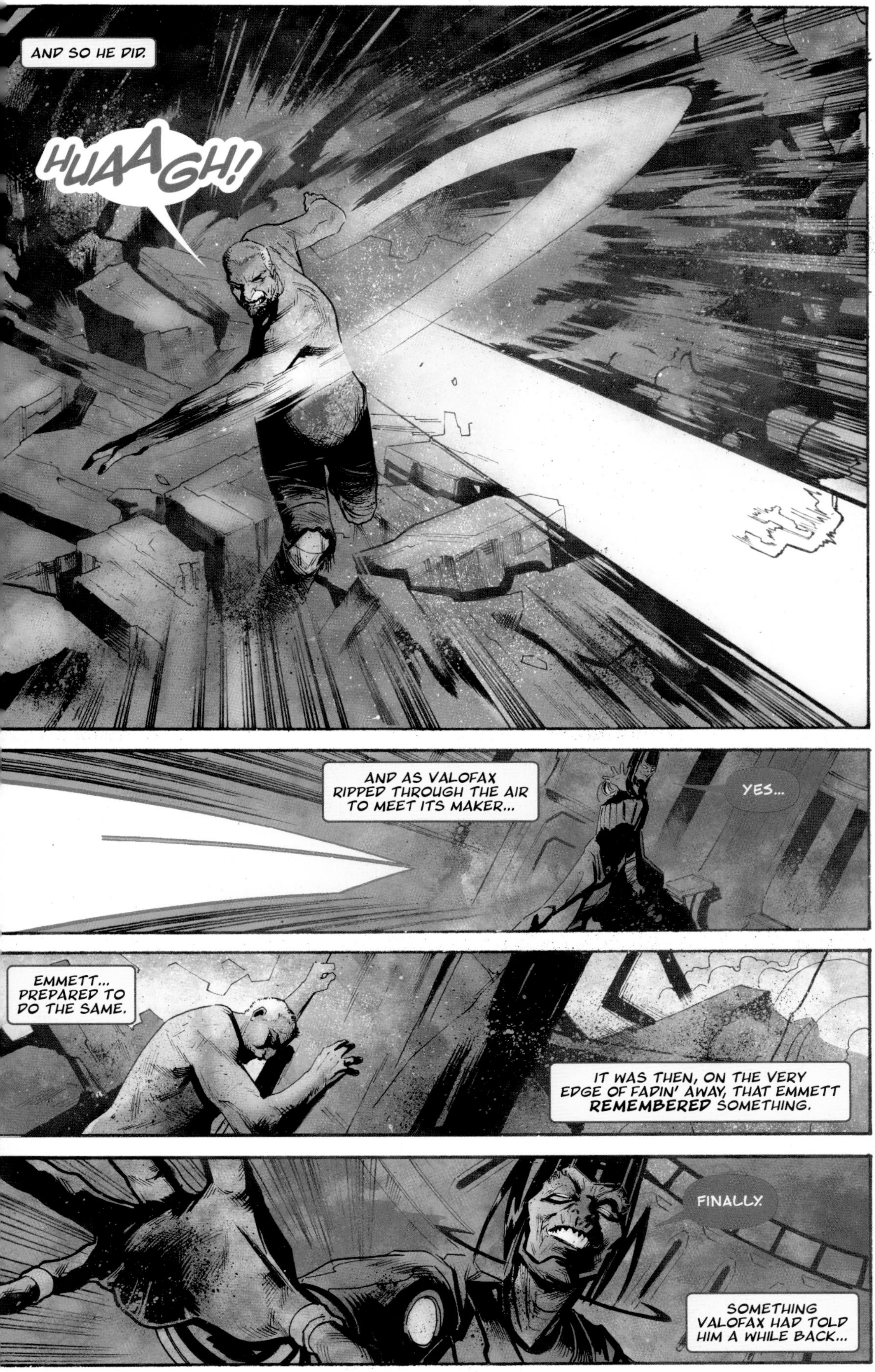
AND SO HE DID.
HUAAAGH!
AND AS VALOFAX RIPPED THROUGH THE AIR TO MEET ITS MAKER...
YES...
EMMETT... PREPARED TO DO THE SAME.
IT WAS THEN, ON THE VERY EDGE OF FADIN' AWAY, THAT EMMETT REMEMBERED SOMETHING.
FINALLY.
SOMETHING VALOFAX HAD TOLD HIM A WHILE BACK...

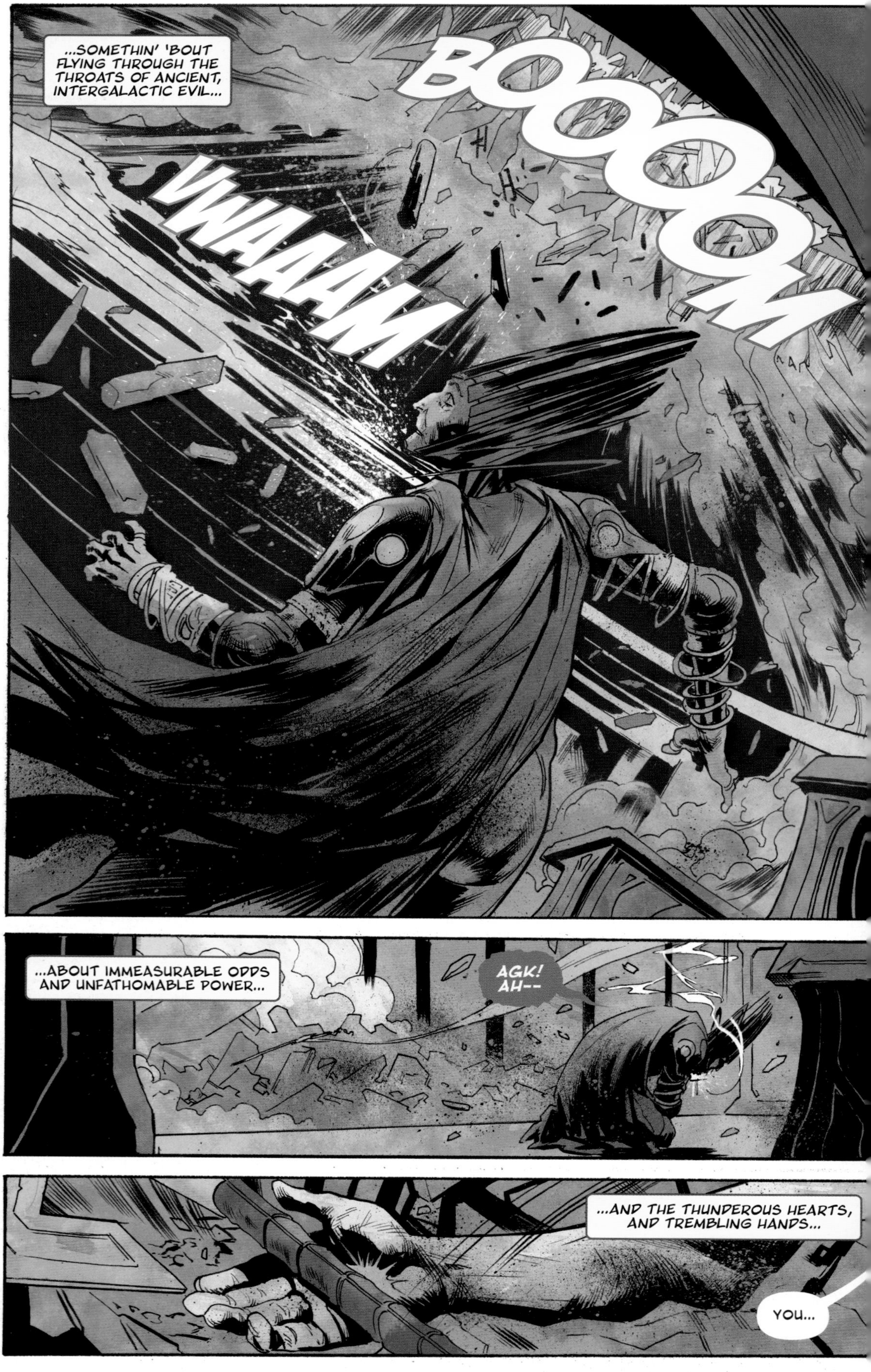
...SOMETHIN' 'BOUT FLYING THROUGH THE THROATS OF ANCIENT, INTERGALACTIC EVIL...
BOOOOOM
VWAAAM
...ABOUT IMMEASURABLE ODDS AND UNFATHOMABLE POWER...
AGK! AH--
...AND THE THUNDEROUS HEARTS, AND TREMBLING HANDS...
YOU...

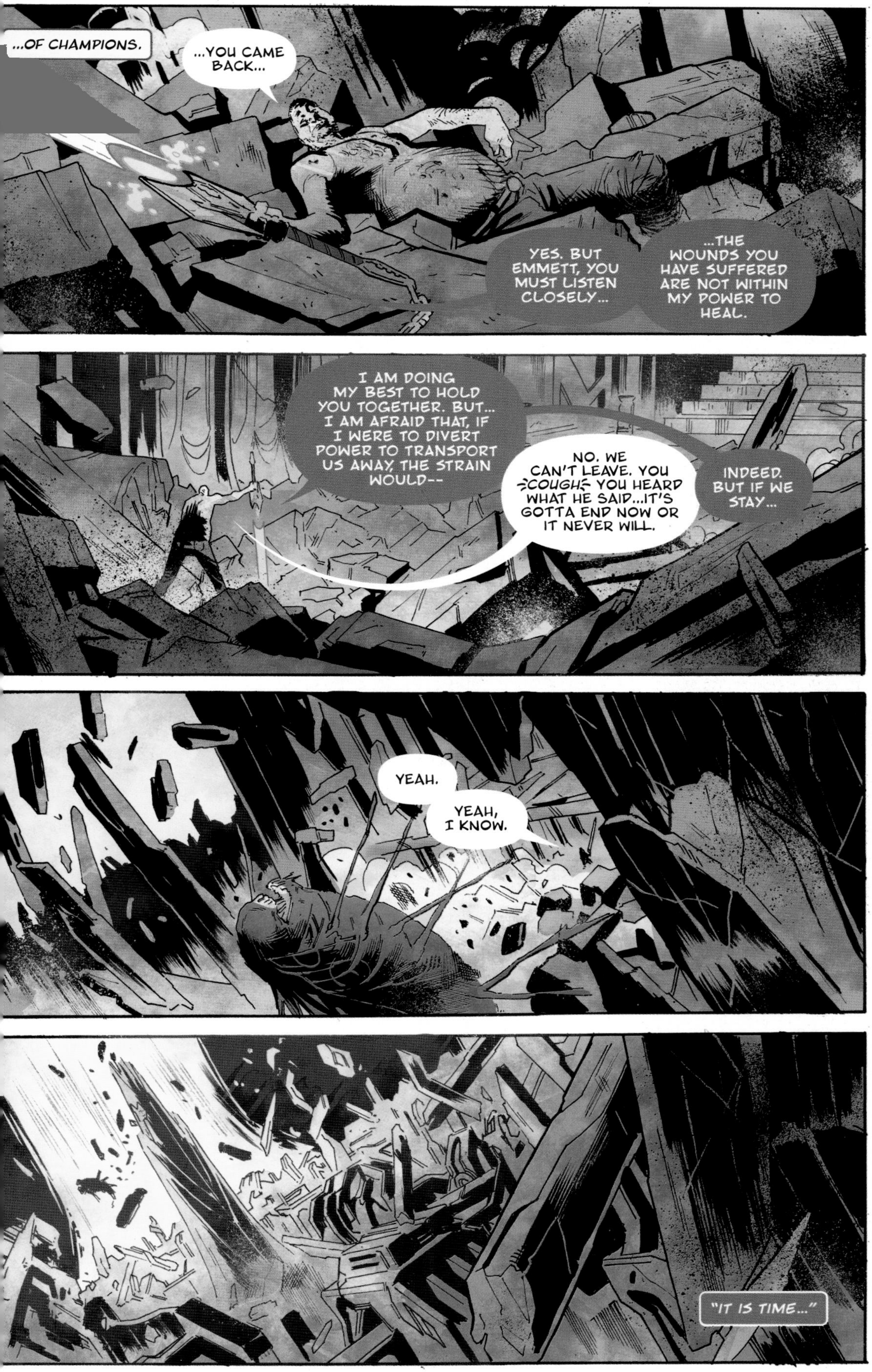
...OF CHAMPIONS.
...YOU CAME BACK...
YES. BUT EMMETT, YOU MUST LISTEN CLOSELY...
...THE WOUNDS YOU HAVE SUFFERED ARE NOT WITHIN MY POWER TO HEAL.
I AM DOING MY BEST TO HOLD YOU TOGETHER. BUT... I AM AFRAID THAT, IF I WERE TO DIVERT POWER TO TRANSPORT US AWAY, THE STRAIN WOULD--
NO. WE CAN'T LEAVE. YOU *COUGH* YOU HEARD WHAT HE SAID...IT'S GOTTA END NOW OR IT NEVER WILL.
INDEED. BUT IF WE STAY...
YEAH.
YEAH, I KNOW.
"IT IS TIME..."

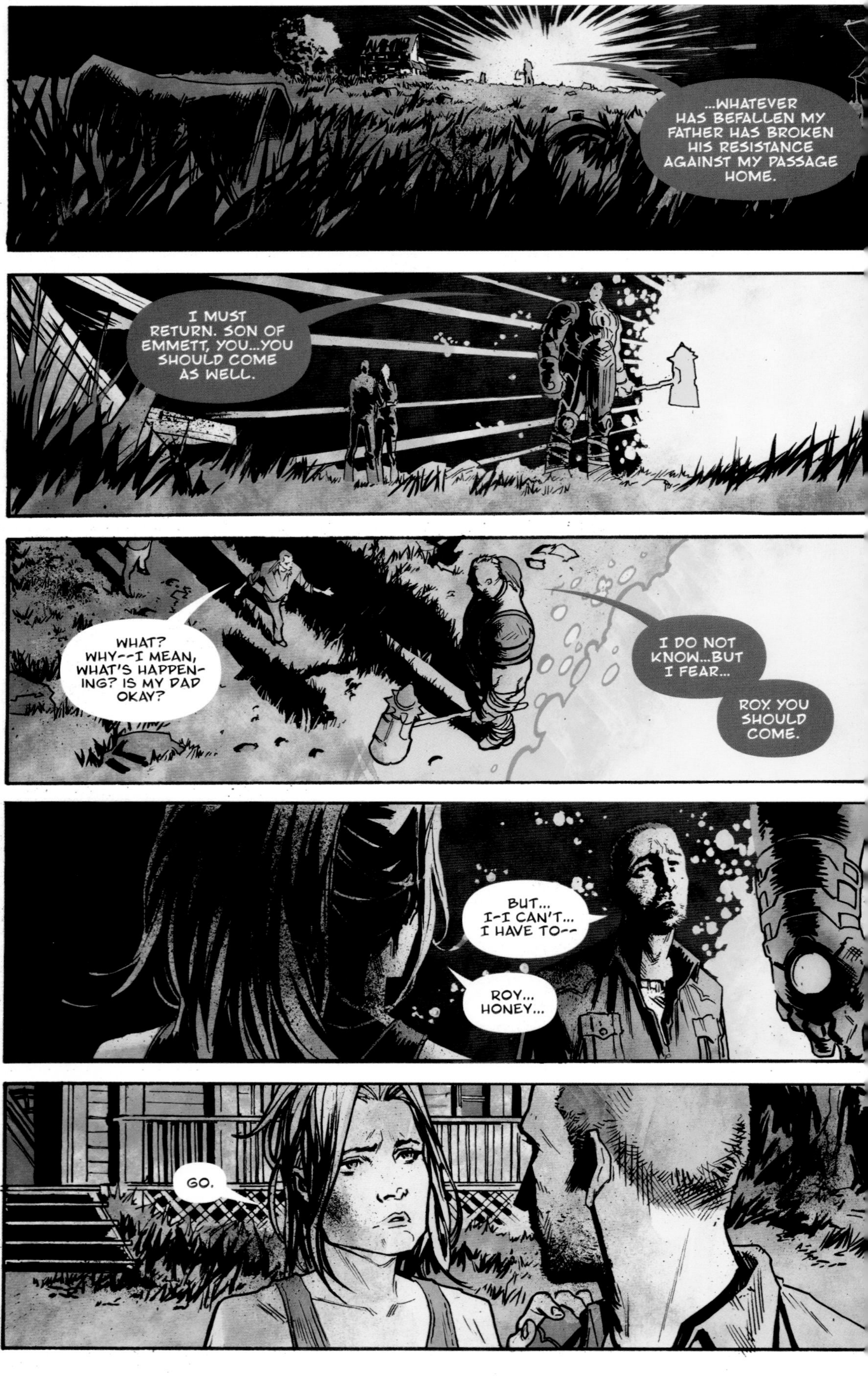
...WHATEVER HAS BEFALLEN MY FATHER HAS BROKEN HIS RESISTANCE AGAINST MY PASSAGE HOME.
I MUST RETURN. SON OF EMMETT, YOU...YOU SHOULD COME AS WELL.
WHAT? WHY--I MEAN, WHAT'S HAPPENING? IS MY DAD OKAY?
I DO NOT KNOW...BUT I FEAR...
ROY. YOU SHOULD COME.
BUT... I-I CAN'T... I HAVE TO--
ROY... HONEY...
GO.

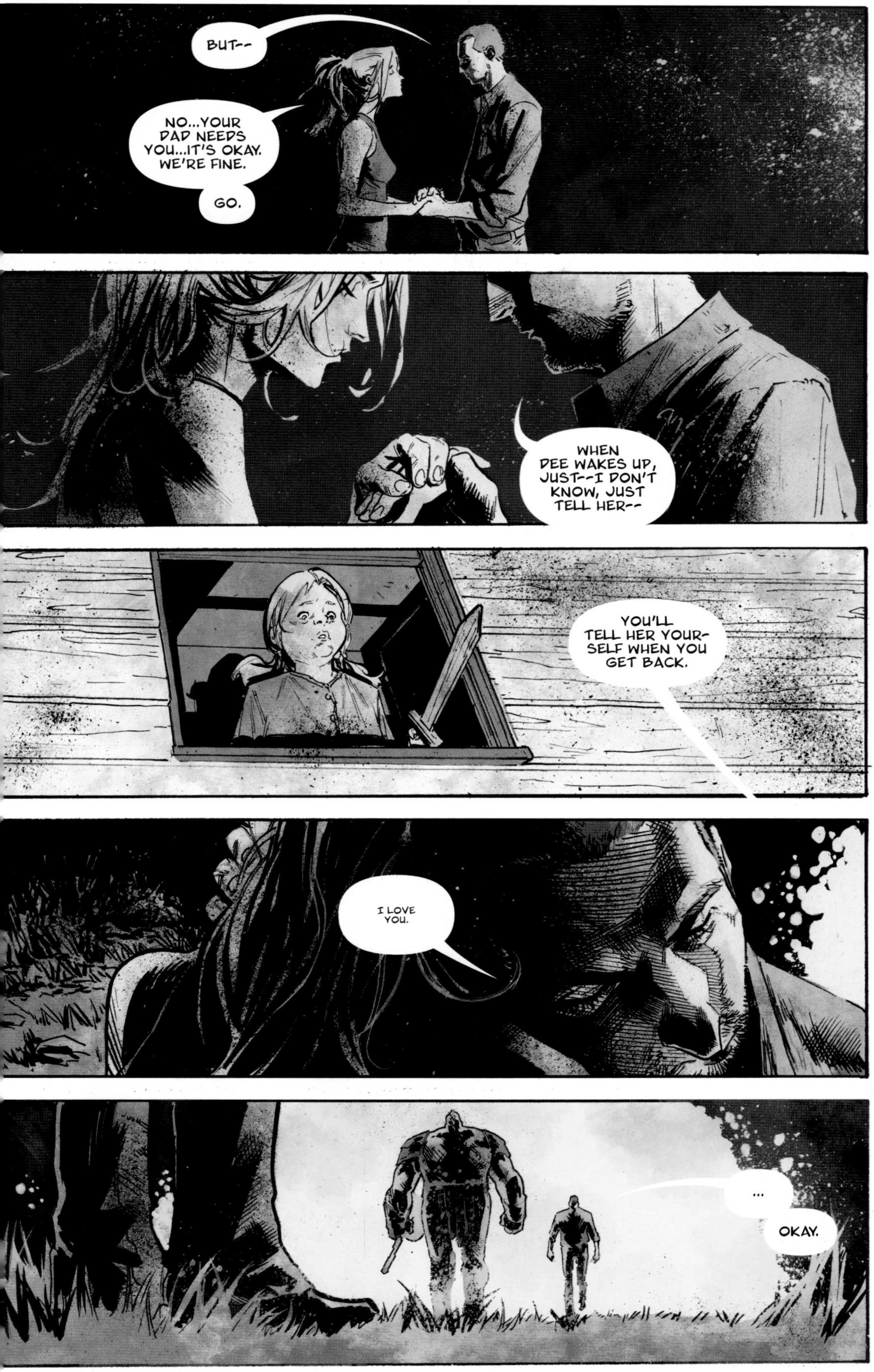
BUT--
NO...YOUR DAD NEEDS YOU...IT'S OKAY. WE'RE FINE.
GO.
WHEN DEE WAKES UP, JUST--I DON'T KNOW, JUST TELL HER--
YOU'LL TELL HER YOURSELF WHEN YOU GET BACK.
I LOVE YOU.
...
OKAY.

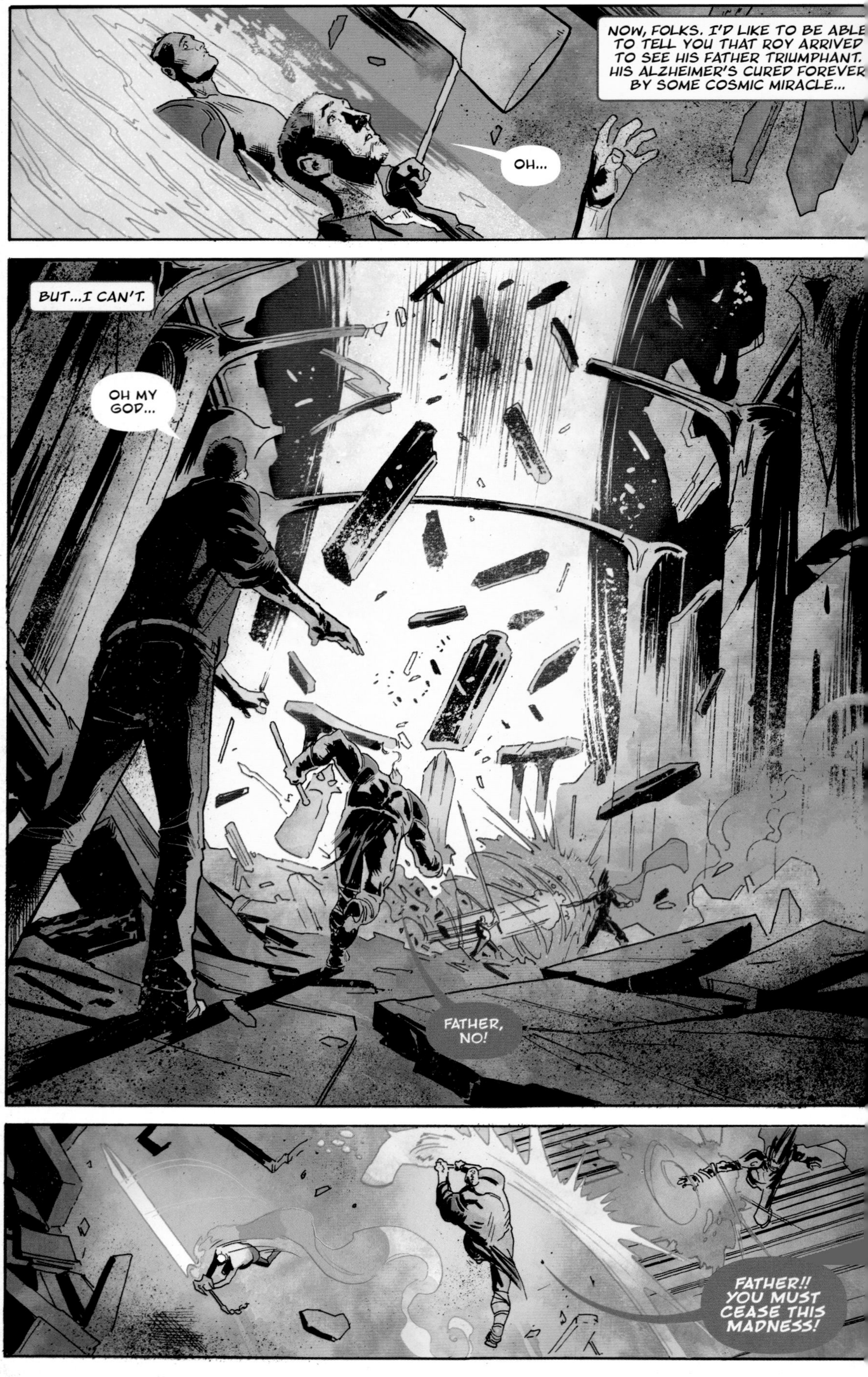
NOW, FOLKS. I'D LIKE TO BE ABLE TO TELL YOU THAT ROY ARRIVED TO SEE HIS FATHER TRIUMPHANT. HIS ALZHEIMER'S CURED FOREVER BY SOME COSMIC MIRACLE...
OH...
BUT...I CAN'T.
OH MY GOD...
FATHER, NO!
FATHER!! YOU MUST CEASE THIS MADNESS!

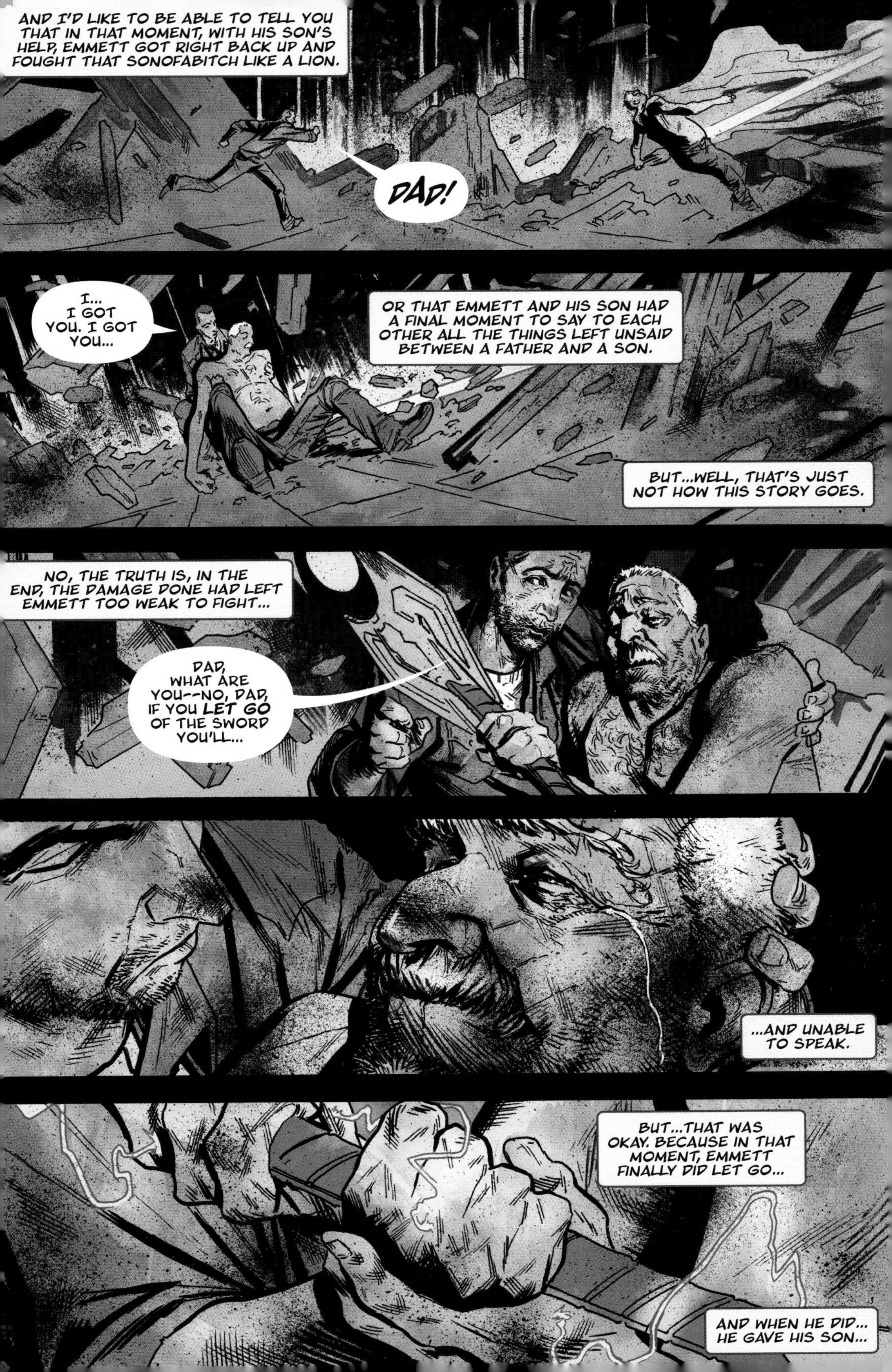
AND I'D LIKE TO BE ABLE TO TELL YOU THAT IN THAT MOMENT, WITH HIS SON'S HELP, EMMETT GOT RIGHT BACK UP AND FOUGHT THAT SONOFABITCH LIKE A LION.
DAD!
I... I GOT YOU. I GOT YOU...
OR THAT EMMETT AND HIS SON HAD A FINAL MOMENT TO SAY TO EACH OTHER ALL THE THINGS LEFT UNSAID BETWEEN A FATHER AND A SON.
BUT...WELL, THAT'S JUST NOT HOW THIS STORY GOES.
NO, THE TRUTH IS, IN THE END, THE DAMAGE DONE HAD LEFT EMMETT TOO WEAK TO FIGHT...
DAD, WHAT ARE YOU--NO, DAD, IF YOU **LET GO** OF THE SWORD YOU'LL...
...AND UNABLE TO SPEAK.
BUT...THAT WAS OKAY. BECAUSE IN THAT MOMENT, EMMETT FINALLY DID LET GO...
AND WHEN HE DID... HE GAVE HIS SON...

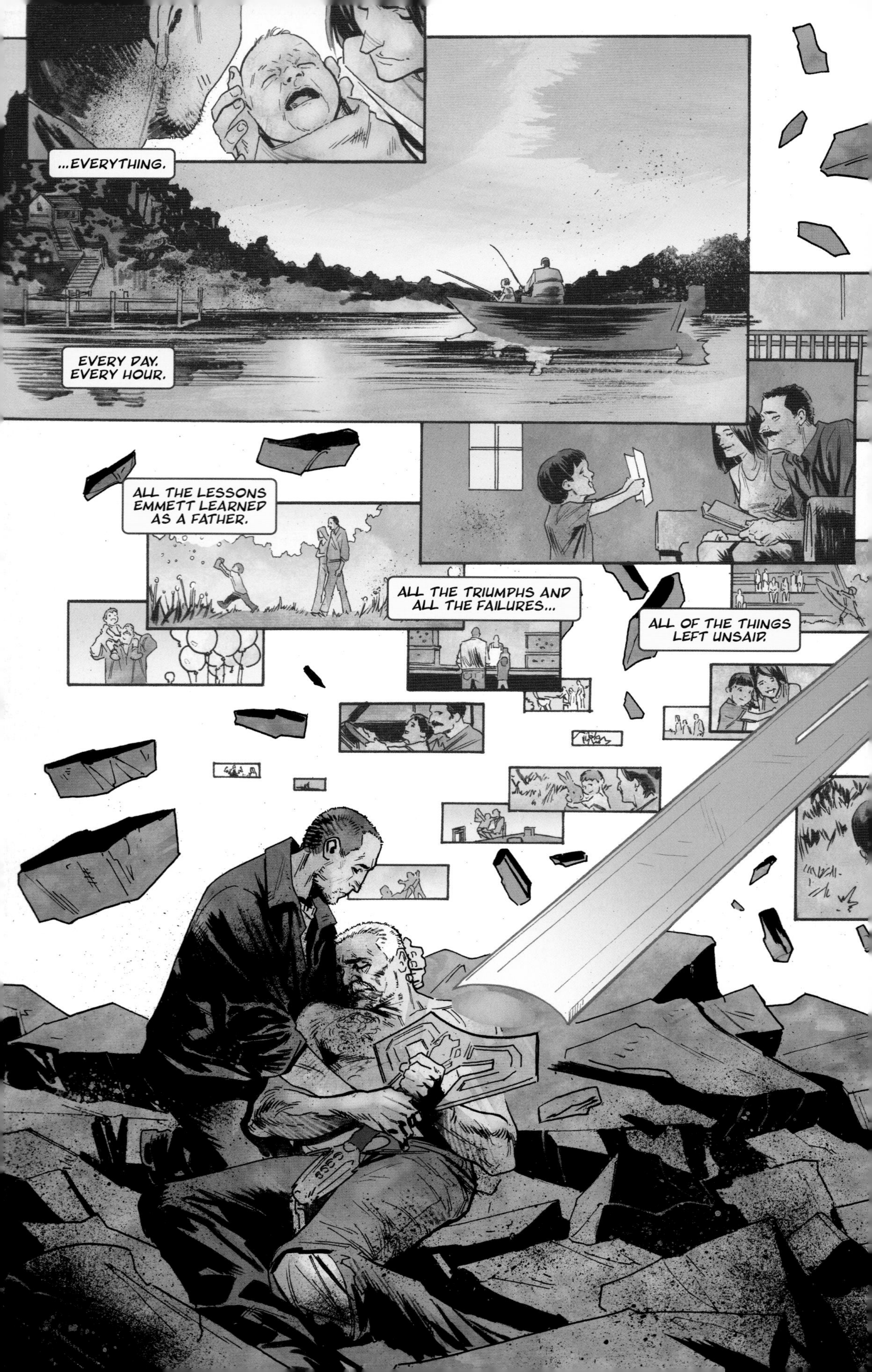
...EVERYTHING.
EVERY DAY. EVERY HOUR.
ALL THE LESSONS EMMETT LEARNED AS A FATHER.
ALL THE TRIUMPHS AND ALL THE FAILURES...
ALL OF THE THINGS LEFT UNSAID.

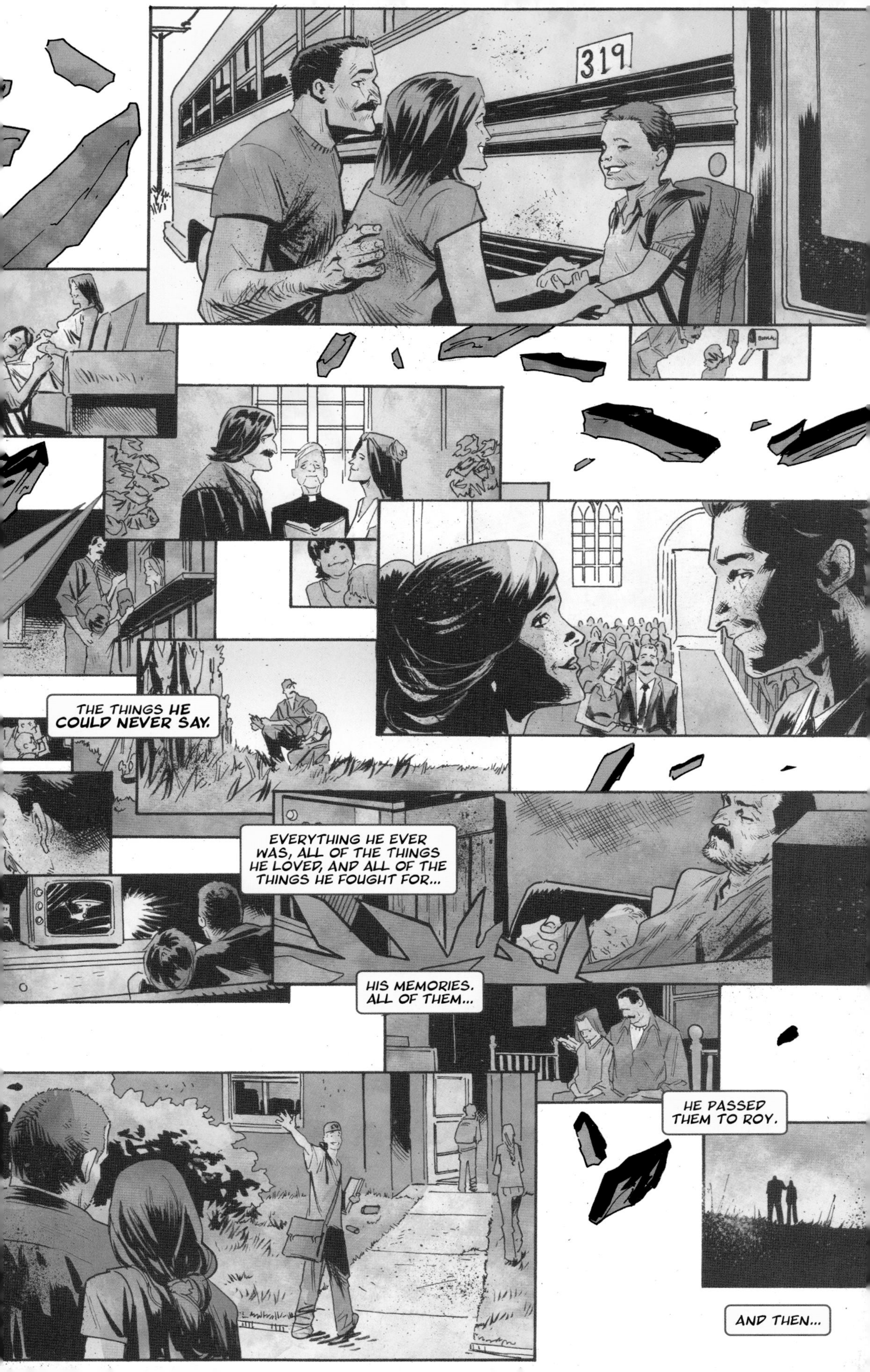
319
THE THINGS HE COULD NEVER SAY.
EVERYTHING HE EVER WAS, ALL OF THE THINGS HE LOVED, AND ALL OF THE THINGS HE FOUGHT FOR...
HIS MEMORIES. ALL OF THEM...
HE PASSED THEM TO ROY.
AND THEN...

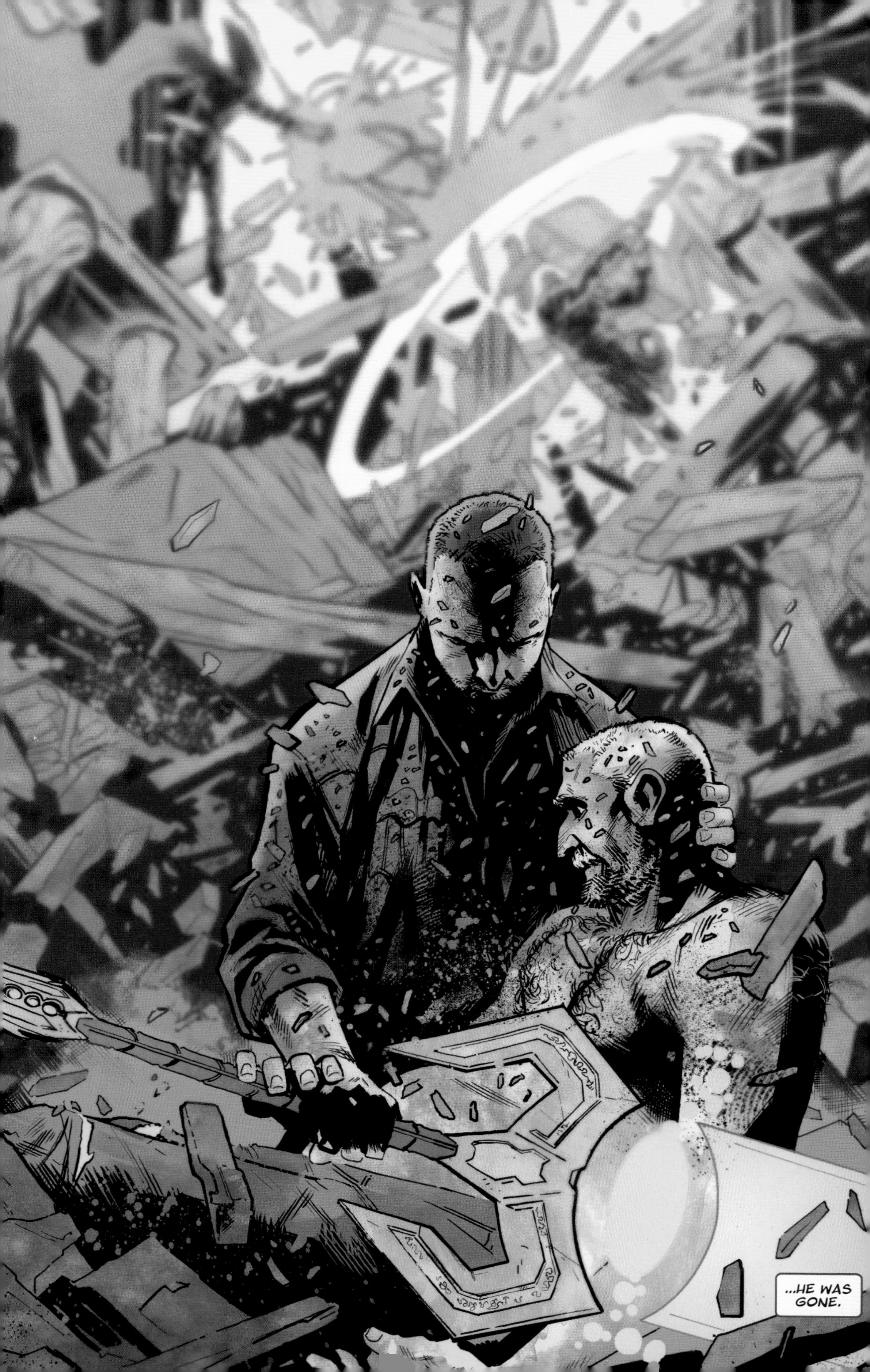
...HE WAS GONE.

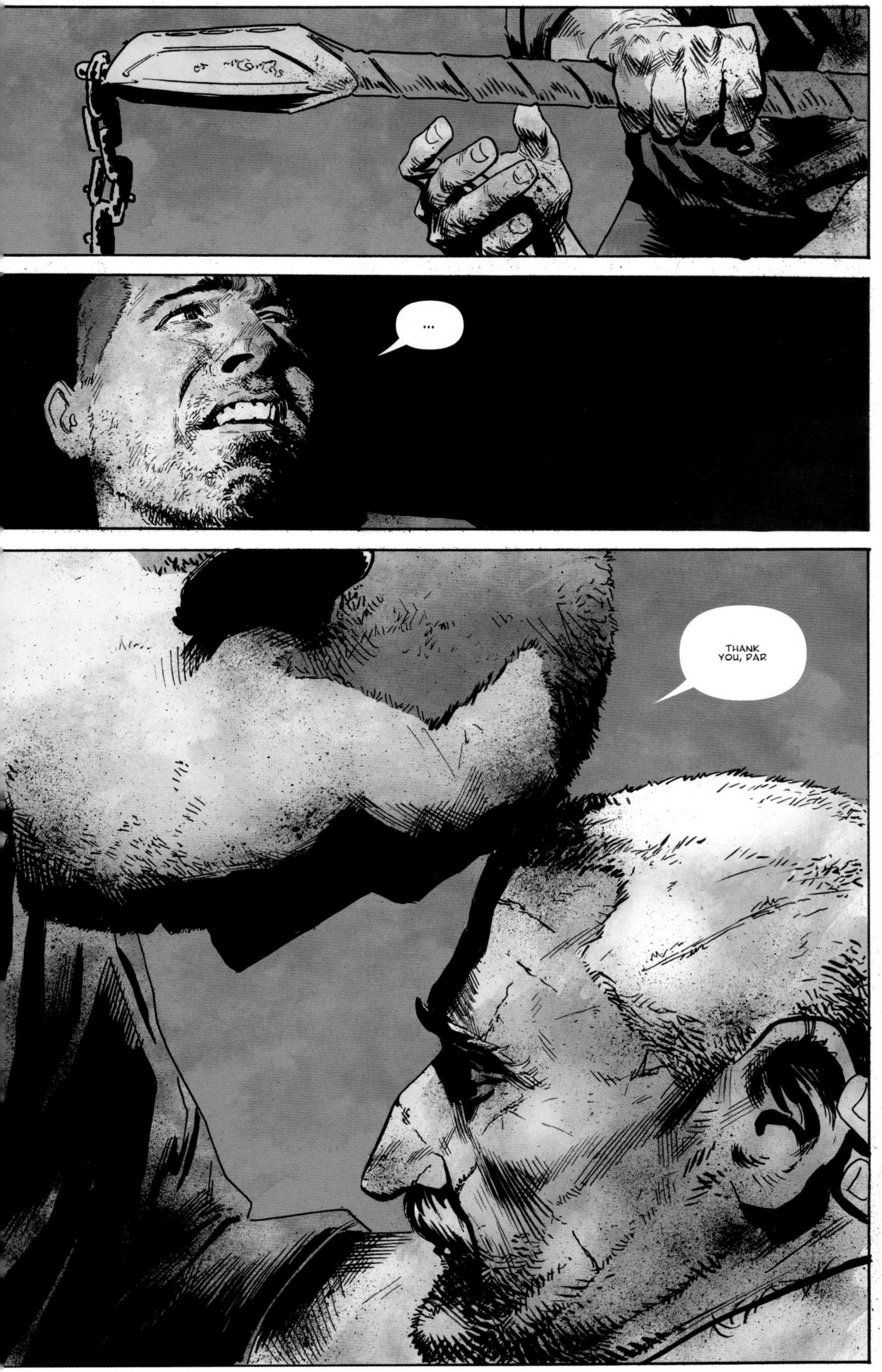
...
THANK YOU, DAD.

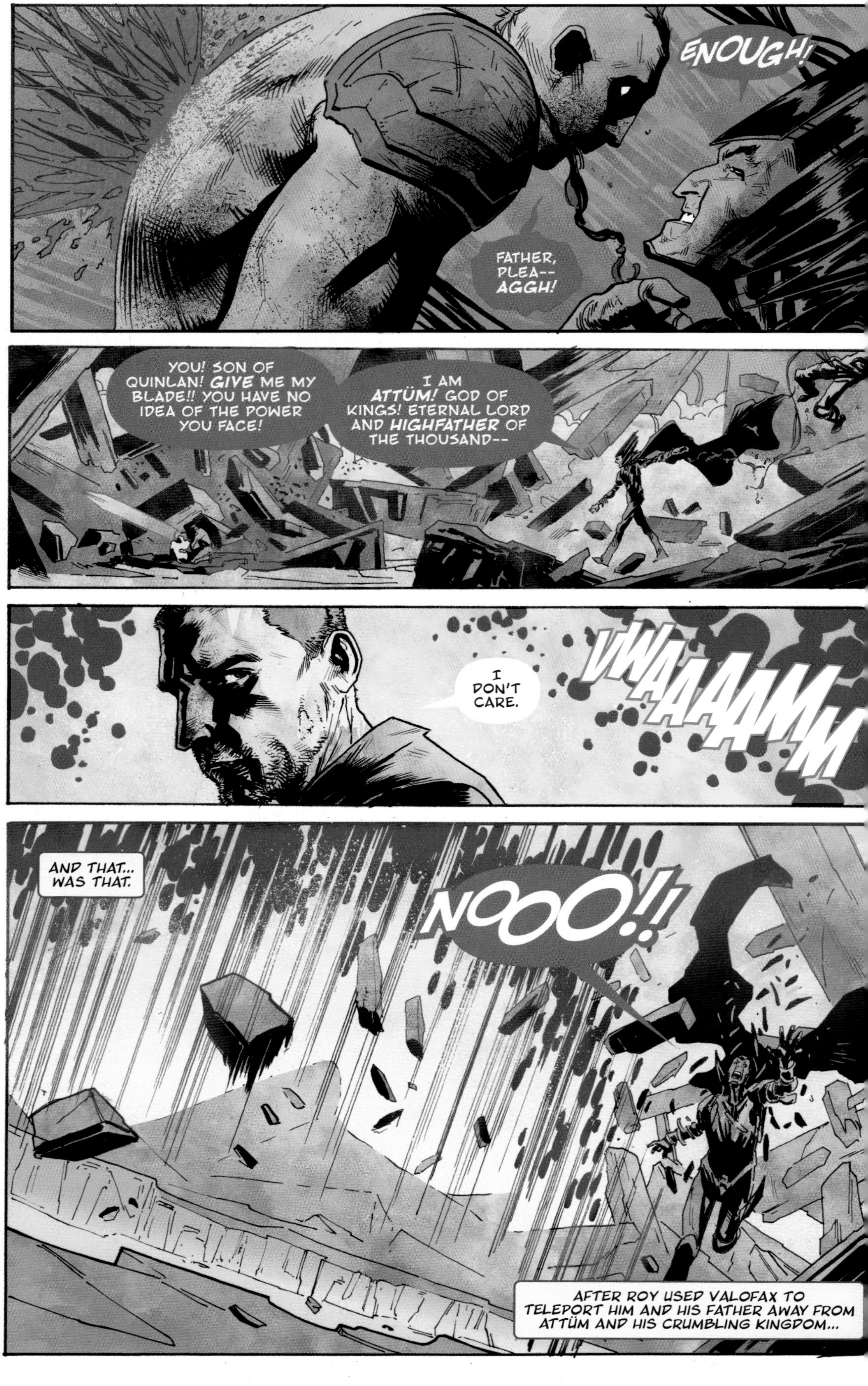
ENOUGH!
FATHER, PLEA-- AGGH!
YOU! SON OF QUINLAN! GIVE ME MY BLADE!! YOU HAVE NO IDEA OF THE POWER YOU FACE!
I AM ATTÜM! GOD OF KINGS! ETERNAL LORD AND HIGHFATHER OF THE THOUSAND--
I DON'T CARE.
VWAAAAAMMM
AND THAT... WAS THAT.
NOOO!!
AFTER ROY USED VALOFAX TO TELEPORT HIM AND HIS FATHER AWAY FROM ATTÜM AND HIS CRUMBLING KINGDOM...

...THE QUINLANS NEVER HEARD FROM THE GODS EVER AGAIN.

AS THE KINGDOM OF ALWAYS SHATTERED AND FADED AWAY INTO THE BLACK...THAT PART OF THE STORY ENDED RIGHT THEN AND THERE...

AND FOR WHAT IT'S WORTH, FOLKS...

I'M SORRY.

I NEVER SAID THIS WAS A HAPPY STORY, ONLY THAT IT WAS TRUE.

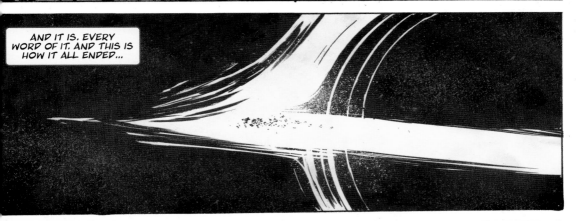

AND IT IS. EVERY WORD OF IT. AND THIS IS HOW IT ALL ENDED...

WITH A FALLEN KINGDOM, A SON...

...A SWORD...

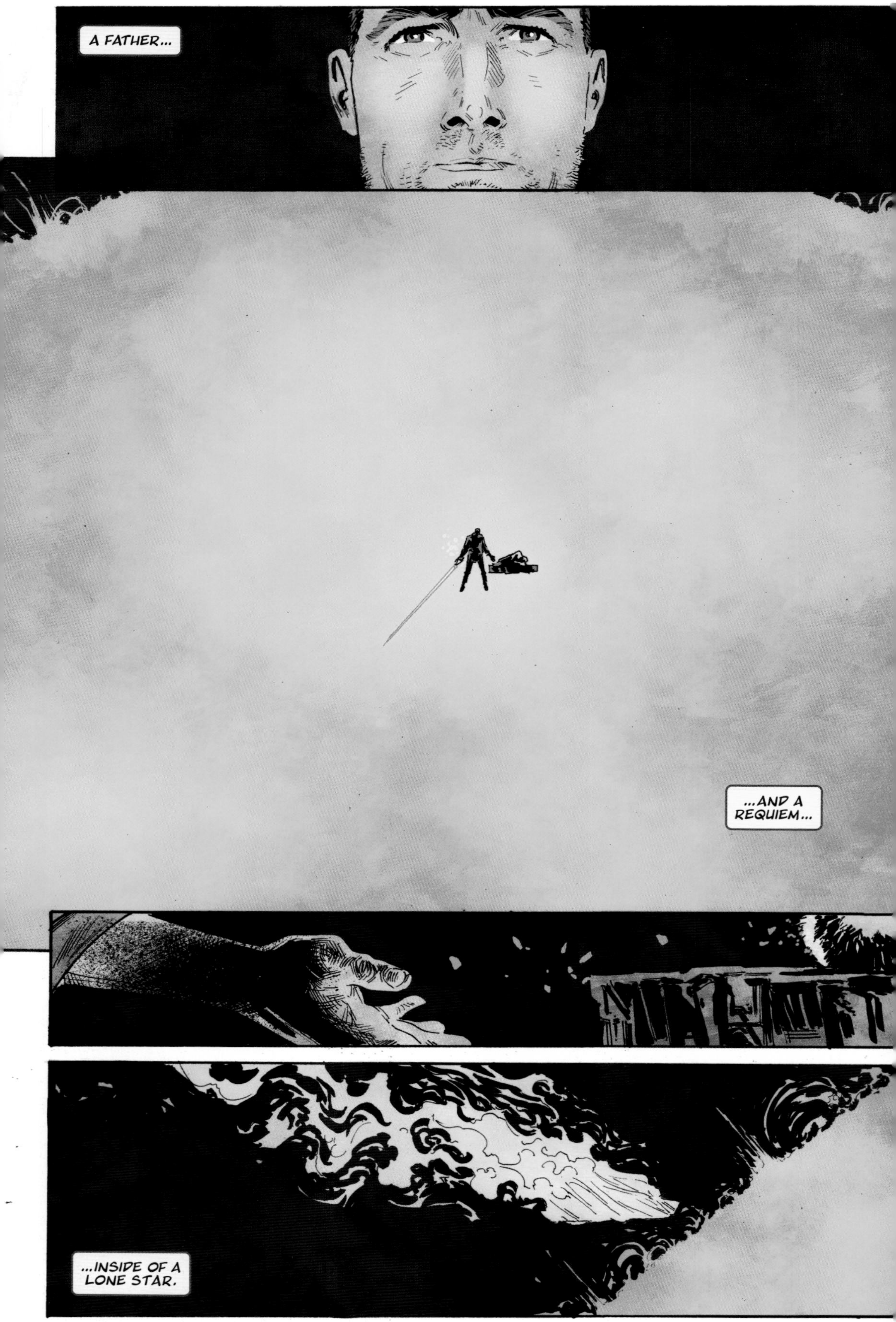
A FATHER...
...AND A REQUIEM...
...INSIDE OF A LONE STAR.

AS FOR VALOFAX...WELL, THIS IS PROBABLY GOING TO RILE MORE THAN A FEW OF YOU FOLKS...

...BUT THEY NEVER SAW IT AGAIN, NEITHER.

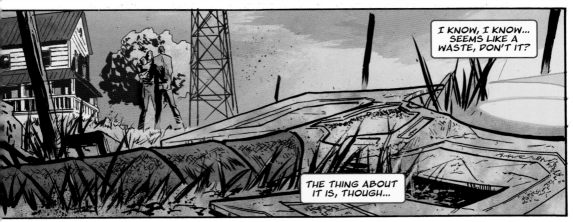

I KNOW, I KNOW... SEEMS LIKE A WASTE, DON'T IT?

THE THING ABOUT IT IS, THOUGH...

THIS NEVER REALLY WAS A STORY ABOUT A MAGIC SWORD.

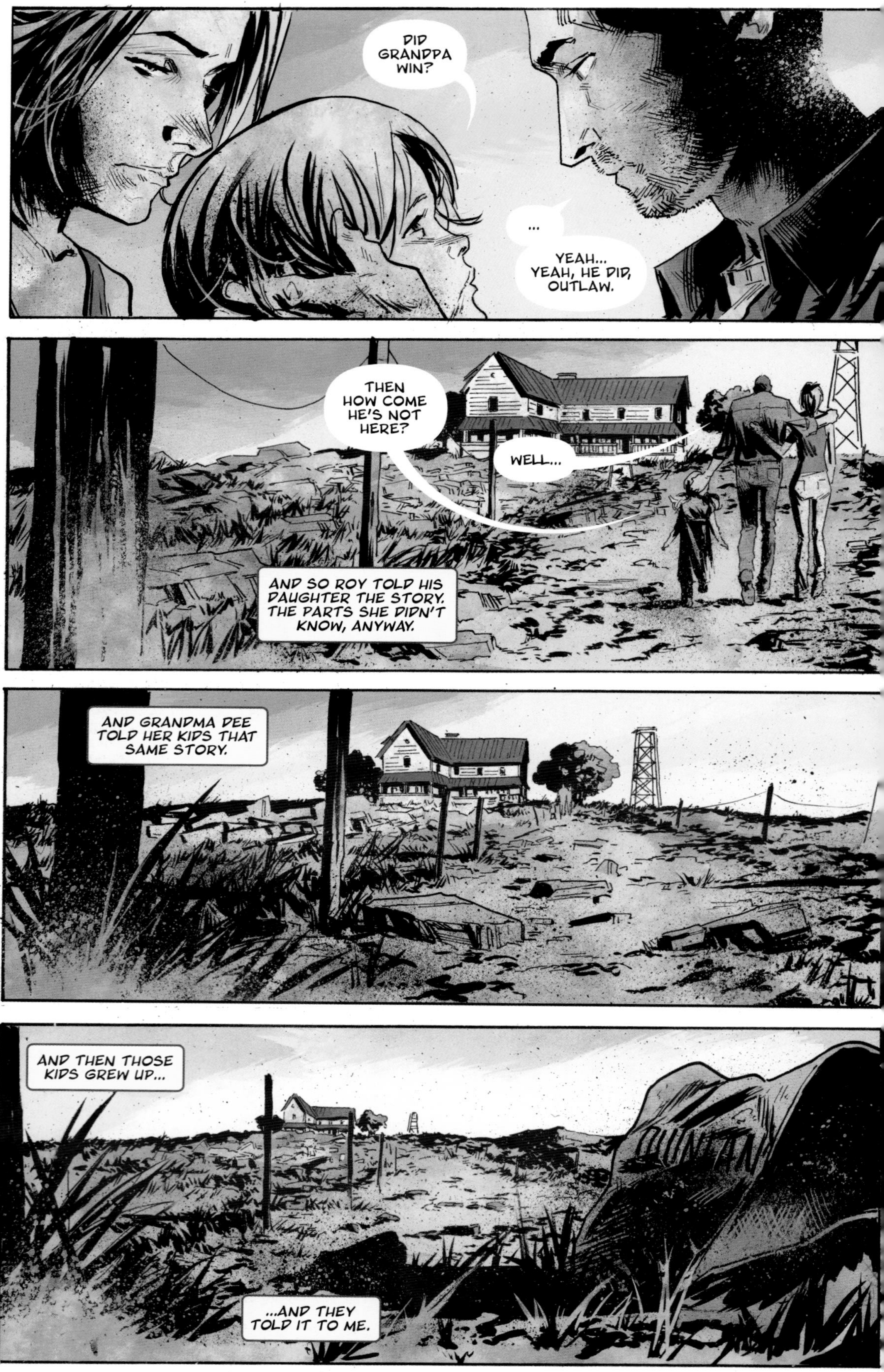
DID GRANDPA WIN?
...
YEAH... YEAH, HE DID, OUTLAW.
THEN HOW COME HE'S NOT HERE?
WELL...
AND SO ROY TOLD HIS DAUGHTER THE STORY. THE PARTS SHE DIDN'T KNOW, ANYWAY.
AND GRANDMA DEE TOLD HER KIDS THAT SAME STORY.
AND THEN THOSE KIDS GREW UP...
...AND THEY TOLD IT TO ME.

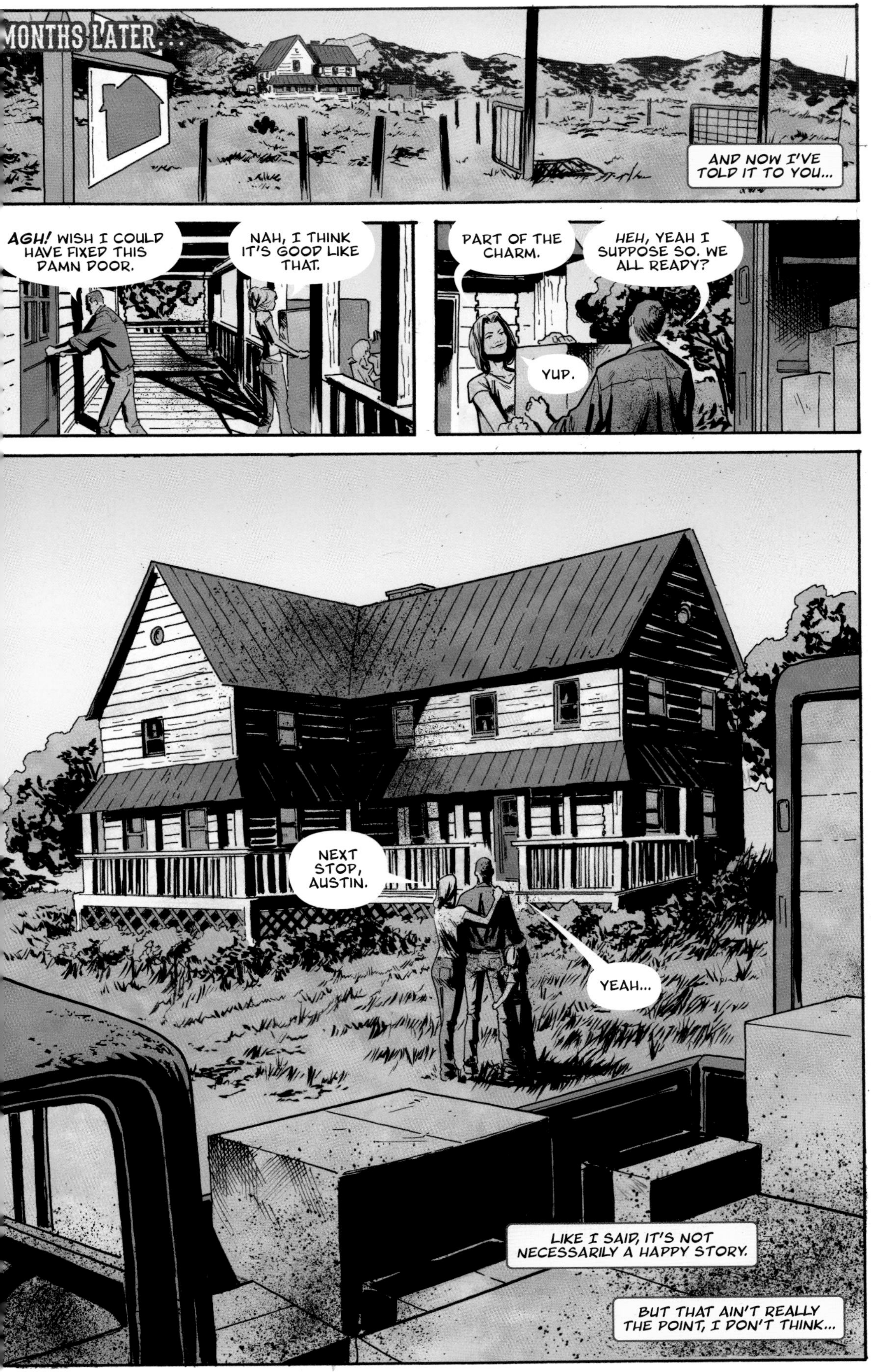
MONTHS LATER...
AND NOW I'VE TOLD IT TO YOU...
AGH! WISH I COULD HAVE FIXED THIS DAMN DOOR.
NAH, I THINK IT'S GOOD LIKE THAT.
PART OF THE CHARM.
HEH, YEAH I SUPPOSE SO. WE ALL READY?
YUP.
NEXT STOP, AUSTIN.
YEAH...
LIKE I SAID, IT'S NOT NECESSARILY A HAPPY STORY.
BUT THAT AIN'T REALLY THE POINT, I DON'T THINK...

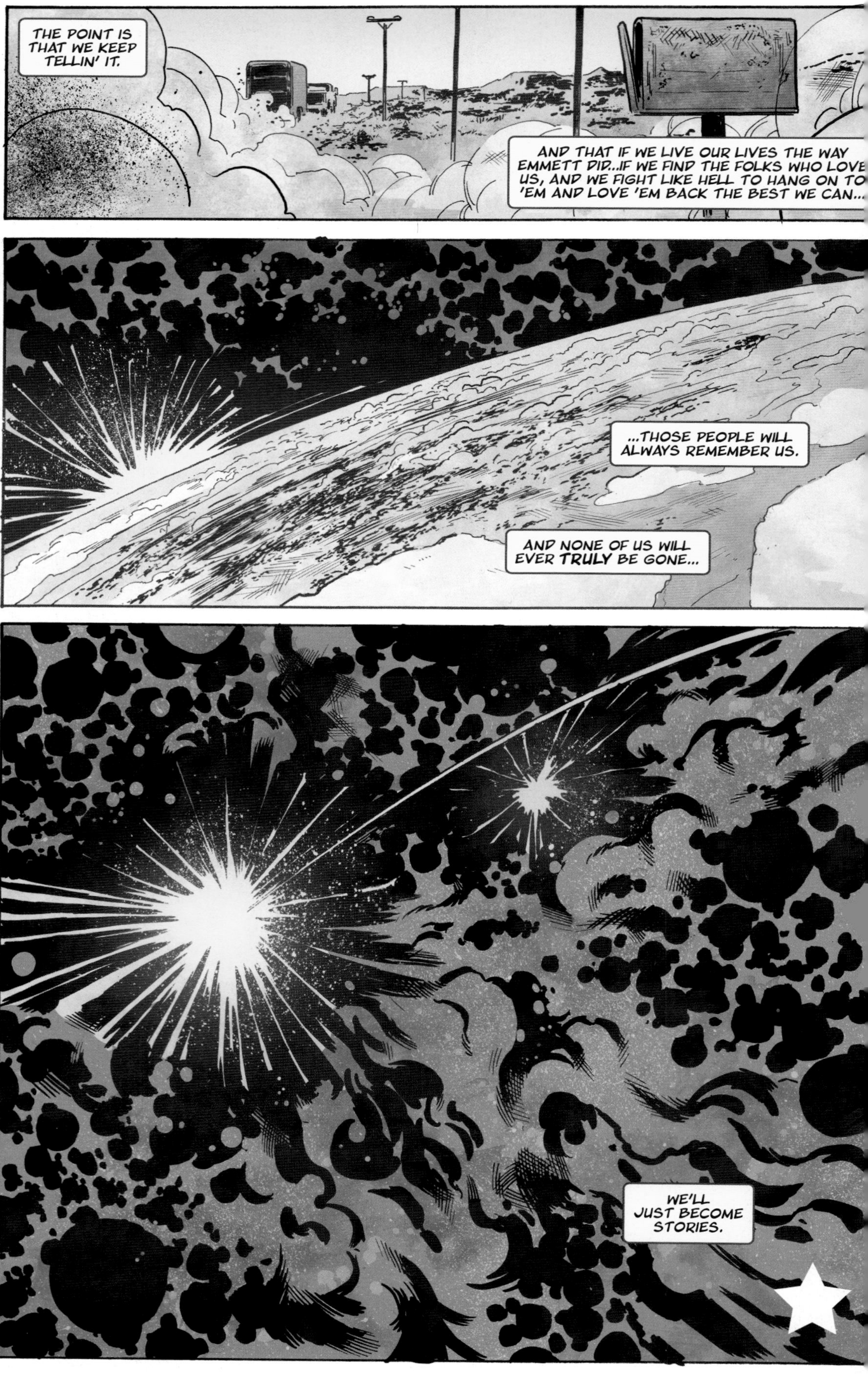
THE POINT IS THAT WE KEEP TELLIN' IT.
AND THAT IF WE LIVE OUR LIVES THE WAY EMMETT DID...IF WE FIND THE FOLKS WHO LOVE US, AND WE FIGHT LIKE HELL TO HANG ON TO 'EM AND LOVE 'EM BACK THE BEST WE CAN...
...THOSE PEOPLE WILL ALWAYS REMEMBER US.
AND NONE OF US WILL EVER TRULY BE GONE...
WE'LL JUST BECOME STORIES.

EXTRAS

VARIANT COVERS / PIN-UPS / DEVELOPMENT & DESIGNS / PROCESS / BIOS

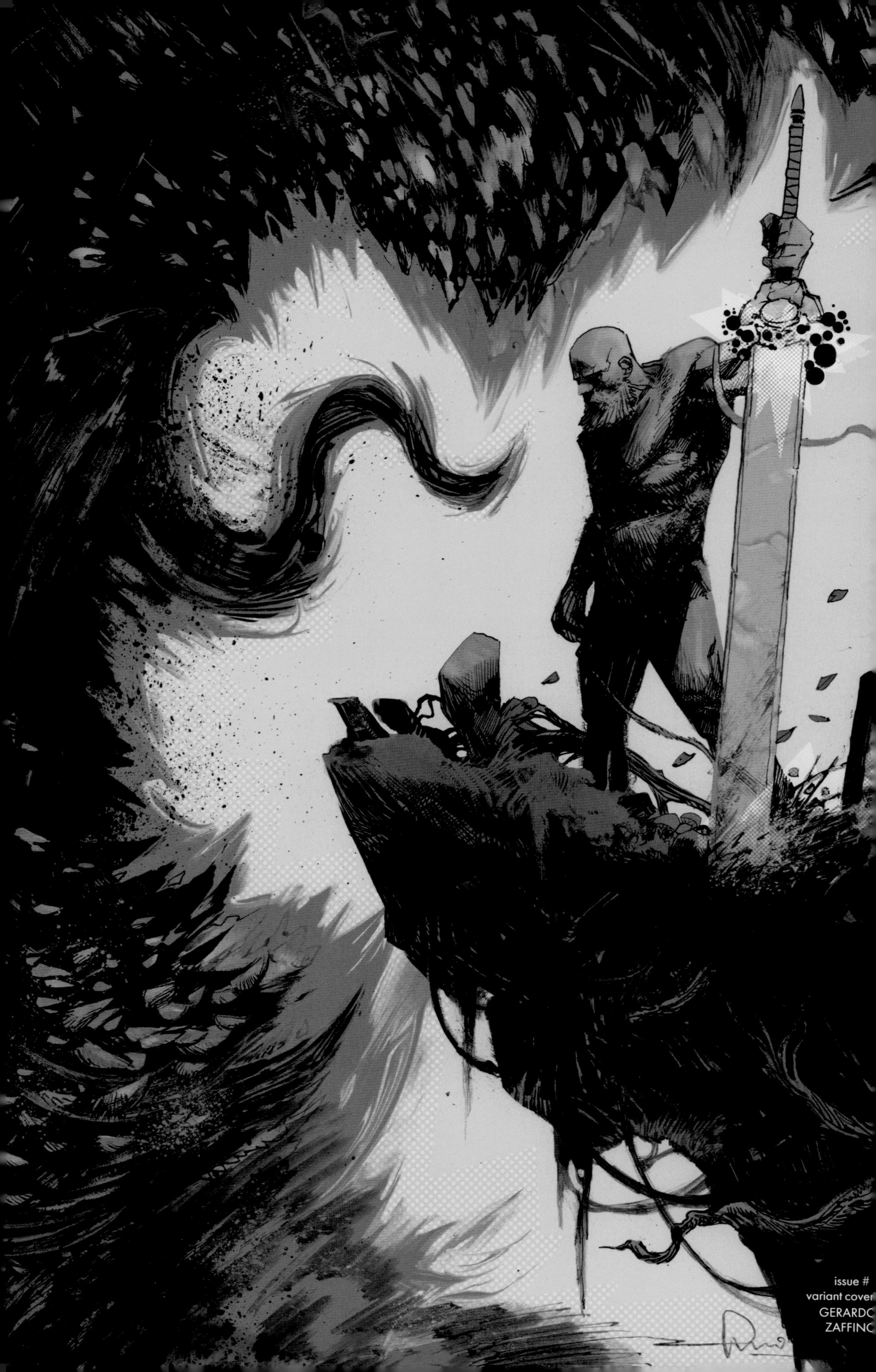

issue #
variant cover
GERARDO
ZAFFINO

issue #1 reprint cover:
GEOFF SHAW

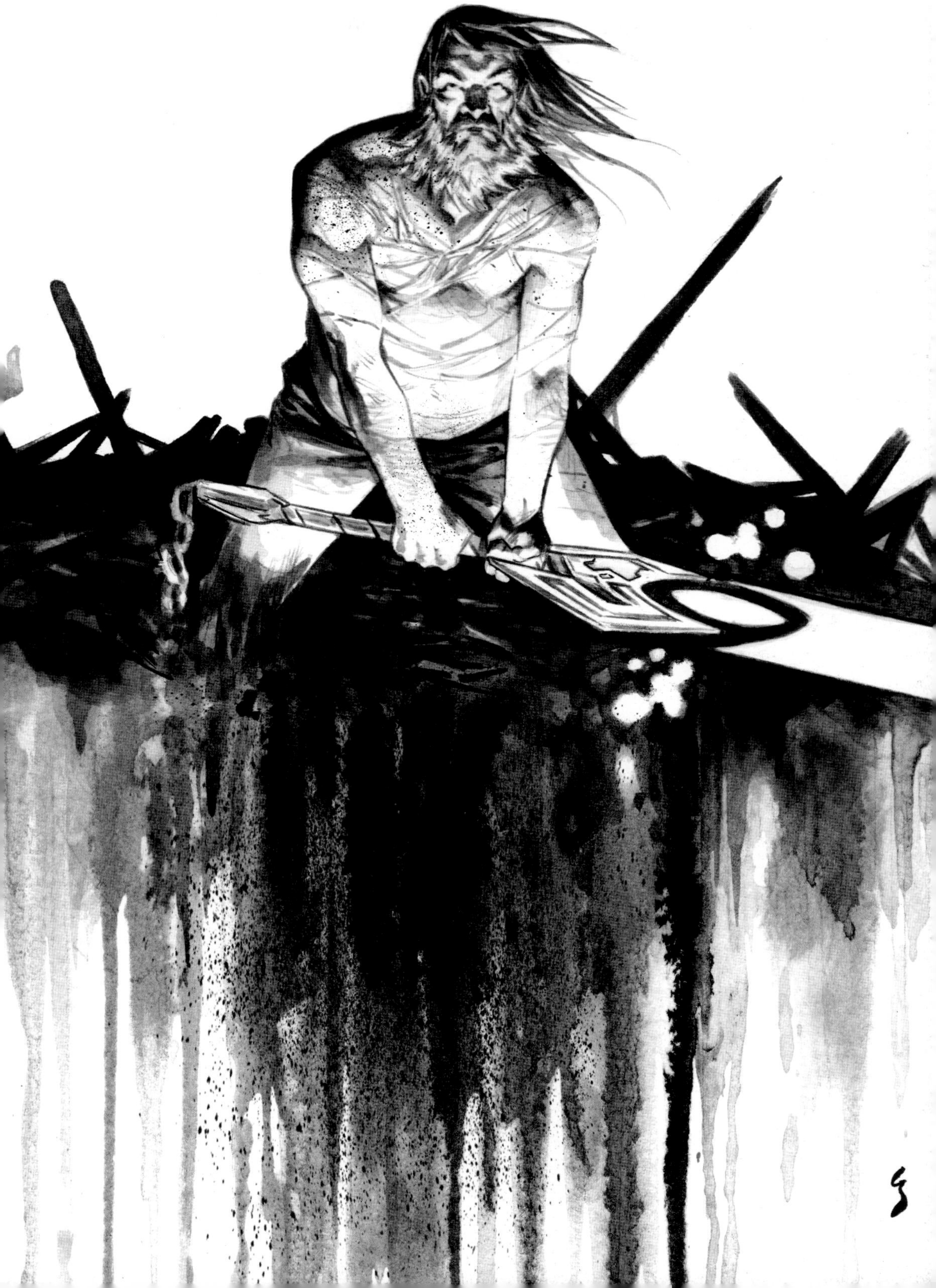

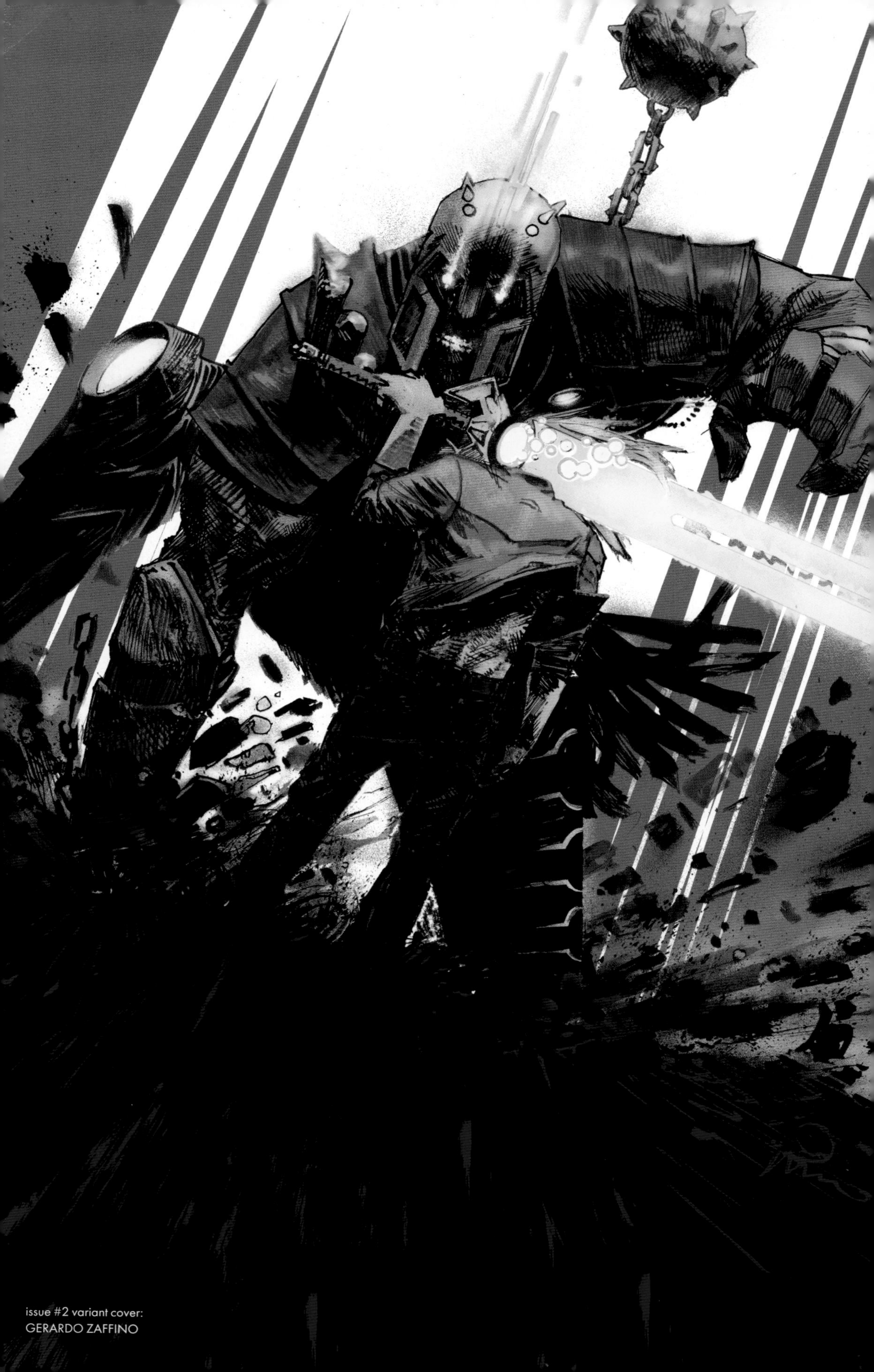

issue #2 variant cover:
GERARDO ZAFFINO

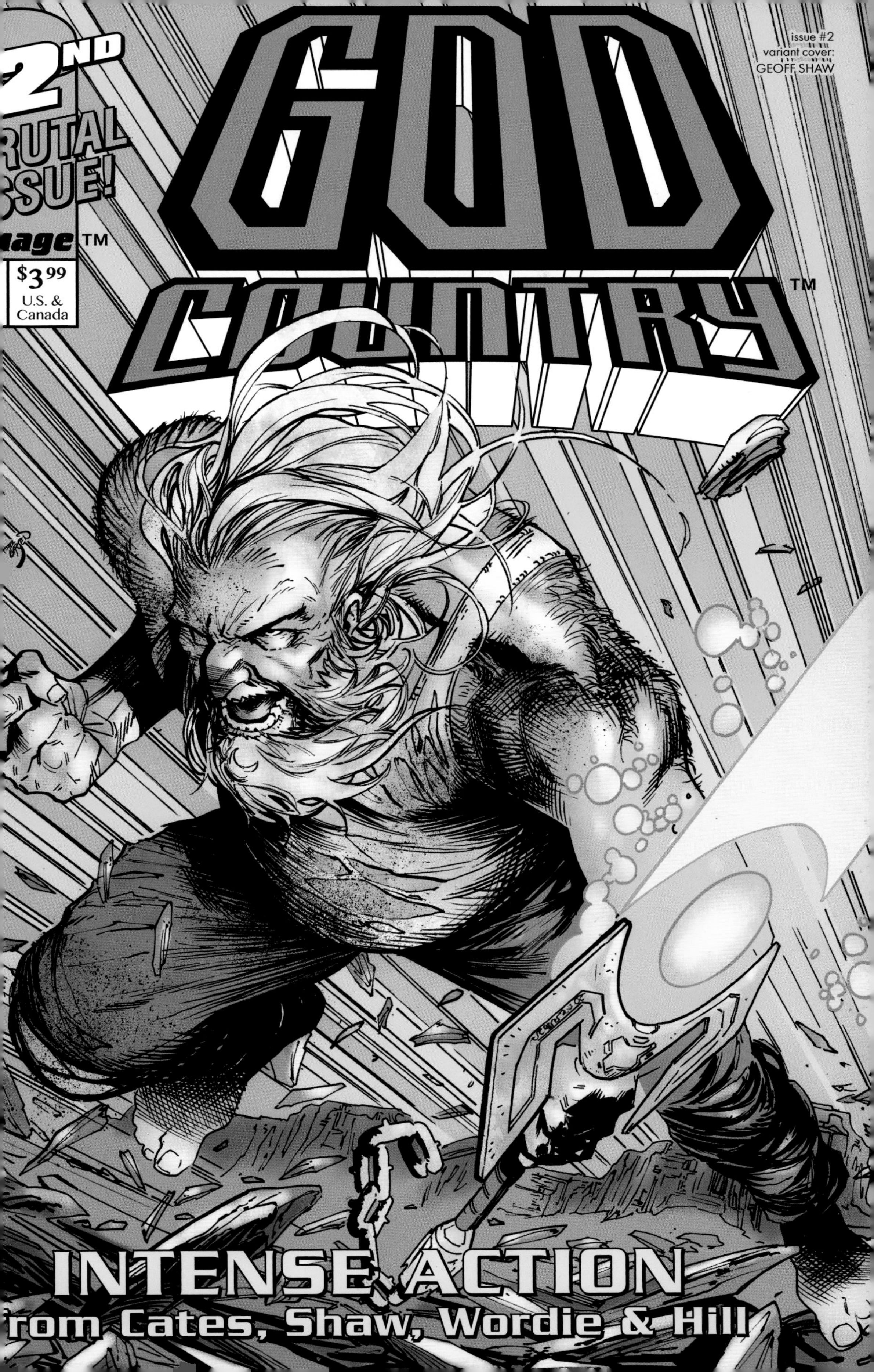
2ND
RUTAL
SSUE!
mage ™
$3.99
U.S. &
Canada
GOD
COUNTRY ™
issue #2
variant cover:
GEOFF SHAW
INTENSE ACTION
rom Cates, Shaw, Wordie & Hill

issue #2 reprint cover:
DYLAN BURNETT

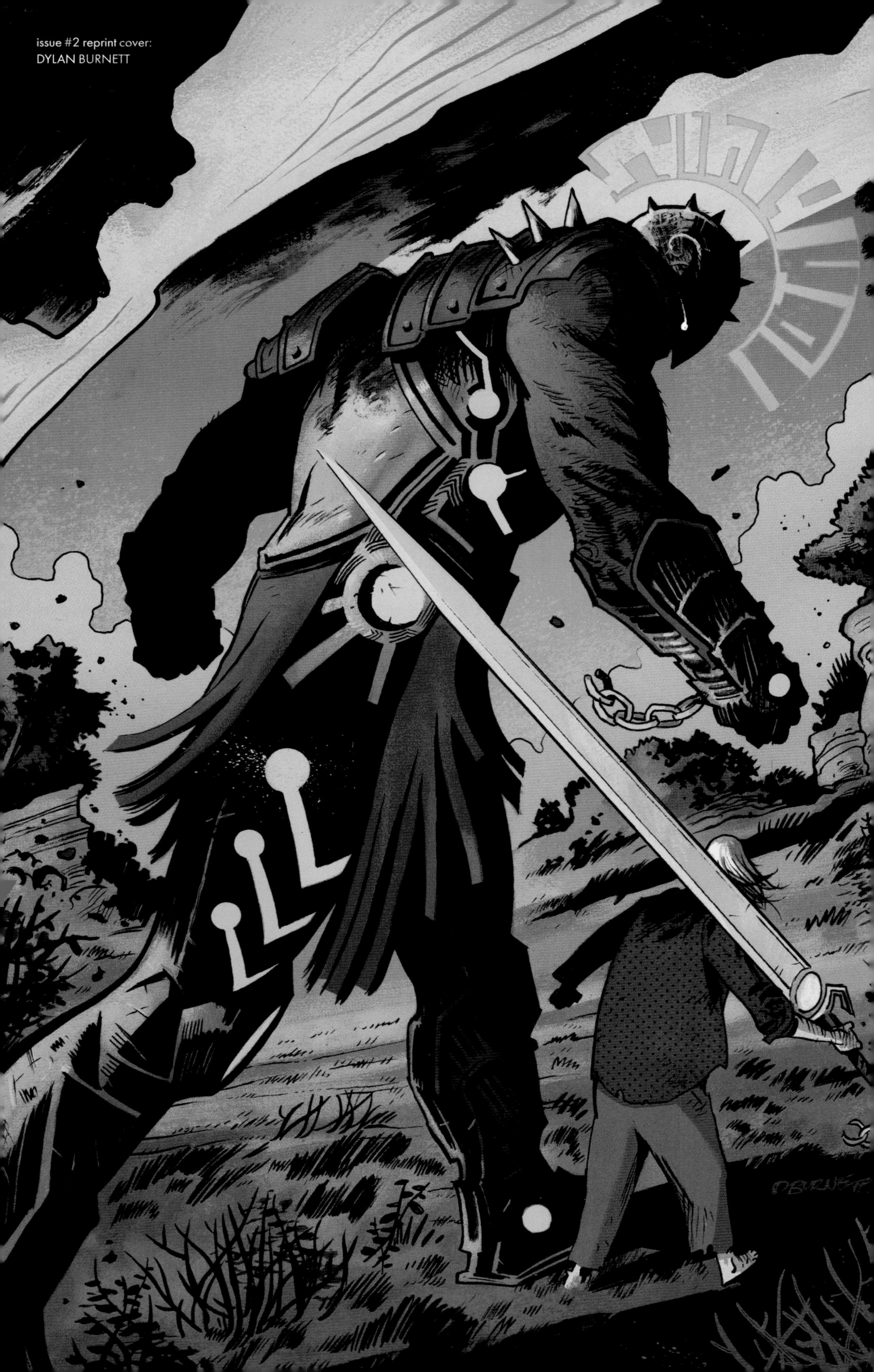

issue #3 reprint cover:
GERARDO ZAFFINO

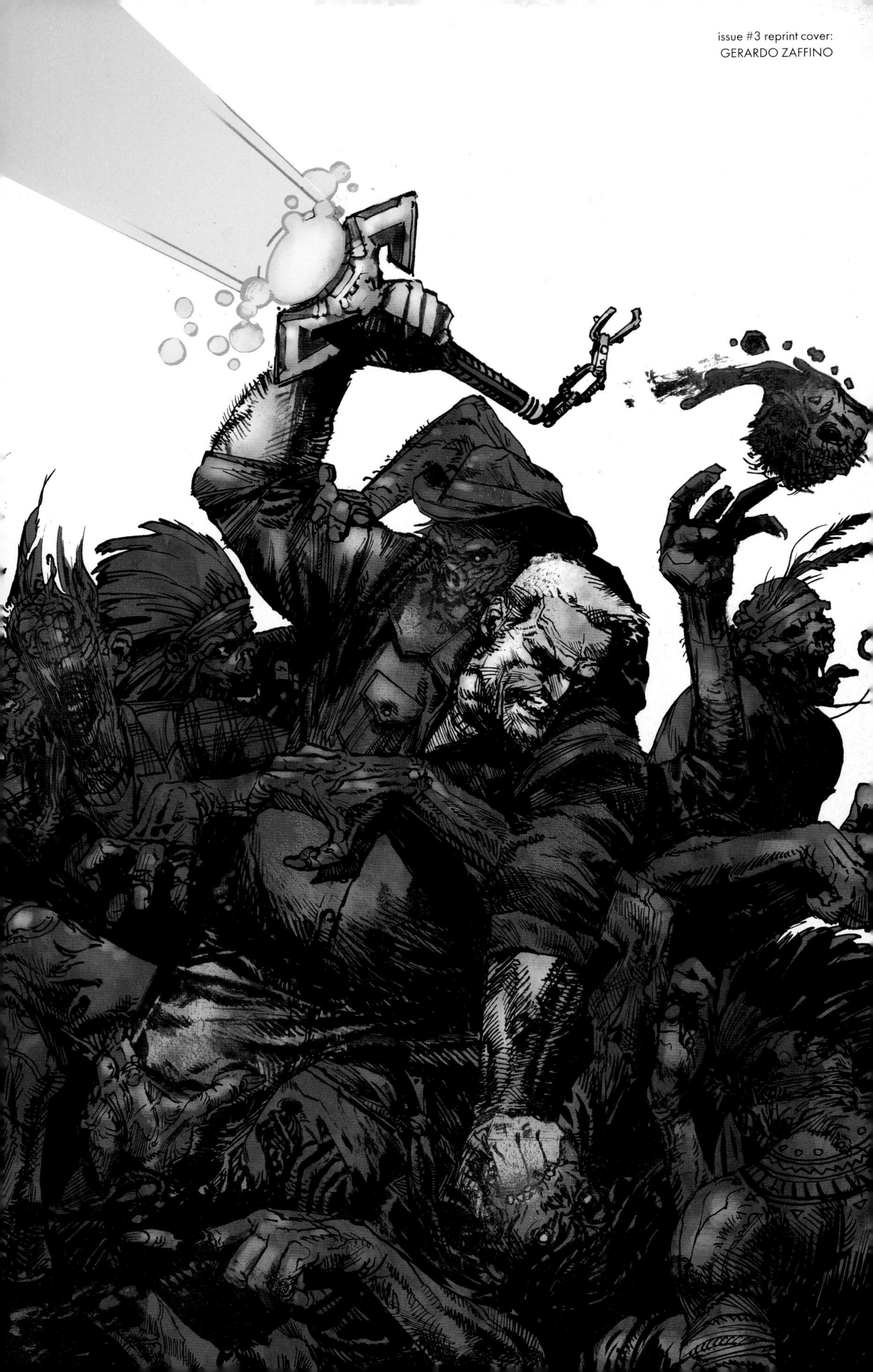

issue #4 variant cover:
GERARDO ZAFFINO

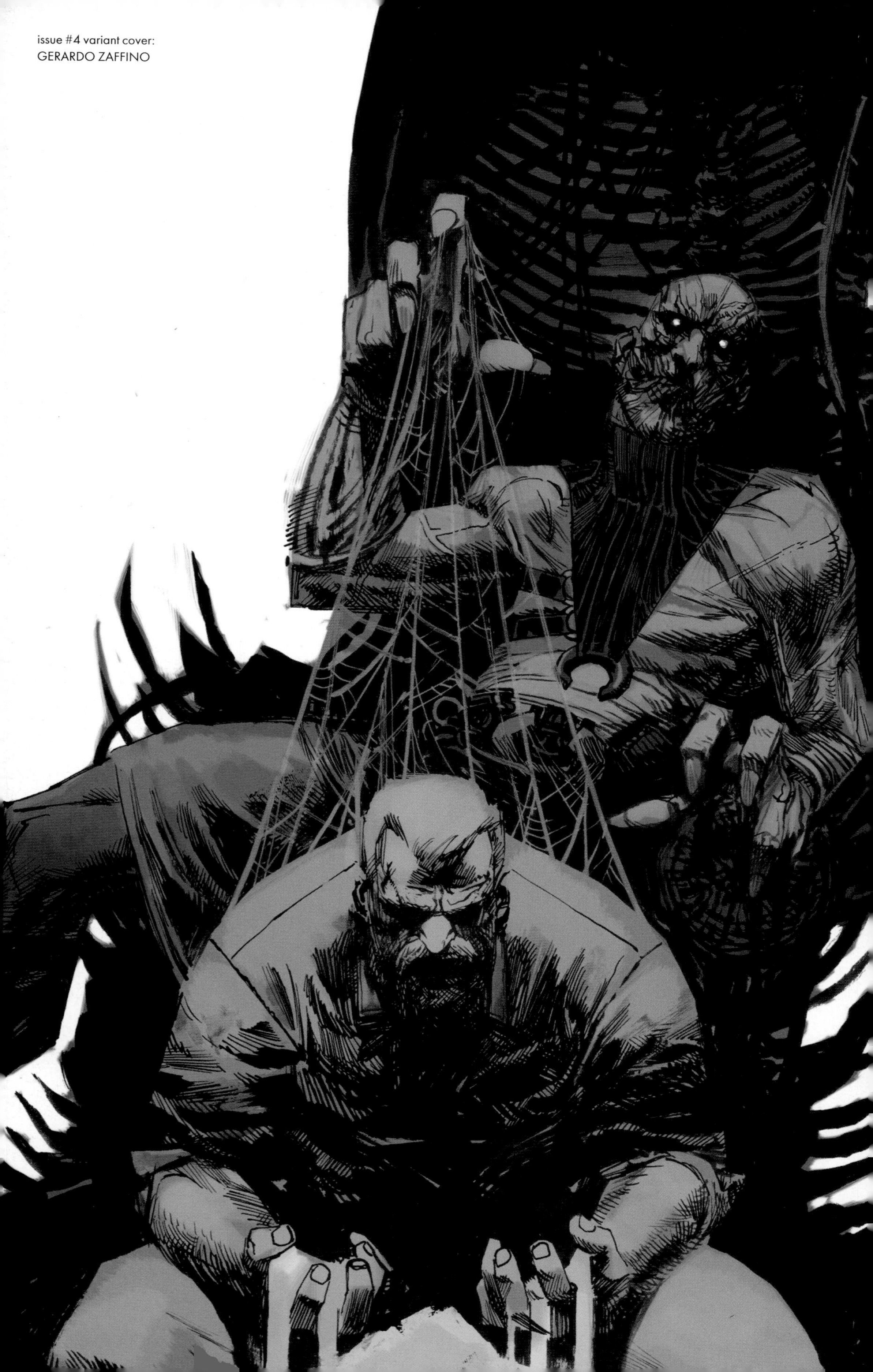

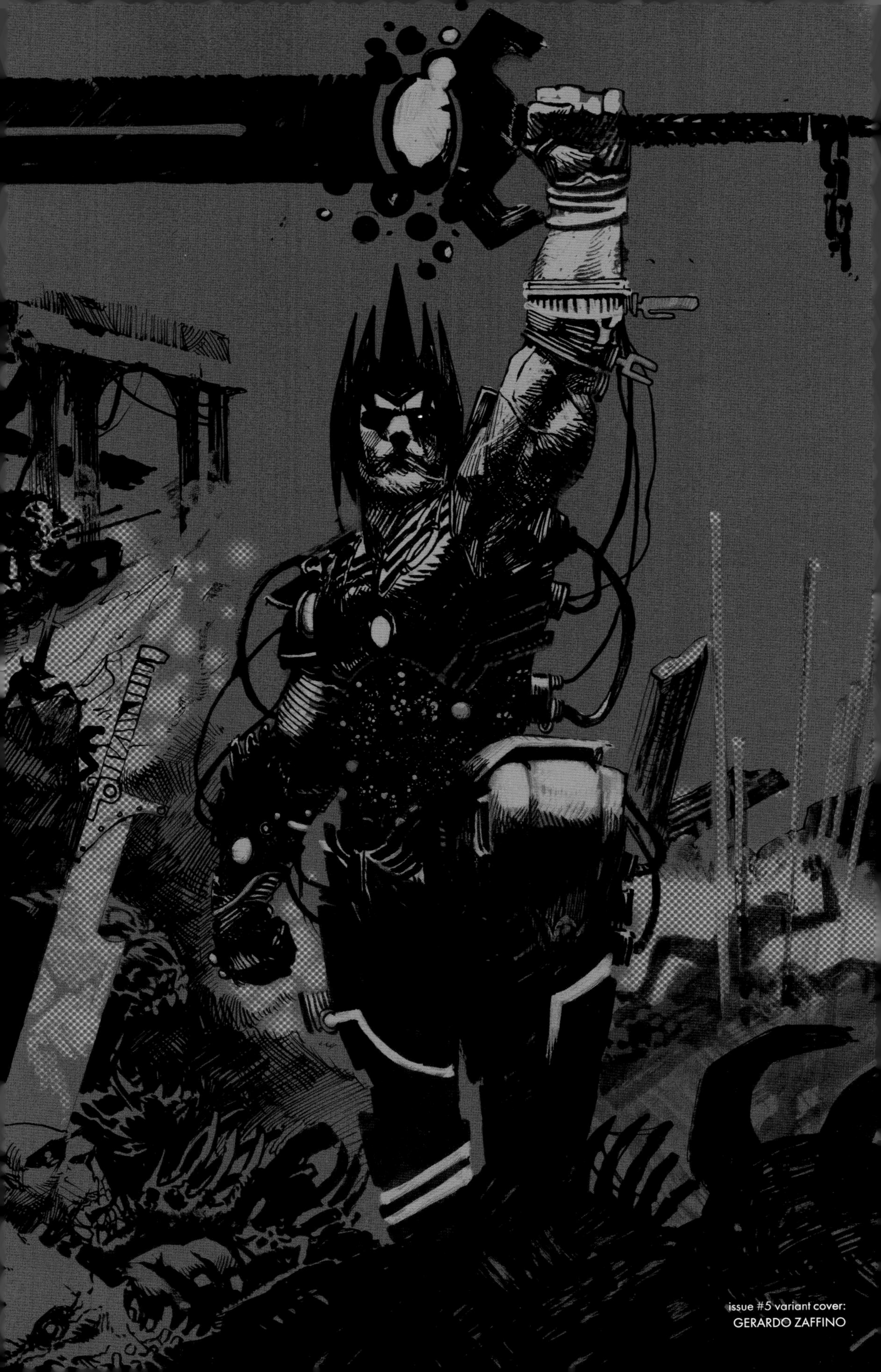

issue #5 variant cover:
GERARDO ZAFFINO

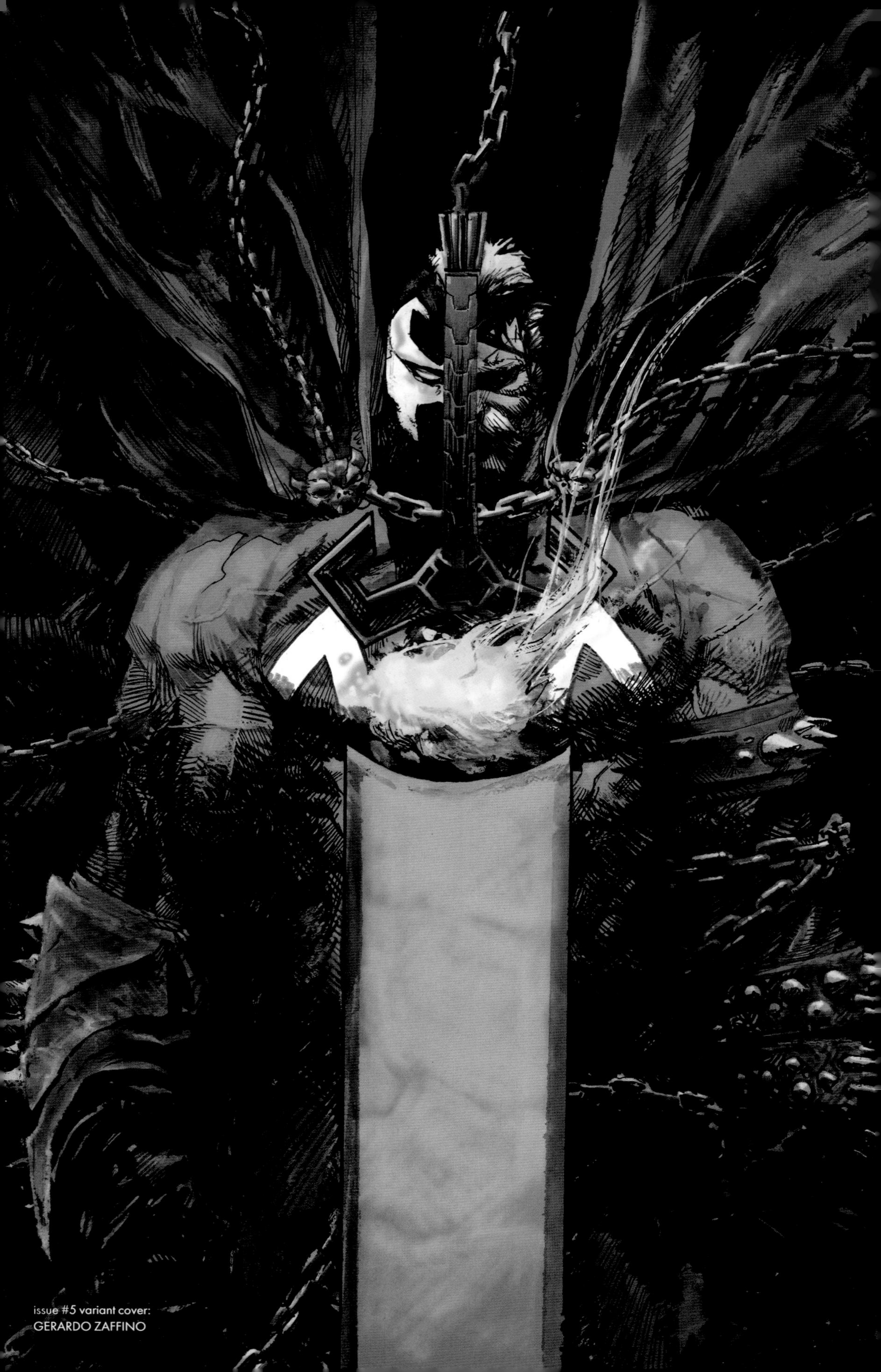

issue #5 variant cover:
GERARDO ZAFFINO

issue #6 variant cover:
GERARDO ZAFFINO

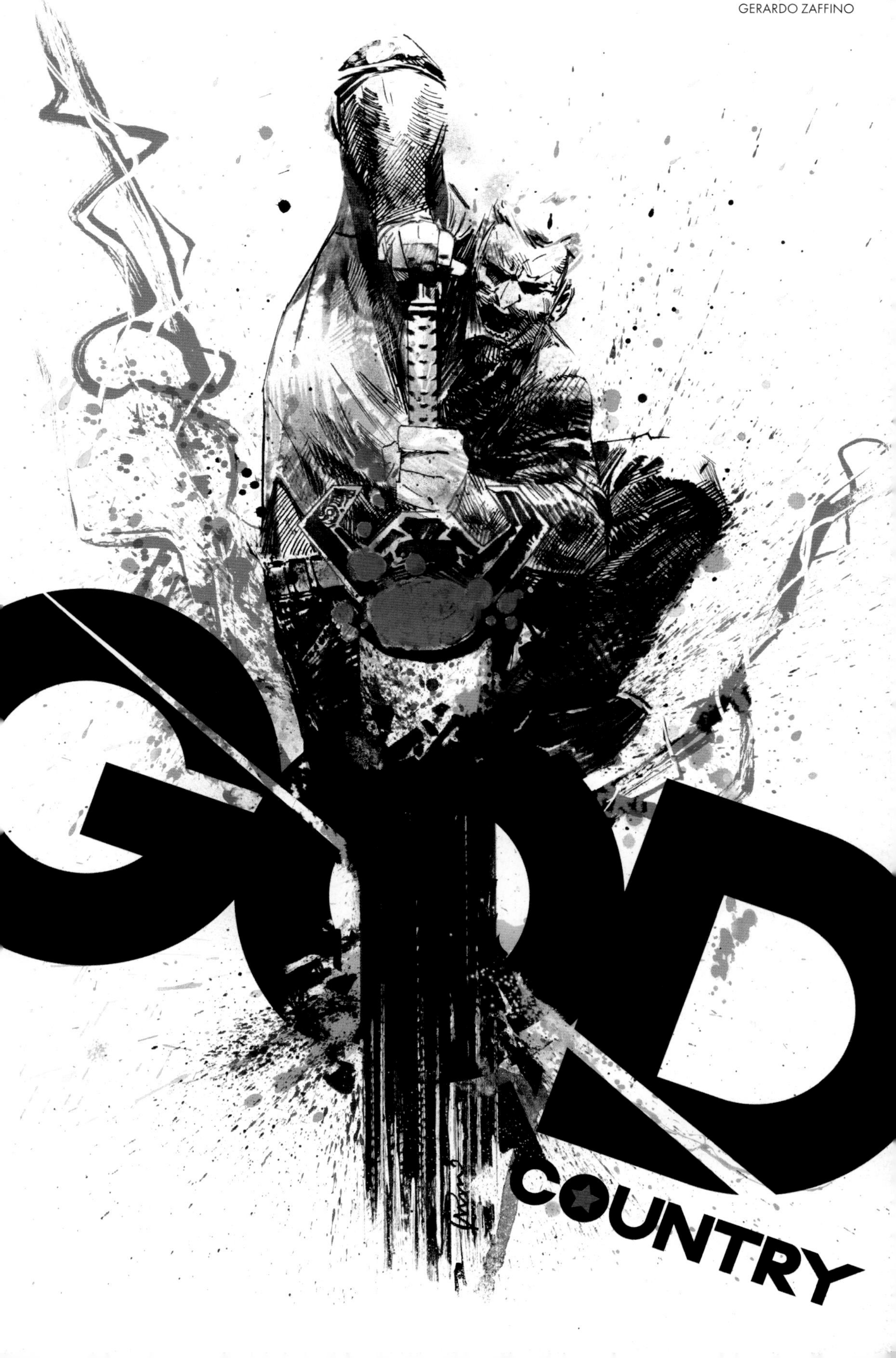
GOD
COUNTRY

pin-up:
IAN BEDERMAN

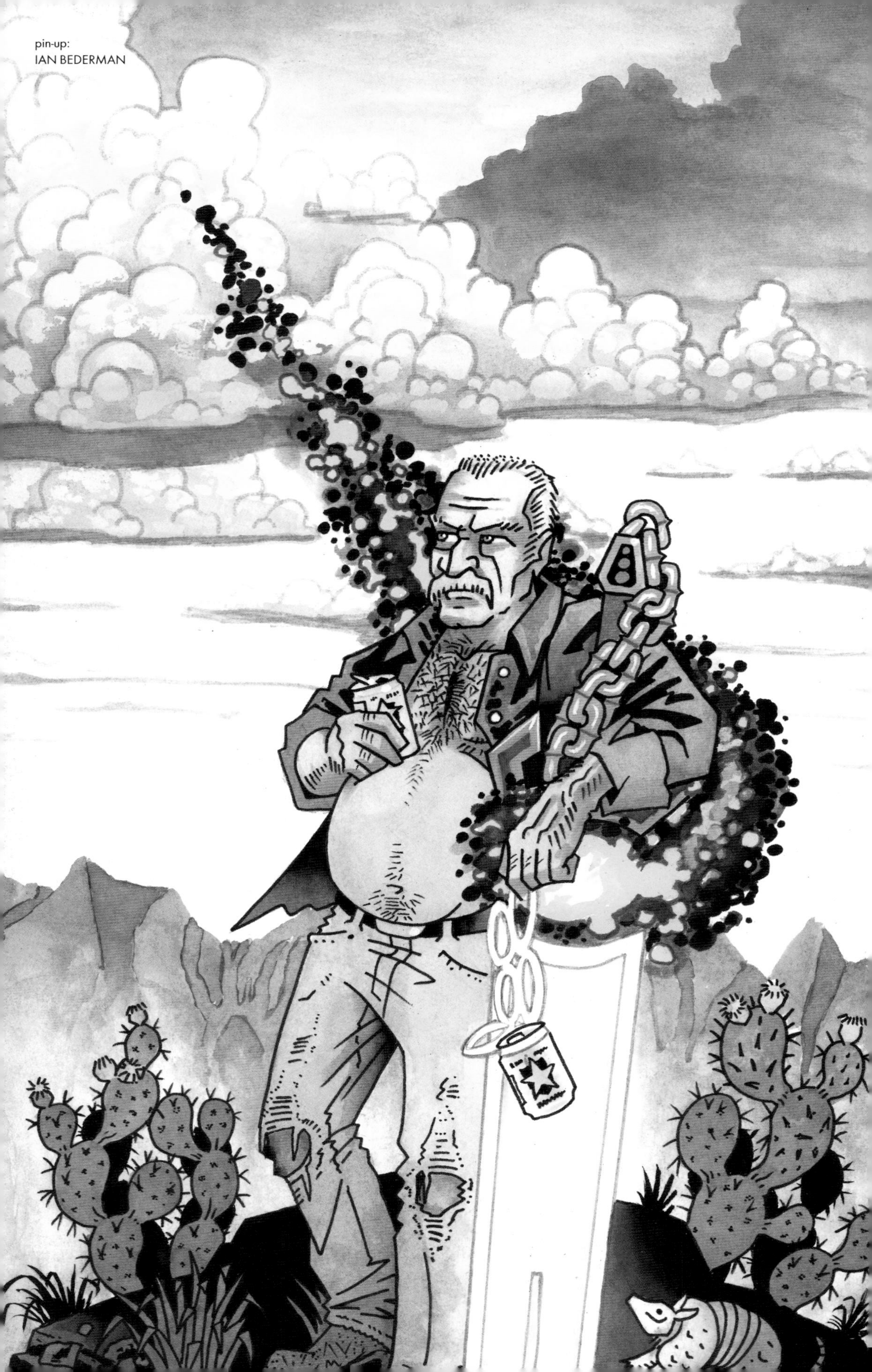

pin-up:
NICK DERINGTON

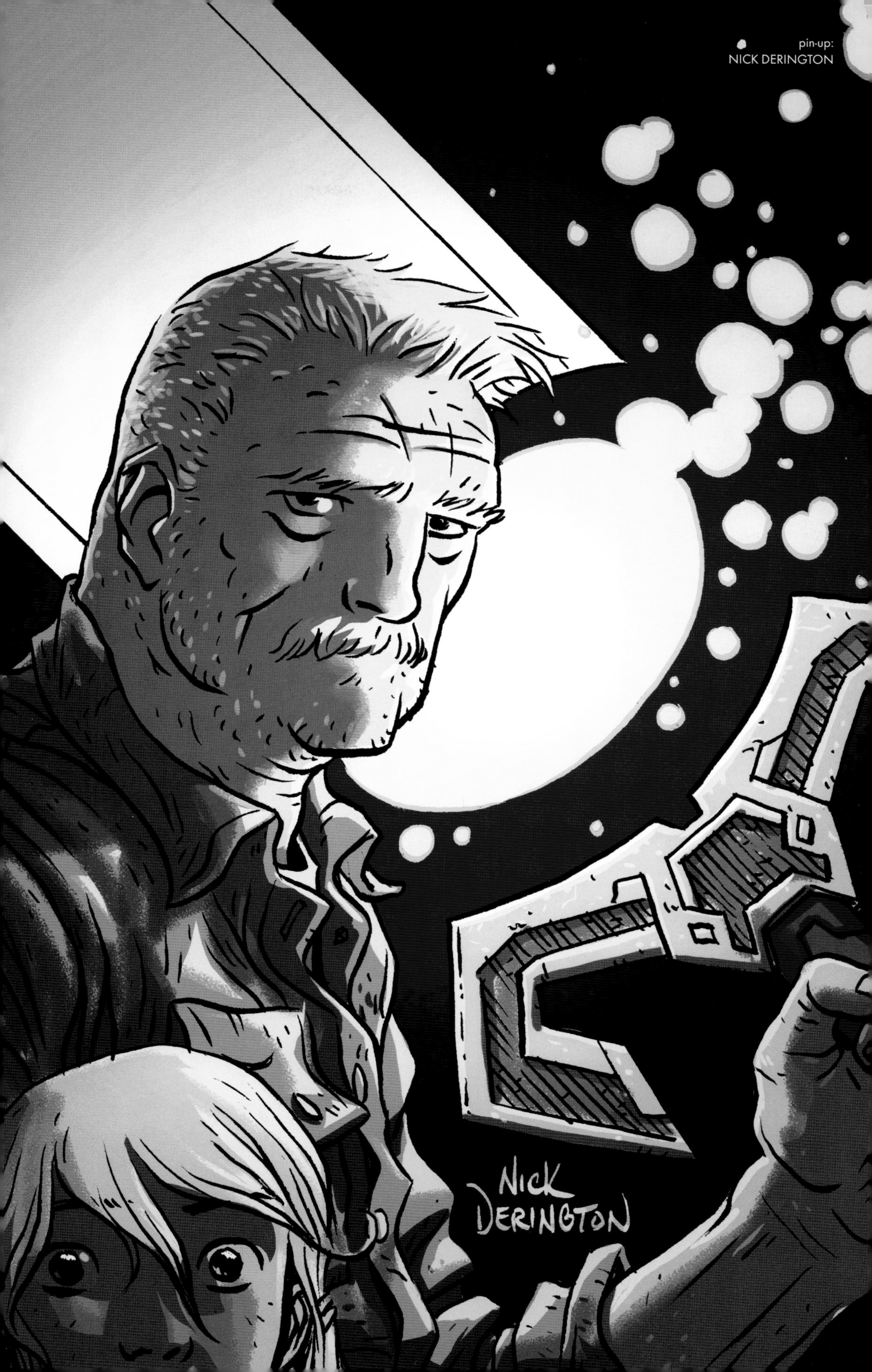
NICK
DERINGTON

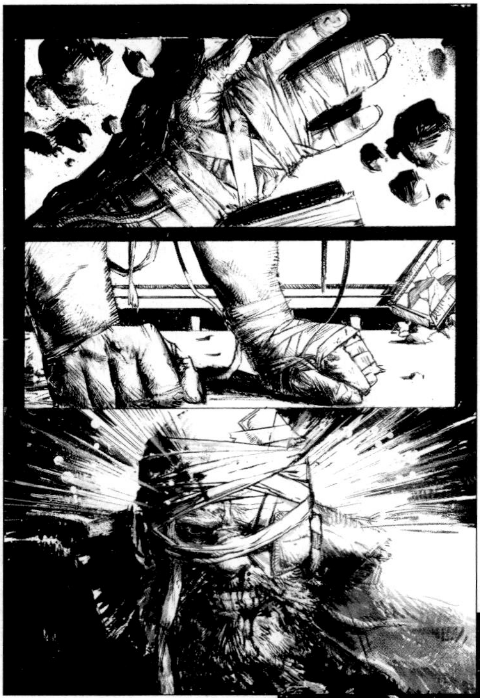

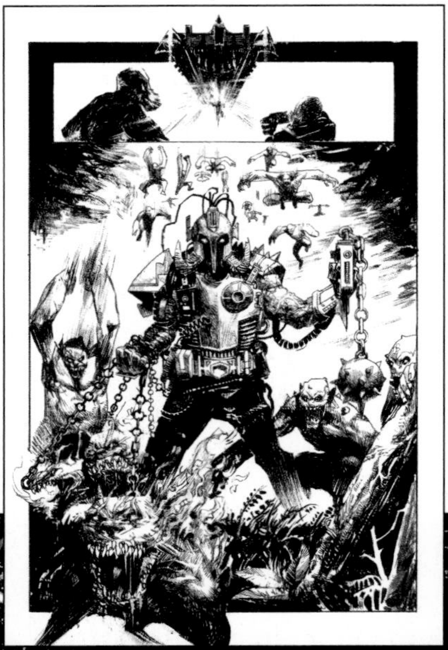

Original series designs
and concepts by artist
GERARDO ZAFFINO

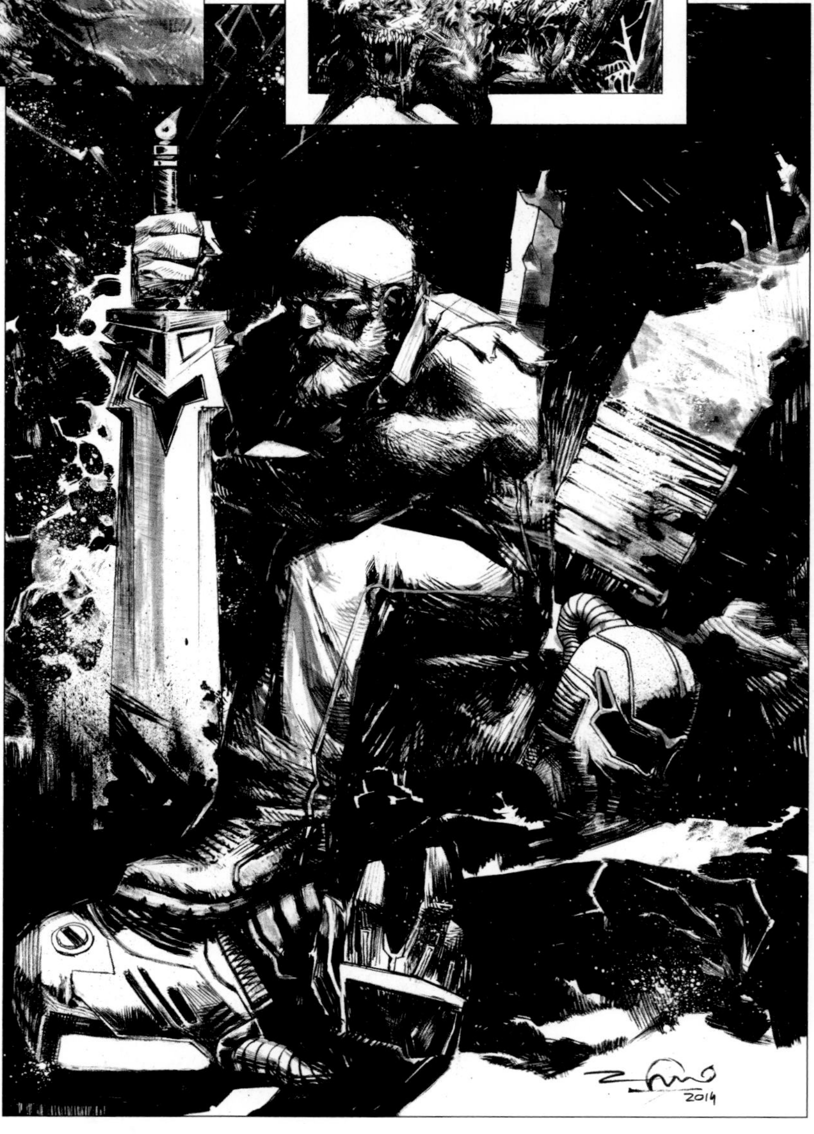

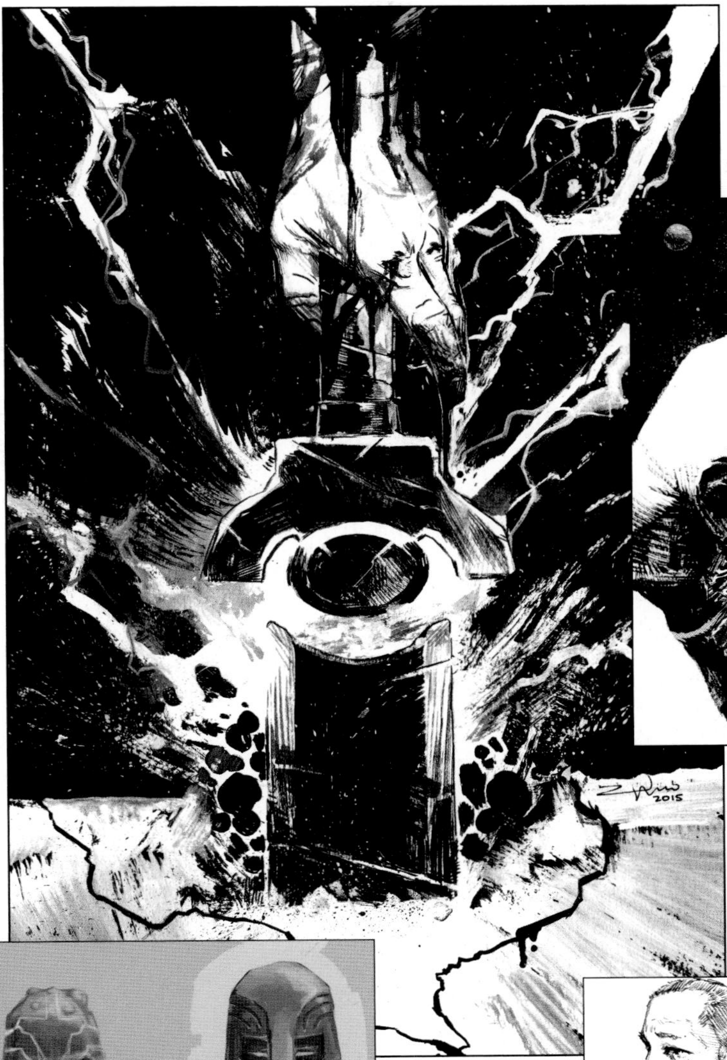

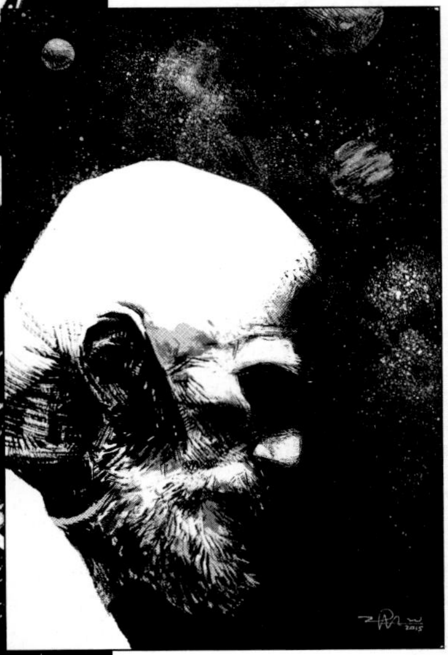

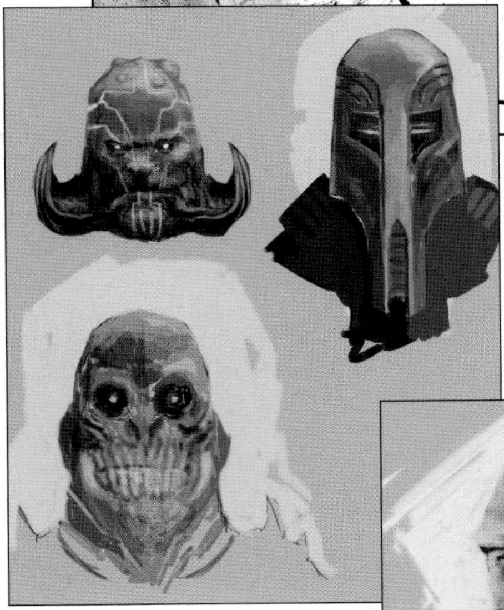

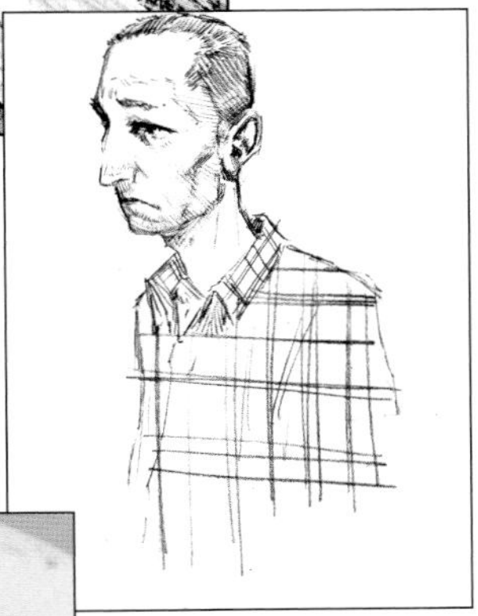

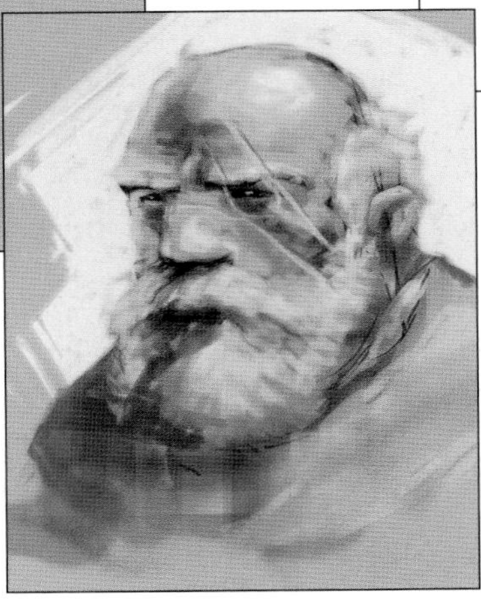

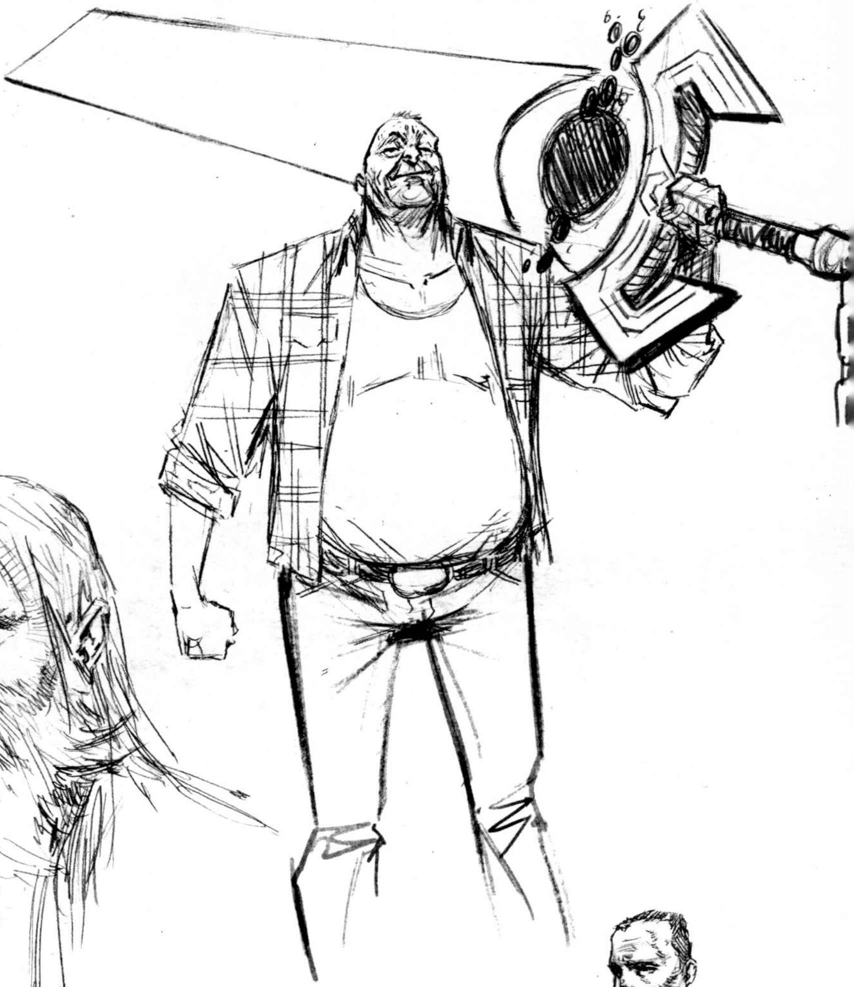

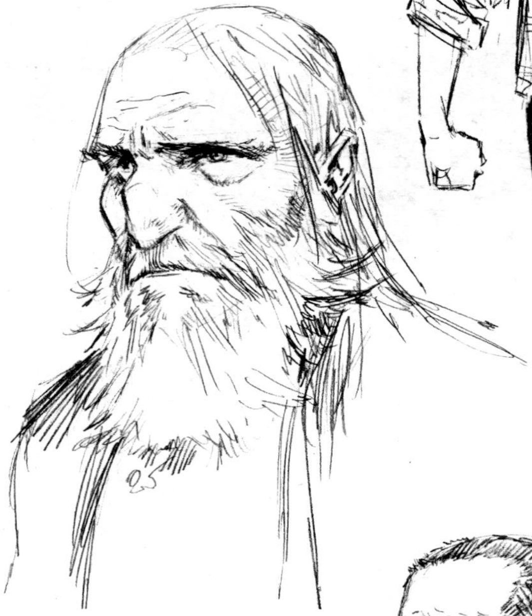

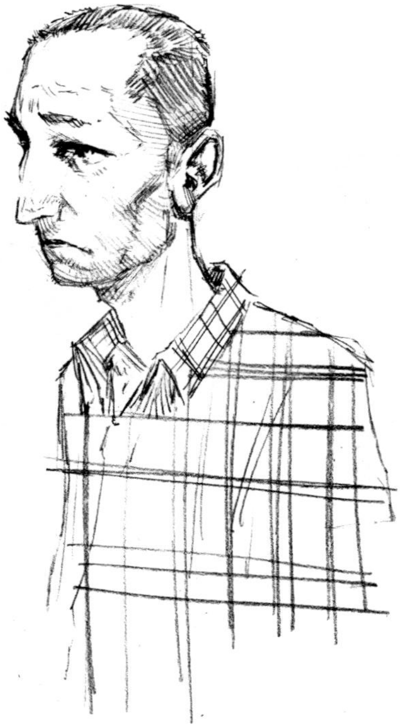

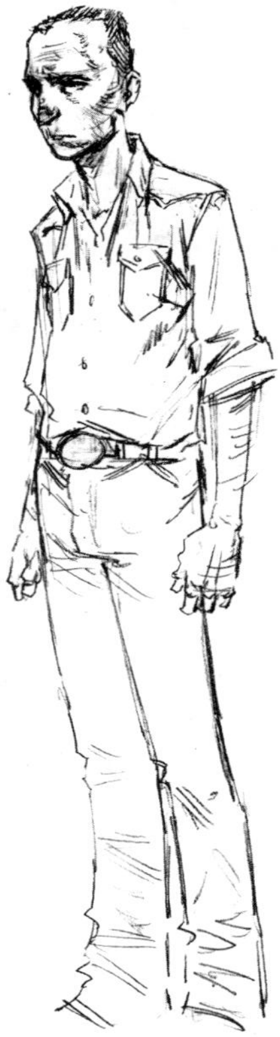

Original series designs
and concepts by artist
GEOFF SHAW

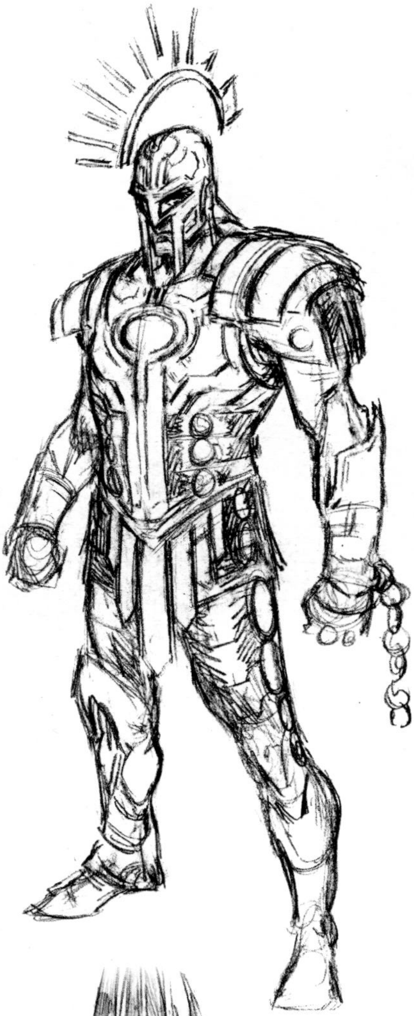

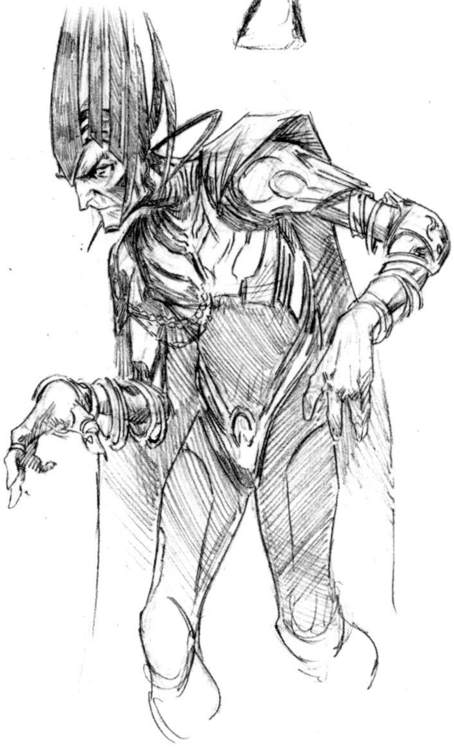

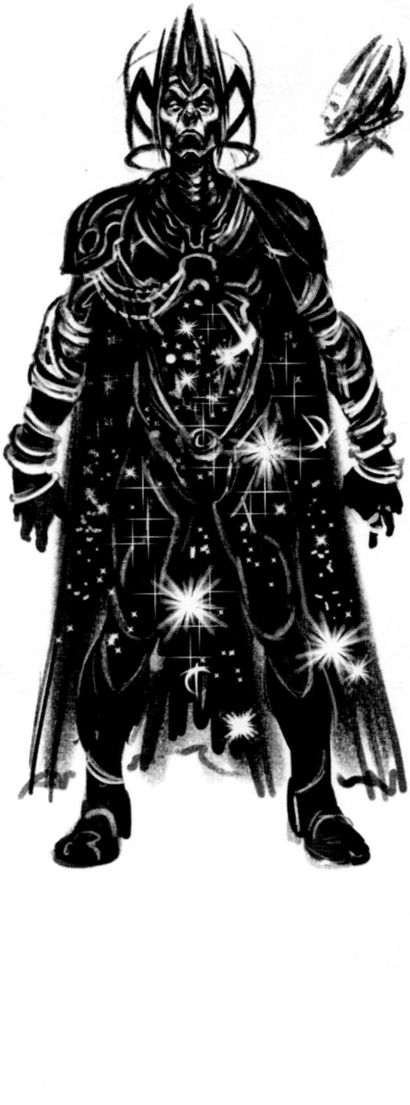

Panel 1 – Pull out a bunch and show Aristus gesticulating wildly. Enthralled in the magic of the story he's telling here.

> **Aristus:** Valofax *is* Excalibur. It is *every* sword that was ever forged, every enchanted blade you have heard of.

> **Aristus:** Every myth, every song, every tale spoken of a mighty warrior and his unbreakable steel…it is and has always been **Valofax**.

Panel 2 – Tight on Aristus, looking down on Emmett and proudly (but not boastfully) explaining things.

> **Aristus:** Just as I live in every war waged, my brother **Balegrim** lives through every rot and death…

> **Aristus:** So Valofax exists in the edge of all blades.

Panel 3 – Tight on Emmett. He ain't buying it.

> **Emmett:** Uh-huh.

Panel 4 – Same deal. Emmett plucks some of the tall grass out of the ground. They are almost at the small graveyard.

> **Emmett:** So where'd it come from? Valofax.

> **Aristus:** My father ATTŪM, lord of the kingdom of always and God of Kings, forged Valofax in the heart of a dying realm.

> **Emmett:** Ah, so it's like a…family heirloom or somethin'? Supposed t' be **yours** now?

PROCESS
Issue 2 page 15

Script
DONNY CATES

Thumbnail / Pencils / Inks
GEOFF SHAW

Colors
JASON WORDIE

Letters
JOHN J. HILL

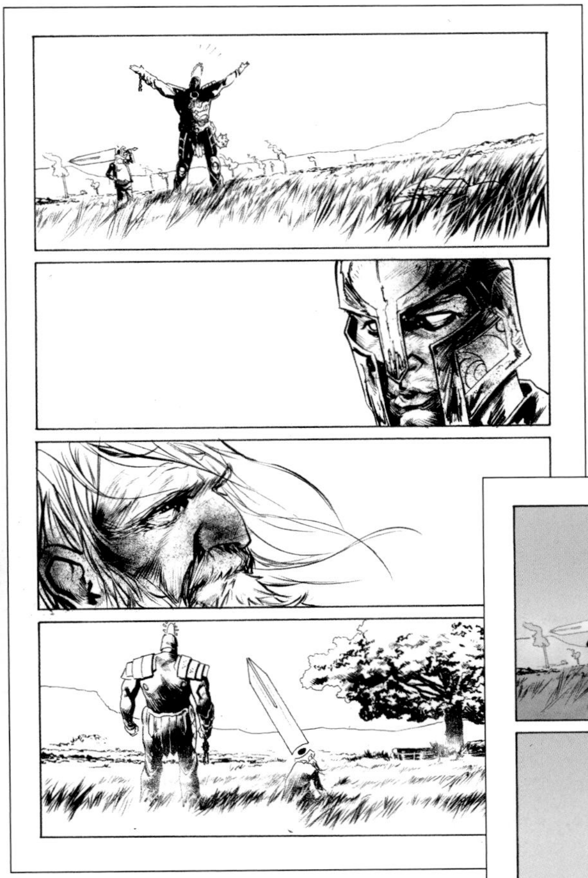

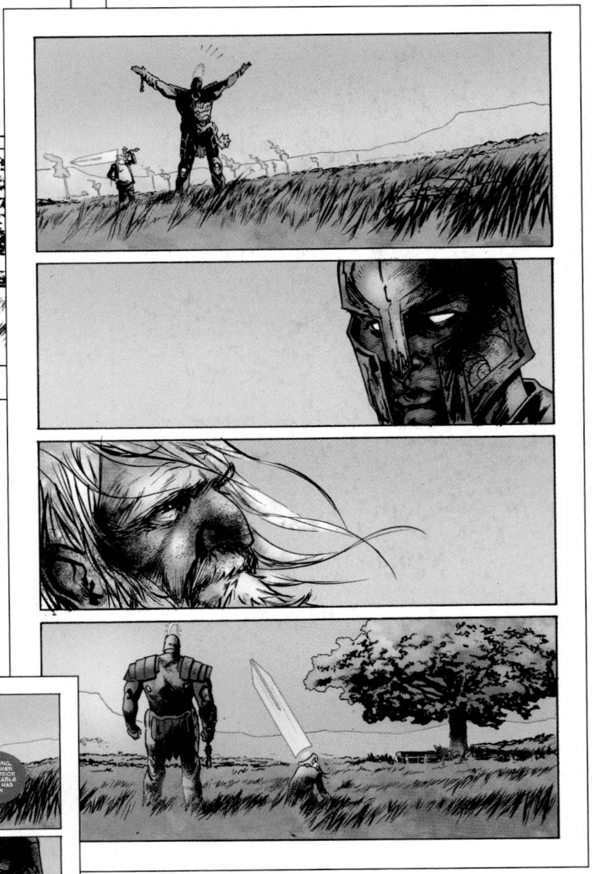

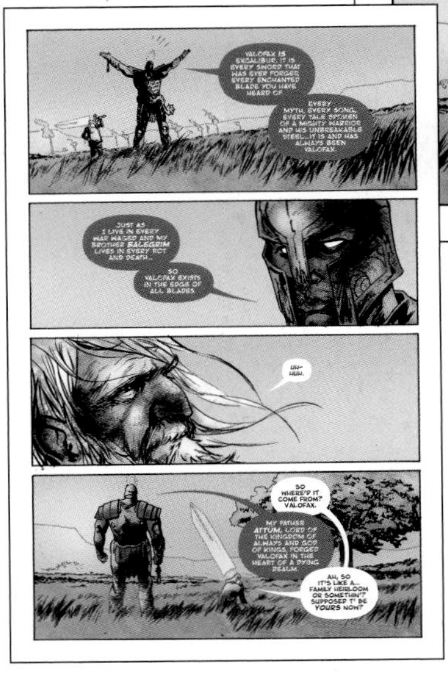
VALOFAX IS EXCALIBUR. IT IS EVERY SWORD THAT HAS EVER FORGED, EVERY ENCHANTED BLADE YOU HAVE HEARD OF.
EVERY MYTH, EVERY SONG, EVERY TALE SPOKEN OF A MIGHTY WARRIOR AND HIS UNBREAKABLE STEEL...IT IS AND HAS ALWAYS BEEN VALOFAX.
JUST AS I LIVE IN EVERY WAR WAGED AND MY BROTHER BALEGRIM LIVES IN EVERY ROT AND DEATH...
SO VALOFAX EXISTS IN THE EDGE OF ALL BLADES.
UH-HUH.
SO WHERE'D IT COME FROM? VALOFAX.
MY FATHER ATTUM, LORD OF THE KINGDOM OF ALWAYS AND GOD OF KINGS, FORGED VALOFAX IN THE HEART OF A DYING REALM.
AH, SO IT'S LIKE A... FAMILY HEIRLOOM OR SOMETHIN'? SUPPOSED T' BE YOURS NOW?

DONNY CATES

Donny is a writer of comic books. His past works include BUZZKILL, THE GHOST FLEET, THE PAYBACKS, INTERCEPTOR, STAR TREK, and ATOMAHAWK. His current work includes GOD COUNTRY, REDNECK, and BABYTEETH, and by the time you are reading this, a few cool things that you no doubt really dig. He's from the town that *King Of The Hill* was based on but lives in Austin, Texas with his wife and his books. He is much more interesting than this bio makes him sound. Promise. Find him on Twitter: @Doncates

GEOFF SHAW

Geoff Shaw began his career on the critically acclaimed miniseries BUZZKILL with Donny Cates. He then went on to pencil the mini-series A TOWN CALLED DRAGON with Legendary Comics. Donny and Geoff teamed up once again for the wildly entertaining (if slightly underrated) series from Dark Horse, THE PAYBACKS. He very much enjoys making comics, and ain't half bad at makin' em'. Find him on Twitter: @GeoffShaw12

JASON WORDIE

Jason hails from Canada. He has done work for Image, Dark Horse, Boom!, and Titan. Some of his works include TURNCOAT, JOHNNY RED, GENESIS, DAWN OF THE PLANET OF THE APES, and TIGERLUNG. Find him on Twitter: @WordieJason

JOHN J. HILL

John is a Portland, OR based freelance creative director working in entertainment and comics. Clients include Adobe, Aeropostale, AfterShock, Atlantic Records, Blizzard Entertainment, Dark Horse, DC, Disney, GM, Legendary, Monkeybrain, MTV, NHL, Radical, and many others. For Image, he has lettered and designed SOVEREIGN, NAILBITER, and GOD COUNTRY (with more to come!). Whenever there's a spare moment John can be found devouring as many cult horror movies as possible and preaching the gospel of Jack Kirby. Find him on Twitter and Instagram: @JohnJHill

GERARDO ZAFFINO

Gerardo was born in 1983 in Buenos Aires, Argentina where he still lives with his wife, daughter, and two dogs. He has worked for Marvel, Vertigo, IDW and Image.